THE DHOW

An Islamic terrorist, waiting in London for other cell members to arrive from the Arabian Gulf, is incandescent with fury when he discovers that his landlady/lover has disposed of one of his possessions; in a rage, he brutally murders her, the reclamation of his Dhow being the key to his mission's success.

Meanwhile, a small eclectic group of Londoners, friends and acquaintances, unwittingly become entangled with the Islamic terrorist's plans. An innocent transaction will bring the group into danger, the terrorist organisation relentlessly pursuing their possession across London, Ireland, then back to London, changing forever the lives of the Londoners.

A bloody trail of mayhem and destruction ensues, with a battle ensuing to prevent the fundamentalists carrying out a major atrocity in the heart of the City.

Also by the same author
The Irish Prime Minister

Fergal is desperate to escape from his Provisional IRA past - having misguidedly attached himself to the terrorist organisation at a very young age - but there is too much in his background that prevents him making a clean break.

The Republican terrorist group have devised a strategy to achieve their goal of a united Irish nation by ingratiating one on their members within a British political organisation, ultimately rising to become British Prime Minister.

Escaping to America, Fergal has to avoid the clutches of the FBI, the British Secret Service, and his old terrorist allies – all of them want information from him, but most want him eliminated.

THE DHOW

Desmond B Harding

ISBN-13: 978-1540488367
ISBN-10: 1540488365

Grateful thanks to my wife Juliette and to our children, Richard and Laura, for their years of undoubted patience!

Chapter 1

Nervously chewing on his bottom lip, the second secretary, commercial, paced the floor, glancing in frustration at his seated companion who was bearing the brunt of the second secretary's anger. The hapless individual replaced the telephone in its cradle and fingered nervously with a pen on his desk. None of this was his fault but the second secretary seemed to want to vent his frustration and ire on his underling, a man only very recently posted out from London.

But it was not good; they had lost contact.

The Agent's mobile had rung but had been disconnected almost instantly, and it had now been two days since they had heard from him. The Embassy in Aden had been alerted and everyone was in a high state of tension.

The second secretary, awakened in the early hours of this morning because there was an alert that their agent's phone had been re-activated, had become angry because there was no news, good or bad, regarding their man. The second secretary – in reality MI6's station manager - was beginning to feel decidedly uneasy; something had definitely gone wrong. The satellite conditions remained perfect but there was just an unnatural silence, a vacuum.

The tracking device initially locating an area over the eastern Yemeni desert had suddenly gone silent, the bleep dying before they could pinpoint a more precise target. It was not his underling's fault, there just had not been enough time to pinpoint a more precise location, but the man had to bear the brunt of his feeling of hopelessness. This was now the second man to have disappeared and there was no doubt now that the mission was a total failure.

In a few hours panic bells would sound in London; they knew they had been close but now it looked dire.

* * *

The air was stifling, the damp heat remaining oppressive. Although late in the afternoon the heat haze rose lazily, but persistently, into the yielding, fatigued air of the clear blue sky.

The stillness was eerie, nothing visibly moving in this baking hot desert area of eastern Yemen. With no cloud cover, the sun harshly and relentlessly beat downward, its unrelenting heat scorching into the desolate surface below.

Stretching for miles, swathes of unrelenting sand, of varying hues, from bleached white to stained yellow, undulated over vast acres of terrain, running up and down dunes, some drifts of sand building hills that rose triumphantly to over 600 feet in height.

Eventually, the sand hit rocks, the desert merging with the mountains that climbed, barren and desolate, into the heavens, seemingly trying their utmost to escape the relentless heat of the hot scouring grains of sand.

A soft breeze emerged ostensibly from out of nowhere, the hot air rising from the desert floor colliding with marginally cooler draughts drifting down from the mountain tops. The gentle breeze, an almost insignificant puff of wind, disturbed some of the yellow sea, resulting in limited swirls of hot sand briefly floating up into the atmosphere before quickly subsiding back in the heated stillness of the baking hot landscape.

The set of tyre tracks cut a path in the desert sand, the tracks skirting the edge of the mountain, crossing a small dried up Wadi, and then onwards across the baked sand until they finally reached their destination, an Oasis containing three unproductive palm trees, a sorry looking gorse bush, and a tiny hamlet of four adobe style dwellings.

The buildings were of very cheap construction, limestone and sun-dried clay, and covered in chipped and pealing whitewash, the 'decorating' having obviously taken place many years previously. The surfaces 'sweated' in the humid air, the moisture sticking like glue to a more accommodating surface than that offered by the surrounding sand.

The hamlet wreaked of desolation, of abandonment, the buildings derelict, the small population having either escaped to a brighter future in the city, or years of in-breeding having caused their demise.

However, the hamlet wasn't entirely deserted. A battered Toyota pickup truck that had seen better days was parked outside the only building that contained any form of air-conditioning - a small, wall-mounted, air-conditioning unit that hummed in desperate effort, battling vainly against the relentless heat. Directly underneath the air-con unit, below the outlet pipe, a small egg cup size pool of water had formed in the sand, its brief existence lasting only whilst the ineffective air-con's unit was switched on.

The stillness was broken by three Arab men, Imam Khalifa, Saeed and Fawzi, discarding their protective suits and gas masks as they exited the defunct dwelling.

Their subsequent sand-carpeted, almost silent, footsteps were disturbed by one of the men as he cleared his throat, the mucus being collected in the man's mouth then spewed out with satisfied venom onto the sizzling sand.

The men were dressed in ankle length 'Kandouras' - loose fittings garments of heavy, hard wearing, cotton material - each wearing a crocheted skullcap which helped to beat off the sun's rays. It was only the leading male, obviously older, his grey-beard hairs snaking down over his chest towards his stomach, who decided that additional protection or respect was required and, accordingly, he removed a blue and white striped 'Gutra' from his pocket, and tied it on his head not bothering to use a woollen braid to secure the head scarf in place.

The two younger Arab men relied only on their skullcaps to ward off the sun's unrelenting rays, and despite the glare of the sun which would normally cause a person to squint or to reach for the closest pair of sunglasses they were wide-eyed with amazement, their faces registering a mixture of shock and awe. In unison, they turned to face their leader, their mentor, the religious man who would guide them to their destiny, the very holy and venerated, Imam Khalifa.

His voice reflecting both solemnity and authority, Imam Khalifa reiterated, "You both now have the knowledge of the poison, and how quick and effective – and pleasingly painful – it can be for use against those who oppress our aims."

Dumfounded by the events he had recently witnessed, Saeed merely nodded in acquiescence, both of the brother's stunned brains still coming to terms with the power of death that they were going to have under their control. Although it had taken the victim nearly an hour to die a painful death – two tiny droplets of the poisonous greenish liquid dropped into his eyes – the Imam assured the brothers that the gaseous form was far more virulent, acting almost immediately, cutting off the victims nervous system.

*   *   *

Inside a room of the vacated house, the ineffective air-con unit hummed noisily, struggling to work against the intense heat, yet the noise did not seem sufficient to disturb a man sitting in the centre of the room. The room itself being bare except for the man and his hard backed, wooden chair.

Closer inspection revealed that the man was slumped, unnaturally, and the only reason that he hadn't fallen, lifeless, to the floor, were the thick ply cord bonds that secured him to the chair. There were actually two separate ropes that secured him to the chair, one binding his legs tightly to the chair's legs and the other round his chest and arms, tied securely to the chair upright.

In the dim light, and despite the beating that he had taken, it was obvious that the man had been of Caucasian origin, his blood-matted fair hair flopping over his forehead.

But his eyes gave the appearance of denying the body's death, like a photograph, they represented a split second in time, the eyes staring out in sheer and utter terror, the reflected image that of excruciating pain and anguish. The man's mouth forged open, face framed in agony and hurt, his lungs crying out for air, his body totally dysfunctional, the howl of pain etched all the way from the man's larynx, over the tongue, all the way through his mouth and engraved onto his lips.

The bruised and battered face, covered in cuts, with a congealed dried blood trail commencing under one eye and downward in a thick line across the man's cheek, shouted in evidence of the severe beating that the man had suffered prior to his excruciatingly painful but, ultimately welcome, release into death.

*   *   *

Imam Khalifa turned to his protégés, sternly advising, "Remember to do *exactly* as instructed; much depends on everyone sticking to the agreed plans and waiting for the final word before proceeding."

"Yes Imam, we do understand, and we are prepared," muttered Saeed, his voice resonating with deep respect.

Fawzi impetuously interrupted, "We drive to Jeddah with our false Saudi paperwork and then onward to Bahrain." Barely pausing for breath, he demanded, "What about Abdullah – where do we meet Abdullah?"

Focusing his malevolent and piercing eyes on the younger,

impetuous Fawzi, Imam Khalifa ordered, "Be patient and listen! Abdullah has his cover already established in London; you will meet up all in good time." Turning to face Saeed, his tone softened, "In Bahrain, you will make contact with Rashid, who will provide you with Bahraini passports. Rashid has booked you both on a flight to London, England, seven days from now. Keep to the schedule!"

Eager to show his mettle and his understanding of their task, Fawzi interjected impatiently, "Yes, yes, Imam, we understand, we have been through the plan many times."

The Imam sighed wearily, glared with menace at Fawzi, but deciding to ignore the interruption from the insolent youth, returned his full attention to Saeed, ensuring that the older brother understood his responsibility of keeping his younger sibling in check, "Make sure that your impetuous and impatient brother follows *exactly* as we have instructed."

His eyes burning with zealous fervour, Saeed proclaimed, "I will Imam. We will not fail."

"Good; may Allah be with you. You know the rewards awaiting you."

Fawzi smiled at the Imam but received only a cold and disdainful response in return, the Imam turning away, having decided that his current instructions had been concluded. It was now up to yet more of his disciples to put his evil plans and schemes into place.

Saeed and his brother climbed into the battered Toyota and firing up the engine, they bid farewell to Imam Khalifa but met only a stony silence in response, the Imam's face registering cold indifference knowing that he would never meet up with the brothers again. They were expendable in his battle of supremacy, yet more foot soldiers indoctrinated into the evil aims of a very small ideological minority. The cold indifference of the Imam's eyes were not matched by the intense and wicked hatred that burnt in his twisted heart and callous, bigoted, selfish mind.

Taking a serrated-edged knife from his belt, his eyes gleamed at the forthcoming satisfaction of sawing the infidel's head from his body. He would have preferred to carry out the task whilst the man was still alive, but the experiment of the poison had been of primary importance in this instance.

Later, the victim's severed head would be displayed on one of the chosen web-sites, announcing yet another milestone in the relentless march of destroying the infidel enemy.

Chapter 2

His stride belying the nervous rumbling in his stomach, Ray Maloney exited the Underground at Embankment Station and walked purposely towards Kerry's Office building.

Buoyed by the forthcoming meeting with Kerry, his mood was swinging between that of euphoria to distress and concern. "What if she turns me down, or worse, laughs at me?" He mused.

Entering the building through the large glass double doors, he passed through the ornate reception area of this outwardly drab, but internally opulent office building; the dull exterior grey having been transformed into bright colours; the walls hanging with colourful tapestries intermingled with expensive pictures housed in gold-edged frames. Pride of place was taken by a scale model of a boat, copied to every minute detail of the original full sized version, and surely worth a few thousand pounds. The scale model had been a gift from the shipyard that built the original full-sized vessel.

However the opulence was of no relevance to Ray, all his thoughts concentrated on his scheduled meeting with Kerry and the words that he would utter. Besides, he had been in this neck of the woods many times previously, thus the familiarity of his surroundings decreased his appreciation of the fine workmanship of the model and indeed of all the other glorious pictures that adorned the walls, all of boats, either under full power or resting peacefully in some exotic port location.

Ray strode towards the reception desk positioned in front of the wall directly facing the large glass doors. Two immaculately attired females, nails manicured and polished to a shimmering degree of shine, bright red lips pouting through carefully applied lipstick gloss, blonde hair gelled and pristine, the sexiness oozing out of their pores, sat behind the oblong Reception Desk. If either Receptionist had been occupied on the phone, the other Receptionist would ensure that any new visitor would be warmly greeted; her practised smile wide, her eyes welcoming, the voice mellifluous.

Fixed on the wall above the Receptionists' heads was a plaque which listed, in gold embossed lettering, the various Group Companies belonging to this prestigious organisation.

Ray ignored the two Receptionists, bypassed the bank of elevators, absentmindedly adjusted his tie, and proceeded to a broad flight of stairs that would take him to the next level and the floors above. He quickly ascended to the third floor, entering into a corridor and walked to the second door on the left - a plaque affixed on the wall grandly announced 'Grosvenor Marine Service'. He pressed the intercom button whilst glancing nervously at his vague image on the plaque, ensuring that the previous tie adjustment presented a suitably suave image.

"Yes?" boomed a voice from the intercom. Ray recognised Siobhan's voice.

"Hello, it's me, Ray...Ray Maloney," he announced, his words revealing his insecurity and lack of confidence.

"Oh Ray, I know who you are without you mentioning your surname," teased Siobhan, amused, "Come in." Her voice was warm and welcoming, and she pressed the buzzer that presaged the click release of the door catch.

Ray boldly opened the door and stepped into the inner sanctum of 'Grosvenor Marine Service', his initial confidence quickly dissipating as his eyes sought out and fixed on Kerry.

The room he had entered was oblong in shape with six evenly spaced desks, each desk equipped with a computer terminal and telephone. Ray breathed a little easier as he realised that Kerry and Siobhan were currently alone in the Office.

Siobhan was in her mid-twenties, with enticingly beautiful green eyes, auburn hair cut to just above her shoulders, pale skin, and a figure to die for. But although of equal beauty to Kerry, Siobhan's looks were lost on Ray; he was totally besotted by the gorgeous Kerry, no-one else being capable of holding a candle against the much desired Kerry.

Both Kerry and Siobhan looked up and smiled at Ray, Kerry being the first to speak, "Hello Ray, long time, no see; where *have* you been hiding?"

Ray, despite his earlier intention to be assertive and positive, withered under Kerry's steady, fixed stare. He merely smiled awkwardly, all his previously prepared words lost in the jumble that had seized control of his brain.

Sensing Ray's discomfort, Siobhan tried to make him feel at ease, jovially taunting, "He's been two timing us with the girls from 'Brannigans'!"

Ray blushed and hurriedly blurted, "Um no, I haven't; I've just been very busy. I had to go and check on a boat in France."

"It's all right for some," grinned Kerry, the idea of a trip to

France being something that she would like the opportunity of doing.

Siobhan's telephone rang and she picked up her receiver, leaving Kerry to stare up at Ray, but Kerry's thoughts were firmly elsewhere, on a trip to France, and with Pete Spratt, now that would be lovely she mused.

Rat fidgeted awkwardly under Kerry's unseeing stare, and he nervously cleared his throat.

Kerry brought back to reality, to the present, was irked at the interruption to her pleasant day dream, her sexual fantasy of Pete Spratt. She brusquely pointed to the chair in front of her desk, ordering Ray to sit down.

Now beetroot red, the colour rising from his neck to the tip of his scalp, Ray smiled shyly, and sat down.

"So, stranger, what can we do for you?" oozed Kerry, but who in reality was not in the least interested in what she or 'Grosvenor Marine Service' could do for him.

"Um, er, do you fancy, um, going out sometime?" he hesitantly began, before being cut off by the impatient Kerry who now had one ear tuned into Siobhan's telephone conversation.

"What? What are you gibbering on about?" she snapped.

Ray lost the last remnants of his courage and immediately changed tack, defensively stating, "Um, actually, I came over to get a quote from you for a replacement engine for one of our yachts."

Kerry was still not giving him her full attention, her ears finely tuned to Siobhan's conversation, "Sure." Then looked up, "Sorry, what did you say?" Ray's words poured from his mouth in a rush of nervous energy, "Kerry, if you can get me a reasonable quote, I'll only have to verify the specification with the engineers and then I'm pretty sure that the order will be yours."

Siobhan's call being terminated allowed Kerry to focus her undivided attention on Ray. "Well," she smoothly uttered, "I wouldn't expect anything less." Although establishing flirtatious eye contact, her smile was without genuine warmth.

Ray nervously cleared his throat and stammered, "I, um, don't suppose that you will be free for a drink this evening?"

Kerry almost laughed at him. "Oh Ray, I'm sorry, I can't," she hastily muttered, "I've already promised Harry Blutter and Pete Spratt that Siobhan I would meet them for a business meeting."

And she quickly added to forestall Ray being included, "I know that you wouldn't want to join us because you and Spratt don't get on with each other."

Kerry smiled dismissively.

Dumbfounded, Ray's face dropped like that of a deprived little boy. All his previous courage had been a total waste of time; he had been rebuffed quite brusquely by the gorgeous Kerry. What didn't help was the fact that she was meeting his arch nemesis and the sexual predator, Pete Spratt, instead! "That'll teach me for setting my sights so high," he thought to himself.

Realising that she had been too discourteous, that she still needed to keep in Ray's good books - he was a valued client - she adopted a more friendly tone, her wily words attempting to pour oil on Ray's troubled waters, "Besides, it is difficult Ray, because Brian doesn't like us getting too familiar with the customers. It could - ultimately - be bad for business."

Ray muttered incredulously, "Really?" But frankly he wanted to scream out, "Then what about you joining Pete Spratt for a drink, surely that's in the same boat?" Bitterly, he bit his tongue.

Kerry re-iterated her chosen tack, "Yes, Brian hates the idea of over fraternisation; god knows why, perhaps he thinks we'll fiddle the prices for you!" She chuckled, amused at her own statement, a forced, affected smile on her lips. "You do understand, don't you Ray?" she added fervently.

Ray was not going to be rude even though he knew that Kerry was feeding him bullshit, "Of course, sorry, I, um, didn't think." He smiled a reluctant and awkward smile and quickly turned towards the door to hide his embarrassment and his evident hurt.

Kerry called out after him, her voice assertive, "I'll work out some prices and get you a quotation first thing in the morning. Don't forget my order Ray. Don't let me down."

Ray nodded meekly, crestfallen, and exited; he knew that the order would still be placed with Kerry tomorrow regardless of her attitude.

When the door closed behind Ray, Siobhan looked up from her desk and murmured softly, "Oh Kerry, you must know that Ray's absolutely got the 'hots' for you."

"Yeah, I know; he's just not exciting, definitely not my type."

"*Exciting* is not everything," she retorted, "Ray's such a nice guy and would make a great partner for you, especially with you and

Sean drifting apart."

"Oh pleeeease Siobhan," Kerry snorted, "I can do a lot better than Ray!"

"Charming! And don't be so sure; poor Ray." As an afterthought, Siobhan quietly added, "I suppose you're thinking you can get Pete Spratt?"

Kerry merely shook her head and laughed, choosing not to reply.

Siobhan was not to be deflected, "Oh come on, you almost dribble with desire for Spratt; but you should be careful, otherwise you genuinely could spoil the working relationship for all of us. Besides, you'll only end up getting hurt."

"Hurt?" queried Kerry, disdainfully.

"You know Pete Spratt's reputation with women."

Kerry was amused, "Ah give over; it's just a bit of harmless fun flirting with Spratt. And I've *never* let a man get the better of me!" Absentmindedly, she pulled a tissue from the box on top of her desk and wiped a fingerprint from her computer screen, "But you're right, I don't think that I want to spend the rest of my life with Sean." She rested her head in the palms of her hands, her eyes drifting off into space, "Sean puts me on a pedestal, and life is becoming so routine and boring. At least with Harry and Spratt's crowd I can have some fun." Kerry giggled, "And if it does all go wrong, well then, as you say, Ray likes like me, so he's always my reserve, my safety net."

Kerry grinned mischievously, smirking at Siobhan, and concluded, "I've never been rejected by *any* man."

"Kerry, you're vain and horrible," retorted Siobhan, but her tone remained affectionate.

Chapter 3

Although having carried out this journey numerous times, the man of Arabic origin was nevertheless nervous, never quite sure if this time he would be stopped, his identity discovered, his mission thwarted.

But guided, he believed, by Allah, he girded his loins and mingling with the other passengers, made his way up the gangway, along the satellite arm that connected to the door of the plane that he had just exited.

Trying his utmost not be singled out, he attached himself to a group of young men obviously returning from a bachelor holiday abroad. Although not of Arab origin, they were tanned a healthy colour and he didn't feel that he looked out of place as he made his way with them through the airport corridors towards immigration and passport control.

Obviously, when they arrived at the Immigration Control area at Heathrow, he had no choice but to separate from his recently acquired 'friends', the young men joining the EEC citizen queues whilst he had to join the much shorter, but non-EEC origin queue.

His queue being shorter, it didn't take long for Abdullah to reach the kiosk and he handed his passport over to the Immigration Officer, a slight twitch developing in his wrist as he did so. His nerves were on edge but he fought to keep himself under control.

The Immigration Officer perused the passport in front of him whilst also glancing towards the computer terminal on his desk, "You are returning to study, Mr Al-Hamzi, Abdullah Al-Hamzi?" He looked up, searching into the face of the man standing in front of him, the immigration Officer's expression more that of supercilious authority rather than attempting to identify a potential illegal immigrant or alien threat. "This is your third year of study in Britain?"

Abdullah's nervousness had begun to get the better of him, a bead of sweat forming on his brow. His voice ringing with tension, he tersely replied, "Yes, Sir."

"Which College?"

"University of East London, Sir."

"Subject?" peremptory snapped the Immigration Officer, the boredom eating into him.

The man's supercilious bullying tone was making Abdullah agitated and confused, "Sorry, I don't understand."

"Subject? What subject...what are you studying?" snapped the Immigration Officer, his uniform making him imagine that he was some kind of demigod.

"Oh, sorry Sir, Civil Engineering; I'm studying to be a Civil Engineer."

The Immigration Officer kept his beady eyes fixed on Abdullah, not saying a word, enjoying making the man feel uncomfortable. He was actually clueless and incapable of determining exactly what kind of threat the man would impose. Fortunately the ice was broken when a colleague called out that the brew was ready.

His thirst overcoming his interest in the 'game', now bored with his victim, the immigration Officer mumbled, "Welcome back to Britain." And stamping the man's passport, he handed it back to Abdullah not bothering to look up as he did so.

Abdullah almost exhaled with relief and grabbing his passport, he hurriedly passed through into the United Kingdom.

"Fools," he thought, "They're more interested in their own authority rather than in identification of enemies. Well, they will pay, oh yes, they will pay. The sinners will suffer."

Almost bounding onward in joy and relief, Abdullah hurried to the luggage hall, collected his bag, and marched through the green channel of Customs, then out into the cold air of west London. He wasn't a great fan of the Underground system because, who knew, there could be other groups with the intention of blowing up more trains and besides he didn't want the possibility of being under surveillance, constantly scrutinised by the numerous CCTV cameras.

Identifying which bus he needed, he joined the line at the bus stop and wrapping his coat around him even tighter, braced himself against the cold air of London which was beginning to bite into his flesh.

Chapter 4

Sean snapped off just over half a poppadum and ignoring the selection of dips, placed the poppadum on his side plate, breaking, then nibbling the residual tiny pieces; he was becoming increasingly agitated.

Naimh exchanged a knowing glance with her husband Brendan, and smiled sympathetically at Sean. She was really glad that they had pre-booked their table because the restaurant was now full, almost overflowing, and there was no way that if they had listened to Kerry's suggestion and turned up together, they could have secured a seat. As it was people were being turned away by the head waiter, instructed that if they insisted on eating at the restaurant, then they were looking at a waiting time of well over two hours.

It had been a choice between the 'Hong King' Chinese and the Indian curry house and Naimh was glad she had made this choice. Although quite expensive and upmarket for an Indian restaurant, 'The Delicious Indian' usually guaranteed beautifully cooked Indian food and was always very popular. Besides, something about the name of the Chinese restaurant, 'Hong King', always put Naimh off - all she could think of was 'honking' up her food. Yuck.

'The Delicious Indian', in South London, was absolutely bustling. Although a Friday night always guaranteed a good turn-out, a full house, tonight it seemed as if it was jammed to the rafters. The place was vibrant, the customers buoyant and bubbling, the staff harried yet remaining efficient and courteous.

Insensitive to Sean's growing discomfort, Brendan reached across the table and helped himself to spoonfuls of onions and mango chutney; he ignored the two other available options of a white sauce and another dish, a dip that reminded him more of bogeys than anything else. None of them seemed keen on starting a conversation, an awkward silence ensuing whilst they nibbled on poppadums, intermittently sipping at their drinks. In contrast to the vibrant and cheerful surroundings, the happiness and joy spilling over in the restaurant, the mood on their table was subdued and visibly strained.

The door suddenly opened and both Sean and Brendan glanced up expectantly but quickly looking away, disappointed, an unknown couple entering through the door. Sean sighed with deep despondency, his brow puckering with a mixture of sadness and annoyance.

Naimh smiled sympathetically, her voice warm and affectionate, "Are you and Kerry ever going to name the day? You've been together for over seven years now and engaged for the last three of them," she grinned. "It's about time that you made a respectable woman out of my closest and dearest friend."

Oblivious to Naimh's attempt at distracting Sean, Brendan interjected, "Before you do that Sean, I'd like to order, I'm bloody ravenous." He glanced purposefully at his watch, "Where the hell is your woman? She's already an hour late!"

"I don't know – that's part of the problem, "Sean lamented as he distractedly fiddled with his fork, his eyes downcast.

Having raised the topic that Naimh had been desperate to divert attention from, trying her utmost to soothe Sean's obvious agitation, she nudged Brendan, angry that he had raised the subject of Kerry's unpunctuality.

Sean continued morosely, "I thought that things were ticking over nicely. We were all set for a May wedding, but, but now..." he paused, a lump forming in his throat, "Kerry seems to want something different. She's finding life boring. She desperately seems to want a change to what she calls our humdrum existence. She wants something 'exciting' or 'dangerous' to happen."

The door opened again and all three glanced up expectantly, but immediately became downcast as the expected person did not materialise.

*   *   *

A black Taxi-Cab drew to the kerb, pulling up a few metres short of the Indian restaurant. Its driver sat, motionless, waiting for one of his passengers to exit, and after what seemed an interminable time the female passenger finally opened the door.

Normally the delay would have annoyed the taxi driver but as the woman was only the first drop off point he knew that the remaining passengers would foot the bill, including the waiting time; his meter was ticking over very nicely thank you.

Kerry, slightly tipsy, laughing flirtatiously, her skirt riding high on her thighs, exited inelegantly, but then leant back into the cab. She kissed one of the men whilst her shoulders shimmied provocatively revealing her breasts through her partially unbuttoned blouse, her bra barely covering her rampant nipples.

Chuckling with a sexy huskiness, she withdrew and waited, unsteadily, as the vehicle started to pull away. Her voice almost slurring, she called out, "Bye lads, see you on Monday."

Quickly alive to her current status, remembering where she was and who she was about to meet, Kerry glanced down at her clothes, "God, I could be mistaken for a 'Prossie' touting for business!" Then she giggled to herself, "I wonder how much I'd earn?"

Hastily re-arranging her skirt and re-fastening the upper buttons of her blouse, she composed herself, cleared her throat, and taking in the ambience of the location, sighed with deep resignation. Walking towards the restaurant door her feet resented each step forward, one foot dragging reluctantly after the other.

Trying her utmost to appear both sober and respectable, Kerry entered the restaurant, a waiter having seemingly appeared from nowhere and opening the door just she was reaching for the handle.

Sean's previously sour and miserable countenance instantly transformed into a beaming smile.

Brendan having carried a lustful torch for Kerry for many years, ogled her, his eyes virtually sticking out like stalks; "One day," he thought, "One day, I'll get my leg over."

As is always the case when a person is trying their best not to make a fool of themselves, to make a seamless, regal entrance, Kerry caught her foot on the carpet and stumbled, managing to steady herself against the side of one the tables. She smiled winningly at the bemused diners then continued on her passage towards Sean.

Sean's welcoming smile withered. He frowned, deep lines puckering his forehead.

"Seano darling," Kerry purred, then hiccupped, giggled, and quickly put her hand to her mouth, "Whoops, sorry." She scanned the surroundings, seeking out a clock, not sure what time it was or exactly how late she was. "Am I late? Had a business meeting; Brian said I had to take his place, an opportunity to impress in my new job. Couldn't phone." Her words rushed out in a tumble of excuses intermingled with the occasional slurred word.

She bent forward attempting to peck Sean on the cheek, but visibly annoyed, he pulled his face away. Oblivious to Sean's distain, Kerry winked salaciously at Brendan. Fully aware of Brendan's desire for her, and though she had no intention of coupling with him, after all Naimh was her best friend, she did appreciate the admiration and liked to play him along.

Brendan glowed at the recognition, the imagined 'come-on' working overtime in his brain.

Ignoring the surface charge between her husband and Kerry, Naimh warmly greeted her dear friend, "Kerry, you're irrepressible. And it sounds as though the new job is going well?" She asked, part questioning and partially stating the obvious.

"Fan...tas...tic! Everyone's been great. I love the job." Kerry added vainly, "And they seem to love me."

"I expect it's because you're dressing more like a tart these days," exclaimed Sean, his tone sour and petulant.

Kerry was indignant, "Like a tart? You cheeky bugger!" Peeved, her tread unsteady, she took her seat, sitting down with a heavy thump on the chair next to Sean.

Brendan couldn't resist adding his two penny-worth proclaiming his partiality for Kerry, "Well, I'm quite partial to tarts and I wouldn't mind 'baking' her; I think Kerry looks great."

Not needing the interjection, Sean glared at Brendan, angrily snapping, "If you don't mind, this has nothing to do with you!"

Ever the pacifier, Naimh playfully slapped Brendan's shoulder, "You've got enough to nibble on with me." She added to Kerry, speaking affectionately, "So Kerry, how are you *really* getting on with your new job? I expect that you've got all those Engineers looking after you, maybe even running around after you. And the Customers, I reckon that they're doing your bidding, eating out of your hands and plying you with orders."

Kerry chuckled, a twinkle of merriment in her eyes; there was no doubt that she had one of the most beautiful, warm, and radiant smiles that Sean had ever seen. His sour expression melted away, his heart unable to resist Kerry's dazzling smile and her balmy, beguiling, deep blue eyes.

"You know you're so very special to me Kerry," Sean said earnestly, the deep devotion written into his face, "I don't ever want to lose you and I do get a little nervous at what could happen." He added somewhat sheepishly, "Because you're so lovely."

Kerry laughed gleefully, tossing her hair, but could not resist exchanging a flirtatious look with Brendan who winked in response.

"The trouble is, Kerry *knows* she can have any guy eating out of her hand!" Naimh, although speaking in a friendly tone, was also telling her friend not to push her luck with Brendan.

"Will you give over, Naimh, I'm not like that, but I do love the new job. It's really fascinating dealing with yachts and boat engineers. It can be exciting at times, and the people I meet are really nice," Kerry paused, taking a sip from her pre-poured glass of wine, "I feel that I've finally got a job where I truly belong."

Sean venomously snapped his poppadum into smaller pieces, "You don't really mean 'nice' people and a 'job where you belong', what you really mean is a job where you can mix with and get to know 'rich' people. Kerry, you're becoming an ambitious social climber!"

Kerry was mildly indignant, the truth hurting, "I am not!" she snapped, but then grinned, "Well, perhaps I am a little bit. But really, the people I come into contact with through my job are actually nice people."

Naimh chuckled, "Of course, those people having money and an exciting and hectic social life, helps!"

Kerry's face clouded, "I'm not that bad; you make me out to be some kind of good time girl. It's just not like that."

Sean had now got the bit between his teeth, "Oh come off it Kerry, you know it's partially true. You *do* want to mix with what you call a 'worldly social circle', the good time crowd."

"There's nothing wrong with ambition," interjected Brendan coming to Kerry's defence, prepared to do anything to show her that her was on her side, which one day, would help him to get into her knickers. "I'd like nothing better than to have those kinds of connections."

Sean snapped sourly, "I wouldn't disagree, but in Kerry's case she feels that her life is not fulfilled, that she's missing out on so much."

"That just isn't true," Kerry protested.

Reaching for his drink Sean almost spilled the glass, his emotions getting the better of him. Deciding not to take a sip, he retorted, "Come on Kerry, you know you've changed. In fact, ever since you got promotion to your new position in sales and marketing, you've become a different person. Now everything that we used to do together, things that you used to find as fun, you now find dull and boring."

"The old routine *is* getting dull; we *always* do the same things!" Kerry replied wearily.

Her words upset Naimh, "Cheers Kerry. If you're not happy with our company, then we don't have to socialise together anymore."

Not wanting to upset her best friend Kerry hastily backtracked, "No, I didn't mean it like that. I just feel that I need something more in my life, a little excitement, or a little danger."

"Terrific! The girl wants danger." Sean sighed in frustration.

Brendan couldn't resist replying, "That's all right with me; I can be very dangerous!"

Sean scowled as Kerry grinned, but Naimh was becoming slightly vexed with her husband, "Not as dangerous as you'd find me, Mister! If you want danger, I can soon show you the sharp side of my kitchen knife!" Then added scathingly, "Besides, Kerry can do far better than an old romantic 'has been' such as you." Having berated her husband, Naimh's tone softened as she said to Sean, "Kerry hasn't changed." Her eyes flicked to Kerry and she smiled, "Perhaps Kerry is a little flirtier than she used to be but she is still the same lovely, genuine person I've always known."

Not knowing what to say, they reached for their drinks, all locked in their own reflective thoughts, particularly Brendan thinking how he was going to get into Kerry's knickers.

Sean grimaced then muttered to Kerry, "I still feel that you are changing, and that you're dressing a lot more sexily these days, particularly when you dress for work."

Brendan's eyes fixed on Kerry, the lust written all over his face, "And you're *complaining*? I keep on to Naimh to experiment a bit more with stuff like stockings and suspenders, crutch-less knickers and..."

Naimh sighed, exasperated, "Shut up Brendan. I don't think that the pornographic gear that you keep buying for me is quite the same thing."

Brendan and Kerry exchanged grins, Kerry replying to Sean, "Besides, I have to dress up for work. Brian tells us girls that the customers expect us to look sexy and attractive."

"Who's Brian?" Naimh asked.

"He's her boss," snapped Sean, "I think he's a pervert!"

Kerry was becoming annoyed, "Don't start on that again. Brian's really sweet."

"And then, of course, there's *Pete Spratt*!" Sean almost spat out the man's name, the bitter anguish and torment evident in his voice, "He's a real lecher, and Kerry always seems to be hanging around his coat tails."

Kerry was taken aback, her protest sharp and overly defensive, "I do *not*! Besides, he's just one of our customers, but is a very important one!"

Naimh had become increasingly concerned, "Come on you two, calm down. If 'Brend' and I had wanted this, we would have stayed home and watched 'Eastenders'."

Kerry muttered an apology under her breath as she and Sean exchanged acerbic eye contact. Fortunately a waiter arrived with their food.

Naimh attempted to lighten the mood, cheerfully advising her friend, "We ordered your usual Kerry."

Kerry, her dander up, the pleasant time spent earlier in the evening with Pete Spratt now becoming a distant memory, glanced disdainfully at the food on her plate, "That's *precisely* what I mean, the same old routine, the same boring things."

Although annoyed at her friend's words Naimh just wanted the evening to be pleasant, thus she merely fixed Kerry with a stern glance, no words being necessary. Kerry muttered to herself, her words undistinguishable, then picking up her glass of wine, she imbibed the red liquid in one enormous gulp.

The extremely sombre mood on their table was in sharp contrast to the mood of the rest of the restaurant, peals of laughter and happiness emanating from the nearby tables.

But danger was coming, an immense danger, and absolutely not in the direction that Kerry was dreaming about!

Chapter 5

Saeed yawned; his muscles ached and his bones felt weary, but at least the end of their road journey was in sight. With his hands gripping the steering wheel, he glanced sideways at his sleeping brother.

Fawzi's head was lolling to one side with his mouth open; he was snoring gently, a tiny drop of spittle leaking from the corner of his mouth, dribbling down his chin.

"Do I wake him, so he can see the wonder of this causeway between Saudi Arabia and Bahrain, or do I leave him to sleep?" wondered the elder brother.

The journey from Yemen to Bahrain had been long and weary, but at least the end of the first stage was in sight.

Initially they had used the old Toyota Pickup truck to take them to Jeddah in Saudi Arabia, then onward to Mecca where they had made their pilgrimage, completing the final task of the 'Five Pillars of Islam'. Feeling cleansed and complete they were prepared for whatever Allah had in store for them and would do their duty as had been instructed by the Imam Khalifa. Fawzi had been particularly looking forward to his reward of twenty-four virgins.

Subsequent to completing their pilgrimage they had driven to a small village just south of Jeddah, where they met up with the designated contact, a friend of Imam Khalifa. Not only had he provided them with fresh clothes, 'Athawbs' woven of the finest, most expensive cotton material as would befit successful Saudi businessmen, but also Saudi Passports and Driving Licenses.

Apparently, the documents had been furnished by a 'tame' police chief through his contacts in the Department of the Interior. A newly registered Chevrolet Caprice Sedan, thirty thousand Saudi Riyals, and business cards that identified them as businessmen from an import company based in Jeddah, were also part of the 'package' given to them.

Transformed into respectable and apparently successful Saudi businessmen, they were then instructed to make their way to Bahrain where they would be issued with fresh papers and new identities. Bahrain was chosen because the Imam felt it would be safer in avoiding the British and other Western Agency Agents who were already watching on the lookout for possible terrorist suspects flying out from Jeddah, Riyadh, or Dammam.

It was mostly Saeed who had driven over the relentless miles of tarmac highway that led to the capital, Riyadh, and then onward to the eastern towns of Dammam and Al-Khobar, finally reaching the King Fahd Causeway that would take them over the sand banks and shallow waters of the Arabian Gulf and into the island state of Bahrain. All along their route they had been housed, fed and watered by friendly souls, all part of the Imam's fundamentalist network.

Dismissing the need to use the air-conditioning system, the brothers had travelled with the windows open, the fine desert dust invading their vehicle and leaving a deposit of yellowy-grey over the cream rear seats and upholstery. The Caprice's cruise control had been both a blessing and a curse; although it had allowed Saeed to relax more whilst negotiating the interminable miles from the west to the east coast of Saudi Arabia - negating the need to concentrate on his speed or regularly adjust his foot on the accelerator pedal- it had shepherded him into a state of drowsiness on many occasions. It was only through the providence of Allah that he had stayed awake, only once driving off the highway, his tyres sinking into the sand by the roadside and dragging him to wakefulness with a sudden jolt.

The earlier dilemma regarding wakening Fawzi was taken out of Saeed's hands. His brother stirred, stretched lazily and yawned, the brother's mouth opening to a wide expanse akin to a fish desperately sucking, trying to breathe when held forcefully in the air. Fawzi's eyes flickered open, then he sat bolt upright, realising where they were. "Why didn't you wake me?" he demanded, the tiredness of wakening from a disturbed sleep making his voice querulous and tetchy.

Saeed smiled at his brother, "So, it's my fault that you couldn't stay awake and keep me company on the journey?"

Fawzi apologised realising that he had let his brother down by falling asleep and not keeping him involved in conversation; thank Allah that Saeed hadn't succumbed and fallen asleep behind the wheel. The miles of boring terrain wore them both down, the shimmering glaring brightness of the sun reflected off the sand and sapped the eyes, numbed the senses, and anaesthetised the brain; persistent, relentless desert interspaced by the occasional and sparse dwelling, making the body want to sink into a somnolent state.

Fawzi was enthralled by the Causeway and the wonders of a city that he could discern in the distance, or at least the tops of the buildings that rose high into the sky. His eyes sweeping left and right, the excitement building within, like a child experiencing its first proper Christmas; there was so much to take in. Fishing Dhows were sailing past larger trading Dhows, and in the far distance he could make out three Ships lying way offshore, safely away from the more treacherous and shallow waters of the coast. His heart leapt with joy as he could make out smoke, and, yes, flame, rising into the clear blue sky. He hoped that it was an American Ship, blown up or sabotaged by one of his Muslim brothers.

Saeed chuckled, advising Fawzi that what he was seeing was an offshore oil well, the excess gases being burnt off in a controlled manner as they escaped into the gulf air.

Stopping briefly at the border post, their papers were given a cursory inspection and their vehicle was checked for any illegal contraband. They were passed through and drove over the remaining distance of the Causeway onto the firm ground of Bahrain. With Fawzi now alert and watching the road signs, in Arabic and English, they drove on covering the relatively short distance of a few miles from the end of the Causeway to Manama, the Bahrain capital.

Continuing their journey to the appointed hotel Fawzi sat, mouth agape, as he took in the sights of western decadence. Manama was a wonderful modern city, yet much of the old heritage had been preserved, the ancient origins of this important trading post not being forgotten. It was Bahrain that first gave the West the flavour of rich Sheikdoms that emanated from oil wealth and prior to that, their pearl divers had given the island a cachet much envied by its larger neighbours; not to mention, of course, the wonderful pearls that had been secured from the sea bed. There was even an offshore fresh water well where, if the tide had been right, people had filled leather bags full of the life giving fluid.

Today, the introduction of cultured pearls, particularly from the Japanese and Far East, together with the over-harvesting of the Arabian Sea bed, had virtually finished off the pearl diving heritage. The divers, and their offspring, had no choice but to seek employment elsewhere, their expanded lung capacity - some capable of being able to hold their breath under water for minutes at a time – no longer being required.

Fawzi was not only enthralled with Manama, its splendid hotels, its tower blocks of concrete, steel and glass that housed businesses as well as residences, the shopping Malls, the all-round evident affluence, but was also shocked, yet intrigued, by the women.

The females were a revelation to him, of every possible nationality and culture. 'Abaya' clad Arabic woman with 'Niqab' veils of various degrees, some completely obscuring their faces, others barely down over their foreheads; there were also other, liberated Arabic females, plus Asian women of all guises from Sari-robed Indians and Sri Lankans, respectful Pakistani ladies, Filipinas, Thais, Chinese, etc, through to Western women with bare arms and swathes of naked flesh exposed. The fair-skinned women filled him with a mix of revulsion and desire. He was appalled at their licentious demeanour, their apparent promiscuity, yet he wanted them, lusted after them, his loins experiencing a joyful life of their own. The numerous virgins that he had been promised when he gave up his life as a martyr would have to wait a little longer he thought as a particular Swedish lady, dressed in tight shorts and a brief tank top, bent over to pick up her dropped car keys.

Chapter 6

Having finished her day's work, which certainly couldn't have been described as arduous, Kerry felt that she needed to reward herself by going for a drink with 'the gang'. She and Siobhan had retired to 'Rosie's' Irish Bar, a popular haunt for many of a similar age in their in their profession.

'Rosie's' was near Charing Cross, thus the location was also suitable for easy access to the London Underground or the Main Line railway station. Many a pleasant evening had been spent getting thoroughly plastered. Everyone enjoyed themselves, making sure that the more inebriated of their colleagues were despatched safely on their way at the conclusion of the evening 'meetings', the few remaining sober people pouring the less able onto their respective trains.

Kerry was ecstatic that Pete Spratt and his entourage were in the Bar and made a bee-line to join them. The bar was rowdy, overcrowded but cheerful, no one complaining about the undue delay in getting served.

As the evening drew on the imbibers gradually thinned out leaving only a sparse few behind. Finally only Kerry, Siobhan, Pete and a couple of other stragglers remained.

With the gradual emptying of the premises, Kerry's group had claimed the bar counter area. Positioning the bar stools into a semi-circle by the counter for easy access, they would also have use of the counter to put down their glasses when not imbibing. Normally, Rosie hated people cluttering up her bar but in this case she didn't mind, both because the place was emptying and because she was extremely fond of Kerry and her friends.

Placing his almost empty glass on the counter Harry's eyes fixed on Kerry, his vision undressing her before he spoke, "Who's for a Chinese then, I'm starving?" His fingers tapping on Kerry's arm, "Come on Kerry, you've got to come with us for a Chinese."

Kerry laughed happily but protested, "I can't. I'm already late and Sean will kill me if I'm much longer."

"Ah, don't be boring," persisted Harry, "I'm sure that if Sean was out with his work colleagues he'd be doing exactly the same as you. Come on, we need you to make the evening fun." Harry interrupted Spratt's conversation with Ibrahim, another colleague. "Pete, we need Kerry...and Siobhan," he added as an afterthought, "To join us for a 'Chinese', don't we?"

Kerry's eyes focused on Spratt, her look one of longing desire. Spratt returned her gaze, smiling beguilingly, making Kerry shiver, a tingle of mysterious pleasure passing down her spine.

Her determination to leave had instantly weakened and with a voice full of lasciviousness she oozed, "I'd love to come boys."

Siobhan fidgeted at her side and with raised eyebrow demanded questioningly, "What about Sean? How are you going to explain that you are letting him down?"

Kerry merely smiled enthusiastically, "That's not a problem, I'll think of something." And with that she flounced off, making her way to a corner recess which was on the way to the toilets and the only place in the Pub where it was possible, barely, to carry out some semblance of a phone conversation.

Having already decided that she was not going to use her mobile phone, Kerry picked up the public phone, inserted a pound coin and quickly dialled her and Sean's home number. She had prepared in her mind's eye the excuse of not using her mobile; having already ignored three missed calls from Sean she would pretend that she had left her mobile in the office.

Her home telephone was answered almost immediately, the person at the other end almost snatching up the phone in unprecedented haste.

"Kerry, is that you?" demanded the breathless and frantically concerned Sean, almost out of his mind with worry.

Unabashed, inconsiderate and without remorse, Kerry merely said, "Hi, Sean darling. I'm afraid I've been held up; it looks as if I'm going to be quite late getting back tonight."

Although Sean was delighted and relieved that it was Kerry on the other end of the line he was dismayed on hearing her words. "No, that's not fair," he protested, "We were supposed to be going out for dinner tonight and I've been waiting for almost two hours to hear from you! I tried your mobile a few times."

"Sorry Sean, I think I left my mobile in the office; it's not in my bag," lied Kerry.

Sean interjected, "You really must take more care of your phone; you don't know when you might need it in an emergency. Buy a spare one; I've been frantic trying to get hold of you!"

"I've told you before; I don't like them very much. They're only necessary for work," she retorted, the thought of Sean being able to contact her at will, being abhorrent to her.

"Where are you now and where have you been?" demanded Sean, almost whining.

"I'm in the pub, at 'Rosie's, a business meeting."

"Well, call it a day and get home will you please, I'm starving, and I would like some of your company."

"I can't just leave; it's business," she protested, "Besides I've had a snack and I'm not hungry."

"Oh Kerry," complained Sean, exasperated but still full of love for his fiancée, "Please come home now. I'll get a take way and then at least we'll spend some time together."

Kerry was determined to not give in, "But...but Sean, listen will 'ya." Sean muttered angrily but paused, waiting for Kerry's words, "Look, I'm sorry Sean but I have to do this for my work. If Brian finds out that I'm upsetting Harry Blutter it could have a bad effect on my job. Please Sean, do understand."

Suddenly alarmed by the mention of Harry's name Sean blurted, "Is Pete Spratt there as well?"

Kerry was taken aback, almost feeling caught out, "What? Er, no, he's um, he's left already."

Sean's concern turned to anger, "What! He was there? You know I don't like you being with him, particularly when I'm not there. I don't trust him!"

"Sean, please! They're waiting for me. It's important for business, for my job. Spratt's not with us."

Sean sighed, muttering with reservation, "Well all right then Kerry, but be careful and try not to be too late please."

Kerry feeling reassured was glad that Sean had acquiesced; but regardless of Sean's objections, there was no way that she was not going to go for a meal with Pete Spratt. "Thanks 'Seano' darling," she uttered with false sincerity, "I'll do my best to leave as early as possible. Bye."

"Bye Kerry, you know how much I love you! See you later," Sean gushed, his tone full of love.

Insensitive to Sean's emotion Kerry merely replaced the receiver in its cradle, Sean's words being cut off in mid-stream. With triumphant joy lighting up her eyes she turned away, her face radiant, and mumbled, "So, Pete Spratt, play your cards right and you could have me tonight."

Grinning broadly, a gleam in her eye, Kerry almost bounded back to Spratt. Their eyes met and she favoured him with a delicious and seductive smile; glowing with anticipation she picked up her coat from a nearby bar stool.

Spratt murmured to Ibrahim, "This is going to be so easy; she's got the 'hots' for me."

"Lucky bastard!" replied Ibrahim under his breath.

"Well boys," announced Kerry exuberantly, "You've got the pleasure of my company. Let's go, I'm famished." She buttoned up her coat in a flash of nimble fingers.

Ibrahim reluctantly declined, "I'm sorry everyone, but the wife's expecting me home."

Dominic, yet another of Spratt's crowd, pointed at the two young females still fluttering in their vicinity, like moths to a light, "What about the girls? They were looking forward to a night of fun and frolics, not a boring meal." The girls smiled in anticipated agreement.

Ibrahim was adamant, but rueful, "Sorry, girls, I have to get home. I'm already in deep shit with my wife for getting back late last night."

"Why worry?" Interjected Harry, teasingly, "I thought that you guys are allowed more than one wife."

Ibrahim responded cheerfully, "One wife and one mother-in-law, is quite enough for me, thanks."

"This 'wife' thing, it doesn't normally stop you taking an interest in the ladies," responded Spratt dryly.

"Ah well, you know how it is," sheepishly replied Ibrahim, "I can only push my luck so far." He grinned, "Besides, aforementioned mother-in-law is coming to stay tonight."

"Ah ha, that explains it!" jovially responded Harry.

"Thus I'm going home, now, to my wife."

"Me too," added Dominic, his eyes fixed on the two younger females.

"You haven't got a wife," Siobhan said, a twinkle in her eye.

"No, I meant I've got to go. I promised to take," Dominic pointed at his two admirers, "Jackie and Belinda home."

"Ah, but whose home?" queried Siobhan mischievously.

Dominic laughed, his two female admirers turning a bright shade of scarlet. With Ibrahim leading the way, Dominic and the two young females exited, leaving Kerry waiting expectantly for Spratt to take her for a meal and then...

Delighted, she declared, "That just leaves the four of us!" Kerry, smiling wickedly, inserted her arms under Spratt's and Harry's arms, leading the men towards the exit. Rosie, although fond of Kerry, shook her head in dismay, not entirely convinced of Kerry's choice of men; besides she actually liked Sean, preferring him to Spratt.

Siobhan, forgotten, was both bemused and slightly peeved but she was hungry and needed some food to soak up the alcohol. Sighing with resignation and exchanging a rueful glance with Rosie, she buttoned up her coat, picked up her handbag, gulped down the remainder of her drink, and followed after her already departed friends.

Exiting with a resigned air, anticipating the potential future repercussions, she muttered, "This could be fun evening, but it could also get very messy, if Kerry's not careful!"

*　　*　　*

Unfortunately, on their way to the Chinese restaurant Harry discovered another bar that he recalled served special cocktails, and without much prompting, he cajoled the three others to join him.

Much later, Kerry and Siobhan, arm in arm with Spratt, led by Harry, stumbled through the opened door of the Chinese. They were in high spirits, laughing boisterously at nothing in particular as only very drunk people do.

The manager gaped with dismay, apprehensive at what he was letting himself in for; on the point of re-directing them back out through the door he glanced over his shoulder at the empty tables, having only sold a few 'covers' that evening. God knows why, but business had been dreadfully slow tonight. Reluctantly and with a heavy heart, he went over to greet his new customers.

Harry, showing off, facetiously demanded, "'Haalow', table 'foh fouwer'."

The manager chose to ignore Harry's crude attempt at humour, replying disdainfully, "Good evening, ladies and gentlemen." He paused before uttering the word 'gentlemen'. "Is that a table for four?"

"That's what I said," re-iterated Harry, "Table for 'fouwer'."

The Manager favoured Harry with a disdainful stare and then glanced at the two ladies in the party. Politely he requested that the ladies follow him, treating Harry and the widely smirking Spratt as if they were invisible. Although there were many empty tables in his path he chose to bypass them all, leading the quartet to a table at the farthest end of the room; then with eyes flickering contemptuously in Harry's direction, he declared, "Here you are. Table for '*fouwer*.'"

Siobhan wishing to atone for her colleagues politely thanked the Manager, then promptly sat down, her tired legs barely able to support her sozzled brain and inebriated body. Kerry followed almost simultaneously, choosing the chair alongside Siobhan. Spratt pushed past Harry and took the seat opposite Kerry, a big smirk still encompassing his face. Harry was irked because he had wanted the seat next to Kerry, or at the very least, the one opposite.

Harry soon cheered up when Kerry winked at him and chuckled, "I don't think that he was too impressed with your Chinese accent."

"No, the boring old fart," he responded, "Some people have no sense of humour!"

The manager had reluctantly taken their drinks order but insisted that they order the food at the same time. Despite Harry grumbling about not having enough time to scrutinise the menu the others were extremely ravenous and accordingly, were more than happy to comply with the manager's request. It had then taken an inordinate amount of time before one of the waiters was permitted to serve the drinks, and in fact, it was only when the manager saw that Harry was about to lead an exodus that he permitted the waiter to depart with his drink laden tray.

Fortunately, most of what had been ordered was generally pre-prepared, thus it didn't take long for the first course to be set in front of the drunken party. As slowly as the drinks arrived at their table the food seemed to arrive quicker, the staff intent in not only filling the drunken customer's bellies with sustenance but also to get them out of their establishment, with bill fully paid, as soon as possible.

One member of the kitchen staff had already included certain unwanted additions to Harry's plate and the manager would also ensure that the end bill would be considerably higher than the four drunken diners anticipated. Harry had been rude and supercilious throughout the meal and payback time was an on-going process as far as the Staff was concerned.

Despite the extra indescribable additions to his meal, Harry had scraped his plate clean, Spratt's plate imitating that of Harry. The two girls had barely touched their food, Kerry with her mind on other things, was more intent on enjoying the drink, a prelude to her giving herself to Spratt later that night. Whereas Siobhan, nervous as to how the evening might end, nibbled at the main course, the starter having been sufficient to assuage her earlier hunger.

The ladies were drinking red wine, the men mixing between lager and red wine, their table covered with empty bottles and glasses. It seemed that the waiters could not keep up with the constant cycle of removing the empties but in reality the boss had instructed the staff to leave the empties on the table thus, hopefully, getting the message across to the party as to how much they were consuming. It didn't work.

Siobhan, sipping at her drink was the most sober, and she decided to crack a joke, "So, why is sex like maths?"

Harry, slurring his words, replied, "I don't know, why is sex like maths?"

"Because add boy to girl, subtract their clothes, divide her legs, and multiply!" She triumphantly explained. The joke amused them, Harry actually bursting into laughter; mind you, in his current state, anything would have been funny so long as the other person laughed as well.

"That's good; I must remember that one," Kerry tittered, her shoeless foot playing footsie with Spratt's leg.

Enjoying the attention, Spratt grinned at Kerry, "Harry's got some new porno DVD's through the post. They're better than the ones that we all watched last week."

Not wishing his thunder to be taken, Harry intervened excitedly, "Yes, they're going to be really good. Do you remember that contact magazine that I told you about? Well, the DVD's came from an advertisement in one of them. They've got the lot, 'lesbo' scenes, bored housewives, oral, you name it, it's all in the films!" His enthusiasm grew, getting quite excitable, "I've even got some contact info for group sex, wife swapping, you name it, it's there!"

Siobhan laughed at Harry's enthusiasm, "Whoa, Harry, don't get carried away. Anyway, for the swinging and wife swapping bits, you need a wife, or at least a female partner."

Harry glanced slyly from Siobhan to Kerry to Kerry then back to Siobhan, "Well, I was hoping that you two?"

Siobhan was tickled, "On your bike. Besides, I'm quite happy with what I'm getting from Danny."

Spratt tore his eyes free from Kerry's eyes; her roaming foot making him feel quite randy. Although he knew that Kerry was a dead 'cert' for him, he actually preferred Siobhan, and turned his attention from Kerry, "Surely you want to experience a few things before settling down with the one man?"

Siobhan retorted pleasantly, "You won't get me on that one. Kerry and I are well taken care of by our fellahs."

"Speak for yourself," Kerry mumbled.

Spratt re-focused his attention on Kerry, Harry eagerly blurting, "Pardon? What did you say?"

The alcohol making Kerry reckless, she snapped, "I said, she could speak for herself." And she exchanged a deep and meaningful look with Spratt.

Harry began to realise that he was fighting a lost cause with Kerry and shrugged, concentrating his attention on Siobhan. "Great, that's one volunteer. Come on Siobhan, you can't let us down."

Siobhan was beginning to feel uneasy, and fixing Kerry with a hard stare, she then smiled sweetly at Harry, "Harry, change the subject; I'm happy with my boyfriend Danny. I've done all the living, and experimenting, that I needed to do before I met Danny. Now I'm strictly a one-man girl. And I'm sure that it's just the booze talking with Kerry."

"It is not!" Her friend retorted childishly.

"Kerry, be careful with what you're saying. And do grow up!" Siobhan's tone was stern, but maternal.

Kerry pouted, an aggrieved expression floating across her face. Petulantly, she picked up her full glass of wine swallowing the contents in one large gulp. Licking her lips, her expression cantankerous, she glared at Siobhan then passed the empty glass to Spratt, declaring, "I'll have another."

Grinning like a Cheshire Cat Spratt took the glass and signalled for the Waiter.

Siobhan sighed, knowing full well that the evening was turning out to be the disaster that she had anticipated; she was losing control in her attempt to protect her friend and work colleague.

His raised arm having been ignored, Spratt whistled to get the waiter's attention, causing Kerry to giggle in 'appreciation' of Spratt's imagined bravado.

The waiter, finalising the bill for another table, glanced up, grimaced and then stared questioningly at Spratt.

Spratt swept his arm above the surface of the table indicating the empty glasses, mouthing for more drinks to be served. Assuming that his message was understood he returned his attention to Kerry, "Do you know Kerry, you would look really good wearing a pearl necklace."

Kerry was delighted and glowed at the thought of Spratt's present, "Why, thank you Spratty – are you going to buy me one?"

Siobhan snorted, laughed, then guffawed. Harry smirked, his eyes taking in the image.

Kerry glanced doubtfully from Spratt to Siobhan's rib tickling amusement, the true meaning of Spratt's words beginning to register. Her face slowly awakened with the realisation of the innuendo of Spratt's words. Although the thought did not displease her she felt foolish at her initial pleasant response to Spratt.

Belatedly, she affected indignation, declaring, "Spratt! You dirty bastard!" But, she couldn't resist smiling, adding, "You are terrible."

Getting jealous, Harry intervened, "Don't take any notice of Spratt. He's getting carried away with one of the porno films that we saw. I think it was called 'Mary gets laid'.

Kerry now highly animated, the booze and anticipated sex making her careless, oozed, "Sounds like fun."

The waiter delivered a fresh round of drinks, Kerry instantly picking up her glass but this time she was unable to down the contents in one go, gagging, almost choking in her attempt.

Despite feeling that she was fighting a losing battle, Siobhan did her utmost to protect her friend, "Hey, easy girl. We'll have to carry you out if you keep knocking them back like that."

"I don't care. Anyway, I can handle my drink!"

"Yea, I can see that!" Siobhan caustically retorted.

Having given up on getting his way with Siobhan, Harry was still hoping to pick up the pieces after Spratt. He glared at Siobhan, "Leave her be, Siobhan, she's fine."

This had the opposite effect on Siobhan, who was now extremely irked. "You would say that; you just want to get your leg over, you dirty old buggers."

Rather than being offended, Harry merely grinned.

Kerry, eyes heavy lidded, foot nestling in Spratt's crutch, stared seductively into Spratt's eyes and ran her tongue over her lips. She could do no more than hand herself to him on a plate but Spratt was enjoying playing the moment, knowing that she was hot for him. Already his mind had moved forward as to how he could get into Siobhan's knickers, the conquest being of paramount importance. Yes, he would enjoy Kerry but she was not of any great importance to him.

Although not interested in either Spratt or Harry, Siobhan was exasperated with Kerry's behaviour. Infuriated, she announced, "Right, my girl; if that's the way you want it." She rose to her feet, Kerry expecting her uptight friend to depart. But with a look of determination on her face, Siobhan stretched across, triumphantly announcing, "Look at this boys!" With a deft tug she pulled open the poppers on the front of Kerry's dress.

Kerry's dress opened fully, revealing her skimpy see-through and lace fringed bra, a brief thong, and self-supporting stockings. Spratt's mouth opened and shut, his eyes lighting up, a lascivious look spreading across every millimetre of his face. Harry, ecstatic, literally whooped with joy.

Although annoyed that it wasn't Spratt who had released her body from the dress, Kerry was delighted at Spratt's joyful reaction and rather than rescuing her modesty, merely flapped her arms about her body, her hands making a feeble and futile attempt at re-fastening her poppers.

Harry's reaction had alerted the other occupants of the restaurant, an excited hubbub erupting almost instantaneously. The manager, caught once again in two minds rushed over to their table, his eyes devouring Kerry never once focusing on her three companions.

Kerry belatedly protested, her protest more of a sham than with heartfelt emotion, "Oh Siobhan, you bitch, how could you!"

The manager finally found his words, his eyes relocating back into their sockets, "Madam, please! You're upsetting the customers!"

Harry switched his vision from Kerry's body to the man's face, gleefully stating, "Oh no, she's not!"

The manager was perplexed and quickly indicated the other Diners, "No, *Sir*, I don't mean you, I mean the *other* customers are complaining!"

Having returned his attention to Kerry's body, Harry reluctantly tore his eyes free once again, quickly scanning the room, "I really don't think that they *are* complaining."

Siobhan grinned mischievously, "Complaining, no; lusting, yes!"

Some of the other female customers began to mumble in complaint, the excited hubbub of their men folk being overtaken by a chorus of female disapproval. A few words such as 'slut' and 'tart' were beginning to rise in the room, reverberating around the restaurant. As much as he was enjoying the view the manager quickly realised that he had to be firm, sternly ordering of Kerry, "Madam, *please;* make yourself respectable."

"Whore!" A forty-something lady cried out, fed up at seeing her husband's eyes sticking out like stalks.

The woman's word hit home, travelling through Kerry's ears to her drunken brain. She glanced downwards at her exposed body, looked up beyond the man standing by their table, and finally became aware of the faces peering in her direction. Suddenly embarrassed and quickly sobering she sat erect, and with new found control of her fumbling hands, she refastened her dress. Her face was now a bright scarlet colour.

Mortified, Kerry muttered, "I didn't realise so many people were staring; how embarrassing!"

Spratt decided that he wanted some of the action that was now hidden under Kerry's dress, "C'mon Kerry, the night's young, come back to my place for coffee."

"I'll come too," intervened Harry, not wanting to miss out on the action.

"Ah, a threesome, a spit roast," gloated Siobhan, doing her utmost to shame Kerry out of Spratt's ruthless intention of bedding her friend.

"Slut!" Persisted the forty-something lady, glaring at Kerry with a look that usually put her own children in fear of not committing a misdemeanour.

As desperately as she wanted to copulate with Spratt, Kerry hesitated, undecided, weighing up her options. But the sea of lecherous faces together with matching disapproving stares and tuts, coupled with raucous laughter followed by a female giggling at a lewd comment from her companion caused Kerry to lose her earlier bravado; her passion being swamped by a growing need to regain her self-respect.

"No; sorry, Spratt...maybe another time." She finally replied, her voice barely audible.

"Come on Kerry, I'll see you home," Siobhan said with smug satisfaction, her action having achieved success. One day, she felt sure, Kerry would be grateful.

Harry was not about to give up, his loins boiling with unreleased longing, "Girls, don't spoil a good evening. The night's still young. We can go clubbing, and then I'll get you both a taxi home."

"Yes, but whose home? The only thing that you'll get us into is a lot of trouble!" Retorted Siobhan jovially as she led Kerry out of the restaurant.

Chapter 7

The sweat was literally dripping from the brow of the Indian worker as he cut slices of meat from a mutton joint that was slowly rotating on an upright spit in front of a vertical, wall mounted grill. In other circumstances, or in other places, the Indian worker might have been described as a chef or at least a cook, but not here. He had not been given any training, merely being employed, like so many of his countrymen, as cheap labour. However, the pittance that he was paid would make him seem like a rich man back in his village home in Kerala, India. He was looking forward to the promised four weeks holiday back home, unpaid; but it would be very special to see his wife and children again; the contract allowed the holiday after completion of two years contract, and he was counting down the last remaining days.

Initially having been brought to Bahrain to work as a labourer in the Port, his sponsor had decided to relocate him elsewhere, and having been handed various assorted labouring duties, he finally ending up working in this Arabic restaurant in the Barbar district of Bahrain.

Restaurant was not really an appropriate description for this particular eating house. The dilapidated building, whitewash peeling from the walls, unwashed plates left on tables, was not hygienic in any conceivable respect. The place was utilised by the Indian labourer employer's assorted staff, plus a variety of local people, consisting mainly of many of the poorer Shi'a Arabs from the area, their annual pay being only slightly better than that of the Indian worker.

The restaurant was quite small, no larger than the ground floor of a terraced house in a British street. There was no air-conditioning, the windows wide open, providing some relief, more from the need to allow cooking fumes to expel rather than to allow the ingress of fresh air.

With the external temperatures vying between forty and fifty degrees centigrade, the restaurant was hot and humid. The front and only door was left ajar, wedged open with an old oil drum.

Flies buzzed happily over the uncovered food dishes placed in the glass fronted, but open topped, display cabinet. Plates of cooked meats lay alongside bowls of various salads, rice, and dips such as Houmas, and on a table nearby was a stack of pitta bread, still hot and fresh from the oven. The bread was slightly too hot for the flies to land on but would soon cool down enough for them to rest their busy wings.

Fawzi sitting at one of the four rickety tables nervously scanned the faces of anyone who entered or passed by the open door. Using a slice of pitta bread he was scooping up his mutton curry from a cracked and chipped bowl, ignoring the flies that gorged on the remnants of dried food stuck to the table.

*   *   *

An Englishman, wearing the uniform of a Chief Inspector of the Bahrain police, sat in the driver's seat of a Landrover, his eyes fixed on the restaurant door. His vehicle was parked under the shade of a canopy attached to a nearby private dwelling.

The Inspector turned to face the two Bahraini policemen sitting in the rear of the vehicle, his expression stern and commanding. Issuing curt instructions he left his two subordinate officers in no doubt of what he wanted them to do, his words heavy with authority, his demeanour exacting.

Following a tip-off they had been observing Fawzi for some time, waiting for the man's accomplices. For two days they had watched and waited, in rota, but no-one had materialised or made contact. The Inspector's patience had finally become exhausted and he determined to pull Fawzi in for questioning. Intense interrogation, with a little knocking about, would actually be the true mode of operation. The Suspects always talked, for even if they weren't guilty he would wring a confession out of them.

The three police officers exited their Landrover and separating as instructed cautiously made their way to the local eating house. The Inspector knew that Fawzi was not a local Arab and there was something about him that bore greater inspection.

He would enjoy making the youth talk.

*   *   *

The sun reflected off the windscreen of a pick-up truck, laden with Calor gas canisters, partially hidden in an open garage near the restaurant.

Closer inspection as the sun's reflection receded revealed a pair of malevolent eyes and the faint image of an Arab face peering from inside the cab.

The man was reciting from the Holy Qur'an, his whole focus and attention preparing him for the task ahead. At the end of this day, he would be with Allah, his purpose served; his life lived in honour of his beliefs.

*　　*　　*

A hand was placed firmly on Fawzi's shoulder; alarmed and petrified he jumped to his feet, ready to fight or flee depending on the odds.

Fawzi almost wet himself with relief when he realised that it was only his brother Saeed, finger to his lips, gesturing Fawzi to follow him.

With Fawzi almost glued to his heel, Saeed scampered to the rear of the building and clambered out of the large open window, quickly climbing onto the flat roof. Keeping low, the brothers made their way to the edge then slid over onto the next building that was separated by less than a foot. Fawzi, terrified, glanced back, relieved that no one seemed to have noticed them. He hastily followed his brother as they scrambled across two more roofs before slipping down a larger gap between the fourth and fifth buildings. Then, crouching as low as possible, they scampered into a drainage ditch, where, with heavy breathing from their exertions, they lay still, Fawzi's body almost deathlike as he didn't dare move a muscle.

Saeed waited, his breathing now eased, and he quietly began praying to Allah, accepting whatever fate had in store for him and his brother.

*　　*　　*

The wait was very short, the English police Inspector, revolver in hand, bursting through the front entrance of the restaurant. The surprised and terrified Indian cook dropped his carving knife, the knife missing his foot by the merest sliver.

Almost simultaneously the two Bahraini policemen entered through the rear window, triumphant smiles of satisfaction and achievement etched on their faces. They had crept round the back of the building totally unseen and undetected, feeling enormous delight in their achievement.

Of course, they had been observed and had been watched every inch of their supposed stealthy progress.

Their delight quickly turned to dismay, for the room was almost empty with the exception of the terrified Indian worker, two customers, and their bemused superior officer. The intended target *had* been in the room and there was no way that the man could have got out undetected.

The English policeman, seconded from Scotland Yard on a very lucrative three year contract, removed his cap, wiped the sweat from his forehead with a handkerchief, and scratched his head bewilderingly. This should have been a very simple exercise, the suspected terrorist detained, a quick journey to his headquarters in Manama, and then the subsequent 'fun' of the interrogation. He had played the day's plan over in his mind; the initial capture followed by the exultation of his peers, the praise from his superiors here in Bahrain and from the Intelligence Services both here in Bahrain and in London and the awe earned from his junior police officers. It should have all been over by two o'clock and then onward to the British Club, where he would have swaggered in, taken his usual place by the bar and bathed in the hero worship and respect of his acolytes, his fellow Europeans who worked for the various government departments or the embassy staff, all of whose workdays finished shortly after one p.m.

But now it had temporarily come to nought. He holstered his weapon, replaced his cap, and fixed a stern and unfriendly eye on the terrified Indian worker. "Arrest him," he commanded to his juniors, "He must have tipped off our 'friend'."

The poor bewildered, confused and utterly terrified Indian worker sank to his knees in supplication and fear, almost crying out in protest of his innocence.

One of the Bahraini policemen, himself an immigrant from the Indian Sub-Continent, his earlier career as a private in the Pakistani army long forgotten where he had been dishonourably discharged for cruelty, took out his truncheon and irrationally hit the already prostrate Indian across the crown of his head, sending the befuddled worker flying back against one the tables. Not satisfied with his initial strike, the immigrant policeman stood over the prostrate Indian, ignoring the man's protests of innocence, the man's futile attempts at defending himself, and struck at him relentlessly. The Indian cook cowered, tried to roll into a ball, his arms attempting to protect his head and body, the blood beginning to seep from his newly created wounds.

Rather than countermanding his overzealous junior officer the Inspector examined a speck of imaginary dirt in one of his fingernails, whilst the third policeman, a Bahraini of Shi'ite faith, just wanted to leave, to get out, for what was happening was totally against his belief and training.

"Someone is going to suffer for this failure," thought the Inspector, "And why not this lowly worker. I'll still have my 'five minutes' of adventure to recount later on at the British Club." The image of the glass of malt whisky warming in his hand gave him a mellow feeling, his initial anger now compartmentalised for reactivation at a later date.

Something interrupted his growing feeling of well-being, a new sound, a raucous noise, the growl of an intensely revving vehicle, the clatter growing, building to a crescendo.

Alarmed, the Inspector turned away from the spectacle of the punishment being metered out to the Indian worker and glanced at his other colleague; they exchanged meaningful looks, recognition and alarm shooting across their faces.

*   *   *

The man sitting behind the wheel in the pick-up truck pressed his foot firmly to the floor, the truck's accelerator pedal almost grinding into the metal of the vehicle's floor well. The rev counter had shot all the way to maximum, the needle jammed hard against the stop pin, the vehicles engine screaming in horrendous protest.

His other foot was depressing the brake pedal, all his energy tied into trying not to let the vehicle loose, the engine desperate to do its work, to thrust forward, to eat up the massive amount of horsepower being generated. Smoke began to ebb from the overheating tyres, the smell of burning rubber assailing the nostrils but of no consequence to the driver.

With his final prayer still on his lips, his maniacal eyes no longer interested in the beauty that this world had to offer, the local Bahraini removed his foot from the brake pedal, and the pick-up, tyres initially spinning in a whining heated protested of scorched rubber and displaced sand, leaped forward like a mad dog, a bull terrier charging after its victim, the blood lust salivating from the corners of its mouth.

The truck, steam rising from the edges of the bonnet, from the radiator grill, and mingling with the burning rubber of the tyres, the engine screaming like a demented demon, drove onward towards the entrance of the restaurant, sending plumes of small stones, sand, burnt rubber and melted tarmac spiralling into the hot and humid air.

Oblivious to the impending threat, the brutal Constable was still carrying out his unjust retribution on the Indian worker, but the Inspector and his other colleague, alarmed, turned to face the entrance and to identify the reason for the growling crescendo. The Inspector realised too late the cause of the approaching howling horror, his feet temporarily immobilised, like lead, as his eyes registered the imminent arrival of the onward rushing vehicle.

Like an express train the truck gathered speed, the driver resigned to his death, a new prayer beginning to form on his lips, a mumble emanating from somewhere deep in his throat.

The Inspector looked over his shoulder and turning urgently gestured to his colleagues that they should follow him and leave via the rear window opening. Before his hands could reach for the windowsill, the previously folded back heavy wooden shutters were slammed shut, the bright sunlight being sealed outside. With a desperation that was beginning to overtake him he pushed at the shutters but was too late, the deafening clunking sound of the metal bars being locked into place assailing his already overburdened ears.

Frantically the three policemen pushed at the locked shutters, their fear and desperation giving them unbridled, but futile, strength. The immigrant policeman clawed and banged his fists on the shutters, pleading for his Moslem brothers to let him out, his fear written over his face.

Fearing the worst, knowing he had miscalculated, the Inspector wheeled round to face the entrance, to make one last attempt to dive out of the room and roll clear of the fast approaching pick-up that had already blocked out almost all the daylight. With utter trepidation and panic the two Constables and the Indian worker cowered under a table at the back of the room, the Englishman running forward, doing his utmost to escape out of the front before the impact.

The fanatical Arab driver smashed his vehicle into the front of the restaurant, crashing through the outer wall. Wood, breeze blocks, plaster and masonry dust flew upward and forward into the room, the impact crushing the front wall in a cacophony of twisted metal, bricks and masonry.

But, miracle of miracles, the front of the vehicle stopped inches short of the petrified Inspector, his cry of resignation in meeting his maker frozen on his lips. His eyes a second before locked wide in utter fear, now narrowed, a malicious glint reappearing, an assertive cruelty reasserting itself in his expression. Emitting a sigh of profound relief he glared at the maniacal face of his Arabic foe, their eyes locking in a mutual stare of hatred, contempt, and loathing.

Lazily undoing his holster, he pulled out his revolver, a victorious smirk gradually forming on his lips.

But something was not right? His enemy did not appear to be afraid, merely sitting quietly still in his cab, the visage of evil intent written on the man's face, the Bahraini terrorist's loathing and hate-filled eyes never once straying from the Inspector's face. The Englishman's expression rapidly changed, the look of confidence and victory altering to one of confusion and doubt, then the realisation of imminent defeat.

A flicker of flame had risen from the back of the pick-up and the Inspector's eyes opened wide, his face registering a belated knowledge, a new set of information which in hindsight would be too late to assist him. He became fully aware of the cargo, his vision taking in the rows of Calor gas canisters, the smell of leaked gas pervading his nostrils. With renewed effort he tried to squeeze past the truck but the gap was not sufficient, the terrorist calmly, serenely, watching his futile efforts.

Annoyed, irked, angry beyond anything that he had experienced previously, he fired at the man, emptying his gun in a burst of rapid fire.

The terrorist died, unconcerned, a bullet penetrating through his forehead with three further bullets smashing his nostrils and his cheekbone. He didn't care, his task accomplished, the flood of pain being instantly extinguished as his pathetically wasted life was brought to an end. For he believed - because it had been indoctrinated into him - that his God would welcome him into his Kingdom. The evil deed that he was carrying out was 'blessed', the infidels' lives being of absolutely no consequence to him.

With his two colleagues by his side, clambering onto the front of the truck, the Inspector began to frantically smash the glass windscreen. Climbing through the broken windscreen into the cab, his clothes torn, deep glass gashes along his arms, he couldn't escape because the doors were jammed solid by fallen masonry.

Preparing to smash his way through the glass at the rear of the cab and exit into sanctuary, the Inspector's face fell, stomach churning in desperate fear.

His certain fate hit him hard, some of the gas canisters were now alight, the smell of gas even stronger. "The bastard opened some of the canisters", he yelled, his face registering known certainty of his demise.

Just as he turned to aim a vicious kick at his dead protagonist the gas canisters exploded, a violent maelstrom of smoke, intense flame and debris dissolving what had been left of the restaurant, its few remaining live incumbents being blown apart, the body remnants quickly devoured by the hungry flames.

The initial eruption was immediately followed by the remaining canisters exploding, the resulting furore, a fireball of unparalleled heat that melted every conceivable item in its path.

With the flames licking hungrily at the adjoining buildings, Saeed, Fawzi, and two accomplices slunk away, disappearing into the warren of the nearby village. By nightfall they would all be spirited away to downtown Manama, the terrible retribution that would be meted out on their Muslim brothers by the deceased Policemen's colleagues of no concern or consequence to them.

Many of the local Shi'a population, guilty or innocent, would be questioned, pulled in, and interrogated by the Bahraini police during the course of the next few days; and the undercover British SAS men, who had provided the intelligence for the police department, were left to ruefully explain to their superiors how they had cocked up on their intelligence gathering.

Chapter 8

Sean was feeling happy this morning; Kerry had seemed as if she was back to her old self, attentive and loving. They had had a tremendous row when Kerry had arrived home at almost midnight last Friday night. She had been drunk and in a foul mood but wouldn't explain to him why. He had ended up sleeping on the sofa whilst she spent most of the night alternating between their bed and the bathroom.

The weekend had passed in a haze, Kerry behaving as if they were strangers but whatever was bugging her seemed to have been ancient history, for yesterday morning she was back to her buoyant, cheerful self. They had enjoyed a romantic evening, doing things together that they hadn't done for a long time, and today he had managed to obtain tickets for the theatre tomorrow night, so life appeared to be back on track.

Sean exited from his car, taking his briefcase from the back seat. The street he was in was typical of the myriad streets of this area in south London. Although all the houses were terraced type, some were dowdy and others spruced up, their owners proud of their homes and their environment. It was also obvious which homes had been purchased by their owners from the local Council, for now many of these privately owned and competitively purchased properties were fitted with double glazed windows and expensive looking front doors.

Sean quickly identified the house that he was seeking, the 'For Sale' sign proudly outside the residence easily identifying the property. It was also the only house currently for sale in this street. Humming softly to himself he approached the front door and pressed the button, instantly hearing the identifying bell that rang in the hallway.

It only seemed to take a couple of seconds before the door was partially opened, the silhouette of a woman appearing in the narrow gap that had been formed.

"Mrs Clark?" queried Sean.

The woman nodded.

"Hello, I'm Sean O'Malley, Surveyor for Mr and Mrs Shoesmith; I believe you were expecting me?"

The uncertain doubt dropped from the woman's expression; she opened the door wider and ushered Sean inside sweeping her arm in welcome, "Come in", she said in a barely audible voice.

Sean entered the hallway but stopped abruptly in his tracks, gulping nervously; the woman was wearing a dressing gown that was almost a negligee, leaving very little to the imagination.

"Um...perhaps I should come back when it's more convenient?" he awkwardly muttered, "I don't want to disturb you." He turned towards the front door.

But before he could take another pace Barbara Clark had pushed past him and firmly closed the opened door. She smiled, a wanton, sexy smile, a smile especially for this young, handsome man who was now standing in her hallway.

"No, you don't need to leave, it's okay. Don't feel embarrassed that I'm not dressed - I was just about to take a shower." Her eyes travelled over Sean's body, "You won't disturb me."

Sean began to perspire, "Um, well, if you're sure?" Feeling quite hot under her intense stare he ran his finger on the inside of his shirt collar in a feeble attempt of letting imaginary cool air invade his heating body.

Keen to make some distance from the woman who was only inches from him, her erect nipples thrusting through her dressing gown like two Exocet missiles seeking their target, he stepped away from Barbara and entered the first room off the hallway; it was the sitting room.

The room itself was dowdy, the furniture having seen much better days. Pride of place was given to a faded old brown leather suite, the three seat sofa having experienced much action in its many years of life. The cushions sagged forward, the material on the arms severely worn with one or two patches of peeled away surface material. If the woman had had money in the past it had obviously long since evaporated. But the room itself was relatively clean.

Barbara followed Sean into the room making him jump out of his skin, the woman only a few inches behind him. He hastily placed his briefcase on the coffee table and hurriedly extracted a note-pad and tape measure. He also had an electronic measuring instrument in his briefcase but in this instance he was happy to be preoccupied in using his tape.

Barbara loosened her dressing gown which wasn't really necessary as already there was very little left to the imagination; she wanted to make sure that Sean realised she was naked underneath and that even at her age of mid-thirties, she still had the firm body of a younger woman.

Seductively, she murmured, "Would you like me to hold something for you?"

Sean was desperate to be elsewhere and without looking round hastily gabbled, "No...no, I'm fine. Thank you."

"I can see that," she oozed.

"Pardon?"

Her eyes feasted hungrily on Sean's body, particularly his bottom as he bent over to place his measuring tape, "Fine! I can see that you're fine."

Sean made the mistake of looking up, her eyes locking onto his eyes whilst she ran her tongue over her lips. He felt as if he had been trapped in an oven and now someone had turned up the heat full blast. His mind was racing and he didn't know what to say, all his desires and wants fixed firmly on the gorgeous Kerry.

Barbara took a step closer and with an almost imperceptible movement of her hand, her dressing gown fell open, her body revealed in its full glory, the Exocet missiles almost leaping off the surface of her well-proportioned breasts; her stomach was smooth and unmarked, her pubic hair neat and tidy, growing back from what had obviously been a 'Brazilian' style. This woman had not carried children.

Sean swallowed hard and perspired heavily; he was out of his depth. Like any man he was sorely tempted, the growth between his legs fighting against the will power of his mind, the smell of the naked woman millimetres from him beckoning him on, a siren calling him onto the rocks. The battle between his senses was almost unbearable, Barbara's hand running across her smooth belly and up to her bosom, the erect nipple becoming seemingly harder under her gentle massage.

Sean's mobile phone rang and he almost sighed with relief, hastily retrieving the ringing phone from his jacket pocket, his penis still protesting through the material of his trousers. "Hello..." his voice was high pitched, nervous, but he cleared his throat and started again, "Um, hello, Sean Maloney." Embarrassed and relieved he smiled at Barbara whilst replying to the voice on the phone, "Yes, yes, I understand. That's okay. Um, could you hold on a moment?" He placed his hand over the phone murmuring to Mrs

Clark, "It's the office I'm afraid. I'll probably be some time."

Peeved and pissed off that Sean had answered his phone when she was about to give him her body, Barbara sourly re-tied her dressing gown, a scowl growing across her face. Taking a few paces towards the door she paused and turned back to Sean, gazed at his disappearing penis and winked salaciously.

Not giving up, she breathed, "I'll be in the shower." She slipped out of her dressing gown, allowing the garment to drop to the floor. "Don't be too long."

Sean inwardly groaned as the woman exited the room and despite his erect penis he continued with his phone conversation, his mind not totally connecting with the conversation taking place.

Finishing the phone conversation he took a pace towards the doorway but a vision of Kerry filled his mind. "Oh, sod it," he thought, "I can't; I can't betray Kerry." And, his mind made up, his disappointed penis now back in its cage, he proceeded to take notes, carrying on with the survey on behalf of Mr and Mrs Shoesmith's Building Society.

*　　*　　*

Sean occupied himself checking every minute internal detail of the ground floor room then thoroughly examined the outside of the building, finally having no option but to re-enter the house through the kitchen door at the rear. He jotted down a final measurement, closed his notepad and re-wound his tape measure, the thought of how he was going to cover the upper floor whilst avoiding the woman racking his fevered brain.

"Coeee, I'm still waiting," called out the ever patient but increasingly frustrated Barbara Clark.

Sean didn't reply, quickly scanning his surroundings for the best method of escape. He would have to return at another time to complete the upstairs and the attic survey, or he could let one of his colleagues take over. Perhaps one of the younger lads, or maybe the divorced middle-aged Henderson, they would surely leap at the chance of a bit of nooky with the nymphomaniac.

Preparing to leave he paused, muttering, "This is silly." Coming to a decision he strode firmly down the hallway and reaching the base of the stairs, called up, "Mrs Clarke?"

Her voice eager, the words spoken as if dressed in honey, she soothed, "Just come up Mister handsome Surveyor, and call me Barbara. Mrs Clark sounds so ancient. My back needs a good scrub, and that's not all that needs attention."

Sean cleared his throat, "Um, I'm sorry, Mrs Clarke...Barbara," adding awkwardly, "You are, um, a very attractive woman...and I may have, er, misconstrued your invitation, but I'm very happily engaged to a beautiful woman." Realising that she might think he's stating that she was ugly, he hastily continued, "Not that you're not beautiful as well, but I'm shortly to be married. I couldn't possibly be unfaithful to my fiancée."

His words were met with silence, stony, unnerving silence. Even the outside street seemed to go quiet.

Sean was unnerved, calling out, "Mrs Clark...Barbara? Can you hear me?"

She did not answer. Sean was about to turn away deciding that discretion was the better part of valour when the woman suddenly appeared at the top of the stairs, her body enclosed in a shift dress, but still no underwear, a wry grin on her face.

"You poor boy," she sympathised, and descended. Sean, embarrassed, looked away. "But, she must be a lucky girl."

"No, I'm the lucky one."

Barbara, having descended, slid her fingers in the direction of Sean's crotch, but he squirmed away, backing from her reach.

"Yes, she's a very lucky girl alright." Barbara sighed with disappointment, "Ah well, I'd better wait for the Postman." She chuckled, "I'll put the kettle on; make you a cuppa."

Unbelievably relieved yet with the slightest tinge of disappointed regret, Sean continued with his inspection of the upper reaches of the house.

Finally concluding his survey, he returned to the sitting room, a cup of tea waiting patiently for him on the coffee table and Barbara sitting on the sofa, legs crossed, her body still inviting.

Sean, making small talk, his vision focused anywhere but on the alluring body of the woman, quickly finished his cup of tea and replaced the empty cup on the chipped saucer. Thanking the woman for the tea he got to his feet, ready and eager to depart.

"It could have been so much more," Barbara wistfully replied.

Sean smiled awkwardly, his eyes not meeting those of the woman, his vision firmly detached from her body, but then an ornament caught his attention, a Silver Arab Dhow resting on a solid wooden plinth, the base placed on the sideboard against the far wall. It was beautiful.

Irresistibly he stepped in the direction of the Dhow. "That really is beautiful." And glancing back at Barbara, "May I look at it, examine it?"

The woman nodded with indifference.

Sean picked up the Silver Dhow ornament and turned it in his hands, admiring its beauty. Heavy and solid, the boat had been crafted in direct replica of an Arab fishing boat, its solid silver sails gloriously reflecting the light emanating from the outside. Sean was absolutely taken by the ornament's beauty and to his unpractised eye he was convinced that the Dhow was made entirely of Silver. "It really is a lovely ornament. I'd love to get one for my fiancée; she works in the marine industry, with yachts and workboats. She'd love this. Did you buy it locally?"

"No, it belonged to my boyfriend," adding scathingly, "Ex-boyfriend!" Her tone became bitter, "The bastard disappeared off the face of the earth three months ago. Now that he's no longer coughing up with the mortgage money, my ex-husband, another bastard, has made me put our jointly owned house on the market. The shit wants his pound of flesh."

Sean returned the Silver Dhow to its place on the plinth, "Um, sorry to hear that," he muttered not knowing what else to say.

"You can have the boat!" Barbara cried impetuously.

"I couldn't possibly take it, it's got to be worth a bit," he protested.

"No, stupid boy, I didn't mean I would bloody give it! What I meant is that you can buy it from me; Christ knows, Abdullah owes me enough."

"Abdullah?"

"Abdullah, my shit of an ex-boyfriend," she snapped bitterly, "He said that he brought the sodding thing in Aden. I think that that's in Yemen or one of those other bloody hot Arab countries. It's supposed to be solid silver, Indian Silver, but worth a bob or two I'm told." Her eyes lit up, "Make me a good offer and it's yours."

Having concluded the deal and paid what he considered to be a fair price for the boat Sean departed from the nymphomaniac's house, grinning like a Cheshire cat, the Arab Dhow and its solid wooden plinth held firmly in his hands, his briefcase barely held by two fingers of his left hand. Carefully opening his car door he lovingly placed the newly acquired Dhow on the front passenger seat, and tossing his briefcase into the rear he gloatingly muttered, "Kerry's going to love this; it'll be part of my wedding present to her!"

Climbing into his car, he fired up the engine and drove away, a song in his heart and a broad smile on his lips. He was doubly pleased that not only had he secured a beautiful present for Kerry, he had also proved that despite the temptation of the very available and attractive Barbara Clark he had resisted and remained faithful to his intended spouse.

If only Kerry knew how much he loved her.

With his thoughts focused on self-congratulation, the joy abounding in his soul, he had no idea, no inkling, of the chain of events that he was about to unleash, his actions of the last hour deciding the fate of so many people within his and Kerry's circle of friends.

Life can go from great heights to utter depths very quickly.

Chapter 9

The week had shot round and once again it was Friday night. Sean was out with a couple of his work colleagues on some kind of self-congratulatory function, something about having achieved record levels of house sales and surveys, the commissions flowing into their pockets. Thus Kerry had the evening to herself, Sean not expected home until around nine p.m.

Determining, however, that she was obviously not going to spend the evening on her own, after all it *was* a Friday night, she had pre-arranged to meet Pete Spratt and Harry at Rosie's Bar, already knowing full well that Harry would not be able to make it as he had a prior engagement and that Siobhan could not interfere as she and her boyfriend were away in Paris for a long weekend.

Not sure if Spratt would come on his own - he always seemed to be followed by an entourage - she was delighted that when he walked through the door he was alone, and my God, did he look handsome. She could feel the stirring in her loins.

Spratt noticed her immediately and made a beeline for her table, a wide grin on his lips matching her smile of greeting. Having almost finished her first drink, the nervous wait for Spratt having made her consume her favourite tipple of Bailey's and ice in copious amounts, Spratt went to the bar and secured a fresh glass for her plus a pint for himself.

Quickly returning to her table, the memory of her almost naked body from the time in the Chinese Restaurant filling his mind and he was beginning to feel quite horny. If he played his cards right maybe, no definitely, he was on a winner. It would harm his chances of getting with Siobhan if Siobhan did find out, but the chances of her finding out were slim as he knew she was away with her boyfriend and Kerry was unlikely to brag. Siobhan was his real target but Kerry would do in the meantime.

He sat down at Kerry's table and they indulged in meaningless flirtatious banter, the conversation of two people skirting round the issue that they both knew was the main reason for them being present. They were like two adolescent teenagers, desperately wanting sex, but neither prepared to blatantly suggest that the deed should be done.

It had been a hot day and was only just beginning to cool, Kerry still feeling warm in her light summer dress, a pair of slip-on sandals on her feet. She felt liberated and exhilarated, the closeness and intimacy of Spratt making her skin tingle with anticipation.

By the time they were on their third round of drinks Spratt had loosened his tie, and the 'designer' stubble on his face appeared much fuller than when he had walked in. Obviously Kerry knew that it hadn't grown so much whilst they had been in the Bar but the evening light, coupled with the internal lighting, made the dark stubble hair look like a worn down scrubbing brush. For a brief second she was momentarily concerned that when they did get together the stubble would mark her skin, the coarse hair causing a rash to develop. She remembered years ago when Sean had started to grow a beard, and the times after they had made love when she had ended up with a rash on her cheeks and across her stomach. Still, what the hell, it would be worth it and she felt a warmth in her loins.

Another aspect that Kerry liked about Rosie's Bar was that although it was a popular venue there was still the opportunity for discreet conversations, the background music sufficient to maintain a small amount a privacy for the various tables scattered throughout the room, yet not loud enough so that people had to shout to be heard.

"So, why did the old man let you out on your own then, and in town, with all us rampant males about?" Spratt asked desperate to move onto the next stage of the 'kill'.

"You've got to be kidding; he doesn't know that I'm meeting you. He thinks I'm out with Brian and Siobhan, business entertaining. He trusts me!" She boastfully concluded.

Spratt smirked, winking at her, "Silly bastard."

Kerry, feeling warm, mellow, relaxed, laughed flirtatiously but suddenly tensed, deciding that it was time that they moved onto what they both knew was the point of the meeting.

"How do you fancy a blow job?" She demanded, surprised at the abruptness of her question and the tone of her voice. Momentarily she coloured, feeling highly embarrassed. "Oh, God, why did I say that?" she thought, "I could have said something much more humorous or romantic."

Spratt's mouth opened wide in amazement and surprise, for although he was confident that she would hand herself to him on a plate he didn't expect her approach to be so blatant. Temporarily taken aback his face soon erupted into a grin followed by an amused smile, quite liking her direct approach.

"I've heard about coming to the point, but you're certainly one who goes straight for the jugular," he smirked.

Kerry, embarrassed, wondered if she had overstepped the mark, had played the wrong game. Perhaps he thought she was a slut.

Spratt seeing the doubt spread across her features quickly added, "You weren't kidding were you? You're not pulling my leg?"

Kerry almost breathed a sigh of relief, the eagerness in Spratt's voice and the cloudy disappointed look in his eyes assuring her that she played her cards just right.

Their eyes locked in an expression of mutual desire, longing and lust.

Kerry smiled, a smile of slow relief with growing profound pleasure, her loins almost burning in anticipation. Seductively, she responded, "I'm not kidding, never been more serious."

With Spratt looking deeply into her eyes she couldn't resist shivering, a tingle spreading from the top of her neck to the base of her spine. God, she wanted him.

Unabashed, she breathed, "I want to give you pleasure Mr Spratt!"

"If you're messing me about, winding me up, I'll kill you," he responded amused, knowing that she was deadly serious.

She smiled at him, pouted and ran her tongue over her lips, her eyes never once leaving his eyes.

Spratt's eyes devoured Kerry and without losing his focus on her and her body he reached for his glass, downing the remaining Scotch in one go. The whisky made his eyes water and he coughed, the drink burning his throat and chest as it made its way to his stomach. Grinning inanely, half out of embarrassment because of the effect the whisky had on him and partially because of his over-eagerness, he rose to his feet, the bulge in his trousers strong evidence of his thoughts and desires.

Kerry's eyes broke free from her fierce gaze on Spratt's eyes and she looked down, aware of the eagerness growing inside Spratt's trousers. She grinned. "Whoa, down boy, I have to finish my drink first."

Delighted at the effect she had created she beamed with happiness and shivered with delighted anticipation. Reaching for her glass she was unable to fully control her trembling hand and took only a tiny sip of her Baileys, shakily replacing the unfinished drink on the table. Desperately controlling her bursting excitement, the tingling anticipation seemingly shooting through every pore of her body, she grabbed her handbag. "I just have to nip to the loo; won't be a second," she almost purred.

Spratt, standing expectantly, the bulge in his trousers beginning to get noticed by other girls in the vicinity of their table, a chorus of feminine giggles wafting in his direction, slumped back disappointed, "Don't be too long." He glanced down at his crutch, "I don't know how long it can wait."

Kerry grinned and, trembling, stepped hurriedly towards the Ladies toilets. Once in the sanctity of the toilet she walked over to one of the two washbasins positioned in front of a large mirror; examining herself in the mirror, she checked her make-up, then taking a hairbrush from her handbag, brushed her hair, tidying the sides that curled slightly in towards her neck. Admiring the finished article, her hair glowing with lustre and shine, she extracted a toothbrush and paste from her handbag and excitedly brushed her teeth, the tense anticipation of her feelings melding with the overheating desire of her loins. As the vision crossed her mind Kerry couldn't help giggling, muttering aloud, "This is crazy, freshening my breath with what I've got in mind to do to Spratt! I can't believe I just came out with it and offered him a blow job."

She was taken aback at the sound of a toilet being flushed in one the cubicles, a middle-aged woman exiting almost simultaneously and glaring with evident disgust at Kerry.

"Oh," said Kerry, taken aback, "I didn't realise that anyone else was in here". Dismayed, she raised her hand to her freshly cleaned mouth.

"Obviously!" pronounced the older female, not enamoured with Kerry, then under her breath muttered, "Slut!"

"Oh!" Kerry was mortified, "I had no idea that you were in there; you were so quiet. Was I talking aloud?" Kerry queried hesitantly, knowing full well that she been speaking aloud. "If I had known, I wouldn't have said..."

Her sentence was left unfinished, the other woman turning her back on Kerry and sternly retorting, "Obviously! Dirty bitch; bloody disgusting!" And with that she strutted with self-important indignation to the door.

Irked at the woman's reaction Kerry snapped, "Anyway, it's none of your damned business."

The woman departed still muttering under her breath; no doubt the whole bar would soon be informed of Kerry's intentions! Kerry coloured, dreading walking back out of the toilet, but she steeled herself, shrugged, and determined that this time no one was going to put her off. She was going to have Spratt one way or the other - perhaps both ways! She giggled. Still, the sooner she got back into the Bar, collected Spratt, and left the arena before miserable madam could spread the word, the better.

Recalling the woman's departure Kerry realised that the bitch had walked straight from the toilet to the bar door, and it was now her turn to shudder in disgust, "She didn't even wash her hands, and I'm supposed to be the dirty bitch!"

Hastily completing her preparations Kerry gave herself a final check up in the mirror; she couldn't help approving, "Well Girl, you look great. Spratt won't know what's hit him. Everything is going to be perfect and after the experience I'm going to give him, he'll just want to make this a long term relationship." She winked at her reflection. "Kerry and Pete Spratt, a couple that would make an interesting combination!"

*   *   *

Ray was stunned, his mind racing and his heart pounding, the hurt quite intense; he felt a churning, gnawing ache in his stomach as he sat and watched Kerry leaving the Bar together with the despised Spratt.

He hadn't wanted to be a voyeur but his eyes had remained fixed on Kerry, pulled there unwillingly by some unseen malicious magnet; the business colleagues who sat with him at his table in Rosie's Bar had long since lost his attention, their jokes and meaningless conversation falling on deaf ears.

When Kerry had walked into the Bar Ray had noticed her straight away, his heart spellbound at her beauty and particularly at how sexy she looked this evening; she was truly gorgeous. He had smiled at her and called out her name, rising to greet her from across the room; but she hadn't heard him, his presence and persona being totally oblivious to her current world. In the process of attempting to leave his colleagues he was momentarily called back, someone asking him the answer to some banal question, and then the moment was lost, Kerry immersed in a conversation with Rosie and another person at the bar counter.

Ray had sat down, determined that when Kerry had finished her conversation with Rosie he would walk to the bar counter in the pretence of getting a round of drinks and 'accidentally' discover Kerry, inviting her to join him and his colleagues.

Unfortunately, Rosie led Kerry to a table and both sat down together, involved in a seemingly intimate conversation. When Rosie eventually left Kerry, to assist serving behind her bar counter, Ray plucking up the courage to cross the room was stopped in his tracks by the arrival of Spratt. The look of pure joy on Kerry's face when her eyes spotted the new arrival cut deeply into Ray's heart; she certainly had been instantly aware of Spratt's presence, Ray's existence having absolutely no meaning to her!

The blood had pounded between Ray's ears as he watched the growing intimacy between Kerry and Spratt and when the couple had left together, the bitterness rose within Ray's chest. He had wanted to jump up and rush after Kerry, telling her not to be so silly, that Spratt was a louche, after only one thing, but he had had to force himself to sit still, his heart aching, knowing that whatever he'd thought to say would have no bearing on Kerry's obvious infatuation.

Chapter 10

Abdullah entered the telephone kiosk, its glass etched with amateur engravings of mostly miss-spelt rude words, the metal scratched and scoured. Placing his overnight bag on the floor he dialled the number from memory, his two pound coins already logged within the pay phone. Abdullah preferred the pay phones as he did not trust any of the systems that required either a phone card or credit card. He wasn't sure whether any of the non-coin systems could be fully traced but he wasn't prepared to take any chances. He was convinced that even the pre-purchased phone cards could be traced back to their shop purchase source and thus ultimately pin pointing the area where the card had been purchased.

He realised that he was probably being over cautious but didn't want to leave anything to chance; the slightest judgement of error could jeopardise everything. He waited a few seconds as the number dialled travelled through the telephone network initially making its speedy way through the underground telephone lines, up into the sub-station, over to the main network, and then beamed up into one of the many satellites navigating the globe. Eventually his call was answered by a familiar voice.

"Ahmed, we have instructions, we need to meet tonight so we can prepare the final arrangements!" Abdullah's voice was firm, his tone commanding authority.

Ahmed muttered in protest, his voice whining in complaint. He wasn't prepared to meet up with his cell leader today, that was for sure; after all, he hadn't expected Abdullah to return to the UK for several more days. It was just not convenient.

Abdullah, instantly angry, belligerently persisted, "We *must* meet tonight! The Imam has sent two more martyrs from the camp." Making the unforgiving mistake of mentioning both the Imam and the words martyrs rather than speaking in code, he could have bitten off his tongue in protest at his stupidity.

Fortunately Ahmed didn't pick up in his error, the man still protesting regarding his ability to meet up today, determinedly intent on seeing through his evening plans without the unanticipated interference of his cell leader.

Abdullah could feel the fury rising within. If he didn't need Ahmed's help then he would have gone straight over to Ahmed's home and helped his erstwhile colleague to join the throng of failed martyrs this very day. But he still needed Ahmed, their task was not let done.

Throwing caution to the wind, his anger transgressing his reason, Abdullah barked, his voice almost growling in an underlying threat of violence, "Ahmed, I don't care what you have planned for this evening, nothing is more important than this and *nothing* must get in our way." His words became icy cold, containing a menace that would have frozen a more understanding or more intelligent man than Ahmed. "Tomorrow is not acceptable! Time has moved forward quicker than we anticipated; with the behaviour of the Americans...and their puppies, the British...the Imam wants action before the end of the month. We have to meet tonight, not tomorrow!"

Ahmed, unperturbed, swore down the receiver, his profanity hitting like a hammer between the two eardrums in Abdullah's head. Momentarily dumbstruck at both the disobedience to his authority and the use of non-Islamic profanities, Abdullah slammed the receiver back into its cradle, his face like thunder, a furious frown spreading across his forehead. Scooping up his bag he stormed out from the phone kiosk, almost ripping the door off its hinges as he pushed it open.

If Ahmed could have seen his leader's face he would have trembled, his plans for the evening being of no consequence to the punishing fate that was now awaiting him, his destiny having radically altered in the space of a few seconds of limited conversation.

Abdullah's face locked into a furious grimace, eyes maniacal, and he stomped off down the road, the thought of the punishment to be inflicted on Ahmed helping to partially sooth him as he made his way to a new destination. Ahmed had just lost his promised virgins.

But what Abdullah didn't know was that Ahmed was intending to have much more fun with a lady, who although almost certainly not a virgin, was about to release the wonders of her body to him. Such heady promises had superseded his religious zeal.

Chapter 11

Laughing like a pair of six year olds, Kerry and Spratt spilt onto the back seat of a London Black Cab. Gradually their laughter subsided and they stared into each other's eyes, a look of unbridled hunger, passion, and desire. Without a word being spoken they succumbed into a glue-like embrace, their mouths firmly attached to one another, their lips like limpets sticking to the hull of a boat.

After what seemed an eternity until they broke for air, Spratt's tongue began to explore the interior of Kerry's mouth, his left hand running through her hair, his right hand starting at the base of her head, running down her back, exploring further downwards. Reaching her buttocks and the worn leather of the cab seat, his hand made its way back up the front of her dress, up to her breasts, massaging and cupping her firm breasts in his hand. His thumb and forefinger kneaded her nipple, the apex becoming rock hard between his exploring fingers.

Breaking free from Kerry's lips, Spratt kissed her chin and then her neck, his free hand venturing along Kerry's leg and up inside her dress, gently caressing as it made its way deeper under her clothing. Meeting no resistance, his caresses became bolder, more strident, his fingers first rubbing her crotch, then exploring inside her knickers, her flesh moist and warm, her voice moaning with want and desire.

Kerry's hands wandered away from caressing Spratt's head and hastily and hungrily made their descent to his trousers, desperately attempting to undo the zip and free the molten lava that was trying to break free from its enclosure. She felt sure that something was about to burst soon and didn't know whether it was the hungry python of her new lover or the rivers of her own unbridled passion.

The Cabbie, becoming aware of the temperature rising in his Cab and the strange noises emanating from the rear, glanced up into his rear view mirror and did a double take, almost swerving across the road in disbelief.

The female passenger had her hand inside the man's trousers, rubbing up and down as if she was polishing a magic lamp, a 'Genie' to be released from the bottle. And the man, well, his hands seemed to be everywhere, under the woman's dress, the man's arms disappearing under the fold of material, his right arm hidden up to the bicep exploring between her legs.

Swearing under his breath the Cabbie muttered, "What the fuck!

Lustful buggers; what the hell should I do?" Correcting his swerve, his eyes back on the road in front of him, he took another lingering glance in the rear view mirror, "Do I kick them out, stop and watch, or carry on with the journey trying to ignore them?" He continued the journey, the indecision assailing him, the doubt making his driving erratic but ignored by his passionate passengers. With eyes continually darting to the view on the back seat before reverting back to the road ahead he came to a decision. "I guess I'll ignore it", he thought but quickly corrected his thought, "No hope of ignoring that! I'd love to get it on video for the lads, they'll never believe it!" Glancing wistfully into the mirror he muttered, "Perhaps I could join them?" But chuckled, knowing his attempt would meet with a swift rejection and probably a punch on the nose.

The Cabbie turned up the heater/demister, the windows of the Cab now steaming up, the heat emanating from within the rear working its way forward in the confined space and seeping into the front compartment. Despite his belated and frantic efforts the dividing glass between the front and rear sections of the Cab clouded over, the glass totally steaming up, condensation dripping down the glass behind the driver's head. The Cabbie mumbled in protest, "Shit; can't see anything anymore."

Having already mentally determined to take his passionate passengers to their requested destination he took a final, futile, glance in his rear view mirror then decided to give his full and undivided attention in delivering his cargo safe and sound, his earlier voyeurism having resulted in a couple of close calls, a jumped red light and a furious pedestrian who only just managed to dive out of the way of the wayward and wildly veering Black Cab. Accelerating, yet now driving in a much safer and controlled manner he continued their journey, muttering, "The sooner I drop this hot couple off the better, at least before they stain my cab."

Oblivious to the outside world and indeed oblivious to their fellow occupant in the Cab, the couple in the back continued their mutual embrace of lust and discovery, their entire raison d'etre being solely occupied on the flesh covering their bones.

Spratt almost fell on the floor when the Cab arrived at its destination, the driver pulling up at the kerb with unbridled haste. The sudden lack of momentum caught him unawares, only Kerry's firm and quick hand pulling him back.

Kerry was oblivious to their having stopped, her quick action merely being to pull Spratt back into their passionate liaison, sensing and feeling that he was somehow pulling away; she wasn't ready for him to stop.

Spratt glanced away but immediately his lips were once again reattached to Kerry's limpet lips, her body wrapping him in her all-embracing passion.

Realising that the sharp stopping of the Cab had not reduced the passion of his passengers the Cabbie realised that more forceful recognition was needed. Accordingly, he knocked on the steamed-up dividing glass.

No response; nothing, other than the erotic sounds of two over amorous individuals.

The driver cleared his throat, knocked more firmly on the glass and not receiving an instant reply, he slid the glass partition open. His eyes almost leapt from their sockets and he felt a stirring of his own. The woman's dress was pulled up above her waist and her knickers were hanging off one foot. The man's trousers were down around his ankles, his boxer shorts pulled so low that the Cabbie had an eyeful of hairy bottom, the revealed bum crack almost totally visible. The Cabbie couldn't take his eyes off the woman's mound of Venus, the man's hand continuously spoiling his vision. Drinking in the scene he was eventually disturbed by the cackle from his radio, the faint voice of the female controller summoning him. Startled, he almost jumped, glancing suspiciously over his shoulder, feeling like a guilty schoolboy watching a couple having sex.

Shaken from his voyeurism he cleared his throat more loudly but was still ignored, eventually barking out, "Oi, you two, we're here, Arcadia Avenue."

Kerry, eyes closed, legs akimbo, groaned in reply. Nibbling her neck, Spratt ignored the interruption.

The Cabbie, although enjoying the scene, was aware that people were passing by on the pavement outside. He didn't want to lose his licence, thus firmly ordered in a loud tone akin to that of bullying headmaster, "Hey, Romeo and Juliet, if you've *quite* finished turning my cab into a brothel, we're at your destination!"

Spratt reluctantly looked up and pulled himself free, giving the Cabbie a full and frank eyeful of Kerry's undressed state. In spite of himself he couldn't resist grinning with unbounded pleasure.

Spratt suddenly found his voice, the Cabbie's words finally piercing into his skull. "Eh, all right, thanks mate." He glanced up realising that they were not quite at his door. "Can you pull in over there?" He instructed the driver, pointing at a house approximately fifty yards further along the road. Catching the man salivating over Kerry's body his tone became harsh, remonstrating at the Voyeur, "There's no need to stare!" And stretching forward he forcefully slammed closed the dividing glass.

The Cabbie was dumbfounded, "No need to stare - cheeky bugger!" But rather than getting out of his Black Cab and thumping the cheeky passenger he merely muttered to himself, "I think the few yards walk would have cooled off the pair of you."

Grating the vehicle into first gear he drove the few remaining yards, the vehicle jerking forward like a Kangaroo taking its first steps.

Despite the erratic movement of the vehicle Kerry managed to rearrange her clothing, her knickers swiftly pulled back up over her earlier revealed 'goodies', the treat with Spratt still highly anticipated, the hors d'oeuvre having merely wetted her appetite. Spratt hastily pulled up his trousers just as the Cab finally stopped. They both exited, Spratt fumbling with his wallet, handing over a twenty pound note and not waiting for his change.

Chapter 12

Abdullah's heart was beating with a furious anger as watched his erstwhile friend and companion, Ahmed, exiting the student hall Bar. His anger rose to boiling point when he became aware that a young blonde woman had also exited, firmly attached to Ahmed, her arm around his waist, the pair of them locked together like Siamese twins, Ahmed's free hand caressing the woman.

Although Ahmed was walking normally it was obvious that the blonde girl had been imbibing copious amount of alcohol, her Arab companion having to make serious efforts to stop the drunken girl from subsiding onto the pavement. The woman laughed joyfully, a meaningless release of joyous mirth that only the inebriated could understand. There really was no reason for her to laugh, the combination of cool night air and numerous Diamond Ice's making her giggle beyond comprehension.

The Blonde was also slightly nervous but exhilarant, having met Ahmed a few days earlier whilst he was delivering snack foods to their Halls, she has cheekily asked for free pack of nuts. They had struck up an instant rapport, and this was their third date, the relationship having quickly developed to such a state that she was more than happy to take him back to her room in Halls.

The woman paused, almost falling over, but Ahmed caught her in his arms, her face embedded in his chest. She looked up at her gorgeous rescuer and brushed the waspish strands of dyed blonde hair from her face. Smiling lopsidedly, her wide and drunken eyes stared into the face of Ahmed and she stood on her tiptoes, planting a long and passionate kiss on Ahmed's lips, the pair sharing a seductive and overpowering moment. Ahmed was beginning to feel new thoughts, emotions that had never touched his life previously, but her public show of affection made him feel self-conscious and he desperately wished for the promised sanctuary and privacy of the girl's room.

Managing to break free from her tongue scouring his mouth he gently pushed her away, her squeals of protest soon hushed when he assured her that he was not rejecting her, merely that he wanted to spend the night in her room...with her.

The blonde giggled excitedly, and full of infatuated expectation she allowed Ahmed to support her staggering steps as they made their short journey back to her room in Halls. Fortunately her room was on the ground floor of the five storey building and he assisted her in getting the key from her pocket, the task not made any easier by her giggling and twitching excitedly as he fumbled in her pocket. He opened the main door of the building and followed her as she led him past six or seven doors before reaching her own room. Fortunately there was no-one about, the thoroughfares of the building being deserted. Even the common room/kitchen area was deserted, most of the students out drinking or clubbing, or visiting their families, or already ensconced with their lovers or friends within their respective rooms. Ahmed could discern the sound of music, a repetitive beat that resounded from somewhere on the floor above and he just made out the sound of raucous laughter before the blonde closed her bedroom door behind them.

If only Ahmed had known, if only he'd been more alert, if only the woman hadn't taken away his caution.

But Ahmed had not been aware that he had been watched every step of the way, a pair of malevolent eyes monitoring his every step, his every action. In different circumstances, in circumstances where the promise of new found love, combined with a couple of small beers, had not been part of his evening, then Ahmed's meticulous training would have forewarned him of the danger that he was in. But no, the lure of the female had weakened him even to the point where he had disobeyed his team leader, Abdullah. A small warning sounded in Ahmed's head but was soon dissipated as the blonde removed her clothes, the blood accelerating from his brain, driving all thoughts of his religion, his mission, to a much more heady anticipation of the wonders of life.

Abdullah had waited outside the halls, watching for a light to be turned on in one of the rooms; it didn't take long before the light was turned on in the blonde's room, the curtains quickly being drawn, cutting out any further possibility of voyeurism. Abdullah's malevolent eyes gleamed with a bitter and intense hatred, his erstwhile colleague and associate no longer considered a loyal friend.

With a harsh tone and a voice as cold as ice he muttered, "So, the dog has become corrupted by Western ways!"
His face registering pure evil, Abdullah, with a chilled anger, considered his next plan of action.

Chapter 13

Spratt arms enveloped Kerry as led her towards the front door of his terraced flat, stumbling across the pavement, their passion and anticipation almost making it impossible to walk normally. Reaching his door Spratt fumbled in his pocket and pulled out his front door key, Kerry giggling with a nervous excitement like a schoolgirl on her first date.

As soon as they were safely inside Spratt grabbed Kerry in a clinch, and they resumed their kissing and fondling as they fumbled their way along the narrow hallway that led to the stairs of Spratt's flat on the upper floor of the terraced house. Groping as they ascended they dislodged a dowdy print of a dual-masted yacht sailing into an exotic Mediterranean harbour, the dust spiralling down from the dislodged print leaving a fine layer of powder on the oblivious duo. Nearing the top of the stairs Spratt almost lost his balance, only Kerry's quick action preventing him from tumbling headfirst all the way to the bottom; steadying him, she pinned him against the wall and kissed him with an almost animal like passion.

Scrambling into Spratt's bedroom they almost ripped each other's clothes off, the encumbrances of material causing them both momentarily frustration. Spratt was staggered at Kerry's passion, her eagerness and wild abandon catching him by surprise, almost making his many years of sexual conquests a succession of meaningless couplings. Barely on his bed they focused on each other's bodies with a voracious hunger, the animal magnetism and lust building to a crescendo.

*   *   *

Dismayed and anxious, Sean paced furiously up and down the sitting-room carpet, his eyes constantly glancing in the direction of the clock above the television. It was almost midnight and the frustration of not hearing from Kerry was drilling into his nerves. He felt sure that something dreadful had happened to her and he had already phoned the police station and the emergency department at the local hospital, but there had been no news, much to his profound relief on that front.

He thumped his first into the palm of his other hand and angrily muttered, "It's almost midnight; oh Kerry, where the hell are you!" The frustration was gnawing and building within.

Resuming his pacing, his eyes shot over to the telephone, the instrument beckoning him like a beacon. Rushing over to the phone he picked up the receiver and listened intently, just to make sure that it was working. "It's working. Then why hasn't she phoned. Phone Kerry, phone, damn it," he cried out. A consoling thought momentarily eased his concerned anguish, "Maybe she phoned when I put the rubbish out." He checked for messages...there were none! "Bollocks! No bloody messages; I hope that she's okay and not lying injured or hurt somewhere." The momentarily alternative thought was instantly replaced by a nagging depression, an image that had been on the edges of his mind and one that he had constantly refused to consider. But the image nagged at him, fighting its way to the front of his mind, to the here and now. "Spratt! The nurses outfit!"

His mind now racing frantically, he rushed to their bedroom and pulling open Kerry's wardrobe with furious aggression he almost ripped the doors from their hinges. The nurse outfit wasn't in there! He rifled through her drawers and even checked through the drawers of Kerry's dressing table knowing full well that the nurse outfit was never in those drawers anyway but he lived in hope that he would find it, the nurse outfit being the special token that Kerry always kept for her 'special' sex sessions.

Surveying the mess that he had created Sean felt a fleeting pang of remorse, "What the hell am I doing?" He muttered, "This is crazy; Kerry wouldn't be unfaithful."

Tidying up the mess, replacing Kerry's discarded clothes and jewellery as best he could, he hurried to his own wardrobe and pulling out a jacket swung it over his shoulder. Determined no longer to sit and wait he was going to do something positive, deciding that he would first check their mutual local haunts; maybe Kerry was drinking with the gang at the 'Cow and Whistle', she always had a fondness for the place, particularly liking a 'nightcap' there with Naimh, and once the two girls got together, time always seemed to be immaterial, to stand still. Many a night he had to go and rescue Kerry and Naimh from their drinking sessions at the 'Cow and Whistle'.

Switching off the lights he left their flat, a new determination in his step.

*   *   *

Ray having drunk himself into oblivion, his two drinking colleagues long since departed, staggered out from Rosie's bar, the fresh air hitting him like a slap in the face.

He had never felt so miserable, the constant image of Kerry with Spratt never leaving his mind, intermittent stabs of anguish excavating in his stomach with huge garden spades.

Stumbling against an outside wall he tripped over his untied shoelace and fell into the gutter. In a haze he attempted to rise but his condition overtook him, his guts taking on a life of their own, great streams of vomit exiting from his mouth.

Retching wretchedly he collapsed back into the gutter, with what was left of his few working brain cells making communication to his limbs virtually impossible; he barely remembered any more, vaguely aware of the two pairs of hands that pulled him from the road. The hands supporting his body and onto a train, a few words being muttered, none of which could be deciphered by Ray's brain.

The people who helped Ray must have known him, because he woke from his comatose state lying on his sofa, fully dressed with one shoe still on. He managed to drag himself to the kitchen, grabbed some paracetamol and a glass of water, and gingerly rediscovered the sofa, his head lolling at a strange angle against the cushion.

*   *   *

Kerry luxuriated in Spratt's bed, revelling in the after-glow of intensive, illicit, sex. She stretched lazily, her body still tingling post-coital and her mind running over the last couple of hours. The initial sex had been frantic, hungry, but later they had slowly explored each other, lingering and enjoying every aspect of each other's body. First Spratt had brought her to an ecstasy of pleasure and then she had reciprocated, giving him untold pleasure, his body almost howling out in unleashed passion, culminating in a mutual, prolonged orgasm.

Spratt wearing only a towel to cover his modesty - Kerry vaguely wondered why - returned to the room with two mugs of steaming hot coffee. Not instant coffee, but Kenyan coffee that he had meticulously percolated in his coffee pot. Spratt was a coffee fanatic, tasting and experiencing all kinds of types and flavours, and he was always meticulous in the preparation of his coffee drinks.

Kerry declined his offer of a liqueur to accompany the coffee, insisting that she had had enough to drink earlier that evening. "Besides," she chuckled, "If I keep drinking I'd be too pissed to leave here and then I'd have to stay all night!"

"Why would that worry me?" smirked Spratt, placing the mugs on the bedside table before climbing back into bed, the towel being discarded just as he had put down the coffee mugs.

"Oh, sure, I can just picture Sean's face if I walk into our flat tomorrow morning. I don't think that he'd believe that my business meeting lasted all night! He's expecting me back around elevenish."

Spratt grinned, "Tell him you've been called away by Brian to a meeting in Holland, or somewhere like that."

Kerry playfully slapped Spratt's chest, snuggled up beside him, then rolled on top. "Spratt, you really are a bad influence," she smiled, "A gorgeous, sexy, bad influence...and I love it." She kissed him on the lips, a long, lingering kiss, affection replacing passion. Breaking free from his reciprocating lips, her eyes met his eyes, her love and ardour boring down into his seemingly fathomless eyes. A smile spread across her lips, her eyes wrinkling in affection before she slowly, ever so slowly, worked her way down his body, her lips re-exploring areas that she had covered in her earlier orgiastic passion. Pausing momentarily she glanced up from Spratt's stomach, "But we will have to do the Holland thing, a whole weekend in Amsterdam, now that would be great." And licking her lips in anticipation she breathlessly added, "I can't wait."

"Neither can I," groaned Spratt as Kerry recommenced her lip and tongue exploration, working down over Spratt's groin, teasing him with her tongue.

Chapter 14

Tired, weary, physically drained, his sports bag beginning to cut into his shoulders, the constant weight of carrying the bag getting heavier as the day had progressed into the deep night, Abdullah finally arrived at Barbara Clark's street.

Skulking close to the brick walls outside each house, he sidled his way up to Barbara's front door and glancing nervously around he rang her doorbell, the familiar chimes echoing out back from her hallway. He kept his finger hard on the button, his impatience demanding an immediate reaction, the chimes resounding through the night air, then he released the pressure on the button.

Although the doorbell chimes had seemed noisy to Abdullah it hadn't woken up Barbara, the inside of the house revealing a silent stillness. The sports bag was really chaffing into his skin and he removed the strap from his shoulder, almost dropping the bag on to the step by the front door.

He tapped his knuckles against the small frosted glass section on the upper section of the door and waited expectantly; Barbara would recognise his familiar little knock. Nothing; total silence! Tired, frustrated and annoyed, he banged his fist against the wood of the front door. Still there was no reply. This time, ignoring the neighbours, no longer caring if he woke them or not, Abdullah hammered loudly on the door, yelling at the same time, "It's me, Abdullah; I'm back, open the door."

After what seemed like an age, an upstairs light was turned on in the house, the light filtering through from the curtains of the front bedroom. Of course it wasn't the only light switched on in the street, Abdullah's noisy banging to announce his return having disturbed most of the surrounding homes.

Eventually a pale, sleep stirred face appeared at the window, Barbara having partially pulled back her bedroom curtain, the woman squinting out into the relative darkness of the street below.

Abdullah stepped back almost into the roadway and looked up, his expression of grimace almost softening into a smile.

Barbara's sleepy, confused face lit up, her shriek of joy clearly heard through the pane of glass. Pulling up the sash window with unseemly haste she almost leaned out too far in her delight and eagerness and cried out, "Abdullah! I'll be straight down!"

Barbara disappeared almost instantly, returning momentarily to slam shut the window and then ran for the stairs, her heart pounding and her desire almost overflowing with anticipation.

"Allah! She's even uglier than I remember from before!" Abdullah scowled and shuddered with revulsion but then his features visibly brightened, "At least I won't have to do this for much longer."

He quickly foraged in his bag and pulled out a small dagger, the dim street light reflecting off the freshly cleaned blade. Gently caressing the glinting metal, his eyes gleamed with fanatical evil. "I will have more need of you soon, my friend," he muttered to the inanimate object, then lovingly replaced the dagger within the folds of a pair of his trousers and quickly zipped up the bag just as Barbara was opening her front door.

Chapter 15

Kerry lying entwined with Spratt suddenly pulled free, raising her upper body. "Christ, Spratty, what's the time?" she asked startled, "Sean will kill me if I'm not back before midnight, especially as he promised he'd stay in so that I don't get home in the dark; I hate being left on my own in the dark."

Spratt picked up his watch from the bedside table. "Relax Kerry, it's only just gone eleven; we'll get you back nearly on time."

Kerry stretching luxuriously, slipped out of the bed and scooping up her discarded clothes hastened to the bathroom so that she could freshen up and remove all traces of her last few hours spent coupling with Spratt. Obviously she knew that very soon she and Spratt would be an 'item', after all how could he possibly not want her after all she had proved and provided to him over the last few hours. But in the meantime she didn't want to push it and would have to bide her time with Sean. "God, how boring!" she thought whilst quickly taking a shower, ensuring that she did wet her hair.

Her toilet completed, teeth cleaned, and re-application of make-up, she felt almost ready to start again with Spratt, the memories of the evening's interlude made her eyes soften with a dreamy quality.

Spratt was in the kitchen, drinking thirstily from a glass of ice cold water, his thoughts no longer on Kerry; he had achieved all he wanted from her, but now he had to have Siobhan, who was his main target. Perhaps Siobhan was the woman who he could give up his bachelor's life for, he mused. "Now don't be silly," he thought, "This preoccupation with Siobhan is getting ridiculous. She's just another woman and when I do make it with her then I'll only get bored like I did with all the rest. Still, I have to find out."

"This screwing can be thirsty business," he muttered and stepping to the fridge/freezer he took out a couple of ice cubes, refilling his glass. Slurping thirstily he gulped down the refreshing liquid, wiping a drop of spilt water from his chin. Spratt grinned in triumph. "Fantastic! Harry will be pissed off. The guys have all wanted a blow-job from 'Sex on Legs' and I've done it, and more than once!" He took another gulp from his glass, "Now I've got to figure a way of how to crack Siobhan."

"What, I can't hear you? What did you say?" Kerry called out as she exited the bathroom.

Spratt was startled, "Shit, she overheard," he muttered in response, "Eh? Oh nothing, I was thinking aloud."

"I thought I heard you say 'Siobhan's name?"

Thinking quickly he replied, "No, I said that we'd better get a move on."

"Oh, all right, I won't be a second; just got to get my bag and coat."

Spratt grinned wickedly.

*   *   *

Against his wishes, Spratt was cajoled in escorting Kerry back to her own flat. Taking the Underground to her stop he felt sure that she be happy if he left her there and could then make his way back to his flat but she was having none of it. It had been a long week at work and although amply rewarded by Kerry earlier that evening, he was exhausted and all he wanted now was to be on his own. The thought of retiring to his bed, alone, was a dominant thought in his brain.

Exiting her tube station, he reluctantly trudged with Kerry through the seemingly monotonous back streets of semi-detached terraced houses, finally reaching Kerry's street. Kerry told him that most of the houses had been converted to dual accommodation, ground and first floor flats, thus helping to both ease the housing shortage and to make the possibility of owning a home more affordable.

Spratt listened to her droning on, his thoughts elsewhere, her blathering of no importance or relevance or current interest to him. In fact he just wished that the silly bitch would reach her door so that he could finally make his way home.

"God, that tube journey took for ever," Kerry muttered, "And you, you clod, didn't help; I can't believe that your watch had stopped," she added with good humour.

"At least you're only late by an hour, it could have been worse." He grinned and winked.

Kerry turned suddenly, pecked Spratt on the cheek, and whispered softly in his ear, "Thanks for a great evening, Spratty; can't kiss you goodbye in case Sean's watching from the window."

Spratt was relieved.

Kerry paused, suddenly stiffening.

"What's up?" queried Spratt tentatively, afraid that Kerry's fiancé Sean had spotted them. He was always wary of angry husbands or boyfriends, his dalliances with members of the fairer sex having put him in a few dangerous situations in the past.

On one occasion, he had just managed to clamber out from a bedroom window as the lady he'd been 'enjoying' was surprised by the return of her burly rugby playing husband and his equally two large brothers, each built like the proverbial brick shithouse. Spratt had been in such a hurry that had had to leave both his trousers and underpants behind, the woman in question quickly kicking his clothes under her bed before her suspicious husband stormed into the room.

Spratt had hidden in the bushes half way down the lady's back garden, his bum scratched and pricked by the rough gorse but luckily his important 'tackle' preserved, cupped safely in his hands. He had waited, shivering, only his thin shirt keeping off the worst of the night's cold until the early hours of the morning, when Sandy, the lady in question, finally sneaked out from her home and locating Spratt, directed him to a spot under her bedroom window. Puzzled, his ardour long since dissipated, he had followed her, not sure why she hadn't brought his trousers. Whispering that the two brothers were obviously staying the night, Sandy had gesticulated to a spot behind a jasmine plant.

"What the hell," thought Spratt, "She can't want me to hide behind that?" Aloud he had whispered, "I was safer behind the gorse bushes down the garden!"

"Shush," Sandy had fiercely retorted, her finger pressed firmly to her lips, and shaking her head she had bent down, picking up Spratt's discarded trousers and pants which she silently handed over. The stupid woman had obviously thrown them out from her bedroom window, straight into a puddle of wet, slimy water. God knows how long they had been there and not only feeling wet and cold, they also stunk of fertiliser. Barely giving him time to slip on his trousers, his underpants were too wet so he put them in his pocket; she had then virtually forced him out of the side gate and into the street. At the time Spratt had cursed Sandy but later he would find reason to be grateful, for a couple of weeks after that incident the local newspaper had reported that a man and his two brothers had beaten the man's wife's lover almost to a senseless pulp, the victim ending up in intensive care in the hospital, his prospect of fathering having disappeared with the beating that he had taken. Spratt had involuntarily shivered when he had read that the woman in question was Sandy and the perpetrators her husband and his brothers; Spratt had had a very lucky escape!

Thus he didn't want to meet Kerry's partner and was more than happy to leg it, to run like hell.

Kerry had stopped in her tracks, her expression one of bemusement, as she stared up into the darkened windows of her first floor dwelling. "The place is in darkness; I wonder what's up? He can't have gone to bed already," she mused, "He always waits up for me, like a faithful dog, or maybe even a keeper." She giggled at her description of the faithful Sean. "Do you mind hanging around for a second? I don't like the dark or going into an empty place by myself, and especially not this night!" Kerry smiled beguilingly.

Not wishing to be there a moment longer Spratt nodded with disinterest. "Yea, okay Kerry, I'll wait by the street corner." Hastily disentangling her arm from under his arm he had sauntered the few yards further along the pavement, Kerry staring wistfully at his departing back then she turned and walked to her front door. Cautiously she opened the door and entered.

Feeling uneasy because of the dark stillness inside her flat, she quietly called out Sean's name, "Sean... Seano...darling, are you there?" Kerry stretched for the light switch, turning on the hall light. "Sean, where are you?"

Walking to the bedroom Kerry peered into the darkness, desperately hoping and wishing to see the shape of Sean tucked up in bed. It didn't look promising, the bed clothes looking far too flat for her liking; with her heart in her mouth she tentatively reached for the bedroom light switch, then resolutely switched on the light. "I'll wake the bastard!" she thought, "It'll teach him not to go to sleep before I'm home, and he didn't leave any lights on for me!"

"Well!" she muttered angrily, staring at the empty room, "The bastard's not here. Where the hell *are* you Sean, you prick?"

Now more angry than afraid she strode to their sitting-room, peered inside, and reached for the light switch. But the sitting-room was also empty, the whole flat encased in an eerie silence. "Damn the bastard!" she muttered, "How dare he not be here for me!"

She retraced her steps, double checking that Sean was nowhere in their flat. "The frigging bastard," she almost shouted, "He's not friggin in! I could have stayed out longer." Piqued, she stamped her foot in petulant annoyance, "Well, *I'm* not going to stay here on my own. Balls to you Seano darling, I'm going out again!"

Furious that her 'pet dog' had not waited faithfully for her, anger evident in all her pores, Kerry stormed out of the flat, leaving all the lights blazing, slamming the front door behind her.

Bemused at her hurried approach and afraid for the consequences, Spratt tentatively asked, "What's up kitten? You look a little pissed off." He didn't really want an answer, fearing that Kerry had told Sean of their liaison and that he would have an irate boyfriend on his tail at any moment.

"The bastard's not in! And he told *me* not to be late!" Her words were spilled with intense fury, the '*me*' almost being spat out. "C'mon, you can buy me a large drink." Without waiting for his response she grabbed hold of his arm, virtually dragging the hapless Spratt down the street.

Spratt peered at his wristwatch. "Kerry I've got to go. I'm up early tomorrow; Harry and I are going down to Brighton. You'll be fine on your own until Sean gets home."

Kerry stopped in her tracks, her eyes blazing. "Pete Spratt, you've had your fun...we both have, but you are not leaving me on my own tonight!" She was determined, adamant.

Spratt attempted to protest but Kerry's fierce glare brought his futile resistance to a halt. He grimaced but then forced a smile.

Seeing that she won this little battle Kerry inserted her arm under Spratt's arm and gazed up with adoration into his eyes. Meekly he allowed her to lead him and they departed, arms entwined, walking down the street like two star struck lovers.

Little did they know what fate had in store!

Chapter 16

Detective Sergeant Morris, called to one of the Halls of Residence at the University of East London, Stratford Campus, was unprepared for the macabre sight and mayhem that greeted him.

The building was in uproar, wailing and screaming girls, shocked and dumbfounded boys, many of the students grouped together, huddling in little clusters, each recounting rumours of the state of Belinda's room and of the terrible things that had been done to poor Belinda. Some of the students were gathered in tight circles of affection and comfort, consoling each other, recounting and embellishing stories of Belinda's time at the University and in Halls. Belinda had not been a shrinking violet and had lived life to the full, at least what little life she had been granted.

There was also a rumour circulating that she had had a man in her room, one of the foreign students, and that he had ritually killed her before doing himself in.

The two girl friends that had discovered Belinda's body had already been taken away, their wails and screams of horror and despair having rung through the halls like wailing banshees, sending shivers down the spines of their unknowing peers. Their wails had blended with the music blaring out from Belinda's radio, a local radio station competing against the terrified duo's screams.

The girls were now in separate rooms at a local hospital, being cared for by a female police constable and a 'Stress Councillor', both of whom were doing their utmost to cajole information from the hysterical and traumatised girls.

Back at the Halls a constable opened the now sealed off door of Belinda's room, the radio still not turned off, a Disc Jockey's ridiculous prattle being incongruously cheerful against the sight that met Detective Sergeant Morris' eyes.

Sergeant Morris carefully made his way over pools of vomit - curry, vodka, and God knew what - that had spewed out from the girls' stomachs as they had ran with sickening haste from Belinda's room, the hallway floor and wall also stained with patches of their previous evening entertainment and consumption.

However that was nothing compared to the sight that greeted him in Belinda's room.

The first thought that struck D.S. Morris was that the murderer was a jealous lover, the murdered male and female victims still wrapped together in a macabre, coital embrace. Their bodies were covered in blood and guts, the slime from the woman's intestines smeared across her midriff and mixing with blood, having seeped into the sheets in a sickening commingling of unpleasant colours and odour. The stench was unbearable. And for the coup de grace the jealous lover had cut off the man's cock and shoved in, deeply, into the woman's throat.

The woman, a young blonde female, had died in instant shock and horror, her young unmarked face frozen in abject fear and terror, her open eyes staring grotesquely upwards.

D.S. Morris could see that the man was clutching something in his left hand. "Perhaps it might be a clue to the killer or killers," thought Morris, but on closer inspection he was disappointed to discover that the man was merely gripping tightly onto an unused condom, the pain and terror of his death making him grip the rubber in a spasm of locked tension. The spittle covered gag that had obviously been forced into the man's mouth was lying discarded on the blood stained sheet.

D.S. Morris, annoyed by the constant interruptions of the prattling radio D.J., grimaced and angrily reached for the radio to switch it off, his irritated enragement causing him to knock the radio off the desk where it fell onto the floor shattering into three pieces, but bringing merciful release to his ear drums.

With the sound of silence now sweeping over the room he turned his attention back to the two corpses, the blood that had escaped from their bodies having dripped onto the rug by the bed, staining the yellow pattern of the rug a dirty crimson hue.

Chapter 17

A moderate breeze blew in from the sea, providing a gentle flow of slightly cooling air to benefit Saeed as he strolled along the Corniche. The sun's rays reflected pretty patterns off the clear blue-green waters of the Arabian Gulf, the sea, although much calmer than the wilder seas of the southern Arabian Gulf, reminded Saeed of his home in Yemen; a home that he knew he would never see again. His heart missed a beat, a great sorrow sweeping over him, but quickly collecting his thoughts he replaced the inner feelings of sadness and despair with a renewed zeal, the promise of serving his Mullah and proving himself to Allah. He praised Mohammed, peace be upon him, for having allowed him to be chosen for this mission. His life was nothing as to the greater purpose of Islam.

Lost in his thoughts, Saeed stepped off the sandy pavement and took a couple of paces into the busy highway. He was brutally jerked free from his thoughts by the sudden and alarming screech of car tyres, the howl of heavily applied brakes accompanied by the blare of a car horn, a long wheelbase Mercedes Coupe swerving, narrowly missing him, the drag of the car pulling Saeed off his feet.

The Arab Driver in the Mercedes leant out from his window, glared at him, mouthing some indistinguishable profanity before speeding away into the distance.

Saeed sat on the pavement kerb, his heart pounding, the thought of his mission being terminated before it had really started causing him to have palpitations. Maybe Allah was not watching over him after all.

The thought of such blasphemy was quickly dismissed from his mind. Allah was indeed watching over him for how else had that crazy speeding driver missed him.

Comforted, Saeed scrambled to his feet and regained the sanctuary of the sand swept pavement, the cracked stones almost making him lose his balance, almost causing him to tumble once more back into the increasingly busy road.

No wonder my brothers have such trouble with the American controlled West and its ways, he thought angrily. That Bahraini could have killed me, speeding like that and he didn't even stop, and he had three young western women crammed into his car with him! The girls were all dressed in identical attire of uniforms he recognised; they were all airline hostesses.

Saeed's thoughts turned back to the fleeting image he had had of the driver, the man's scowl, his angry, twisted face swearing at him. I hope his day of judgement comes very soon, he thought. But something about the man's face was troubling him though, niggling at the back of his mind; he recalled that face from somewhere but from where, and why? Was it someone he had met in Bahrain? Perhaps he had met the man in Jeddah or somewhere else in the Western province of Saudi Arabia?

And then it hit him...hit him like a bolt from the blue.
He knew where he recognised the man's face from and Saeed's blood began to boil. Great swathes of anger and malice swept through him, his hands beginning to shake with a sudden rush of nervous adrenaline. "Oh, now I will have my vengeance," he muttered, "London can wait. What I have in mind for *that man* is far more important." With a steely glint in his eye and jaw set like granite he went off in search of his younger brother.

*   *   *

Fawzi couldn't believe it. "Prince Faris? It can't be, he lives in Riyadh."

"Believe me, Fawzi, it was Faris; that man's features are indelibly registered on my mind."

"But what's he doing here in Bahrain?"

Saeed stared with contemptuous disdain at his brother, "What do you think he's doing, you imbecile, he's screwing western women and drinking alcohol."

"What!" expostulated Fawzi, "Impossible! He had our father imprisoned and flogged for selling alcohol."

"Oh don't be stupid, Fawzi," Saeed exploded, his anger rising once more, "Prince Faris *ran* the major liquor rackets in the northern expatriate compounds around Riyadh; it was only because our father failed to collect money from three western families that Faris had him arrested by the Religious Police. Those bastard families promised to pay our father but left the country before he could collect; it was a sizeable debt. Father was always supposed to collect the money before delivering the alcohol but he had trusted the three Western men."

"I knew that father had been given a five year prison sentence, five hundred lashes and then he was to be deported, but I never knew the circumstances," replied Fawzi softly as he sat down with a troubled thump onto the chair. "But surely our vengeance is against the three Western families, not Prince Faris?"

"Both!" snapped Saeed, "Faris was the one who betrayed our father and arranged for such a long sentence and the harsh flogging. He also arranged for all our family's money to be confiscated. If you remember, we were deported from Saudi within two days of father being sentenced even though our mother was eight months pregnant. The situation and the awful journey home caused her to miscarry, our little sister being born dead."

"Yes, I remember we were escorted from the country in a hurry but I never knew the whole story," Fawzi uttered, his brow puckering.

"Father died in prison, unable to survive the fearful persistent flogging, they never let his wounds heal properly before recommencing the punishment. That's what killed our mother; she never recovered from his death or the death of our unborn sister."

"The bastard!" It was Fawzi's turn to get angry, the fire rising through his veins. He leapt to his feet. "So, what do we do?"

"Do, my brother?" retorted Saeed, "We will take our vengeance."

"But what about London...our mission?"

"London can wait," snapped Saeed, the blood pounding through his overheated temples. "London can wait; first we will have our vengeance against the mighty Prince Faris!"

Saeed's eyes became hard and cruel, the fiery religious zealot in him being replaced by a cold, furious and intense hatred. Even his younger brother Fawzi, staring into Saeed's cold and malignant eyes, could not resist a fearful shudder, the soles of a thousand hob-nailed boots seemingly scraping up his spine.

Chapter 18

Bernie Delaney, raised in a small provincial town in the south of Ireland, had been enjoying the best year of her life.

Reasonably successful whilst at school a couple of years ago she had secured herself a place at University in Dublin to study economics; her parents and family had been so proud of her, the first of the family to have taken such a step. But when Bernie had seen the advert for cabin staff for an air-line in the Middle East, with the promise of international travel, she had leapt at the opportunity. Bernie's blonde hair, beauty, and her ample figure had never left her short of male admirers and thus it was a relatively easy task for the interviewing panel to assess her 'abilities', passing her as a suitable candidate to fill one of their vacancies.

Turnover of the female cabin staff was always high, some of the girls being snapped up by Gulf Arabs whose promise of a better life quite often ended in tears for the girls, ultimately ending up in a society where women had virtually no effective rights. Some of the girls however did enjoy successful lives and careers, moving on to other air-lines or meeting up with and marrying the man of their dreams, usually a successful different kind of high-flyer who could provide them with the necessary comforts of wealth and security.

For Bernie it had been a fairy-tale of revelation, the initial training in Bahrain, the handsome Arabs drooling over her and her colleagues, the entertaining, the wealth, and the presents. The parties had been numerous, huge formal occasions or private little soirees, and the yachts, the parties on the yachts had been awesome. The 'rest' days could be spent alternating between sun-bathing on the highly polished decks - their every whim catered for by the army of Indian workers that buzzed aboard the boats like drones - or swimming in the azure, shallow waters of the Arabian Gulf. Some of the wealthy young Bahrainis and other Gulf Arabs possessed a multitude of water toys and Bernie had learnt to water ski and had had great fun shooting over the waves on one of the high powered water scooters. To cap it all she had seen so many places in the world that she could only have dreamt about if she stayed in Ireland. One day she would go home, a rich husband in tow, and settle down with three or four kids but for now she was going to milk it for all she was worth.

Although she had been in the job for little over ten months she was feeling more and more that this was her lucky year, everything was on the up and up. She and her best friend Kylie, a petite red haired girl from Stirling in Scotland, had suddenly been thrust into the first class compartment, the senior cabin crew for the flight from Jeddah to Manama being taken ill as a result of a severe case of food poisoning; someone had recommended some fresh oysters that turned out not to be fresh at all. Thus it was that Bernie and Kylie met up with Faris, a seriously wealthy and handsome Arab, who soon had the two girls eating out of his hand. It was a bonus when they discovered that he was a Saudi Prince to boot!

They and another girl, a sultry looking female from Shanghai, with gorgeous long dark hair that stretched half way down her back, spent that first night with Faris in the royal suite at a five star hotel. Their 'rest' period had gone by so quickly, the three day R&R passing in the blink of an eye, or more correctly, through untold sexual positions. Bernie had learnt a good deal about herself over those three days and had even been encouraged by Faris to explore and experiment with her friend Kylie and the dark haired Chinese woman. At first she had been revolted but under Faris's cajoling and with his gorgeous eyes directing her on, she had gone through with it. It had aroused Faris even more than their earlier love making, and the screwing that third night had been phenomenal.

The next two weeks had passed with a blur and even the stop-over in Singapore had not interested her this time. All she wanted to do was to get back to Faris. Every time she thought of Faris she fingered the heavy gold necklace that he had given to her and which must have been worth over a thousand pounds (he had told her what it cost in Bahraini Dinars but she couldn't remember the exact figure).

She hadn't seen Faris for over a month, the disappointment of him not being in Bahrain when she got back cutting through her like a knife. The mobile number that Faris had given her was always answered by a message service and despite the numerous messages left he had never returned her calls.

Thus, when Bernie received that call on the Friday morning, the last day of her current rest period, she leapt out of her bath, dressed in record time and was waiting eager and expectant outside her apartment by the time that Faris's black-tinted glass limousine arrived barely fifteen minutes later.

The driver had opened the rear door of the vehicle and Bernie had stepped expectantly inside, "Faris darling," she had uttered but then the disappointment had hit her visibly, a wet rag slapping her bright, burning cheeks; she felt such an idiot.

Rather than rushing into the welcoming arms of Faris she met the grinning features of her friend Kylie and that damn Chinese woman! Both of them smirking up at her, like Cheshire Cats; the bitches! She had wanted Faris to herself but the Chinese girl made her quickly realise that all three girls came as 'package', an amusement for their handsome Prince who already had four wives back in Saudi Arabia and was not about to take on a fifth...certainly not a westerner, particularly in view of the current political situation in his country. The driver dropped the girls at Faris's Bahrain residence.

Bernie had spent the journey smarting but Faris's warm, brown eyes had soon melted her ire; he transferred the girls to his Mercedes Coupe. She had looked on with astonishment at Faris's reckless driving, at one stage he almost knocked down a local Arab who had inadvertently stepped off the pavement, Faris swerving at the last instant, the poor pedestrian being sent flying into the gutter. Faris had continued his journey unabated, a mere glance in his rear view mirror and maniacal laughter accompanying his forward progress. For a fleeting second Bernie had been given an insight into the disdainful and cruel nature of this handsome man but a glance from his warm, brown eyes soon had her weak at the knees and she snuggled closer, her hand on his thigh, delighting in the fact that she had beaten the two girls in getting the front passenger seat.

*   *   *

Through their contacts Saeed had found out where Faris moored his yacht and he had waited patiently all day, without food and with only a small bottle of water to sustain him. He had even ignored the protests from his brother Fawzi, concerned and fearful that they had missed their flight to London, the furious phone calls from Abdullah demanding to know why they hadn't boarded and the consequences that awaited them.

Saeed had been oblivious to it all, his only focus now being on vengeance, revenge against the man responsible for his family's misfortunes. For the umpteenth time he checked the packet of explosives, the timer device set for less than two minutes but not yet primed. There hadn't been enough Semtex available to blow up

Faris's boat but it would certainly destroy the man's car.

Beginning to fear that Faris was not coming back to shore this night Saeed's heart sunk, the daylight giving into to twilight and then into the darkness of the night.

And then his heart soared, his hopes rising as a large yacht drove into view, the helmsman steering the boat in the direction of Faris' mooring.

Saeed left his position; to onlookers it was if he was apparently sleeping amongst a row of metal refuse canisters, and he sauntered in the direction of Faris' parked coupe. Sliding under the car Saeed fixed his home made package under the Coupe, secured to the front axle as close as he could get it to the driver's side of the vehicle. He waited patiently for Faris to return, barely daring to breathe, the time interminable until he heard the familiar voice of his target accompanied by three twittering, giggling females. He felt the car move as the girls climbed aboard and waited until he heard the clunk of the doors closing. Then he set the timer on the detonator. It was only just in time, Faris firing up his engine and engaging the drive control in the space of seconds.

The Mercedes Coupe roared off into the night leaving a foolish looking Saeed lying prone on the tarmac. For a moment he remained stationery not daring to move, the speed of Faris's departure catching him unawares. Luckily no one was looking in his direction and he quickly scrambled to his feet, disappearing behind the refuse bins and onward into the deeper recesses of the working part of the harbour.

*   *

Bernie was glowing, her year excelling beyond expectations. Faris had taken her aside and promised that he would take her to his estate in California where they could spend a week, just the two of them, together. Her thoughts soaring, her heart filling with joy, she reached for Faris' hand, slipping her fingers and then her hand into his.

She smiled. For a second Bernie's heart seemed so full of joy, the overflowing emotion seeming to blow her head off but then the pain hit her, the realisation that what she was experiencing wasn't joy but something else. It wasn't the happiness exploding within that was causing this feeling but something from outside, something that ripped through her, causing unbelievable pain. She screamed, the agony, the shock, the pain, all simultaneous but fleeting, her heart stopping seconds before her body was blown apart.

It had been such a good year.

Chapter 19

Abdullah's mood had not been helped by Fawzi's failure to explain why he and his brother Saeed had not made the flight to London. Having already lost one member of his team, the weak and corrupted Ahmed, it now appeared that the brothers were about to let him down. He would have to make a call to the Imam Khalifa and find out if any replacements were possible from the various sleeping cells already based in England. There would be hell to pay for this failure but Abdullah would make sure that it was Ahmed's family who suffered, not him. After all, being a devout Muslin, married to the cause, he was willing to give up his life for Allah; it was his various appointed cell members who were succumbing to temptations of the flesh.

Abdullah himself had spent some time in Bahrain so he knew of the multitude of sins and temptations available on that small island state for those whose faith and beliefs were like that of the infidels. He thought of Barbara Clark and involuntarily shuddered; yes he was using her but it was only for a purpose, for the ultimate good of his mission.

As if on cue the thought of Barbara seemed to draw that awful woman into the room. Abdullah repressed a shudder of revulsion but also ignored her, staring purposely at the living room window, looking out onto the depressing terraced street outside.

Barbara, in her dressing gown, wet hair dangling in an untidy mess down to her shoulders, cigarette clamped in her mouth, bent over a magazine rack. She glanced up staring wistfully at Abdullah's naked back. She could feel the desire rising within her.

"God, Abdullah," she almost purred," It's so good to have you back. You don't know how much you mean to me. The love, the sex, it is always really special between us."

He hated her using Allah's name in such a way and coupled with a sentence using the word sex! Allah would surely punish her; if only Shari'a law was effective in this country. He would then have the pleasure of watching this woman being buried up to her neck, then stoned to death. Oh how he would enjoy casting the first stone!

Barbara's face clouded, "But why did you disappear...leave me, and for so long?" Her face transformed from that of a doe-eyed deer to an expression of rancour, "Three bloody months without a word, and no bloody sex! Where were you? Where have you been?"

"So many questions, so much yakking," he retorted dismissively, his face registering anger.

Barbara was suddenly afraid that she had been too harsh, quickly stubbing out her cigarette, stepping towards Abdullah and wrapping him into a tight embrace. This time he couldn't resist the shudder that ran through his body, but Barbara merely took that as a sign of his affection, his body shaking with eagerness from her touch. She began to caress his back, running her fingers across his shoulders and down his spine.

She looked into his eyes, "At least you're back now, and I won't have to sell this house."

Abdullah did not respond, his thoughts concentrated on trying not to scream out, only wanting to throw this repulsive creature off him. He was also worried more and more concerning the impending failure of his mission.

Barbara pulled away, her hands gripping tightly onto Abdullah's forearms, her face scanning his, "Abdullah, you are back, permanently, aren't you?" Her eyes misted, "You're not going away again? Oh please say no, I just couldn't bear it."

Abdullah removed her fiercely gripping hands, freeing himself from her closeness and took a step back. "I can't stay. I've only come back to get a few personal things. My family needs me back in the Yemen."

Barbara almost screamed and rushed forward, grasping hold of Abdullah in a vice like embrace, her cheek almost glued to his naked chest. She pleaded hysterically, "No, Abdullah, no! You can't go again. What will I do? I'm lost without you!"

Abdullah's reply was cold, dismissive, he had determined that he could no longer stand being near this woman; she had served her purpose, "That's not my problem, woman." He would collect his possessions and find a new location whilst he waited for a fresh team to be assembled. His vision travelled to the sideboard, focusing intensively, a frown spreading across his forehead. Wrestling free from the woman's embrace, a terrible concern swept through him, from the tip of his forehead travelling through his heart and hitting him in the guts like a punch to the solar plexus. "Where's my Dhow?"

Abdullah pushed Barbara away, almost sending her sprawling, a dire anxiety enveloping him.

Barbara stared up at him, her expression varying between anguish, confusion, sorrow, and fear.

"My Dhow, you stupid woman," his voice was venomous and angry, "Where is my Dhow?"

Her mind working furiously, Barbara quickly realised what he was asking. "Oh, you mean your bloody boat." She smirked with self-satisfaction, a chance to get her own back for his harsh words, "I sold it, to help pay the mortgage."

Abdullah exploded, "You did *what*!" He was almost apoplectic with rage, "You had no right; that was *my* boat...my Dhow!" He took a step menacingly towards her, "Where is it? Who did you sell it to?"

Suddenly afraid at the maniacal expression on Abdullah's face and the evil reflected in his eyes, Barbara backed away, her own eyes registering fear parallel to the rising anger and venom in Abdullah's eyes. Nervously, she retorted, "I really don't know. I had to sell it, to make ends meet."

Abdullah advanced on Barbara, a fury in his eyes that she had never witnessed previously. She stood frozen, petrified.

Abdullah grasped her by the throat and with a voice as rough as a metal saw grinding on metal, demanded, "Tell me where my Dhow is? Now!"

Barbara, white with fear, barely able to speak, muttered, "I sold it to the man who came to survey the house for the Buyers." Her eyes felt as if they are about to pop from her head, Abdullah's hot breath like a furnace and his face inches from hers. She was now very afraid and desperately squeaked, "I can try and get it back." Her knees were beginning to buckle, her breathing more difficult, "I have the man's card."

Abdullah shouted into her face, "*Where?*"

Barbara's water-filled eyes glanced in the direction of the sideboard, "Over there, in the drawer."

Abdullah looked over his shoulder at the sideboard, loosened the fingers that had been squeezing tightly on the woman's neck and gradually released his grip from Barbara's red and bruised skin, his eyes boring with intense hatred into her petrified irises. He stepped to the sideboard, yanking out two drawers, the drawers falling heavily on to the carpeted floor, before he found the one containing the card.

Dazed, confused, and afraid, Barbara leant against an armchair, gathering her thoughts, her breathing becoming easier. She glanced at Abdullah's back, no longer with yearning, nor with sexual desire, but with an anger that was growing inside her.

The pig was no longer interested in her, he obviously had found what he wanted and was scrutinising the Surveyor's card. Her hackles rose, "No man treats me like that!" she thought angrily, and making the biggest mistake of her life she charged at his back, screaming with intense fury, "You bastard; you fucking bastard, how dare you treat me like that!"

Abdullah spun round before Barbara could sink her claws into him. Calmly, he extended his arm, fist clenched, and caught her cleanly on the chin, the force jolting her head backwards. The woman, shaken, stunned, did not have a chance to recover. Abdullah smashed her across the face with the back of his hand, sending her flying across the room and tumbling backwards over the two-seater sofa.

Tumbling backwards over the sofa, Barbara cracked her head against the wall and remained still, disorientated and semiconscious, her breathing coming in shallow gasps and her prone body dripping blood from the gash at the back of her head.

Abdullah's intense anger was replaced by a calm, cold, heartless demeanour and he strode over to the woman.

Barbara imagined that he was coming to say sorry, to help her to her feet; he had obviously become overwrought and over tired. Perhaps she shouldn't have kept him up all night making love. But it had been a long time since she'd had a man. She wouldn't forgive him straight away; no, she would make him grovel first but then, later, much later, she would make her peace and invite him into her bed. In her semiconscious state she managed a flicker of a smile as Abdullah's hand reached down towards her.

He straddled her limp body, placing his hands round her neck, compressing tighter and tighter until the life was squeezed from her pathetic body, her eyes opening wide in shock, the smile slowly transforming into a grimace, the mouth finally forming a silent scream as her lungs fought desperately for breath. She wriggled once, a desperate attempt to crawl free from the clamps squeezing her neck, then her left leg kicked out involuntarily as her body gave in, the life sucked from the body's sad and depressing existence. For Barbara there would be no more worries about paying the mortgage, with or without the house sale.

Gradually Abdullah released the pressure from Barbara's neck, sure that the awful woman was now dead. He had felt his hands locking in cramp, the fingers losing their feelings. Although he was convinced that Barbara had died fairly quickly, he had kept the pressure on her neck for well over five minutes, determined to take no chances of the bitch being able to make some sort of recovery. Also, he felt a justification in prolonging her 'punishment', even though her only crime was that she was in the wrong place at the wrong time, but to Abdullah she signified everything that was going wrong with his plans.

Finally his cold eyes re-focused on the woman and he rose, stepping clear of her body, staring down with utter loathing and contempt at her lifeless form. "Pathetic harlot!" he snarled in disgust.

Abdullah turned away from Barbara's lifeless body, her existence no longer of any interest to him, and walking leisurely to the sideboard he retrieved Sean's card placing it in his pocket.

Abdullah exited the room, his face registering an expression of hatred and intended malice. "The Surveyor," he murmured, "The infidel thief has my property...but he will be sorry that he stole it from me...his judgement day is also coming!"

Chapter 20

Ray had a thundering, tumultuous hangover thrashing in his brain when he woke in the early hours of dawn. In addition to the pounding in his head his heart was in his boots; he had never felt so low. To have seen Kerry and Spratt leaving Rosie's bar, arm in arm, had caused him such unexpected anguish and sorrow.

He climbed stiffly to his feet, rubbing life back into his joints, his muscles stiff and frozen, the doorway having provided only limited shelter.

Although he had known that Kerry was engaged to Sean he had held out hope that maybe, one day, she would notice him and he could woo her away from Sean. But now that he had seen Spratt with Kerry and the way that Kerry had reacted to Spratt, her moon filled eyes wide in adulation, made him realise that Spratt had already succeeded in getting Kerry under his spell.

Ray knew that Kerry would get hurt and despite his anger, his heart was filled with compassion for her. He knew that she had lied to him about Brian telling her not to get involved with customers and he knew that she merely used him to secure orders, but he didn't really care about that. To have seen her with Spratt, leaving together as they did, their intentions plain for all to see made his heart feel like a heavy lead balloon. "Oh, Kerry," he mused, "I thought you were stronger than that!"

In spite of his anger he knew that he would be around to help Kerry pick up the pieces; he would be unable to see her suffer.

*   *

Taking his seat on the British Airways flight to London Heathrow Ray had had a whirlwind trip, inspecting two yachts in a little over thirty-six hours and was now on his way back from Bahrain.

The reports would be compiled by the time he returned to his office and the trade-in valuations assessed and agreed prior to completion of the two new-build contracts. One of the boats belonged to a wealthy Bahraini businessman, his high-jinks being curtailed by his new wife - the man's third - and rumoured to be an Iranian lady of exceptional beauty.

For a few years at least she would rein in his tendencies of 'entertaining' the various air-hostesses that stopped over in the Arabian Gulf. The Bahraini businessman's new boat would be a much more boring affair, a family designed boat that would not see much usage. The second boat belonged to a Saudi, one of the numerous Saudi Arabian Princes, and with the death of his father this particular prince wanted to upgrade to a much more luxurious affair.

Ray became progressively aware of the passenger sitting in the seat next to him, the man causing Ray to feel increasingly uncomfortable. The man shuffled nervously, his feet sliding backwards and forwards, his body constantly fidgeting. An unpleasant odour began to emanate from the direction of the man's armpits, sweat beginning to form on his brow. The man was highly agitated, possibly in fear of flying.

Normally Ray was not too fussy were he sat on a plane but this time it was really beginning to bug him, the thought of sitting next to this passenger for the almost seven hour flight making him feel increasingly uncomfortable. The man also had a bowel problem, his nervousness releasing a cloud of unpleasant gas - and they hadn't even taken off yet, the aircraft still taxiing down the runway. He knew that there would no possibility of changing seats, his business class ticket obsolete as the flight had been fully booked, the only spare seat available being next to his unpleasant fellow traveller. He could have waited for tomorrow's flight, but there was so much to do back in the office. So he gritted his teeth, determining to ask the stewardess for a strong drink the moment that they were in the air. "Surely, my business class ticket will earn me some concession?" he mused.

The man sitting in the window seat turned away from his scrutiny of the airport activity and breathed a sigh of relief as the wheels left the ground, the plane climbing into the sky. He glanced at his nervous companion in the middle seat and spoke a few words in Arabic, his tone harsh and acerbic.

Foul-stench man muttered a few words in reply but quickly became silent as the Arab in the window seat continued his tirade, obviously berating his companion for being so weak.

Ray sighed, a plaintiff tired sigh; it was going to be a long journey.

*   *   *

Fawzi had never flown before, the butterflies in his stomach flying back and forth for all they were worth. He had already emptied his bowels three times that morning and vomited twice, but still he felt as if he would need the toilet again. It was only Saeed's insistence, plus the threat of what would happen to their remaining family in Yemen, that persuaded him to finally board the plane, his feet feeling like lead weights as he climbed the steps to the aircraft. Just before entering the plane he had frozen in fear, bringing the long line of embarking passengers to a crushing halt and attracting the attention of many people in their vicinity.

Saeed had whispered in his brother's ear, at first cajoling then threatening, and when he spotted a vigilant police officer looking up at them, the strap of his machine pistol being lowered from his shoulder, Saeed finally manage to half push, half convince Fawzi to enter the plane, a terrible stench left in their wake as Fawzi emitted a fart of indescribable odour.

Little did all three passengers sitting together realise how intertwined their lives would become in the very near future, the stench that Ray was now experiencing akin to a garden of roses compared to events that were destined to occur!

Chapter 21

It hadn't taken Abdullah very long to locate Sean's Office Block, a prestigious building just south of the City's square mile.

Having drawn the sitting room curtains he had left Barbara's body where it lay. The curtains being drawn during daylight hours wouldn't attract any undue attention from the neighbours, Barbara's reputation for 'entertaining' male friends being quite legendary in the area.

Abdullah had taken a quick shower and gathered his few meagre possessions. Having emptied Barbara's purse, gaining a few measly pounds and hardly worth the effort, he had left the house. His first priority was to retrieve his Dhow then he could seek out fresh lodgings. He knew of two sympathetic possibilities that would provide him with shelter but the future was meaningless without the Dhow. It was all about the Dhow; he must retrieve it then he could re-plan the mission. That fool Saeed and his brother would soon be on their re-arranged flight to London and the three of them could, and should, carry out the appointed task.

Although feeling more tired than he had ever been he determined to keep going, purchasing an A-Z of London. After a few wrong turnings, including once having caught a Tube in the wrong direction, he finally located Sean's office block.

Biding his time Abdullah had watched the building from a café near the entrance and had noted that every so often the stern looking, middle-aged Receptionist was replaced by a younger woman who seemed more interested in catching the eyes of the post delivery boy rather than being effective in her duties. Thus he would wait until the next time that she was on duty. Then he would make his move.

It had all gone according to plan, Abdullah having entered the building carrying a note pad and holding a pen in his hand. He had convinced the disinterested girl that he was in the premises to prepare a quotation for a new air conditioning system and that he needed to re-check some dimensions. The girl, now engrossed in a private telephone conversation, waved him through.

Whilst talking to the temporary Receptionist he paid particular attention to a wall mounted board that detailed the various Companies resident in this building and in particular the organisation that employed Sean. Quickly ascertaining that Sean's company's offices were on the ground floor he studied the board in greater detail, identifying the various Partners together with their relevant Office numbers, each room including the meeting or board rooms being given an alpha-numeric address.

Deciding that hiding on the ground floor would limit his chances of being discovered Abdullah checked out the floors above, no one questioning his right to wander through the building. "Fools", he thought, "It will be so easy to plant explosives anywhere in this pathetic City and destroy many of these decadent Westerners!"

On the third floor he located a large gentlemen's toilet with fifteen urinals, six cubicles, and a maintenance storeroom. Ignoring the cursory glances of the three men pissing at the urinals he found that the storeroom door was unlocked. Quickly pulling the door open he tugged at a piece of string hanging down from the ceiling, a muted bulb reluctantly popping into light. Abdullah made pretence of recording the storeroom's contents, jotting down the quantities of soap, toilet paper, bleach, and other detergents/cleaning agents that were located within. As soon as the Gents was empty he pulled the storeroom door closed behind him, jamming it shut with a folded piece of cardboard. Then he turned off the light and sat, waiting patiently for the building to empty, his luminous watch helping him keep track of the time.

Time had dragged and despite Abdullah's best intentions he had fallen asleep, his head propped against a stack of toilet rolls, his feet in an empty bucket that still smelt of the disinfectant previously used to clean the toilets. He didn't wake until his watch registered well after midnight, the building in total darkness, an eerie silence pervading.

It took Abdullah nearly half an hour to locate Sean's office suite, everything looking so different in the darkness. It was a further ten minutes before he had identified Sean's office.

Not finding his Dhow, he risked turning on the light but it didn't improve matters, the Dhow being nowhere in sight. He ransacked Sean's office, turning out all the drawers, filing cabinets and a small cupboard that only housed Sean's personal tea-set. He smashed the cups and saucers in frustration because of his failure to locate his former possession. The offices of Sean's partners, and indeed all the ground floor rooms, met with the same fate. Oblivious to the threat of being discovered Abdullah tore through the ground floor rooms like a whirling dervish.

He searched for almost three hours then the twittering of an early bird made him realise that it was getting lighter outside and that he would have to leave, the risk of being discovered putting a total end to the intended mission.

Reluctantly Abdullah made his way back to the building entrance and checking that the coast was clear, he exited the building, disappearing off into the growing light of the early dawn.

*   *   *

It was a further two days before Abdullah dared to venture back, to return to the scene of his chaos.

Having entered through the large double glass doors of the prestigious and opulent building he approached the main reception desk, behind which sat an imperious looking middle-aged female, her glasses perched half-way down her nose, her eyes boring into his, a warning of not to waste her time, she being a supercilious and busy lady.

Abdullah leant forward over the main reception desk, encountering a 'tusk' of disapproval, his face inches from that of the Receptionist. "People should know their place," she thought, "He should be standing a good foot away from my desk, not leaning over me like some ignorant oik."

She was about to speak, to protest, her stern glance and expression of disproval meeting with nonchalance, a disinterest, the man ignoring her discomfort; but the man spoke first, his tone low, confidential, *foreign*, "I need to speak to a Sean O'Malley."

The Receptionist drew back, creating a small distance between her and the rude foreign gentleman. "Do you have an appointment?" she demanded, her tone icy.

"No, but I need to speak to Sean O'Malley."

"I'm sorry but we operate a busy office and if you haven't got an appointment, then I'm sure *MR* O'Malley will be unable to see you." The Receptionist stressed the Mister title, adding formality to the exchange of words, reasserting her authority. "Perhaps I can forward a message for him," she added as an afterthought, just in case this foreign gentleman was a potential customer.

"It's a private matter," snapped Abdullah, "And has nothing to do with you."

The Receptionist kept her tone calm but firm, the authority of her important vetting position adding a gravely determination to her voice, "I'm afraid that I am not going to disturb Mr O'Malley unless you can give me more information. At least tell me who you are, and your business with Mr O'Malley?"

Abdullah fixed the female Receptionist with a hard, threatening stare, but being used to coping with the toughest of individuals she didn't bat an eyelid. He was beginning to feel hatred for this overweight western female; how dare she question his demands, thwarting his wishes? His eyes pierced like two orbs of burning suns but she just looked away, ignoring his threatening malice. He bunched his fists in frustration and through clenched teeth, growled, "I have something that belongs to him."

"What is it?"

"I can't tell *you*," he snapped in response.

The receptionist was becoming irked, her fastidious aloofness being replaced by impatience, "Don't be ridiculous. Unless you give me more information I will phone Security and have you removed from this building." She reached for her telephone.

Abdullah clamped his hand, tightly and fiercely, around her wrist.

The Receptionist semi-rose from her seat, bristling with indignation, "How *dare* you; you're hurting me!"

Abdullah realising that he was fighting a losing battle, released his grip and stepped away from the reception desk. He smiled benignly. "Okay, okay, I'm sorry," the words tumbling from his mouth without sincerity, "I will tell you. But it's private."

The Receptionist was still fuming at his behaviour, glowering with indignant anger and was severely tempted to call Security, but hesitated as he continued, "When your Mr O'Malley surveyed my partner's house he left his watch in my...partner's bedroom. We have an...open relationship." The implication being that Sean had behaved with impropriety to the visitor's partner.

The Receptionist, eyes blinking in disbelief, her face displaying a mix of hurt, anger, wariness and shocked amazement, rubbed her sore wrist; she was shocked momentarily, not knowing what to say.

Abdullah then pulled a wad of ten pound notes from his jacket pocket. "He also left behind a lot of money." The Receptionists eyes widened, her open lips unspeaking. "And that's why I need to make sure that Mr O'Malley gets his things. With respect to you," He smiled at the Receptionist, "I don't know you and wouldn't want Mr O'Malley to lose anything."

"Well!" Her composure was totally destroyed. "Well!" she

repeated, gob smacked as Abdullah smiled again, a knowing, secretive, nudge-nudge type of smile that she found offensive. The Receptionist, shaking her head in amazed disbelief, picked up the telephone receiver and pressed the digits for Sean's extension.

Feeling confident that he was getting somewhere Abdullah stepped back from the reception desk whilst the woman engaged in a muted, discreet conversation with a person on the other end of her phone. Occasionally she glanced up at the man standing in front of her desk but quickly looked away before eye contact could be made, her eyebrows arched in a mixture of shock, revulsion, and disgust.

Abdullah took the opportunity to make sure of his bearings, scanning the lobby and the stairway that led to the floor above. If he couldn't get hold of that thieving Surveyor today then he would get the man later that night.

The Receptionist, back to her haughty persona, replaced the receiver and favoured her uninvited visitor with a scowl. "Mr O'Malley claims not to know who you are or what you're talking about!" She announced with frosty aplomb, adding triumphantly, "And he's in a meeting at the moment!"

Abdullah's face fell. At the very least he expected to have the opportunity of meeting the thief and having the prospect of recovering his Dhow.

Saddened that she could not enjoy her triumph any longer she finally managed to pass on Sean's subsequent instructions, "I hope, for your sake, that you are telling the truth. He seemed very angry at my call. However, he will have a word with you on the phone in a couple of minutes. Although his office is on this floor he can't get away, but a coffee break is scheduled." The internal telephone on the Receptionist's desk rang almost immediately, the woman passing the receiver to Abdullah.

The subsequent conversation with Sean did not go as Abdullah had planned, the 'thieving' Surveyor insisting that he didn't have time to meet Abdullah and didn't know what he was talking about. Abdullah persisted with his story that Sean had something that belonged to him and that he in turn, had money, a lot of money that belonged to Sean. The conversation was interrupted, a muffled voice informing Sean that the meeting had recommenced. Cutting their weird conversation short, Sean politely informed Abdullah that he needed to terminate the conversation, and besides it was obviously a case of mistaken identity. However, if the gentleman was prepared to wait until the meeting was concluded then Sean would have a brief word to find out what this was all, advising the furiously protesting Abdullah to leave his name and address if he couldn't wait. Actually, becoming extremely irked, Sean was bloody annoyed that this person had erroneously labelled him as an adulterer, also inferring that he had removed a third party's property from a house that he had valued. He would have it out with the man as soon as he could. He terminated the conversation, the man's harsh voice still insisting that he needed to speak to Sean immediately.

Furious, Abdullah slammed down the receiver, the Receptionist almost leaping out of her seat in surprise.

"How dare you," she protested, "You nearly broke my telephone."

"Oh, shut up, woman!" he yelled at her, the fury rising within his breast, "Before I shut you up!"

The Receptionist, determined not to be spoken to in such a manner, picked up the receiver and dialled an emergency number; the dialled number requiring no words to be spoken. With arctic glee she looked up at Abdullah, "Someone will be along in a minute then we'll see how brave you are."

Abdullah thinking quickly, smiled at the Receptionist, scanned his surroundings then rushed forward, a malevolent expression on his face. The Receptionist made a belated attempt to rise from her chair, her face registering fear and panic, but the man reached her before she could fully rise, administering a 'rabbit punch' to the back of her neck, then he snapped her neck with practised ease. She collapsed, slumping lifeless to the floor. Insensitively he rolled her body almost double and shoved her as far as possible under the reception desk, replacing her chair in front of the desk; then turning, he virtually leapt up the steps to the floor above.

Heart racing, adrenalin kicking in, he reached the first floor landing, and ducked down behind a large plant pot that gave him cover yet permitted him the ability to peer through the gaps of the ornamental metal supports of the wooden bannister. Focused, angry, dangerous, he stared intently into the reception area below just as a door opened at the side of the reception lobby, a security man rushing into the empty room. He was followed almost immediately by a second individual, this one wearing an expensive looking suit.

"Where's Mrs Styles?" asked Sean to the bewildered security officer who had stopped in his tracks, confused by the empty lobby. Seriously concerned and not a little bemused, Sean had been unable to continue with his meeting and had asked to be excused, feigning a sudden case of food poisoning as a result of last night's Chinese meal. Quickly excusing himself from the meeting, he and the security officer arrived almost simultaneously.

"Don't know, Mr O'Malley," responded the confused Security Officer, scratching his head in confusion, "She typed in an alarm code, but she's not here."

"Well, this is crazy; what the hell is going on? She just phoned me to tell me that I had a visitor and now they've both disappeared?" Bemused, Sean strode to the building entrance and checked outside. No one; even the pavement was deserted. Bewildered, he muttered under his breath, "And I excused myself from an important meeting just to have a quick word with that rude, lying prat!" He made his way back to the door at the side of the reception lobby, the bewildered security officer following in his footsteps.

Abdullah involuntarily sucked in his breath. He had finally got sight of his prey, his sharp eyes peering through the stairwell railings, absorbing every facet of Sean's identity; he scowled and murmured, "So, Dhow thief, you *will* lead me back to *my* Dhow. Then your life will no longer have any meaning!" With the immediate coast clear he rose to his full height, a vicious gleam in his eye, and slowly and calmly walked down the stairs and exited the building.

He would be back, oh yes, he would return, and then...

Chapter 22

The flight to London had been everything that Ray had feared, the Arab Man sitting next to him only managing to hold on to the contents of his stomach for just over two hours. The man had turned paler and paler, his brown visage becoming increasingly tinged with green. Ray had become progressively concerned, his journey increasingly uncomfortable.

Twice Fawzi had pushed past Ray, any semblance of courtesy and manners of secondary importance to his headlong rush to the toilets. On the man's return Ray had requested the stewardess to provide another sick bag for the man sitting next to him. Goodness knew, the aircrew must surely have already been aware of the man's stench, and his rumbling stomach must have been evident every time he rushed down the aisle to the toilets. The man's green gills and puce colour had Ray almost on the verge of joining his fellow passenger in a 'technicolour yawn'. But the stewardess had scowled at the request; she was busy serving drinks and would return as soon as she could.

As luck would have it, the flight attendant arrived far too late, Fawzi once again leaping from his seat, this time the bile rising far too quickly in his throat, his lips desperately attempting to contain the flood of liquid that shot up from his stomach and into his mouth, his cheeks puffing up like that of a hamster storing its food. Attempting to pass Ray, Fawzi could no longer keep the bile in his mouth and a stream of semi-viscous fluid spurted onto Ray's lap, continued onto the aisle carpet and yet there was a sufficient quantity to just catch the arm of a woman sitting in the aisle seat directly opposite, her shriek of disgust not entirely in harmony with the remaining fluid from the retching Fawzi still dripping onto the aisle carpet. Far, far too late, their stewardess almost ran forward, berating Fawzi for his disgusting behaviour, and was brusque to the point of rudeness with Ray, not acknowledging that her tardy response had exacerbated the situation. Totally in conflict with his character, Ray swore involuntarily causing the now truculent, hostile stewardess to remonstrate with him concerning his language; to cap it all, trying to offload any responsibility, she threatened to call the captain.

A stand up row was brewing amongst the mayhem but fortunately the senior flight attendant arrived on the scene and quickly calmed the remonstrating stewardess, cleaned the woman passenger's arm of vomit, and then the furiously irate Ray was led away, the senior attendant very solicitous, the woman intent on cleaning him up as best she could. Mollified but embarrassed, standing in the galley area with a tea-towel protecting his modesty whilst the flight crew cleaned up his trousers as best they could, Ray enjoyed the soothing effect of a large scotch. One of the crew added a few drops of Opium perfume onto his trousers with the intention of dowsing the stench of vomit, holding her nose while she did so.

When Ray did eventually return to his seat almost half an hour later the sickly smell of vomit and perfume accompanied his every step. Fortunately the crew had cleaned up the area around his seat and his Arab 'companion' was now sitting, seemingly calm; but in actual fact the man had been sedated, a mild tranquilliser sending him into the warm and soothing comfort of sleep, the Arab man's brain no longer concerned with the turbulence of the journey.

The second Arab man sitting next to the window apologised to Ray, explaining in broken English that it was the first time that he and his brother had flown and that they had also come through a recent family bereavement. Ray grudgingly accepted the apology and when the man sitting next to window finally fell asleep as well Ray spent the remaining part of the journey in blissful peace, even refusing on behalf of himself and his two sleeping fellow passengers any further sustenance. He certainly didn't want either man to be awakened until they had touched down on English soil!

When they did touch down, the plane finally taxiing to a halt alongside the appointed landing pier, Ray never knew such relief as he waited in his seat, the two Arabs having pushed passed as soon as the fasten seatbelt sign had been extinguished. He most probably would have been as keen to exit the plane but his hand luggage was in an overhead locker further down the cabin, all space in the overhead lockers in his immediate vicinity having been fully crammed when he originally boarded and took the final available seat.

With hindsight he wished he had waited for the next flight!

When the cabin had almost emptied Ray went to the rear of the plane, to his locker, and recovered his briefcase and coat. Returning forward to exit the plane he noticed that his fellow passengers had left something in the seat pocket. Reaching down Ray pulled out a hard covered brown book, the words adorning it in Arabic. As much as he wanted to ignore the men's possession - after all he had made his journey most unpleasant - he decided that two wrongs didn't make a right and accordingly determined that he would catch up with the men in the baggage claim area and hand over the book, Ray realising that it was obviously a personal copy of the Holy Koran.

But by the time that he had cleared Immigration and reached the baggage hall there was no sign of his two fellow travellers; they seemingly had disappeared off the face of the earth.

Weary and exhausted, with the combined smell of perfume and vomit exacerbating his nostrils, Ray shrugged, put the copy of the Koran in his briefcase, collected his suitcase and exited. The thought of the two Arab men receded in his mind as he put distance between himself and airport, the pleasant smiling image and essence of Kerry filling his attention. He was so looking forward to seeing Kerry tomorrow; he would make some excuse, find some pretence to visit her. Although utterly exhausted, his face lit up, a smile spreading across his mouth, his eyes brimming with love and devotion.

Chapter 23

Kerry was first out of their flat closely followed by Sean, who pulled the door too, then double locked it with both a Yale key and an ordinary key. In the past neither of them had paid too much attention in securing both locks on their front door but with everything that had happened recently, Sean was not about to take any chances.

Kerry turning to watch Sean locking their front door gave way to an involuntary inexplicable shudder.

The man watching from a vantage point further along the street, leaning apparently nonchalantly against a red letter box, saw them exit and snorted, then curled his lips in contempt at their excessive efforts in protecting their property. With his collar turned up on a thick, heavy duty coat, baseball cap pulled low over his head, Abdullah stepped back into the shadows cast by a sun canopy of the nearby small grocery/ newsagents store. His eyes glittered malevolently, reflecting a mix of evil and hatred as he focused on Kerry and Sean walking along the street.

Kerry could not help shuddering, a feeling that someone was walking over her grave, a sense of intense foreboding building within her. "Is it guilt?" she thought, "Am I regretting my sojourn with Spratt?" Then she smiled at her ridiculous thoughts and this time tingled with pleasure as she recalled her 'forbidden' lovemaking with Spratt.

Solicitous, Sean looked at her, enquiring with affection if she was alright? Was she feeling cold? Without waiting for her response he lovingly wrapped his arm around Kerry, comforting her, keeping her safe and warm.

Kerry's eyes looked up at him but she did not smile in response to Sean's warm grin of affection. Instead her expression was one of worry and concern, her eyes clouded. "No," she responded hesitantly, "I was just thinking about poor Mrs Styles; she was your principal receptionist for two years wasn't she?" Without waiting for a response Kerry added, "And then there was also the earlier break-in at your offices. It gives me the shivers. Do the police know what's going on? Have they said anything; have they found out what's going on?"

"Nothing tangible," responded Sean dubiously, "They haven't got a clue as to why Mrs Styles was murdered; she didn't seem to have any enemies herself, so it has to be connected with the guy who was trying to see me that day. All we know is that he was foreign, his English not brilliant. The police grilled me because they thought I must have known something, particularly because of the way that my own office was ransacked. But as for the break-in at the company offices, nothing was stolen. The whole place was trashed but there doesn't seem to be anything missing. My office seems to have received the worst of the treatment. There just doesn't appear to be a plausible explanation."

"Maybe it was kids trying to find cash for drugs?"

Sean shook his head negatively, "No, the police don't think so; it has to tie in with Mrs Styles murder and somehow connected to me or something that I've done, but no-one from the police really seems to have any idea."

Kerry shivered again, this time only from fear, her earlier thoughts of Spratt contained to a secret memory. "Well, just you be careful."

Sean smiled at her words of concern, "I will." And then he kissed her lovingly on the cheek.

*   *   *

This was the second day that Abdullah had watched Sean's flat and the second time he had noted their efforts in securing their flat. The first day, he had thoroughly reconnoitred the area, scouting along the main street and then from the street that ran parallel behind. But there was no access from the rear, the tiny walled gardens of the properties being totally overlooked by the neighbours. Abdullah had been in the process of climbing on a dustbin with the intention of scaling Sean's back wall but a pair of curious eyes had focused on him, the woman from two doors down the street watching his every movement, the bawling baby in her arms temporarily forgotten as she watched the stranger. Abdullah had sheepishly skulked away, momentarily thwarted, but he knew he would return.

And now it was today and still there were too many neighbours, too many people, too many eyes watching the neighbourhood. Thus he would have to rethink his strategy, find a new method, garner more information regarding his enemy and the enemy's woman. He would studiously collect all the information that he could find out about the infidel scum and then he would work out a new plan, a new strategy. Properly prepared, he would get back his precious property, but first he would make them pay, make them truly suffer, for delaying his mission, his purpose.

With a renewed determination in his step, the malice growing within his heart, he followed Kerry and Sean to the tube station. Staying as unobtrusive as he could, years of blending into the background helping him, he followed unobserved, remaining on the Tube as Sean exited the carriage, the man planting a swift kiss on Kerry's forehead. Abdullah switched trains as Kerry did, following, always from a discreet distance, then trailed her all the way to her office block.

He was about to follow the woman inside the building but the siren of a hastily approaching police car baulked him, unnerving him, and he made a quick but discreet turn around, hurriedly strolling away, his hands deep in his pockets, his shoulders hunched with a combination of frustration and trying to keep a low profile. Merging with the crowds, he disappeared back into the London Underground network.

    *   *   *

"Did you get it?" asked Fawzi, his eager voice raised in hopeful anticipation.

"No, I didn't," snapped Abdullah in response, "If I had it would be with me now, fool!"

"There's no need to speak to my brother like that, we need to work together in harmony, as a team," remonstrated Saeed, the hurt expression on his brother's face making the elder sibling rise to his brother's defence.

Irked and frustrated, Abdullah reeled round to face Saeed. His eyes blazing, he almost shouted, "Don't tell me how we need to work!" He gestured furiously, his arms raised to the heavens. "You and your brother almost jeopardised this mission, overstaying in Bahrain. And then to kill Prince Faris...unbelievable!"

"He was a bad man," protested Saeed. "It was a '*just*' killing."

"Nobody denies that he was a bad man," shouted Abdullah, his angry face inches from Saeed's face causing Saeed to back away a small step. "But because of your reckless stupidity, you caused mayhem to our brothers. The Bahrain Government had a team of British SAS soldiers operational in Bahrain, and together with the internal security services being fired up, they quickly located our cell. All our brothers are either dead or in the hands of the British and Americans!"

"I had no idea. I didn't think of the consequences," meekly protested Saeed.

"Exactly, you fool!" Abdullah shouted, the spittle from his angry mouth leaving a speckle of residue on Saeed's face. Saeed dare not raise his hand to wipe the spittle from his face just in case Abdullah might think he was preparing to strike out.

"Once our mission is completed here we will go on to other things and, Allah permitting, there will be the opportunity for vengeance against the pretenders, the fake guardians of the Holy Mosque, of Mecca and Medina!" Abdullah's voice was raised in maniacal fury, "Not only would Prince Faris have been dealt with but all of the family who claim guardianship over our Holy Shrines!"

Fawzi nervously wrung his hands; he wanted to go to his brother's defence but knew that Abdullah was *the* king pin, *the master* of this operation. If he or Saeed messed up then the repercussions against them would be horrendous. There would be no hiding place and particularly in this foreign land where they didn't really know anyone. Their only contact, besides Abdullah, was the Imam of the mosque in this area of north London. The Imam was providing them with lodgings, their accommodation consisting of a shared room in the basement under the mosque.

There was another person who they knew, or in truth who seemed to know them. This man, an Indian initially from Gujarat, was apparently now working with the British social services. He had good connections and not only had he met them at the airport, he was the one who had arranged their papers and brought them safely to this mosque.

But that was it; even at prayer times the brothers were kept separate from the other worshippers, the minimal possibility of being observed a key to their mission. Prayers had been carried out in the basement, Fawzi having been loaned a new copy of the Korean as he had carelessly left his own personal copy on the plane. That had really irked him as the book had been given to him years ago by his father's brother and it had accompanied Fawzi everywhere. But no more; he felt a deep sadness at losing what he considered an old friend, his comfort, his safety blanket.

"Forgive my carelessness," meekly implored Saeed, "I will not act independently again."

"It may be too late for forgiveness," snapped Abdullah, the

harshness heavy in his tone.

Fortunately for Saeed the Imam descended the stairs from the Mosque, and although imbued with an unchallenged authority, he spoke softly, "Abdullah please keep your voice down. Even though you are speaking in Arabic many of my people speak the language and not all are loyal to our cause."

"Only those who have been corrupted by the West would be against our aims!" spat Abdullah, but he did not shout, his voice now calmer, moderated.

"No, Abdullah," the Imam riposted, "Most believe in the sacred tenets of Islam but they do not wish any harm to their fellow British citizens. They would be happy to convert the population to the Islamic faith by peaceful means."

"Pah!" protested Abdullah, "We don't need such weak people. We will achieve our aims without them!"

"That's as may be," persisted the Imam, "But let us eat then talk of other matters. Maybe we can jointly think of the best way to recover your Dhow."

Fawzi almost smiled with relief, the Imam having subdued Abdullah's rant, and, yes, his stomach was rumbling; a meal would be most welcome.

Chapter 24

Ray had visited Kerry's office a few times over the previous couple of days in meaningless pretexts of trying to solve pricing or technical issues. But each time he had visited Kerry was either out of the office or involved in a meeting, so he had had to spend his time with Kerry's boss Brian, who although a good friend, was not really the person that Ray had wanted to see. Brian was also becoming suspicious of the amount of times that Ray had visited their offices, particularly at the meaningless questions that he was being asked by his supposed intelligent friend.

Overhearing from Siobhan that a group of people from the marine business where meeting up that evening, Ray managed to inveigle an invite for himself from Brian. Rushing straight home from his umpteenth meeting in Brian's office He had showered, splashed on copious amounts of Calvin Klein aftershave, and dressed in what he considered one of his snappier outfits, tight fitting trousers and a beige moleskin jacket and rushing like man running from a swarm of bees he arrived breathless, but ruggedly smart, at the appointed venue and at the scheduled time.

Espying Brian's group in the waiting throng on the pavement Ray rushed over, his heart thumping, face visibly eager at the thought of seeing Kerry. Brian, Siobhan, and two other girls from Brian's office greeted him with warm smiles, the girls praising his handsome appearance. Siobhan even favoured him with a salacious wink. But there was no sign of Kerry and his heart shrivelled from its earlier euphoria. He almost blurted out, "Where's Kerry?" But held his tongue; maybe she was late, maybe she'd turn up in a minute. Then he spotted Spratt's crowd heading over towards them; Spratt accompanied by his shadow, Harry Blutter, and the entourage of girls and acolytes that always seemed to affix themselves to Spratt.

Ray and Spratt exchanged desultory greetings, neither keen on the other. Harry Blutter taking heed of Spratt's indifference, just totally ignored Ray, warmly greeting everybody in Brian's party except Ray.

Already beginning to feel down in the dumps at the lack of Kerry's presence, Ray was now totally fed up. An evening with Spratt's crowd was not what he wanted and he determined to make his excuses and leave as soon as it was polite to do so. Even if Kerry did turn up now he didn't want to hang around because he knew that she and Spratt would most probably make a bee-line for one another.

The party settled onto a series of tables grouped together on a higher floor that overlooked the dance floor area, one or two of the younger set occasionally disappearing down to the floor below to 'strut their stuff'.

Harry's eyes fixed on a particularly scantily clad girl who was gyrating energetically on the dance floor and for some reason it made him think of Kerry; wistfully he sighed, "It's a shame Kerry isn't here; I really fancied a dance with her, a nice slow, sexy grope on the dance floor. Where is she anyway?"

Ray's ears picked up, he desperately wanted to know where she was as well.

Knocking back a mouthful of White Diamond, Siobhan grinned at Harry, "Her fiancé Sean wouldn't let her join us; they're having some kind of romantic dinner tonight." She replaced her drink on the table adding with amused disdain, "Besides, Kerry wouldn't look twice at any of you lot."

Spratt smirked and cockily retorted, his voice almost boastful, "That's what you think. I..." He instantly stopped himself, not wishing to spoil a good thing, the promise of future 'goodies' from Kerry and possibly Siobhan. Fortunately the music grew louder as the D.J. cranked up the tempo. Spratt had to raise his voice to be heard, "Anyway Siobhan, what happened to your own boyfriend, Danny? How come he's let you out with us reprobates?"

"Oh, Danny's lecturing on a business seminar in Spain," her reply was equally loud, "He left yesterday. But he knows I won't let him down."

"In Spain; it's a good life for some!" Ray interjected, not unpleasantly, "But I'm glad to hear you're both getting it together. You do make a great couple, you suit each other."

"Well, thank you Ray," responded Siobhan, smiling, "That's very sweet of you, and I think that we do to."

Dominic, one of Spratt's acolytes, edged closer to Siobhan, putting his arm around her shoulders and resting his other hand on her thigh. "Well, darling," he suggestively oozed, "I can make it an even better life for you." He nuzzled her neck.

Siobhan recoiled, instantly pushing him away. "Get off will you!" she snapped, "If you guys are going to start that then I'm off. We're supposed to be having a fun night out, as friends, nothing else!" She got up, reaching for her coat.

Harry grasped her arm. "Hold on Siobhan," he pleaded, "It's not like that." He glanced at Dominic, shooting him a withering glance of contempt, not because he didn't approve but because Harry felt it was he who should enjoy some time with Siobhan. "Dominic's only being a bit of a prat. Besides, in his pissed state, he wouldn't be much use to anyone." Harry smiled, "Please don't go."

Siobhan glanced dubiously at Dominic's leering features, sighed, and agreed to stay. After all, it was still fairly early and she didn't want a long evening on her own. Picking up her empty glass and with a forced smile on her face, she passed the glass to Dominic demanding, because of his rudeness, that he should get her a drink.

Harry and Spratt re-iterated Siobhan's demand, adding their own orders, and insisted that Dominic should buy the round of drinks; the others in the group agreeing, a baying chorus of demands that sent Dominic, against his wishes, towards the bar.

Ray stood up intending to sit at the temporary vacant space by Siobhan but Spratt, as if reading his intentions, leapt up and sat at Siobhan's side. Ray scowled, nonchalantly picked up his pint, and focused his attention on the dancers below.

"Sorry about Dominic annoying you," Spratt's voice was warm and affectionate. "Do you fancy a turn on the floor?"

Harry interjected, "No, Siobhan promised me the first dance, a nice slow one!"

"Now boys, no fighting over me," purred Siobhan with humour, "But if you want a slow one Harry then you'll just have to wait." The pounding of the music over the speakers was very far from being a slow ballad.

Spratt smirked, "Well I guess I'll have to go first." And with a broad grin on his face he stood up, reached for Siobhan's hand and pulled her to her feet.

Harry was visibly annoyed but he knew he had shot himself down with his request for a slow dance.

Spratt led Siobhan to the dancing area, edging their way to a small space amidst the middle of the gyrating throng, Siobhan just ducking in time as a wildly swinging arm nearly decapitated her. Barely had they started moving when the record finished, and the D.J. decided to change tempo, finally playing the slower records that Harry had been desperately waiting for.

Spratt grinned, "I actually prefer these slower records; I much prefer to feel the woman I'm dancing with." He placed his arms around Siobhan, holding her very close. Siobhan, very slightly, pushed him away. As they danced, almost imperceptibly, Spratt held Siobhan closer. Siobhan began to relax, becoming aware of his warmth and closeness; she looked into his dark eyes. Beginning to feel a bit too cosy, her consciousness alerted her that she was going to have to be very careful of Spratt. She could understand why he'd had so many conquests but she was determined that there was no way that she was going to be yet another one.

Spratt stroked her arm, his lips close to her ear, his other hand holding her at the base of her spine. "Siobhan," his oily, seductive voice, spoke softly into her ear, "You know I'm in love with you. You're the only woman for me; the only woman who could ever tame me and make me content."

"Yea, yea, I'm sure," she replied sarcastically, "And you'll make me happy ever after." Spratt held her tighter, not picking up on her sarcasm.

She pushed him slightly away, looked into his face, and smiled, "You know that kind of smooth talking bullshit won't work with me; I'm not some young, soft chicken waiting to be plucked. I've been around a while."

"No, seriously Siobhan," Spratt persisted, "I've laid off sex for two months now. I just can't do it with anyone else. You're all I ever think about...I've become totally fixated by you." Although flattered, Siobhan snorted in response.

Spratt pulled her closer again and caressed her back whilst nuzzling her neck. This time she didn't pull away, beginning to relax with the moment. They danced almost as lovers; with Spratt's affectionate hands stroking her, his lips caressing her neck, the slow movement of their entwined bodies rubbing against each other, she was beginning to feel warm and sexy. Wrapped in their tight embrace Siobhan nearly succumbed to Spratt's technique. But the slow music suddenly halted, the lights brightened, and the D.J. yelled out the title of hard hitting 'rap' record, instantly shattering the romantic mood.

Siobhan pulled herself free from Spratt's firm grip. "That felt too good Spratt. I'm going to have to watch you, you smooth bugger."

"Shit," muttered Spratt, "Almost had you sucked in."

"What?"

Spratt startled, not realising that he'd spoken aloud, quickly recovered, "Oh nothing; I said I wish the D J would pack in playing the 'Rap' or 'Garage' records when people are trying to have a romantic dance."

Siobhan not convinced, frowned, "Come on; let's get back to the others. I could kill some more of that wine that Dominic bought." She grasped Spratt's hand leading him, reluctantly, from the dance floor.

Suddenly an attractive Blond stopped them in their tracks. Ignoring Siobhan as if she didn't exist, she focused her attention on Spratt. "Hello Pete, I've still got your 'boxers' at my place. When are you coming back to collect them?" She winked salaciously.

Spratt ignored the blond bimbo, attempting to push past her without recognition.

The Blonde was not giving up so easily. "Hey Pete, are you trying to ignore me?" Finally seeming to acknowledge that Spratt was not alone - his hand in the grip of another woman - the Blond bimbo's eyes flicked contemptuously over Siobhan.

Spratt continued, unabated, pushing past, muttering from the side of his mouth, "Not now, Mel, not now."

The affronted woman snarled back, "Oi Pete, you don't just ignore me you know. Come back here, now!"

Siobhan turned to face the snarling menace, leaving Spratt with no option but to stop in his tracks, his face a picture of panic. Siobhan looked at the snarling female antagonist and then at Spratt, immediately recognising that a relationship had existed between the pair of them. Calmly, she released her grip on Spratt's hand, "God, Spratt, I don't believe how close I came to being sucked in; you very nearly trapped me in your web."

Dismayed, Spratt protested his innocence, "But...but, Siobhan...I don't know who this girl is."

Siobhan grinned, retorting with wry humour, "Pete, I'll see you back at the table; I think you've got things to sort out here." Grinning, she turned away, leaving Spratt to face the wrath of one his previous conquests.

Spratt began to panic; he'd had his enjoyment with Mel and as far as he was concerned, the woman was history, "Hold on, Siobhan, wait for me." He turned, intending to follow Siobhan.

The Blond grabbed hold of his shirt sleeve, yanking him back.

Spratt was annoyed, his voice filled with ire, "What the hell do you want, Mel?" Adding, "Why don't you sod off, you sad old slapper!"

Now her dander was up. That he had initially ignored her she could forgive, but not this. How *dare* he! "Pete Spratt, you're in great danger of getting your balls cut off!" She paused, smiling grimly, then continued in a mellow tone, "But of course, you're not worth the hassle." She smiled with seemingly loving affection, reached up to embrace Spratt as if to give him a farewell peck on the cheek, placing her arms on his shoulders, and moved her face closer to his.

Spratt's nervous demeanour broke into a leering grin; he leant forward to receive her kiss of farewell.

Suddenly without warning the Bimbo swiftly brought up her knee, and holding Spratt firmly by the shoulders, she kneed him, with tremendous force, in the bollocks. Spratt caught totally unawares, doubled up in excruciating pain, "You bloody cow!" His protest was barely audible due to the stinging ache in his balls. He dropped to the floor, gently cupping his throbbing genitals.

The woman stood over him, smiling triumphantly, hands on her hips as a club Bouncer rushed to the scene, and taking in the vision of the very sexily attired lady, skirt hardly below her bum, he grinned like a maniac, her curvy figure making him feel quite lustful. He glanced down at the prostrate Spratt. "I think you should disappear, luv." The Bouncer grinned at the Blond and then unceremoniously hoisted the resistant, aching, Spratt to his feet.

Spratt, still gently cupping his testicles in belated protection, spluttered indignantly, "Aren't you going to do anything about her? She attacked me!" Another sharp twinge of pain shot through him and he groaned pathetically, "Didn't you see what the stupid cow did? Chuck the silly bitch out."

The Bouncer stood grinning at Spratt and winked at the Blond.

Spratt almost wailed in frustration, "Aren't you going to do anything?"

"Sonny," replied the huge man with total disdain, "Are you telling me a little female beat you up? I suggest you forget about it and go back to your friends – if you have any!"

Spratt, his throbbing testicles making it difficult to stand erect, glared daggers at the woman. She merely grinned in response, blew him a kiss, turned on her heels, and nonchalantly strolled away. The Bouncer chuckling, shaking his head in amusement, watched with pleasure as her departing buttocks swayed from side to side.

Groaning, moaning, doubled up like a hunchback, Spratt returned to his table, a chorus of raucous banter and derision greeting his arrival. Ray was in stitches, his delight at Spratt's evident discomfort giving him his only highlight of the week.

Chapter 25

The news emanating from home had not been good for Abdullah; so much was now resting on his shoulders.

The government in Saudi Arabia was clamping down on Abdullah's comrades in the Kingdom; even the vociferous Mullahs had to hold their normally outspoken tongues, their poisonous rhetoric being reduced under the watchful eyes of soldiers of the Saudi National Guard. Abdullah was convinced that this was because of the pressure put on the ruling Al-Saud family by the American government and their Western puppets.

Also, things in Yemen were looking quite bleak. American and British Special Forces were working in tandem with the Yemeni authorities, seeking out supporters of Al-Qaidah and Da'esh and the other pro-Islamic groups who advocated violence against the heretics of the West and their evil, corrupt ways.

All along the network, from Afghanistan, Iraq, Lebanon, Syria, Palestine, things were looking bleak. So many being betrayed, others hunted down by undercover agents of the West, and although recruitment was magnified almost tenfold for every Islamic 'soldier' taken out of action, it took time and resources to train the recruits. Training had been much easier in the days when the 'Taliban' ran Afghanistan, the camps operating with little or no interference. But now everything had to be effected much more discreetly, the training limited both in terms of quality time and in terms of numbers capable of being trained in the new smaller camps. Fortunately, his 'brothers' were able to function at a fairly discreet pace in the Kashmir territory under Pakistan control as well as the mountainous terrain that bordered Afghanistan.

The news coming from the East made Abdullah ever more determined to carry out his mission, to really punish the American lackeys and their British allies for supporting the President of Western evil that defiled their beliefs. Oh yes, he would make a statement on behalf of his 'brothers', a message that would send shivers down the backs of all the corrupt Western governments. But first, he had to have his Dhow.

Abdullah smashed his fist into his hand, the venom rising within his breast, the evil pouring from his eyes like smoke seeping from a dampened fire. "That bastard Englishman who has my Dhow, by Allah, he will pay! He has cost us so much time!" Abdullah's muttering voice growled akin to a low tone of rippling, aggressive thunder, his differentiation between English or Irish irrelevant. Any white person in this country was English as far as Abdullah was concerned.

Saeed and Fawzi, as intent in joining Abdullah in carrying out their appointed task, physically quaked in their boots. They knew how dangerous their new leader was, and how cruel he could be. Although both of them were equally capable of killing an opponent, neither harboured any illusions of the ruthless determination that emanated from Abdullah, his callous disregard for any friend or foe who got in his way.

Abdullah had taken great delight in recounting to them of how he had disposed of his very own cousin, Ahmed, who had not followed the discipline necessary to be successful. Ahmed's pleas for mercy had fallen on deaf ears, Abdullah determined not to be crossed or disobeyed. And the Western harlot who had led him astray, well, the tale of her demise had made Fawzi feel slightly sick.

Saeed, aware of the growing malaise and anger that was building within Abdullah, quietly led his brother from the room, leaving the ranting Abdullah to take out his growing frustration on the hapless cleaner, a man of simple mind and limited education, who eked a miserable pittance working as a general dogsbody for one of the more important devotees of this particular mosque.

Being an illegal immigrant the cleaner was virtually a slave, working for a pittance, being provided with only the basic rudiments of board and lodging. If the Imam had been fully aware of the status of the worker 'volunteered' by one of his flock he would actually have provided the man with a better standard of living, for although against the wicked ways of the West, he believed in equality for those of the 'faith.'

By the time that Abdullah had wreaked his ire, working out his intense anger, the pitiful cleaner had a broken finger, a bloody nose, and two cuts across his bruised and battered face. The poor man limped from the basement room, his bruised left dead-leg barely able to carry him up the steps.

                  *   *   *

Sean, miles away, ensconced in his flat, shivered, an intense feeling of unknown dread sweeping through him like a dose of diarrhoea.

Kerry, laughing gaily, oblivious, took another sip from her glass of Baileys, and picking up the remote control, changed the channel on the television.

Sean just could not shake off the feeling of doom that was enveloping him, growing like a heavy blanket, a pervasive fog that smothered him in uneasy dread.

Chapter 26

Ray bounded up the steps, sometimes taking two at a time, sometimes three, as he climbed to Kerry's office. Feeling sure that Siobhan would have recounted the exploits of the other night and particularly Spratt's embarrassment, he was convinced that Kerry would welcome him and understand that his feelings were more genuine than those of Spratt. Feeling in a much better frame of mind than he had felt for such a long time, he was so looking forward to his arranged meeting.

But suddenly he stopped in his tracks. Although his mind had been playing over and over, pleasantly recalling the soothing melody of Kerry's voice, something jarred his thoughts; something was not right. He realised that he could actually *hear* Kerry speaking, the sound of her voice no longer being played only in his head but actually assailing his ears. The words that he was hearing were not pleasant, nothing like those that he had been pleasantly imagining, longing to hear.

Almost reaching the landing of the third floor, he peered up into the hallway above. Kerry was standing in a corner recess, her back to him, and although her voice was low, discreet, he could catch every word that she was saying as her voice tumbled out with a mixture of seductiveness and conspiracy, her mobile phone held tightly against her ear.

"Spratty," she oozed, "I haven't heard from you since our little session last week. Are you avoiding me now you've had your oats?"

Ray couldn't hear Spratt's response but what Kerry said made his heart sink to his boots, a big hole appearing within him, threatening to devour his sanity.

Kerry persevered, her voice heavy with nervous doubt, her words hesitant, Spratt's response not filling her with confidence. She was used to men falling at her feet and Spratt's almost indifference was nagging at her stomach, causing her feelings of discomfort and anguish that were totally alien to her being. "Anyway, after the special 'present' I gave you last week…"

She paused as Spratt interrupted but then continued breathlessly, her confidence returning, the knotting in her stomach dissipating, Spratt's words obviously akin to what she had wanted to hear. The confident enthusiasm was back in her voice as she continued their conversation, "It's more of what I can do for you. You see tonight is my keep fit night. I always go to the gym on

Tuesday evenings. But I've thought of a better and more pleasant way, of keeping fit."

She paused again as Spratt interrupted.

"Whoa, boy, whoa." Ray noticed that Kerry's eyes were twinkling with amusement as she half turned in his direction, then she turned her head back towards the recess, not spotting him staring at her.

Her voice soft and low, oozing sexy seductiveness, she almost purred, "Look, I can't talk much longer; they'll wonder where the hell I am. Just to let you know, instead of my gym gear in my sports bag, I've brought along my nurses outfit. A little *Kerry* treat, which I'm sure you'll love."

She laughed out loud at whatever Spratt had said.

"Sure, I'll give you some 'special medicine', especially the oral kind!"

Ray finally managed to move from the spot that had him rooted, his head in a spin, his heart seemingly in a wringer, his feet like lead. He turned on his heels and almost ran down the stairs, Kerry's final words chasing his reluctant eardrums as she made her arrangements for the evening, "So, I'll meet you at Aldgate Station at six thirty? Okay? See you later."

Kerry discontinued her call, totally unaware of Ray having been party to her conversation. Frankly she wouldn't have cared less anyway, her whole focus being on securing Spratt for herself. She exhaled deeply then grinned with anticipation.

Ray ran from the building, his world in turmoil, the bemused faces of the receptionists staring at him as he departed the building like a scalded cat. A car almost hit him, the driver pushing on his brakes in a squeal of tyres as Ray ran into the road trying to get past a mother pushing her pram along the pavement. He ran until he was exhausted, his brain pounding, his heart bursting, and his breath wheezing, his mind questioning over and over, "How could Kerry be so stupid? I can't believe she's allowed herself to get sucked in by Pete Spratt!"

*   *   *

The large clock mounted on the tower of the nearby bus station was marching inexorably towards seven o'clock. Kerry glanced at her watch, looked up and down the street, and kicked out at fresh air; she was extremely annoyed. She didn't like to be kept waiting. How dare he? Once again she looked at her watch, checked the time against the tower clock, stamped her foot in anger and frustration, then walked to the Tube Station entrance, peering inside just to make double sure that Spratt wasn't waiting for her inside the building.

"What if he's not coming; he didn't seem very keen at first? I'm not used to this. I've *never* been stood up in my life! If Pete Spratt turns up now he better have a good excuse." Kerry spoke out loud not caring about the strange glances she received from passing strangers. She turned away from the Tube Station, walking to a nearby low wall. "Perhaps I got it wrong," she thought, "Maybe he meant Aldgate East Station?"

She sat on the wall, tried for the umpteenth time to ring Spratt on her mobile, but he either had his phone switched off or wasn't getting a signal because he was already on a Tube on his way to her. God she felt frustrated, staring angrily into space. "Bloody little shit!" She murmured almost at the same time that Spratt exited the Tube Station arm in arm with a busty young female, wearing a skirt with a split that Kerry thought almost went up to the girl's waist.

Spratt and the girl were talking in a very intimate manner and Kerry's heart did a lurch. "Who the hell is that slapper? What a trashy looking slut!" She muttered, but a dull ache was developing in her stomach. "Perhaps he's forgotten we were to meet and he's going off with her?" Kerry thought with growing horror.

Almost reluctantly, she rose up from the wall, face like thunder.

Spratt, feeling tranquil, looked up from his intimate conversation and spotted Kerry; he led the girl to where Kerry was standing, hands on hip, her expression a mixture of concerned doubt and growing anger.

As they approached, Kerry stared scathingly at the girl, looking her up and down with total disdain and utter contempt. Getting closer Spratt was suddenly aware of Kerry's expression and the danger signals emanating from her eyes. He quickly disentangled himself from the girl, whispering to her, "Sorry Monica, that fiery looking woman ahead of us is my hot date for this evening, but she doesn't look very happy at me being with you." He edged away from Monica. "I'm not brushing you off but you can't expect me to miss a sure fire opportunity; that woman is sex mad, she's insatiable for me." He winked at Monica, who although disappointed, smiled faintly in response.

Kerry's scowl broadened but Spratt called out in greeting,

realising that he'd better say something to break the obvious nascent tension, "Hello Kerry. This is Monica. She's new in our office and I'm showing her the ropes." Monica smiled in greeting, the smile quickly disappearing at Kerry's curt nod and scowl in her direction.

"Really?" Kerry snapped, her voice heavy with caustic sarcasm, and then retorted, "It seemed if you were not just showing her the ropes but more like tying them around you both!"

Monica frowned nervously as Spratt edged towards Kerry, pecking her on the cheek, and put his arm round her shoulders. With an amused tone and winking at Monica, he said, "Take no notice Monica; our Kerry can have a touch of the Irish spleen at times but she's as gentle as a mouse really. She has a great sense of humour." Spratt grinned affectionately at Monica then smiled seductively at Kerry.

Kerry's hostility melted into a beaming smile that lit up her eyes.

Knowing that he could charm the pants off her, literally, he smoothly added, "I've been looking forward all day to meeting my favourite woman,"

Kerry almost purred in response, "Ah, sure, you're a smooth one, Spratty." She glanced triumphantly at Monica, smiled with superior contempt, and wrapped her arm around Spratt's waist. Monica's earlier feelings of happiness disappeared. Kerry was not finished with her young potential usurper, imparting with condescending disdain, "Bye; mind you don't catch your death of cold with that skirt. You *young* teenagers still seem to dress as if you were still in the sixth form, bless you."

Monica feeling belittled, close to tears, meekly said, "Bye, Pete, see you in the morning." And without a word to Kerry she turned away just missing Spratt's conspiratorial wink; she stalked off without a backward glance.

Now that the upstart girl had departed, Kerry felt it was time to vent her spleen on the late arriving Spratt. "I was getting worried. Where the hell have you been? You kept me waiting for half an hour!"

Spratt was diffident in his reply, "Oh, you know, stuck in the office. It was one of those days."

"Stuck in the office? Stuck in the Office!" She almost bellowed with indignation. "You kept me waiting for half an hour and you didn't even try to phone me!"

Spratt grinned sardonically, the twinkle in his eye demonstrating his amusement at Kerry's little tantrum. That only served to fire her up even more as she ranted, "It seemed more like you were stuck to that young girl's flaunted body rather than stuck in your office!" Then spluttered, "It's crazy what these youngsters wear, or should I say what they don't wear! And she's barely out of school clothes by the look of her. You're almost a paedophile!"

"Yea, very funny," retorted Spratt not amused. "We were just very busy and time went by."

"Busy cradle snatching I guess!"

Spratt was no longer smiling, his eyes clouding in anger. He snapped, "Do you want me to push off? Call the evening off?"

Kerry fixed him with a steely glare, "Do you want to go?" She stared daringly at Spratt, her expression a mixture of petulance and ire.

Spratt suddenly realised that his 'sure thing' was in danger of disappearing and thinking of his loins, he mellowed, determined not to let Kerry rile him. Meeting her eyes he looked endearingly at Kerry, an affectionate gleam in his eyes seemingly growing more adoring, boring into her irises and melting her anger. Her resistance totally melted away as he enveloped her in a loving embrace, whispering words of loving endearment into her ear.

Kerry wrapped in Spratt's apparent loving embrace, sparkled with relief and expectation; lifting her head she stared into Spratt's eyes. They grinned at one another. The tension totally melted. "Well, Spratty boy. Take me to your love nest before I change my mind," She purred, "And as a special treat I may let you give me a pearl necklace."

Spratt's face erupted into a lascivious smirk and they sauntered off, arm in arm. "This is so easy," thought Spratt, smirking internally, almost licking his lips in anticipation.

Chapter 27

Abdullah's patience had finally run out. He had spent days stalking Sean, checking the man's routine, looking for any avenue of opportunity. Even the man's woman had been followed, the shameless harlot, for Abdullah had marvelled at her over-friendly behaviour to other males. But the woman had not given any clues to the whereabouts of his Dhow.

One of their 'tame' sympathisers, a successful businessman, his fortune made in property speculation, but increasingly imbued with idealist tendencies, had arranged an appointment with Kerry's Company on the pretext of investing in a small yacht. Because of the need for absolute discretion, Abdullah had made no direct contact with the successful businessman, leaving it to the Imam to impart a full description of the missing Dhow, in verbatim detail as earlier related by Abdullah to the Imam.

But the businessman had reported back that there was no evidence of the Dhow being in the woman's office. Indeed, there were numerous models of various boats, of various shapes, sizes, and designs, but none matched the description of the precious, missing Dhow. So now it was time for decisive action. Abdullah was totally convinced that his precious Dhow was in Sean's home and he determined that today, this very day, would be the moment in which he repossessed the item that truly belonged to him.

He had observed Sean and his woman leaving their home, and had then waited, watching, as he had done many times before. This time though, there would no indecision. He knew that there would be no discreet access to Sean's flat, so first he had to remove the obstacle of the people in the flat below Sean's.

Rather than wait in the one spot for hours on end Abdullah had paced the nearby streets, returning every so often just to make sure that nothing untoward was happening, and that no apparent change in routine was occurring. Fully conversant with the routine of the people from the ground floor flat, he knew that the woman's husband left a little before nine each morning. He also knew that the woman carried out various chores, shopping or meeting up with friends for coffee, usually returning to her flat just before lunch.

Today was no different, the husband had left as usual, and the woman had departed with her baby a little after ten thirty. He had followed her from a discreet distance, making sure that she was sticking to her repetitive daily schedule; first the local supermarket and then meeting up with two equally drab friends, whereupon all three retired to a bustling coffee shop. Abdullah had left the cackling women to their devices, returning to his patrol of Sean's street and the surrounding area.

With immaculate timing he returned to Sean's street just as the mousy haired woman turned the corner, returning just before one p.m. and pushing her child buggy in front of her. Her western brat of a baby was fast asleep, head lolling delicately to one side, the child's wisps of red hair wafting across its forehead, softly scuffed by a gentle breeze.

Abdullah felt no emotion for the action that he was about to take, his doctrine and his mission being of sole importance. The woman's life meant nothing to him; she was an obstacle, evil that had been put in his way in an attempt to prevent the fulfilment of his God given journey. He would sweep her aside, and her baby too, and that would be two less individuals to spread the evil corruption of the West.

With microscopic timing, a result of the research carried out over the last few days, Abdullah paced himself, his approach coinciding to meet up with the mousy haired woman at the precise moment when she had put her key in the lock of her front door and opened the door, ready to push the child buggy in front of her.

The woman didn't even get a chance to scream, Abdullah's hand firmly clasped over her mouth, his other hand pushing her sharply in the back. The door being slammed shut behind them. The terrified woman was more concerned for her baby, the buggy tumbling forward, rolling upside down, the baby strapped inside suddenly awoken from its slumber in a confusion, its lungs giving vent to anger and confusion. The mousy haired woman wrestled free, squirming away from Abdullah, firstly to rescue her baby and then to vent her fury on what she presumed was a man intent on a sexual attack, a rapist. She was going to fight him for the sake of her child.

But as she broke free she felt a sharp pain piercing up through her rib cage, the cold steel of the six inch blade slicing into her. Shocked, surprised, stunned, and momentarily in agonising pain, she felt the warm blood oozing from her, her voice beginning the sound of a scream to match that of her baby.

Quickly withdrawing his knife, he sliced across her throat,

slashing it open like a piece of paper sliced in two. The woman's shocked and terrified eyes glazed over, the scream frozen on her lips, and she slumped to the floor, lifeless. Leaping over the woman's prostrate body Abdullah grabbed the baby's buggy, and without any attempt at righting the bawling infant, he calmly slit the child's throat.

Dragging the two bodies away from the entrance door he pulled them callously into the first room that he came across, the woman's sitting room, a residue of blood and guts smearing across the woman's hallway.

Abdullah washed the blood from his hands and face, and hastily searching the woman's home, located some of her husband's clean clothes. Although the clothes weren't an ideal fit, they would suit his purpose for the moment.

Having striped off his blood stained clothing, he waited for the husband to return. But the cold began to bite deep into him, making him feel drowsy, thus he wrapped two of the woman's blankets around himself and waited in the darkened sitting room, curtains drawn, his macabre companions of no consequence to him.

When he had got rid of the husband, then he would feel more confident in dealing with the Surveyor and his woman in the flat above.

When the husband was dead there would no one to hear the screams of pain and torture that he would inflict on that infidel who had stolen his Dhow. Oh how he was looking forward to the evening ahead, and his vengeance for the wasted days!

Chapter 28

Sean pushed himself up from his armchair, picked up the remote and switched off the television. He looked at his watch for the umpteenth time that evening.

It was almost twelve o'clock! "Not again Kerry," he mumbled angrily, "Where the hell are you? That's twice in just a few days!"

He tried dialling her mobile, leaving yet another message to go with the eight or nine that he already left on her answer service. Kicking out in frustration at the pouffe, Sean stomped from the sitting room, hastening to the bedroom. Furiously he yanked open Kerry's wardrobe, separating the hangers/clothes, checking for what may be missing; then he rummaged carelessly through her shelves, not knowing what he was looking for and or what was actually missing. Something was nagging at the back of his mind. But nothing special seemed to be missing.

Pausing, he stepped back, his eyes quickly scanning the top of Kerry's wardrobe. Relieved, he noted that her gym bag was missing. "Well at least she's taken her sports bag," he muttered, "So she can't be clubbing with that in tow!"

He remained motionless, hands on hip, frustrated, worried and confused. A sudden thought shot through him. "The nurses outfit! Where does she keep that?"

He re-checked Kerry's wardrobe with greater thoroughness. Then stepping to a chest of drawers, he hurriedly opened and pulled out the contents, a pile of Kerry's clothes ending up in a discarded heap on the floor. "Damn it," he muttered, "It's not here! The lying cow; what is she up to?"

He searched frantically through all Kerry's possessions but there was no sight of the nurse's uniform. "Right," he cried out, his voice raised in anger, "I'm going to find out where she is!" Thinking distractedly, he rushed from the bedroom, immediately turning on his heels in the hallway, returning to the bedroom, almost running to Kerry's side of their bed. Sean tipped out Kerry's dressing table drawer, hastily locating her prized address book. He held it up triumphantly. "Got it," he almost cheered, "Now to nail you, you pair of bastards!"

Pulling a can of lager from the fridge to steady his growing nerves, he opened it, taking a large swig. With the lager still dribbling down his chin, Sean tentatively opened the address book, quickly scouring the pages. Having checked the obvious first, he didn't find any reference to Pete Spratt under 'P' or 'S'. "Of course, she'll be more devious than that," he mused and almost simultaneously located a name and number that was not familiar. "'P.Smith' - an unlikely name - I bet that's Spratt's number!"

Picking up his can of lager, he marched from the kitchen and strode purposely to the telephone, almost snatching up the receiver in his eagerness. Quickly pounding the buttons, Sean dialled the number gleaned from Kerry's book and took another large gulp from his can of lager; misdialled. "Shit!" he exclaimed as the mechanical recorded voice of the BT operator informed him that such a number did not exist. Dialling more carefully the second time he was pleased to hear the ringing tone. "Come on, answer, you bastard!"

"Hello?" mumbled a sleepy male voice.

"Is that you Spratt? You bastard!" roared Sean.

"Who...what?" mumbled the sleepy voice.

"Spratt, Pete Spratt," furiously snapped Sean, "That is you, isn't it, you piece of shit!"

The voice at the other end of the phone was now more awake, retorting with anger, "Look friend, I don't know who you are but there's no character by that name here. Have you any idea of what time it is?"

"Of course I know what the fucking time is? I want to speak to Kerry!" Sean responded, his voice almost screaming in fury.

"Kerry? You've got the wrong number pal," replied the voice calmly, obviously recognising Kerry's name otherwise he would have slammed down the received on the apparent nutter who was incorrectly phoning him. "Kerry's not here; she doesn't live here." He paused, now fully awake, "Anyway, who the hell are you? Yet another sex starved male trying to get his leg over the slapper?"

Sean taken aback sucked in his breath, "The slapper?" He continued with growling ire, "What the hell do you mean? How dare you call her a slapper!"

Now the voice was getting really pissed off, "Who the hell is this? And get the fuck off my line. I'm tired and want to get back to sleep, you pissing moron!" And with that, the person slammed down the receiver.

Sean, dumbfounded, stared at the phone in his hand, muttering over and over, "He called my Kerry a slapper - a slapper; the fucking twat!" He was about to redial then realised that he was still looking for Kerry, so slammed the receiver back into its cradle. He remained standing, staring in anger at the telephone. "Slapper!" He repeated, "How dare that bloody bastard say that about my woman!"

With a heavy heart and a mixture of worry and anger in his belly he trod wearily to his armchair, slumping down. Staring into space, he sipped his lager with disinterest, the address book hanging limply in his left hand. The book fell from his grasp landing with the upturned pages open. He reached down nonchalantly for the book and suddenly his eyes focused on the initials 'P.S.'. With unseemly haste Sean scooped up the book. "Ah hah, 'P.S.'; that's it, P.S., Pete Spratt! Under 'A' for affair I guess, that's clever," He ranted to himself, "Right Spratt, you little shit, time for discovery!"

Sean dialled the number, tapping his foot impatiently as he waited for a response. "Come on, come on; pick it up, you shit."

His heart fell as he heard Spratt's voice, his whole being desperately not to be proved right, his gut knotting in fear of the truth, "Hello, Pete Spratt..."

Sean cut in, "Spratt you utter shit, is..."

Spratt's voice interrupted him, "...I'm not in, but you can either leave your number or a message after the tone and I'll get back to you."

Sean stared at the receiver in his hand, hating and loathing the innocent tool of the voice. "Fuck off!" he shouted down the line and once again slammed the unfortunate receiver into its cradle. "Bloody bastard! What are you doing with my Kerry?"

* * * *

Luxuriant smile on her lips, Kerry quietly opened her front door and as silently as possible, stealthily entered. Closing the door quietly behind her, she tip-toed up the dimly lit stairway.

"Sean?" she whispered, and not receiving a response queried in a slightly louder voice, "Sean, are you awake?" It was well after midnight and although she knew that Sean would be furious, she was pleasantly surprised to find the flat quiet, the sitting room in darkness but the hall light left on, presumably Sean having gone to bed. "Oh, good," she thought, "At least I won't have to face him this evening and give him that cock and bull story I made up; sucker."

She almost jumped out of her skin as she suddenly noticed a

shadow, a shape emerging from out of the blackened sitting room. Her heart stood still, fear enveloping her every pore. The newly encountered form flew out of the darkness and a pair of fierce, gleaming eyes pierced into her, the ethereal shape seeming to take on the shape of an ogre as it pounced in her direction.

Then she emitted an immense breath of relief; it was only Sean. But as quickly as she had realised that the 'ogre' was not an 'ogre', the look on Sean's face told her that she was in dire trouble; the terrifying fear of the supposed unknown, the imagined 'ogre', was now replaced by a different fear, a fear of discovery and retribution. "Does he know?" she thought to herself, "He looks mad as hell!"

Her earlier confidence evaporated and the smile that had formed when she realised that the 'ogre' was only Sean, instantly faded from her face. She quickly racked her brain for the excuse that she had carefully prepared earlier.

"Where the hell have you been? I've been worried sick. I've phoned *everyone* we know!" Sean's tone was a mixture of anger and relief. Although undeniably pleased to see her return safely, he was never the less aware that she must have been up to something and his stomach knotted with jealous anger.

Kerry stuttered, unnerved, "What..."

"You've been late twice in so many days," snapped Sean, "Are you having an affair? It's Spratt isn't it?" His searching eyes narrowed. "Where's your Sports bag?"

"Sean, please."

"And the nurse's uniform, where is it? It's gone!" he persisted, his brow furrowed and his tone querulous.

"Look Sean, you don't own me." Kerry decided that she had no option but to brazen it out - at least until Pete Spratt could offer her some kind of commitment. "Besides, I was out on business, and the nurse's uniform is...is...at the cleaners; I dropped it off there last week." Thinking quickly, she blurted, "If you can remember, you did a Bill Clinton on it," concluding with venom, "And unlike Monica Lewinski, I wanted the stains removed!"

Angry on the surface but scared stiff inside, Kerry forced her way past Sean. But he gripped her shoulder, determined that the discussion was not over.

"And why didn't you bother to phone or acknowledge the messages I left on your mobile? I've been out of my mind with worry; what have you been up to?" he demanded with petulant ire.

Kerry reeled round to face him, her eyes blazing, face full of rancour; with spleen she snapped, "I really have had enough of you not trusting me!" Then she softened her stance, adopting a mistrusted and unloved demeanour, forcing a tear to form in her eye. "I've had a shit evening and was really looking forward to getting home...to you...and now *this.* "She almost wailed, "*This* constant questioning, this doubt, the constant mistrust. You know I wouldn't do anything."

Sean was abashed, mortified that he had upset his beloved, "I'm sorry Kerry; it's just that I was so worried, because you know I care for you so very much."

Kerry let the tears fall. "How could you not trust me?"

"Stupid of me, I know," he lamented, "But I'm always afraid of that letch Spratt hanging around you."

Kerry's heart skipped a beat at the mention of Spratt's name. "Don't be silly," she soothed, "He means nothing to me."

"Anyway, why are you so late," he asked kindly, "And where's your sports kit?"

"Um," Kerry could have kicked herself for forgetting. She had left her sports bag in Spratt's flat. Her expression of momentary doubt alerted something inside Sean. His eyes narrowed, looking into her eyes, searching her soul. Flustered, her face turning crimson, she began to imagine that he could read her mind, see the pictures of her and Spratt copulating. "Um", anxious and embarrassed, she was losing the ability to think on her feet. "I, er...."

"Kerry?" Sean's firm, questioning tone was making her uneasy, his eyes penetrating deep within her psyche.

Kerry now genuinely upset, tearful, bewailed, "I had to cancel my keep fit, and I left my sports bag in the office. We had a potential new customer phone us at five this evening. Brian said that it wouldn't take long, a seven o'clock meeting at the Tower Hotel." She was amazed how quickly the made up words of her lie tumbled from her mouth with effortless ease, "The meeting went on for ever! But I really didn't realise that it was this late. I'm so knackered, and starving. I didn't have a chance to get anything to eat."

Sean was now absolutely mortified at his apparent lack of understanding, "God, didn't Brian buy you a meal? The tight bugger! Oh, my poor darling. Go and rest your feet, I'll get you something now." He pulled Kerry close, wrapping her in a loving hug, his head against Kerry's head. Kerry's face, hidden from Sean, broke into a wicked smile, her mind chuckling, "Thank God I forgot to bring the nurses uniform back from Spratt's!"

"Go on, sit down and I'll rustle something up for you." Sean said lovingly, as he pulled away looking with deep, unconditional love, into her eyes.

"I need the loo first," Kerry purred, "I'm bursting!" And pulling herself free, she turned on her heel, smirking broadly, as Sean headed for their kitchen. Still smirking, she leant against the wall and kicked off her shoes. With the smirk being replaced by a dreamy expression, she hummed to herself and stretched luxuriously as she headed towards the bathroom.

She was still in the bathroom when her mobile phone rang, Sean rushing in from the kitchen to answer it. "Who the hell can it be at this hour," he grumbled as he reached for the phone left by Kerry on the hall table.

"Hello, it's me," said Spratt, "You've left your bag here."

"Who's that?" demanded Sean, "Left her bag where?"

"I..." quickly realising his error, Spratt disconnected.

Sean scanned the call record and locating the last received number, pressed dial. The call was not answered. Rushing to the sitting room where he had left Kerry's address book, he checked the number with the number that he had dialled earlier on the house phone. With trepidation, a dreadful sensation of almost paralysis enveloped him - it was Spratt's number. So, his worst fears were realised.

Kerry returning from the bathroom, seeing her mobile phone in Sean's left hand, her address book in his other hand, froze in fear, her eyes opening wide, contrasting to the narrow slits that Sean's eyes were now.

His voice cold with fury, his very being controlled so that he resisted hitting out at her, ordered, "Get out Kerry; get out now." His emotions were running wild and although he wanted to smash up the place, do anything to vent his anger and frustration, to appease his broken and betrayed heart, he forced himself to be civilised. "Not only have you obviously been unfaithful, you've lied to me; treated me like a fool."

"No, Sean, it's not what you think," protested Kerry, no longer knowing what to say and fearful that he might arrack her.

She backed away; his clenching and unclenching fists making her feel extremely uneasy. "Sean, I sorry," she pleaded, "I didn't want to hurt you."

"Shut up Kerry," he replied with calm fury, "No more lies. I've had enough."

Kerry began to cry.

"You can have our bedroom tonight," he stated in a matter of fact tone, belying the raging turmoil eating at his insides, "And I'll sleep on the couch."

"But, Sean," wailed Kerry.

"In the morning, one of us has to leave." Pausing momentarily, he added, "I'll go."

"Please Sean," pleaded Kerry, "I can't afford the rent on my own."

He looked at her scathingly, "Is that all it comes down to? I was only useful to help you living here...while you screwed other people."

"Other people!" she protested, "Other people; there's only been one, and it only happened once."

"Yea right, sure!" Sean mocked scathingly, "Somebody else I phoned earlier this evening when I was looking for you, called you 'the slapper Kerry'."

"The slapper Kerry!" retorted Kerry indignantly, "Who was that; who called me that?" she demanded, her belief in her unsullied reputation causing her pique. "How bloody dare they; who was it?"

Sean turned his back on her. "Forget it Kerry, I no longer believe anything that you've got to say."

She leapt at his turned back. "How dare you. I'm not a slapper!"

Sean ignored her, not making any attempt to remove her hands gripping fiercely on his arm and shoulder.

"Don't you turn your back on me," she snarled, "I'm twice the person you are."

He was cold, aloof. "Leave me alone Kerry, I'm no longer interested in what you say or do, or who you really are."

"Right!" she snapped letting go of him, but quickly scurried round to face him, her face inches from his. "And Spratt's a better lover than you," she snarled with contempt.

That hurt him like an arrow piecing his heart, but with a steely determination he turned away from her once again, muttering, "I'm really not interested." The pain of her words ripping through him like a skewer traversing his body, travelling through his intestines and out of his bowels.

Furious that he had once again turned away from her Kerry reached up and gouged his face with her nails. She wanted him to hit her, to bruise her, to give her vindication with her peers, justification of why she was walking away from him. But he did not rise to the bait. The more she scratched and struck at him the more he drew himself into himself, until the pain of the scratching was beginning to get too intense. Then he held her arms, and pinioned her to the sofa until she finally calmed down, her struggles of protest growing weaker and weaker.

After a few minutes of inflicting an intensive death stare, she finally calmed herself, remaining motionless, her energy spent. Satisfied, Sean cautiously released his grip on her and pulled away.

His heart sunk when Kerry leapt up but instead of attacking him again, she screamed, "I'm leaving here. Leaving now, tonight; I can't stay another moment."

"But where would you go this time of night," protested Sean, "It's not safe."

"None of your fucking business," she snapped, "I'm going."

"Don't be silly Kerry. I'll go."

"No, fuck off," she yelled, determined not to give him the satisfaction of the 'higher ground'."

Despite Sean's futile protests, Kerry packed a small bag of essentials, just stuffing in the minimum amount of clothing without thought or plan; none of the clothes were folded, just crammed in the bag.

Stomping to the bathroom, she grabbed a few of her feminine essentials and her toothbrush, and jammed those into her already overfull bag. Without speaking again to the protesting Sean, she stormed from the flat, slamming the front door closed behind her, the door smashing into the door frame in a cacophony of sound, like a boulder smashing into a tree.

The vibration shot through the building, travelling upwards and laterally, almost shaking the front of the house and causing a pane to rattle in the front room of the ground floor flat.

Sean sat, bemused, befuddled, wretched and broken hearted, hurting internally and externally. "Where had it all gone wrong," he thought over and over, his fists clenching and unclenching in frustration, fatigue, heartbreak and anger.

Chapter 29

Abdullah woke with a start; he felt as if the ground had almost moved under him. Dazed and confused, he tried to focus his eyes in the dark, nonplussed as to where he was, his fuddled, sleepy brain adding to his disorientation. Slowly gathering his thoughts he remembered. "But was he now in trouble? Was that the police trying to break down the front door?"

He resisted the urge to leap up from the armchair that had comforted him to sleep, and waited patiently, his ears picking up any noise; sounds that would tell him if he was surrounded or if there was still an avenue of escape.

Almost not daring to breath, he waited, counting the seconds. There was only silence now.

Gently he removed the blanket that had kept him warm and rising, he stepped disdainfully over the dead body of the mousy haired woman's husband. The man had let himself in the flat just after six p.m. and amazed by the unexpected silence in contrast to his usual welcome, his ears normally being assailed by the baby's hungry cry for food, the man had rushed into the sitting room. There he had died, stunned, terrified, the fear and anguish barely having had an opportunity to work on him, at one minute past six.

The death had been instant, swift, Abdullah plunging his knife with unbelievable force into the man's heart.

"But what *was* the noise that had woken him with such a start; it surely couldn't have been a dream?" Abdullah mused, and shrugging his shoulders he stepped towards where he remembered a table light had been.

Cautiously feeling his way Abdullah almost tumbled over the table, almost knocking the lamp to the carpeted floor. Hastily reaching out for the toppling lamp he steadied it then flicked on the switch, a subdued light piercing the blackness of the room; the light threw out its illumination, revealing the macabre image of the three deceased bodies, their blood dried across their wounds. The white light reflected red, seeming to ripple over the pools of blood that surrounded the woman and her child. Surprisingly the man hadn't lost too much blood, what little blood he had lost being soaked into his clothes and overcoat.

Abdullah shrugged with disinterest. He checked his watch and was annoyed that he had allowed himself to fall asleep. He had been asleep for nearly five hours, Allah knew he was tired, having had very little sleep over the previous three days, but nevertheless he was annoyed that he had succumbed to weakness.

Now it would be more difficult to gain access to the Dhow stealer's house, certainly at this time of night. The man was sure to be cautious, wary, a knock at his front door sure to arouse suspicion.

*   * * *

Despite his heartache and anger Sean could not resist a feeling of euphoria on hearing his front door bell ring. A smile played across his lips and his heart lurched from utter depression to a feeling of immense joy at the thought of regaining a dear thing lost.

"Kerry's back," he mused, "She's realised that she's been stupid, running off in the dead of night like that. Well, I won't make it easy for her, but we can rebuild our relationship." With a skip in his step he leapt up from the armchair that had been his black hole, his pit of depression and desolation, only a few seconds before. Although his emotions were swaying wildly between anger at her betrayal and joy at her return, he knew that his love for Kerry would let him forgive her.

"God," he thought, "My life had seemed to be so empty, so meaningless, only a few moments ago; now it has a renewed purpose."

His spirits soaring with a rediscovered belief, hope for the future, Sean raced to the front door, his heart pounding in a mix of anticipation and vigorous energy.

He flung open the front door, crying out, "Kerry, so glad you're back..."

But his spirits sank, his joyous face disappearing in a mask of total disappointment. Once again his heart sunk, dropping like a stone into his slippers. He stared in annoyance at the dark skinned stranger standing at his door.

"Yes?" snapped Sean, ready to punch out the features of this stranger who had caused him such disappointment. "Have you *any* idea what time it is?"

"I am sorry to disturb you," responded Abdullah, his voice soft, soothing, "But I have something that belongs to you."

"What? What is it," snapped Sean, still angry at the man for causing his disenchantment.

Abdullah reached into his pocket and pulled out his knife,

suddenly thrusting forward into Sean's abdomen.

As the knife sliced cleanly into his soft belly, Sean, mouth gaping open in complete surprise, staggered backwards, caught totally unawares.

Abdullah leapt forward seizing the initiative that he had already established, knocking Sean to the floor.

Sean had a ridiculous thought that things were turning out not to be his day. Lying face upwards on the floor he tried to pull out the knife with one hand whilst fighting his attacker with the other. But in his condition and with the initial disadvantage he was no match for his assailant. He could feel himself growing weaker, the loss of blood draining him.

The stranger was now spread-eagled on top of him, the knife embedded in Sean's gut right up to the hilt. Sean was powerless and now that the shock had passed, the pain was beginning to bite into his consciousness.

Abdullah's face was pressing against Sean's cheek, the foul breath making Sean want to retch. He spoke quietly, but with menace, in Sean's ear. "So thief, what have you done with my possession?"

"What..." stuttered Sean, "What are you talking about? I haven't got anything of yours...I...I don't even know who you are?"

"Liar", barked Abdullah, slapping the back of his hand across Sean's face.

"Who...who are you?" pleaded Sean, "I've done nothing to you."

Abdullah stared into Sean's fearful eyes, his look neither one of concern, pity, understanding, nor compassion, but a look of intense hatred, of vindictive malice.

"Please," Sean beseeched, growing weaker, "I really don't know what this is about."

"Yes you do, liar!" and with that Abdullah administered another back handed swipe across Sean's face, breaking Sean's nose, an unpleasant crack echoing in the hallway. "You stole my Dhow!"

"Your Dhow?"

"Yes my Dhow, my boat!"

"I don't know anything about your fucking boat," protested Sean, wheezing, his words uttered between shooting spasms of pain, "What the hell are you talking about?"

"Don't lie to me you thieving western infidel!" snapped Abdullah,

"You have my boat; Barbara Clark said it was you who took it."

"Barbara Clark?" queried the increasingly weakening Sean, just wanting this to be over. "What have I done to deserve this?" He thought to himself.

Abdullah's eyes stared at him with a hatred that Sean had never experienced before and the man raised his hand to strike another blow across Sean's face, the blood already dripping out from Sean's broken nose.

Sean stared up incomprehensively; then slowly, so slowly, realisation hit him. His eyes registered understanding, the iris widening in recognition.

Abdullah recognised the change in Sean and lowered his arm, the blow not followed through. "So, I can see that you know. No more pretence," he growled, "Tell me where it is."

"It's not here, I gave it to..." Sean shut up, immediately realising that if he told Abdullah that he had given the boat to Kerry as a gift then her life would also be in danger. As much as he had been betrayed by her he still loved her like he would never love another, and there was no way that he was about to put her precious life in danger.

"What? What were you about to say?" demanded Abdullah, frustrated, so close to the answer, "Who has got my Dhow?"

"I...I sold it," responded Sean thinking quickly, his mind trying to override the pain racking his body.

"Liar, you were going to say a name!" shrieked Abdullah, striking Sean fiercely across the face, knocking out a tooth, blood now leaking from his victim's mouth.

Sean's teeth had snagged the back of Abdullah's hand, tearing a three millimetre strip of skin, the graze seeming to enrage Abdullah even further. He laid into Sean's face, pummelling with his fists, reducing Sean's face to a bloody pulp.

Sean succumbed into unconsciousness, the repeated blows rendering his body into silent stillness.

Abdullah looked down with disgust at this meaningless individual underneath him but then he paused, realising that his anger could defeat his objective. He had not yet found his Dhow and if it wasn't here, he needed Sean to be alive so that he could question him further. Rising, he sucked the back of his hand, cleaning the leaking tear of skin that Sean's teeth had caused. Then, like a raging lion, he tore through Sean's flat, searching, ransacking demonically, the destruction growing to an increasing frenzy as he failed to find the Dhow.

Oblivious to the noise he was making, knowing full well that the three occupants in the flat below would not interfere or object, Abdullah reduced Sean's flat to a tangled mess of debris and destruction.

But there was no Dhow.

"In the prophet's name, where is the Dhow?" he queried, then returned to the comatose Sean, almost tripping up in his haste. He pulled the unconscious Sean up by the front of his shirt and with his face millimetres from Sean, almost screamed, "Where is my *Dhow*! And where is *your* woman!"

Of course Sean could not answer and Abdullah shook him like a rag doll, Sean's head flopping from side to side, but his body no longer willing to partake in this world. With a last gasp of foul air from his lungs, Sean's eyes opened wide in recognition of finality and his mind switched off, his soul departing to a more peaceful world of death.

Furious, berserk, Abdullah let Sean's lifeless body drop with a thump, knowing that he would get nothing more from this stupid man. Frustrated, he kicked and kicked, repeatedly smashing his foot into Sean's lifeless body.

Fury vented, he stood motionless, staring down at Sean's battered corpse, his mind racing, fathoming out his next possible course of action. He bent down and with a determined tug, his foot on his victim, he managed to free his knife from Sean's body, quickly wiping it on a clean patch of carpet. Venturing to the kitchen he thoroughly cleansed his knife, washed his face and hands, and returned to the sitting room where he had already located an address book.

Scurrying to the bedroom, to the discarded pile of clothes on the floor, he grabbed and put on Sean's Crombie overcoat, hiding the blood stained clothes underneath, the clothes that he had already stolen earlier that night from the flat below.

Tucking the address book in overcoat pocket and spotting Sean's mobile phone, Abdullah picked it up, putting it in another pocket. He would need all the information that he could gather if he was to find his Dhow.

But first his new target would be the woman, the woman who,

sometimes, seemed to belong to the Dhow thief. "Where was she?" he pondered.

With nothing further to be gained from this place Abdullah took one final kick at Sean's lifeless body, and rushed from the flat, slamming the front door behind him.

The door already suffering from Kerry's earlier harsh treatment did not shut properly, merely jarring against its frame, the lock not catching, and as Abdullah ran away down the street the door slid open, leaving a six inch gap of light leaking out onto the street, the flying night life already taking an interest in the contents of the lifeless flat.

Chapter 30

Kerry stifled a yawn. God, was she bored and tired and although it was only just after ten o'clock in the morning, she wished that the day was over so the she could succumb to a nice warm bed. She had been unable to postpone her meeting with Ray, and as such he was sitting the other side of her desk droning on and on with some meaningless technical data. God, she was bored, but he was boring.

She couldn't help releasing a wide, tired yawn, her face screwing up with weariness.

Ray smiled at her, "Sorry, I'm boring you, but although I've written all the details down I do need to go through some of the points with you."

"If you must," she yawned, but to ease her words she favoured him with a small smile.

"You looked knackered," he responded solicitously, "Shall we have a coffee break? Rather than your own stuff how about me taking you to the Espresso bar. I'll get you a coffee and a croissant and we can finish our meeting there. The change of environment and fresh air will do you good."

That sounded ideal to Kerry. Anything to get her out of the office, and at least she would have some other distractions at the coffer bar rather than just having to listen to Ray droning on and on. "Good idea," she smiled, "I'll get my coat."

Ray beamed with pleasure; this was the first time that she had ever favoured him with one of her warm, genuine, smiles. His heart soared.

It had been a hell of night for Kerry. After her row with Sean, and her foolish departure from the flat at that time of the night, she had reached the locked Tube Station which quickly brought her to her senses, realising that her knee-jerk action had left her temporarily homeless. The dilemma of where to stay, and who would put her up at that time of night, hit her like a brick wall.

Her first thought had been Spratt and she had phoned him, telling him what had happened and that she needed a bed for the night, her mind racing ahead to the possibility of the continuation of pleasure that they had both shared earlier that night. But Spratt's reaction had disappointed her, like a blow to the solar plexus. He had explained that he didn't think it was a good idea, what with her just having split from Sean. He added that Sean would be bound to tromp round to his place and the scene that would follow would be embarrassing for all concerned; it would be preferable to leave it for a few days, to let things cool down. Despite Kerry's protest that Sean wouldn't hurt her, Spratt insisted that his suggestion was the best. He added that it was very late and that he had an important meeting scheduled for first thing in the morning. And then he had disconnected the phone; he *disconnected* from her.

She was furious and stood staring, mouth agape at her mobile.

Kerry tried to phone her friends Naimh and Brendan but there had been no reply. Then she remembered that they were home in Ireland, visiting relatives. Tired and tearful, beginning to feel sorry for herself, she had then telephoned Siobhan. Danny, Siobhan's boyfriend had answered, and on Kerry explaining who it was he had grumpily handed over the phone to Siobhan.

Quickly waking, Siobhan had sympathised with her work colleague and friend and assured her that there was always a bed available for Kerry. Siobhan had then got out of bed, much to Danny's annoyance, and had made herself a coffee as she waited for her friend's arrival; she almost fell asleep, sitting in her armchair, whilst she waited for nearly an hour before she heard Kerry's soft knock on her front door.

The two girls had then spent the next hour discussing their lives, in intimate detail, as only women can do, Kerry explaining her split from Sean, the acrimonious departure, but not mentioning the real reason, her liaison with Spratt. That was another matter for another day; she still hadn't given up on her personal dream of securing Spratt for her own. Getting a taxi that time of night had also been a problem, but at least she had got there.

Kerry and Siobhan didn't get to sleep until gone four in the morning and it was barely three and a half hours later that they were up and on their way to work, both looking as if they had spent the night on the tiles.

On their arrival their Manager Brian had made a few disparaging comments about their appearance and what they must have got up to the previous night, but their shared scowl and grimace of disapproval quickly stopped his ribald comments.

Thus Kerry was very pleased that Ray had given her the opportunity of taking a break. As she and Ray left the office, with Brian's consent, Siobhan had glared at her, wishing that she too could leave and get some fresh air, the lack of sleep making her eyelids seem overly heavy.

The meeting with Ray had gone well. Kerry had actually been kept awake, interested. His conversation, splattered with humour, had kept her attentive, entertained. He was not that bad after all she mused, and certainly could be amusing company. They had dallied over the meeting, sharing quite a few coffees so Kerry was almost on a caffeine-high as she and Ray made their way back to her office almost an hour and a half later. But on reaching her office they were startled to see a plethora of activity, the area cordoned off, police cars surrounding the building.

"What the hell's going on?" muttered Kerry as she rushed forward, Ray hot on her heels. "I hope Siobhan and the others are okay."

They were stopped from entering the building, a burly policewoman who would have made a grown up Billy Bunter look like a dwarf, blocking their passage. "You can't go in there," she ordered, her dictate more akin to a bark.

"But my office is in there," protested Kerry, her voice filled with genuine concern, "What's going on? I need to get in, to find out if my colleagues are okay."

"And you are?" demanded the blockbusting policewoman, her eyes flicking from Kerry to Ray.

"I don't work here, I'm a customer of this lady," he indicated Kerry, "My name is Ray Maloney; Kerry and I were having a meeting."

"Kerry?" The policewoman's eyes narrowed, "Are you Kerry Murphy?"

"Yes, yes," replied Kerry anxiously, "Why, what's happened? Has something happened to our office? Are they okay?"

"Come with me," instructed the policewoman, her expression one of utter distaste and contempt.

"Charming lady," muttered Ray, but loud enough for the colossus to hear. The Policewoman's back stiffened but she didn't turn round, merely leading Ray and Kerry to a group of police officers, some in uniform, but three in suits.

The policewoman spoke to her colleagues, her thumb indicating the couple behind her, "This is Kerry, Inspector. The guy with her is called Ray Mahoney."

"Maloney," corrected Ray. "It's Ray Maloney."

The Inspector momentarily surprised, quickly rushed forward, his baleful eyes flicking from Kerry to Ray. Initially ignoring Kerry, he demanded of Ray, "And who are you?"

"I just told you, Ray Maloney."

"Don't get smart with me son," snarled the Inspector, "I didn't ask for your name. I need to know *exactly* who you are? What's your relationship to this... *this* woman," he added caustically, his contempt for Kerry obvious from his tone.

"Relationship?" interjected Kerry, "We don't have a relationship; he's just a customer."

The words 'just a customer' wounded Ray; he had been hoping that he could be more than 'just a customer'.

The Inspector ignored her interruption, demanding of Ray, "Where were you last night?"

"Why? What's this about?" Ray queried.

"Just answer the question," snapped the Inspector, his uniformed colleagues now surrounding the concerned, but confused Ray and Kerry.

"What is going on?" insisted Kerry, "What the fuck is this about?"

"Watch your language, lady," interposed the second of the three 'suits', "Don't speak to the Inspector like that."

"I was at home," replied Ray, his response doubtful, "I had an early night."

"Can you prove it," demanded the Inspector.

"Well no, but..."

The Inspector ignored his reply, focusing his attention on Kerry, "And you? Where were you?"

Kerry's mouth opened and closed; she didn't know where to begin, where to start. "I was...um.."

"Right," snapped the Inspector, "I'll think we'll pursue this matter down at the station."

Kerry stood, dumbstruck, still trying to figure out what was happening; what was it all about.

"We have a right to know what is going on; why are we being questioned, about what?" demanded Ray.

The Inspector grimaced at the pair of them, his eyes already having already decided that they were guilty. Turning to the 'suit' on his right, he instructed, "Caution them." And glaring at Kerry and Ray he replied in a matter of fact tone, "You're helping us with our enquiries."

Without further ado Ray was unceremoniously manhandled into a police car, the burly policewoman keeping him company on the back seat. Kerry was bundled into the subsequent police car, a uniformed police officer sitting either side of her as if she was some desperate criminal. The two police vehicles sped away, sirens blaring unnecessarily, the officers triumphant in their capture.

* * * *

It had been a harrowing experience.

Ray felt like a washed out rag. He had been interrogated, finger printed, a DNA sample taken - the inside of his mouth still felt raw - and they had stripped him of his clothes, temporarily providing him with a very uncomfortable jump suit made of disposable paper. He had felt extremely self-conscious and highly embarrassed as they marched him between the holding cells and the interrogation rooms.

Twice he had been put in a cell that stank of stale sweat or vomit - he couldn't quite discern the odour - and twice taken to an interrogation room, where he had been on the end of an intense grilling, receiving a verbal onslaught that had him almost believing that he was guilty of some crime. The first interrogation had been by a Detective Sergeant, in the presence of a female uniformed officer, which only served to embarrass Ray even further, particularly because he felt the disposable jump suit was not the most modest of garments.

The second interrogation had been carried out by the supercilious Detective Inspector with the Detective Sergeant also present.

It had been a shock to Ray when they finally explained to him the reason for his 'assisting them with their enquiries' as the Inspector put it. He could not believe it, Kerry's fiancé murdered, brutally by the sound of it. Although the Police hadn't revealed details, the intensity of their questioning and the distaste evident, made Ray realise that Kerry's fiancé had not had a pleasant ending to his life. Ray didn't know the guy that well, only having met him on a couple of occasions, so he was more mortified for 'being in the frame' for killing him than sorrow at the man's demise. He then felt guilty at his lack of compassion, and began to feel painfully sad for Kerry. He was also convinced that Kerry was not the sort of person who could carry out such a deed.

It was four long hours before a knock on the interrogation room door brought him relief from the incessant questioning, the Inspector departing the room to take a message from a uniformed constable who had stuck his head in the doorway. Still being confused and dazed Ray had not thought to request a lawyer, convinced of his total innocence, thus he sat still, waiting, sure that his ordeal would soon be over.

He almost cried out with relief when the Constable returned to the room carrying Ray's clothes, bundled, and sealed in a large, heavy duty, plastic bag. The police constable did not speak to Ray only directing his conversation at the Detective Sergeant, "Inspector Symington says he can be released; nothing to tie him with the murder."

Forensics had also given his clothing a clean bill of health, and his movements of yesterday tied in with his statements. There was no reason or evidence to implicate Ray.

The Sergeant reluctantly accepted the instructions passed to him from his junior and fixing Ray with a look of pure contempt, growled, "It seems that you may be in the clear for now." Without any apology he turned to the Constable, instructing, "Take him to the duty sergeant and arrange for the return of his other possessions, and his release."

Ray smiled in relief but this seemed to anger the Sergeant who added with a determined threat, "Don't think you're totally in the clear yet! Don't think of leaving the area; we'll need to talk to you again." The Sergeant pushed past Ray, exiting the interrogation room, leaving the bewildered Ray to meekly follow the Constable.

*   *   *

For a further two hours Ray had sat in the public area of the police station, waiting to hear what they were going to do with Kerry. Luckily for her, Brian had arranged for a solicitor, and there had also been a stream of ready support, Siobhan and other colleagues turning up at various intervals, all being quickly chased away by the civilian clerk stationed at the entrance desk.

Siobhan was now sitting next to Ray, having returned to the police station only five minutes earlier. Waiting in a cafe nearby, she had been summoned by Kerry's Solicitor who had informed her that Kerry was being released on police bail. Apparently her Solicitor felt sure that the entire case was nonsense but the police were not giving in so easily.

Ray had been shocked to learn from Siobhan that forensics had found traces of Sean's skin under Kerry's fingernails, and having taken Kerry's clothing from Siobhan's home, they had identified minuscule traces of Sean's blood on her blouse; the DNA analysis had quickly identified that it was Sean's blood!

It didn't look good for Kerry and her legal man had battled long and hard, fighting tooth and nail on behalf of his client; he had kept Brian and Siobhan fully in the picture during the breaks from interrogation. Kerry had explained that the blood on her blouse was obviously when she had wiped her hand after scouring Sean's face with her nails Now it seemed that they had turned the corner, the solicitor's call to Siobhan giving cause for relief.

It was only a couple of minutes later that the Solicitor exited from the main body of the police station, greeting Siobhan with a smile and a warm hand shake. She almost felt like hugging the man. He grinned, stating that he was convinced Kerry was in the clear, but the inexperienced, fast-track, Inspector had not been quite ready to give up on his suspect, still insisting that Kerry be released only on police bail until further enquiries had been carried out.

Evidently the denouement had been the discovery of the three dead bodies in the flat beneath that of Sean and Kerry; the police 'Socos' team, Scene of Crime Officers, having forced their way into the flat after their repeated knocking had not produced any response. The macabre scene that met their eyes had had even these hardened men reaching for their handkerchiefs and rushing outside for gulps of fresh air.

A set of unidentified fingerprints also matched a fresh set of prints found all over Sean's flat. In addition it was quickly determined that the fingerprints were already on file, matching those of the recent grisly student murder at one of the residential Halls at the University of East London.

It later transpired that a heated telephone conversation had taken place between the 'fast-track' inexperienced Inspector and Sergeant Morris, the experienced detective from East London. Morris had not hidden his contempt for the senior officer, who may have been adept at politically correct crimes, but totally incompetent in the matter and investigation of protecting the public from criminals.

*　　*　　*

Kerry's legal man departed, leaving Ray and Siobhan to wait nervously for Kerry's release. It seemed to take an indeterminable time before Kerry emerged, her face tear-stained, her eyes registering shock and incomprehension.

Siobhan rushed forward embracing her friend in a motherly hug, Kerry bursting into tears, no longer able to hold back the emotion of the last twenty-four hours.

Ray remained standing, clenching his fists, feeling hopeless, but desperately wanting to cuddle and console her. Siobhan finally pulled free from Kerr's embrace and Kerry looked up, her tear filled eyes focusing on Ray. She smiled weakly and mumbled, "I'm so sorry Ray, I'm so sorry that you were dragged into this."

"I don't care," he soothed obsequiously, his eyes like puppy-dog orbs, "It's not important; so long as you are okay?" And he almost ran forward in his haste to hug her.

Kerry wrapped her head into Ray's shoulder, releasing a fresh torrent of tears. Initially her tears were mainly for herself, reflecting her selfishness, her self-pity, but as time developed the tears grew for Sean, the grief of his death hitting her like a ton of bricks. Kerry's immense feelings of grief and guilt welled up inside her like an inflating balloon.

The civilian duty officer, no longer content to abide the weeping woman and her two companions, chased them out from her police station.

Chapter 31

Saeed made excuses to keep well out of Abdullah's way, his brother Fawzi following his example, their leader having returned in a foul and murderous mood. He hadn't told them too much other than the obvious fact of his having failed to locate the Dhow. The mission was looking decidedly tenuous and Fawzi had quietly questioned his elder brother as to whether they should remain in England or make their way back to the Middle East where they could be of more use. Fawzi advocated going to Iraq, to work with others in bringing death and destruction to the infidel American and other Western soldiers and all their allies who worked with them in the puppet Iraqi government and police force.

It had taken Saeed some while to calm down his fiery younger brother, warning him of the immense danger of upsetting Abdullah who was a dangerous man, quick tempered and psychotic, bordering on insanity. Besides, Abdullah was well connected with the hierarchy of Al-Qaeda and the brothers didn't need to put themselves in greater jeopardy. Saeed and his younger brother were both strong in their beliefs, intent in following the true teachings of Islam, convinced in the purpose of submitting their mortal lives for the greater good of the 'cause'. But Saeed also knew that there were other men, guided by more extremist views, fanatics who would not allow any person to stand in their way.

Fortunately Abdullah, subsequent to a hasty meal of pitta bread and halal mutton, had rapidly submitted his tired and weary body to a tossed and troubled sleep, his tortured and twisted mind succumbing to a series of convoluted nightmares, his body tossing and turning like a demented demon.

The brothers decided to become scarce, avoiding any possibility of being in Abdullah's vicinity when the man woke up and guaranteed still to be in foul temper.

Leaving a hastily scribbled note explaining their intentions of carrying out a thorough analysis of the London Underground and bus system, ensuring that every aspect of their mission was being researched, the brothers crept silently from their liar, silently closing the front door, fearful of waking Abdullah from his restless and troubled sleep.

The brothers spent the entire day and most of the evening travelling on the tubes and buses, criss-crossing the various routes of the inner London transport system, their 'oyster' travel cards allowing them unlimited access over the network. Plying the various routes, they familiarised themselves with every possible nuance of their allocated potential targets and the escape routes to be taken.

Satisfied that their part of the mission was fully explored Saeed led his brother back to the safe house, still feeling uneasy at the 'welcome' to be garnered from the increasingly irrational Abdullah. On their way past Kings Cross station a lady of the night winked at Fawzi, her cleavage exposed to barely above her nipples, her skirt scarcely below her crotch. Fawzi paused staring hungrily at the woman but Saeed, taking a firm grip on his brother's arm, dragged him away, reminding him of the virgins waiting for him in heaven.

With a backward glance Fawzi reluctantly followed his brother.

Chapter 32

The next few days had passed in a whirlwind of frenzied activity. All Kerry's circle of friends, acquaintances and business colleagues had been interrogated. Although Ray had been eliminated fairly early from the police investigation, he still felt great concern for Kerry and, together with Siobhan, had proved a real tower of strength, always being available whenever Kerry needed a shoulder to cry on.

Siobhan had imparted some of the details of Kerry's fall out with Sean on the night of his death and even though Ray had not been an integral part of Kerry's inner circle of friends, he had done his best to give her as much moral support as he could. Because they had both been arrested together there had also developed a small mutual bond between them, albeit a fragile and rather limited bond. Thus Ray had spent more time mixing with Kerry and Siobhan, something that he had been craving for some considerable time but not in the circumstances they were experiencing at present.

Ray had felt that they were under constant scrutiny, being constantly watched, but despite his vigilance he could never discern anything or anybody in particular. Never-the-less his sixth sense, supported by Kerry's and Siobhan's observations, convinced all three that they were under some kind of microscope; they felt, no doubt, that it was the police, and their feelings of discomfort grew in equal proportions to their annoyance. It was exasperating that despite all the pointers to the contrary, the 'fast-track' Inspector still seemed to be pursuing his interest in their direction.

*   *   *   *

To comply with the wishes of Sean's family it was agreed that Sean would be buried in Ireland, at a cemetery in his home village near Limerick. Despite the protests of Sean's immediate family, who had learnt of the falling out prior to Sean's demise, Kerry determined that as she had shared a fundamental part of his life and that she had an indispensable right to be there when he was finally laid to rest.

Not being willing to share a vehicle containing Sean's body, Kerry had flown to Shannon Airport together with Naimh, who provided her with moral support. It was left to Naimh's husband Brendan, together with one of Sean's many brothers, to take Sean's coffin on the ferry from Anglesey to Dublin and then onwards to Sean's parent's home.

The funeral had been held in the village church, where Kerry had had to endure many pointed fingers, together with a torrent of frosty disapproval. But she had been determined to be there when they put Sean's body to rest; it was her way of saying sorry and a recognition of the many years that they had spent together. Maybe they hadn't got married but for all intents and purposes they had lived together like any married couple. It was sad that their relationship had finished on such a bad note but there had been many fond memories that she could recall in her moments of pathos.

Irrespective of the presence of many of her own family who lived nearby Kerry would not have been able to cope without the moral support of Naimh and Brendan. It had been a harrowing experience and her nights were spent in restless slumber, tossing and turning, her dreams mixed up between Sean and Pete Spratt. It was always Spratt who finished uppermost in her mind. When this was all over, when the dust had settled, she would make sure that Spratt would really find out what a great catch she would be.

With that final thought she drifted into a more restful sleep, a smile playing on her lips.

*   *   *   *

Whilst Kerry was in Ireland, Ray determined to find out more about the police investigation; accordingly he contacted his friend at the Telegraph newspaper who owed him a favour or two. Although his journalist friend was involved in the travel and leisure side of the newspaper, the man knew who to contact on the crime desk for the necessary information.

Wheels worked within wheels and favours were called in by others, and as such Ray found himself together with one the newspaper's crime reporters, sitting across a bar table from Sergeant Morris of the Metropolitan Police. Sergeant Morris explained that he was no longer involved in the case and he could not state if Ray, Kerry or Siobhan were under scrutiny even if he knew. That information was confidential and there was no way he would compromise an on-going police investigation.

However, as the evening wore on and the single malt whiskies expanded into doubles it was obvious that Sergeant Morris was becoming increasingly bitter about the new persona at the forefront of her majesty's constabulary. His role, and those of his peers, were no longer concerned with apprehending what they perceived were true criminals, and in protecting the public, keeping the streets safe, but were now increasingly occupied in the investigation of meaningless crimes, many of them labelled as ' hate' crimes but which in actual fact were people merely expressing their dislikes for one another. Obviously if that dislike manifested itself into something stronger than Sergeant Morris was happy to apply the full force of the law, for no matter what colour, creed, or race, Morris hated bullying and he was first to defend anyone picked on.

But now his beloved police were playing at law enforcement and the leaders that they seemed to be recruiting, each armed with a degree that bore little relevance to the actual good work of proper policing, were turning the force into a political tool. Policing had now turned itself away from crime solving, side stepping to political correctness, with personnel no longer being promoted on their ability but more on their profile to fill positions in a politically correct police force. Quotas had to be filled and investigations tuned to the individual whims of senior politicians or the new cadre of police officers who were quite happy to police by statistics, massaging figures to suit their own personal agendas.

It was not that Sergeant Morris hated degrees per se, in fact he held in great admiration many of those who had attained degrees but his beef was that obtaining a degree was not a panacea for successfully running a police force. Sergeant Morris reserved his greatest bile for Detective Inspector Symington, the 'idiot' who was running the investigation on Sean's death. Morris had been convinced that the trail of murders was something to do with a fanatical movement but he had been unable to follow through, having been forced off the case by D I Symington and Symington's connections with the new breed of 'career fixers' at the Metropolitan Police.

Morris's thorough investigation of the two murders at the University of East London had exhausted all possible enquiries, leaving him convinced that the murdered female student had merely been incidental, unlucky enough to be in the wrong place at the wrong time. The real target had been the foreign student, Ahmed, but all leads had hit a brick wall. Even Ahmed's background had shown many blanks, numerous periods when he had left the country, his destinations unknown; also, his actual lecture attendance records and submitted course work indicated a serious lack of interest in attaining his degree. The man had spent more time doing part-time work, including delivering supplies to his own University. Although apparently investigated by the security services, Ahmed had been labelled as 'little or no risk', his existence dismissed and quickly forgotten by those who, perhaps, should have known better.

Morris was angry and upset that under the new police prevention of terrorism powers more people had been detained for expressing their views and opinions on the Government than the small handful who had been detained under the true threat of terrorism. The new powers were not being used to prevent terrorism but rather were being abused to prevent the people having freedom of thought and ideas, a tiny cadre of authority holding carte blanche over the majority of the population. The argument that the Law had been brought into being by a large majority Government didn't wash with Sergeant Morris as he reminded his detractors that the people who voted for this 'large majority' were actually approximately only thirty per cent of the population.

When Sean's murder had been flagged at his station Morris was instantly alerted to the similarity of the murders of those at the University. He had immediately contacted Inspector Symington's team and offered his assistance.

The more Morris found out, the more he was convinced that Sean and/or his Company held the key to solving the crimes. The Sergeant had spent a great deal of time investigating all of Sean's connections, his Company, and his customers. When he discovered the details of Barbara's Clark murder he knew that he was on the right track.

But Inspector Symington adopted distaste for the practical and experienced detective, the Sergeant's actual ability belittling the lack of talent of the senior officer who had only been taught to police by rote. It didn't take the Detective Inspector very long to get Morris taken off the investigation, removed him from his secondment to Symington's team. Symington than pursued his own enquiries, knowing that his superiors were looking for a high profile race case. Accordingly the investigation veered in a fresh direction, Symington's team sure that Sean had killed Ahmed and Mrs Clark because he had 'discovered' that they were having a liaison and this interfered with Sean's affair with Barbara Clark. Thus it was obviously a race crime, but now Symington had determined that he needed to find out who had taken retribution on Sean. Symington was convinced that the answer lay with Kerry and Ray.

Ray departed the meeting with Sergeant Morris; he was developing a sour taste in his mouth and a growing knot in his stomach. Kerry was due back from Ireland tomorrow and if Morris's comments were correct, than anyone connected to Sean was in danger - and Kerry had had the strongest connection! Also, he knew that under Detective Inspector Symington's investigation there was very little or indeed no protection to be afforded from Her Majesty's Constabulary. In fact the police were putting them in greater danger rather than assisting them; but that was irrelevant to the new breed of police personnel such as Inspector Symington for they considered that as long as the police were seen to be acting in a politically correct manner then everything was okay.

Even if the investigation was eventually found out to be incorrect, no doubt when they were all dead, than a report would be commissioned, a few knuckles rapped, Inspector Symington promoted, and the whole incident either brushed under the carpet or quickly forgotten.

Ray racked his brains of what to do, how he could protect the woman who had filled his mind over the previous many months. He was sick with anxious apprehension and foreboding, his brain reeling.

Chapter 33

Abdullah had spent his days watching, monitoring every aspect of Sean and Kerry's world. From his previous observations of Kerry's life he was pretty sure that Ray was not going to be the key that he was looking for. No, the answer still lay with Kerry; she was the one who knew where his Dhow lay.

The bitch would pay!

He had to be ever more discreet, more alert, because Kerry and her friends were also being watched by the police. The imbeciles, they had no idea of what they were up against; they would never catch him, certainly not alive!

But the money was beginning to run short, the reserves eaten up by the excessive delay in accomplishing the mission. To help the financial situation and to alleviate the increasing boredom that was enveloping the imbecilic brothers, Abdullah's contacts had arranged for Saeed and Fawzi to work at the local laundry; no questions were asked and false papers were arranged. "It is so easy to adopt a new life, and a new identity, in this corrupt western country," Abdullah mused, grateful yet contemptuous.

Nonetheless his financial needs were growing and he needed a lot more capital. Accordingly, a meeting was arranged with their appointed financial link, a man who was only to be contacted in situations of extreme urgency. Abdullah now considered that they had reached such a scenario. The call was made and the meeting arranged for that day. Abdullah had been surprised at how quickly the contact responded on receiving the code word and how readily he was willing to meet. He knew his holy mission was important but this put a new slant on it; the man was virtually falling over himself to help. Abdullah's increasing feelings of paranoia and intense anger melted away. He *was* important, a chosen one, and his brothers were obviously committed to give him maximum support.

*   *   *

Salman Khan ran a successful export-import business, mainly trading with the Middle East and the Indian Sub-Continent. Although his principal activity involved machinery spare parts he was not averse to trading in any product or any commodity.

When only three years old Salman had arrived in England with his parents in the nineteen-seventies and equipped with their new British passports they became fully fledged members of the British community. His parents immersed themselves in the British way of life but without losing their roots. They were firm believers in respecting their neighbours' way of life whilst remaining true to their own principles. The family grew in size, and grew in success, Salman's father's hard work reaping its rewards. Salman had been educated within the British education system but maintained a strong bond with his Muslim background. Like his parents he had his beliefs but fully respected others in following their respective teachings.

After leaving University Salman had soon tired of working for others and through his father's connections he had secured a loan to start up his own Company, importing assorted spare parts from India. Again through his father's connections, accompanied by a lot of hard work on his part, he had grown his Company beyond recognition, a multi-million pound trading business. The operation had grown steadily over the last eighteen years and Salman now employed over twenty staff.

The oil boom in the Arabian Gulf countries had really opened up his opportunities and, being a very clever individual, he had snapped up every opportunity that came his way. His contact list ran from Rulers to back street Traders, all relying on Salman's service and discretion. It was the discretion aspect that put him in contact with a wholesale operation in Sharjah, in the United Arab Emirates. The operation was funded by money from Saudi Arabia and although trading successfully in a diverse range of products, the main reason of the operation was to launder money and to provide financial support to Al-Qaeda operatives overseas.

Salman had inadvertently been sucked into the net, initially by supplying Arms shipments that ultimately ended up in Afghanistan. Unable to obtain the necessary licences from the British Government, Salman had arranged supplies via factories in Poland and the Eastern Block, supplemented by various French-Algerian shipments that were diverted to different destinations. The operation in Sharjah had taken care of all the necessary paperwork, providing Salman with the requisite documentation to fool the authorities.

Initially it had been the money that drove Salman on but it wasn't long before he began to espouse the cause, becoming increasingly bitter at how he saw the West treating the Palestinians and his Muslim friends. Torn between his feelings for his adopted country - he was British for goodness sake - he could not stand by idly whilst misguided, delusional politicians wreaked havoc. Sometimes the West's security services would actually encourage and support the Mujahidin, then at other times they would attack them with the full force of all the facilities available. It was a game, a group of people playing cat and mouse.

Thus against the tenets of his upbringing, and in total anathema to his parent's strict moral code, Salman threw in his lot with the Islamic fundamentalists.

Various bank accounts had been set up at the Hong Kong & Shanghai Bank in London with parallel accounts in the various branches of the British Bank of the Middle East in the Arabian Gulf territories. Although the HSBC Bank, now headquartered in the Channel Islands, had relinquished its name in its overseas branches in the United Arab Emirates, Salman was used to calling them under their original titles, the BBME.

It was one of the HSBC London Accounts that he was now going to hand over to Abdullah, together with a bank card. The Account had been kept ticking over, transactions of various values being effected over the last two years, but it was one of three accounts that Salman and his paymasters had kept on standby, ready to assist their Islamic brothers in the field. He had never met Abdullah but he had been forewarned that the man might contact him and that Abdullah's mission was of great importance, a mission that would have an even greater effect and drastically overshadow the attack on the Twin Towers in New York.

*   *   *

The meeting with Abdullah had made Salman feel very uneasy, the man's hostile attitude and patent hatred of everything pertaining to the West making him feeling decidedly nervous and uncomfortable. Salman had never encountered any of the fanatics, all of his previous dealings having taken place with pleasant businessmen or financial bankers for the terrorists.

The downmarket venue chosen, a grubby café in the East End of London did nothing to enhance Salman's feeling of wariness. Although gladly handing over the card, together with the pin number, Salman left the meeting with a doubtful disposition and a heavy heart.

For the first time in many years he was beginning to doubt his life choice; he actually felt unclean.

Chapter 34

Abdullah drove his battered Peugeot 207 into the hotel car park in Limerick, Ireland. He was tired, weary, exhausted like he had never felt before. The Peugeot that he had hired from a car rental company in Barnet, North London, had started out in pristine condition, polished and clean, bearing no scratch marks or any other identification of wear or tear. Indeed it was Abdullah's lack of experience of driving that had resulted in the car looking like an old banger, his previous driving experience having mostly involved steering left hand drive cars across the open roads of Yemen and Saudi Arabia.

Although that silly woman, Barbara Clark, had allowed him to take the occasional turn behind the wheel of her very old Ford Focus, Abdullah felt aggrieved with the woman, blaming her for his deficiency in right hand drive expertise, plus his lack of experience of congested traffic conditions. His inexperience had proved a greater obstacle than he had originally anticipated.

Less than a mile from the car hire depot Abdullah had lost his nearside wing mirror, a BMW coupe removing it clean off his car as he tried to park in a Tesco car park. Not wishing to draw attention to himself he sneakily departed the car park, knowing that he would have to stay hungry and thirsty for a little longer; besides, his watch told him that the people picking up Sean's body would soon depart from the funeral parlour. Having kept tabs on Kerry, he knew all her plans and all the arrangements for Sean's burial. These people were not going to thwart him, no matter how many he had to torture or kill.

Driving a few more miles, always remaining a few cars behind the vehicle carrying Sean's coffin, he followed them into a motorway service area and watched as they parked up. By now, not only desperately thirsty, he also needed the toilet, the pressure on his bladder only countermanded by his desperation not to wet himself. Hastily reversing his car into a space between two other vehicles, he badly misjudges it, driving with some force into the back of a transit van, his bumper locking onto to the transit; the horrendous grinding noise made him quake in his boots as he revved his car forward desperate to release himself from the transit, his car suddenly freeing itself in a cloud of smoke and dust, the Peugeot's rear bumper separating and remaining locked on the transit.

Embarrassed but determined not to give up, he moved his vehicle to another parking spot and, to allay the concerns of nearby motorists, returned to the Transit, pretending to write a note admitting culpability, leaving it tucked under the windscreen wipers of the transit. The paper was, of course, blank. Resisting the urge to run he just made it in time to the toilet, then grabbed a bottle of water and a vegetable sandwich from W H Smiths; quickly returning to his Peugeot, he sat and waited, for all intents and purposes giving the impression that he was waiting for the return of the transit van driver. Concerned now that he might have missed the people driving Sean's body he was quickly relieved when he spotted the man friend of Kerry, a man he had heard Kerry call Brendan, and the other man travelling with Brendan return to their estate car, Sean's coffin wrapped in blankets in the rear so that it do not draw too much attention from fellow travellers.

Once again Abdullah had ground the gears of his hire car as he set off in pursuit of Sean's coffin, but the most recent mishap had been when Abdullah was parking below decks in the Ferry, the side of his car veering too close to the deck wall, a deep gouge, surrounded by myriad scrapes, running along the side of the vehicle. All in all, Abdullah didn't really care what happened to the hire car, the documents he used having been forgeries, the driving licence itself bearing a picture that held very little resemblance to himself, and the credit card used was a stolen one, not the one given to him by Salman.

Because he had spent a considerable time in scrutinising Sean and Kerry's friends and colleagues Abdullah had a fairly good background of Sean's life; thus, it was relatively easy for him to ingratiate himself into the funeral party, no one paying too much attention to his presence. Indeed, a couple of the younger Irish fillies imagined that the tall, dark stranger would make quite a handsome catch and they spent much of the 'wake' trying to get to know him better. This suited Abdullah because he used the familiarity of the younger girls to take the opportunity of exploring Sean's family home, searching everywhere for his Dhow.

Kerry, the one person who might have been suspicious of this total stranger, was too grief stricken, coupled with feelings of guilt and remorse, to notice the unknown presence. Her attendance at the subsequent 'wake' had been curtailed, Sean's family making her decidedly unwelcome. Accompanied by Naimh and Brendan, Kerry retired to the hotel bar, where they held their own 'wake' in respect of Sean's memory, but without the body being present.

Thus when Abdullah, exhausted, returned to the hotel, he managed to slip unnoticed past the drunken funeral party. Making the most of his opportunity he entered the unlocked bedroom of Brendan and Naimh. His search of the room revealed nothing of interest; he was getting used to failing in his searches. Quickly formulating an idea, he rifled through a handbag that he found hanging by its strap on the back of a chair.

Striking lucky almost instantly Abdullah identified Brendan's and Naimh's address in England via Naimh's driving license and located a set of house keys, tucking them in his pocket. Now, knowing their address, entry to their property could be achieved with relative ease and at a time and moment where absolute caution and discretion could be observed.

Happy for the first time in days, a plan formulated, he retired to his own bedroom, locked the door and dropping exhausted onto the bed, settled into a deep and refreshing sleep, his body giving in the weariness of its limbs. The increasing noise of the 'wake' did nothing to disturb Abdullah's deep sleep, the funeral party continuing until the early hours of the morning.

Abdullah woke, refreshed, in the first light of dawn, his head totally clear, unfazed by the presence of any alcohol. Creeping down to the empty hotel kitchen he located what he hoped would be there, a very sharp carving knife; then sneaking out the front door, he crawled under Brendan's car, spending the next forty minutes patiently sawing through a hydraulic break pipe. Finally achieving his aim, a trickle of hydraulic fluid spitting gently onto the ground, he clambered to his feet, furtively checking that no one was watching. Dirty and sweaty, he threw the knife in a nearby bush and re-entered the hotel, his intention to have a quick wash, eat in his room, then he would follow Brendan's car on its return to England, waiting for the inevitable.

Chapter 35

Ray's business meeting had dragged on far longer than he would have wished; glancing at his watch he saw that the time was racing towards seven in the evening. Feeling a great thirst come upon him and not wanting to go to his flat alone he decided to pop into one of the 'watering holes' that was a popular venue to his peers in the marine business; also swaying his decision was that he knew this particular Pub, 'Rosie's Bar', to be a favourite of Kerry and Siobhan.

He couldn't believe his luck when he spotted Siobhan leaning against the bar counter chatting to Rosie, the Publican's wife, after whom the bar was obviously named. He quickly scanned the venue for Kerry; disappointed, he realised that the woman of his dreams was not with Siobhan. Still, he felt like company and Siobhan was always friendly so he approached, greeting her and Rosie almost in the same breath. Another subconscious reason for his decision to stay was to find out from Siobhan how Kerry was getting on and if she was back from the funeral.

Ray struck up a conversation, not believing his luck when he learnt that Kerry was back from Ireland and was due to meet up with Siobhan at the Bar, apparently, Kerry like Ray, had had a late meeting. They retired to one of the pub tables, awaiting Kerry's arrival. Siobhan was also grateful for Ray's company and had never understood Kerry's contempt for Ray.

It wasn't long before Kerry made her entrance, sweeping into the pub like a 'Diva', her outer appearance belying the inner turmoil of her recent life. Spotting Ray and Siobhan a broad smile lit up her face and she rushed over, bestowing a cheery wave and a mouthed 'hello' as she caught Rosie's eye.

His heart pounding at her presence, Ray leapt up and decorated her cheek with a warm and welcoming kiss before offering to buy a drink. Removing her coat, Kerry draped it over the chair but insisted that she wanted to go to the bar with Ray as she wanted to say hello to Rosie. Ray felt like a million dollars as he stepped to the bar with the gorgeous Kerry walking by his side, her perfume assailing his nostrils, her aura filling his senses.

Rosie was busy serving a large round of drinks so Ray and Kerry spoke to Pat, Rosie's husband. "Hi, Pat," trilled Kerry, relieved to back in familiar surroundings after the trauma of the last few days.

"Hello my beautiful colleen," gushed Pat. "Sure, it's always good to see one my two favourite girls." Pat beamed like a benevolent father. "What'll it be, you're not after the Guinness are you?"

"No, thank you," grinned Kerry, "We'll have a half of lager and a Bailey's, I have a great thirst!" She then glanced at Ray suddenly remembering his presence, "And a pint for the man who's paying!"

Pat adopted a kindly expression, broaching the subject of Kerry's recent loss, "So, how's the world treating you today? Has everything been sorted out?"

A tear of self-pity formed in Kerry's eye, "Yes thank you," she almost sobbed in response, "But it was all very difficult, what with Sean's family knowing of my split from him." As an afterthought she added, "I shall miss Sean very much. You just don't forget so many years."

A lump formed in Pat's throat, Pat being just another of Kerry's acolytes, yet one more sucker male who Kerry had eating out of her hand.

Having finished serving her large order Rosie hastened over and although she had a great fondness and affection for Kerry, she knew that Kerry's heart was not so heavy, her feelings for Sean having long since waned; besides, she knew Kerry's character and knew of her resilience, an inner strength that would soon make the young woman bounce back. Determined to lighten the mood, to break the solemnity that had quickly formed, Rosie squealed, "I expect you've been collecting a few more male hearts in Ireland. How was the old country?"

Kerry took up the baton, answering in a jocular manner, "Sure Rosie, you know it's your Pat that I'm really after. What a fine man." Pat's chest almost swelled, whilst Ray stood like a spare piece of pork at a Jewish feast.

"But of course," continued Kerry, "I know I'm too late," she winked at Pat, "Rosie having already taken your heart."

"Away with you," scolded Rosie affectionately.

Ray and Kerry returned to the patiently waiting Siobhan, who got to her feet, wanting to nip outside for a cigarette. "It'll be only my second today," Siobhan uttered defensively, their disapproving stares making her feel guilty. I don't think I'll ever be able to give up but at least I've cut down to only four a day."

"Siobhan you know it's not good for you," admonished Kerry, "That really is a filthy, unhealthy habit. Doesn't Danny say that he hates you smelling like an old ashtray?"

"That's not a problem today!" snapped Siobhan indignantly, "Danny's across in Madrid." But she sat down peeved, yet resigned, and fiddled with a beer mat instead.

"Anyway," Ray mumbled somewhat self-consciously whilst adopting a very serious expression, wondering how to impart his concerns to Kerry. How could he explain that he felt Kerry's life was in danger without putting the heebie-jeebies up her. "We need to talk," he added, his tone very serious.

"Oh, God!" thought Kerry, dreading what he was about to say. "He's going to try and ask me out. I couldn't bear that. I'm just going to have to be brutal with him." But she smiled, saying out loud, "God, you do look serious...you aren't going to confess to Sean's murder, are you?"

Ray was shocked about how she could joke about such a subject. "No...no, of course not!"

"God you're so boring," thought Kerry, still smiling sweetly.

"No Kerry, I'm serious; but it is about Sean."

Kerry giggled, relieved; "Thank Goodness he isn't going to proposition me," she thought, adding out loud, "You and Sean were lovers?"

"Kerry," snapped Siobhan, "Ray's trying to be serious. He's got concerns about your safety."

Kerry turned her attention to Siobhan, glanced at Ray, then back to Siobhan. Both Ray and Siobhan were wearing extremely serious expressions which only served to make Kerry giggle.

"Kerry!" admonished Siobhan, "Ray is really worried."

"Yes," Ray persisted, his anxiety not helped by Kerry's jocular approach. "Whilst you were in Ireland I had words with a police contact. We both feel that there was more to Sean's death, and those people in the flat under yours, than meets the eye. I think you're being stalked."

Kerry didn't need whether to laugh out loud, merely glancing in Siobhan's direction whose severe expression didn't help. Kerry took a sip of her drink to stop herself giggling.

"So," persisted Ray, "I feel that you and Sean are the key to..."

Ray didn't get the chance to finish his sentence, Spratt's friends Harry and Dominic and a female, Monica, entering the pub. Harry instantly noticed Kerry and Siobhan. Harry's face lit up; smiling broadly, he hurried across, gleefully gushing, "Hi-ya girls; I thought that you might be here." He stared longingly at Kerry, totally ignoring Ray. "Do you mind if we join you. I'm with Dominic and a new girl from the office," Harry pointed at the couple who were still making their way across the bar.

When the girl with them neared, Kerry's face froze; she recognised Monica from a previous evening with Spratt. Ray was startled to see Kerry's warm welcoming smile disappear, immediately being replaced by a look of pure hostility. The colour also drained from Monica as she quickly recognised Kerry, the woman's previous hostility making her feel terribly awkward. Dumbfounded, aghast, she muttered under her breath, "It's that old bag again. Damn it; I was so looking forward to an evening of fun."

Dominic glanced quizzically at Monica.

Cognisant of Kerry's instant change in mood, the anger blazing in her eyes, Harry glanced back over his shoulder. But Kerry, unable to withhold her rancour, witheringly snapped, "Oh, we've met already. She's the new 'attraction' in your office."

It was Harry's turn to be dumbfounded, "Well...but...how?" he queried.

Kerry blanched, suddenly realising what may be revealed; in the process of preparing a really biting, caustic and sarcastic comment, she bit her tongue.

"What's up with you Kerry, you look as if you've seen a ghost?" queried Siobhan.

"You've met Monica before?" questioned Harry staring curiously at Kerry, waiting for an explanation.

Kerry fidgeted awkwardly, not knowing how to extricate herself from a potentially embarrassing situation. If they found out that she had had a liaison with Spratt before her split with Sean then her name would be mud and a lot of the sympathy that she had garnered subsequent to Sean's death would quickly dissipate.

Meanwhile Monica, realising that she had nothing to fear from Kerry whispered in Dominic's ear, "I've seen that red-head before. She was really horrible to me." Monica chuckled, delighted in her new ascendancy, adding with her lips tingling against Dominic's ear, "Wow, of course! It must be a secret, a secret about her and Pete Spratt!"

"You *what*!" exclaimed Dominic out loud, "Come again?" Monica now totally emboldened, cheerfully declared volubly, "Oh, I met Kerry one night just over two weeks ago."

Kerry was mortified, wishing that she could disappear, her normally quick witted personality drying up, not knowing what to say or how to stop Monica.

Monica noting Kerry's discomfort continued gleefully, "Yes, I've met her before; it was when Pete Spratt travelled with me to Aldgate Tube. He told me that he had a hot, insatiable date with a woman who was 'gagging for it'." She watched maliciously as Kerry paled, happily pointing at Kerry to reinforce her words, "And it was her!"

"Oh!" uttered Kerry, distressed beyond measure, the back of her hand shooting to her mouth, not knowing what to say.

Ray's jaw dropped, his face crumpling like a screwed up bag. Although he had suspected it, he had never wanted to hear actual confirmation of a relationship between Kerry and Spratt.

"What!" Siobhan exclaimed.

Harry was also deeply shocked, "You're kidding! Pete never told me; the sly old fox!"

Not knowing what to say, Ray muttered, "Kerry you can do so much better for yourself, better than someone like Spratt." He didn't say it for his own benefit, the words being involuntarily uttered because of his genuine sentiment and true concern for Kerry.

In a mix of confusion, dismay and almost in shock, hands fumbling, Siobhan reached for a cigarette, her disturbed mind making her light up in the bar.

Kerry, a sea of disbelieving faces staring at her and the gleefully grinning minx Monica gloating at her in the background, leapt up from her seat. Her face scarlet, close to tears, the shocked expression on her friend's faces making her feel dirty and tarty. "I feel sick," she mumbled, and made a headlong dash for the ladies toilet.

Siobhan was furious and glared with malice at Monica, "I don't know what's going on boys but I can assure you that Kerry would not get involved with Spratt. She's got more sense." Favouring Monica with a withering stare, Siobhan followed Kerry to the toilets.

Both Harry and Dominic, determined to know more, turned to face the now hesitant Monica, Siobhan's expression having terrified her. Ray merely sat motionless, stunned, crestfallen and morose, his thoughts leaping all over the place.

Dominic cheerfully demanded, "Right Monica, spill the beans. But first I need a drink. Come on, tell it all...all the sordid details...but wait until we get a get a drink."

Harry merely mumbled, "God, I'm amazed! I *do* need a drink."

Ignoring Ray, oblivious to his sadness, the three of them disappeared to the bar.

*   *   *

Kerry's face was ashen as she leant over a washbasin; she looked up as Siobhan entered the Ladies toilets, their eyes meeting.

"You okay?" asked Siobhan, concerned.

Kerry nodded in affirmation but then shook her head negatively. "No, not really." She paused then blurted out, "I can't believe that Spratt spoke about me like Monica said, 'gagging for it'."

"Well, we know it's not true," retorted Siobhan but something in Kerry's eyes made her ask, "Tell me that it's not true, is it? You and Spratt, you didn't? You haven't?"

Kerry stared forlornly at Siobhan, not answering.

"Oh Kerry, how could you have been *so* stupid? I did warn you so many times not to get involved with Pete Spratt in that way."

Kerry almost wailed, "Don't preach. Anyway, what's wrong with me having a relationship with Spratt?"

"R*elationship*?"

"Yes," Kerry meekly responded, "A relationship."

Siobhan snapped, "Spratt doesn't have relationships. He has one-night stands, or liaisons with women who are readily available for sex; but relationships, no, never...at least not in our sense of the word. If it wears a skirt, is not totally ugly and says 'yes', then Spratt is interested. You should know that. God, you should *know* that!"

"It was going to be different with me."

"He told you that did he?"

"Not in so many words."

Siobhan was exasperated, "Well, in how many words then?"

Kerry, beginning to feel defensive, raised her voice, "This is none of your business."

"It is my business," retorted Siobhan, "You and Spratt, and the crowd; we're all part of a circle of friends and business colleagues." She glared at Kerry, frustrated at her friend's naivety, "You could spoil everything and I had warned you not to get involved with him, mostly for your own sake!"

Kerry re-joined childishly, "You're only jealous because you fancied Spratt. I know you wanted to shag him."

"Oh Kerry don't be so stupid. Grow up."

"Don't tell me to grow up! I've had enough of this. Why should I be concerned what that silly little Monica said. It's me Spratt wanted, not her, or you."

"I didn't want to say this," replied Siobhan in a low voice, "But I guess I'm going to have to tell you."

Kerry's heart skipped a beat; maybe Siobhan was about to reveal her own relationship with Spratt, "*What?* You haven't?"

"Of course not; but Spratt did try it on with me."

Kerry's already ashen face turned paler, the remaining colour draining away like bath water when the plug is pulled. "You're just saying that, you're lying, making it up."

"Sorry, it's true. He told me that I was the only woman that he *really* fancied, and that the other women had meant nothing to him."

Kerry was close to tears. "No! It's not true; it can't be." She looked away from Siobhan and then looked up, a plaintiff expression on her face, "You didn't...you didn't...have sex with him did you? Tell me the truth."

"I've said already. No! Of course not! But *you* did."

"Twice; actually more than twice, but on two different occasions."

"Oh Kerry! For your information, when we all went out on that weekend a couple of weeks ago, he told me that he hadn't had sex for a long time, that he was waiting for me and, maybe, if I'd had a few more drinks, and if I didn't have Danny, then I might have been sucked in; the lying little sod!"

"Two weekends ago?"

Siobhan nodded in affirmation.

The tears welled in Kerry's eyes, "Obviously, we had sex before and after he tried it on with you. The first time was the Friday before and then the Tuesday afterwards, both times in his flat. It felt so perfect, so romantic. I really thought that with me it would be different for him. I can't believe how stupid I've been. And it was me who asked him." She wiped away a tear, "He didn't ask me; I virtually begged, offered myself to him on a plate. God, how easy I made it for him!"

Siobhan embraced her friend. "You silly, silly, poor cow." With genuine warmth and affection she tightly held the crying Kerry, stroking her friend's hair trying her best to comfort her friend.

Kerry sobbed into Siobhan's shoulder, "God, I'm a fool."

"Yep."

Kerry pulled her head free, staring pathetically through her tears at Siobhan, "Thanks."

Siobhan smiled ruefully, "We've all been there; at least once in our lives."

Not feeling inclined to smile, Kerry permitted a faint grin to spread across her lips, wiping her eyes with a tissue, "You're a good friend Siobhan."

*   *   *

Harry, Dominic and Monica returned with their drinks; Ray remained seated, immobile, still stunned, his expression dazed, his thoughts lost deep within his spinning mind.

Returning from the 'Ladies' Siobhan shot a look of pure malice at Monica.

Ray glanced up, his expression expectant; whatever happened, he still needed to warn Kerry, to make sure she was okay.

Harry grinned sheepishly.

Dominic wanted to make the most of the situation and gabbled, "Have you girls finally finished? Sorted yourselves out? I can't believe how you take so long in the ladies, particularly as we are waiting to hear Kitty's version of her night of elicit passion."

Ray, pale and visibly upset, frown creasing his forehead, swallowed nervously.

Siobhan paused as she reached the table, a look of pure malice shooting in Monica's direction; Monica recoiled, fearing for her well-being. Siobhan snapped at Dominic, "It isn't funny Dominic," and staring witheringly at Monica she added, "Kerry's in a bit of a state."

"Not in a such a bad state as she obviously was a couple of Tuesday's ago, I expect," retorted Dominic animatedly, "We hear that Kerry likes pearl necklaces!" Dominic burst into laughter.

"Hah, bloody hah," Siobhan retorted, her voice heavy with anger, "I don't know what this little trollop," She glared with venom at Monica, "Has told you, but she can't know."

Monica snapped back with indignation, "I'm not a trollop; it wasn't me who wanted a 'good seeing to' and a...pearl necklace' to boot!"

Siobhan, her face inches from Monica's face, threatened, "Why, you little..!"

Monica shrank back, afraid, blurting, "Anyway, it was Spratt who told me, before, and after, his sessions!" It was Siobhan's turn to recoil, horrified, her mouth attempting to form an unspoken word, her brain dazed, she was speechless.

Dominic defended Monica, "Take it easy Siobhan. Monica was just in the wrong place at the wrong time, but aren't we glad. What a story."

Siobhan reeled round to face Dominic, her voice deep with fury, "If you, or that that little tart, say anything..."

"Don't get so upset," appeased Harry.

"Look," interrupted Siobhan, her eyes blazing, "If any of you say anything, to anyone, I'll never forgive you and you will be sorry. I promise."

Unable to stop himself Dominic chuckled, "Wow, I like a woman with spirit. What are you doing later?" Siobhan attempted to slap him across the face but Dominic, grinning wickedly, swiftly ducked, his head moving out of Siobhan's reach.

"Grrr, oh you, you men; you're impossible." She regained her composure, "Please Dominic, not a word to anyone; promise?" Adamantly persisting, "Promise!"

Dominic sighed. "Okay." Of course, he had no intention in keeping silent on the subject. Siobhan glanced at Ray and Harry, seeking affirmation, her expression conveying the same demand as she had put to Dominic.

Harry, still surprised, nodded in affirmation.

Ray, remaining dejected, dumbfounded, nodded, but asked, his voice morose, "Where is Kerry? I still need to talk to her about my concerns."

"Now's not the time, Ray," responded Siobhan kindly, "Kerry's nipped out the back. I'm going to take her back to my place."

"That's a shame," replied Harry, "Tell her to comeback in and we can all have a chat about it. We're all mates together." He rose from his seat, "I'll go out and fetch her."

"No, leave her be," ordered Siobhan, "I don't think she can face company, especially not mickey taking company such as you lot."

"I do think you should talk to Kerry," implored Ray, "You know, what we were speaking about earlier."

Harry glared at Ray, not understanding, and hastily intervened,

"Seriously Siobhan, Kerry must know how *I* feel about her. I'll give her all the support she needs."

Siobhan grimaced, "I think she's been taken in enough already by you guys. You wait until I get hold of Pete Spratt, I'll rip his balls off!"

Dominic winced, "Ouch; I can feel his pain already."

Harry persisted, "Siobhan I'm being genuine."

"Yea, sure," gleefully laughed Dominic, "You lecherous old dog; you just want your own piece of the action, a portion of pussy; you just want a shag!"

"I think you guys have said enough," growled Ray, the menace evident in his tone.

"Oh, yes?" Harry snapped, rising to his feet.

"Leave it Ray," Siobhan stepped between Harry and the rising Ray, Ray's face incandescent, the blood vessels in his neck bulging with anger. "I know you've got Kerry's interest at heart. "She put her hand kindly on Ray's arm, "And I'll talk to Kerry about what you said."Turning to the bristling Harry she winked, "Forget it Harry. Ray, like you, is concerned for Kerry. I'm taking her home. The last thing on her mind is to talk with any of 'the gang'; it's just all too personal."

Harry persisted, "But, I want her to know that I really care."

"You guys are not in favour at the moment, particularly after what Spratt said to me the other night. How I was the only one; how he hadn't had sex for ages, etc. All complete bull shit!"

Dominic emitted a throaty chuckle. Harry, in spite of his attempt at genuine concern, could not resist a little smirk.

Siobhan scowled, "It's not a laughing matter."

"We're not laughing at you, or Kerry," defended Harry, "It's just what you said about Spratt." He grinned affectionately, "That's just typical 'Spratt'. And, lucky bastard, it usually works for him."

"Well, it didn't work with me!" Siobhan responded tartly as she picked up her and Kerry's handbags and turning on her heel, she exited.

Ray's head was pounding and he remained sitting dumbstruck for a couple of minutes, oblivious to the babbling conversation around him, then making his excuses, he departed, leaving the three remaining people to their lurid conversation. In a daze he made his way home to the comfort of a bottle of Glenlivvet.

Chapter 36

Subsequent to Kerry's departure back to England Abdullah had waited patiently for his plan to work but Brendan and his wife had remained in Ireland, visiting family and friends, the car mostly remaining idle in the car park.

Three days had passed but still the man's car hadn't failed. Abdullah was beginning to think that his plan had been a waste of time; with hindsight he had had more than enough time to return to England, rifle through their house and get out before anyone discovered his presence. Irritated beyond measure and about to call it a day Abdullah was relieved when he saw that finally Naimh was packing the car, obviously preparing for the return journey.

Aggrieved that the brakes had still not failed on the very short journeys already undertaken by Brendan, Abdullah was in a quandary of what to do next. He didn't know if his task had been unproductive because he hadn't cut the right pipe or if it was because the roads were not that busy, or because Brendan was driving very slowly, ultra-cautious, very rarely having to bring his brakes into play; certainly not in the squeal of heavy pressure that Abdullah had been wishing for.

Brendan's slow driving speed was certainly helping Abdullah to keep up, particularly as he did find it extremely difficult driving on the wrong side of the road compared to his previous experiences in the Arabian Gulf. He had assumed on the journey over to Ireland that Brendan had been driving slowly because of the coffin in the back but now he knew better. The man was just such a pedantic driver.

Abdullah's frustrations increased as he cursed his continual failures, his run of bad luck. "Right," he shouted, "In the name of the Prophet I will make it happen!" And with that he accelerated, the road ahead being free of oncoming traffic, and he sped past the dawdling Brendan, scowling at the man as he overtook. His sideways glance had caused him to swerve, almost taking him off the road, Abdullah having to fight with the wheel just to stop his car going over into a shallow drainage ditch.

Brendan, with the sleeping Naimh beside him on the front passenger seat, breathed a heartfelt sigh of relief. He had been annoyed at the car that had been following them for mile after mile. Brendan knew that he wasn't a fast driver and usually people were on his bumper, trying to urge him forward. But this time, no matter if Brendan had slowed, the following car always seemed to keep pace. Initially comforted by the thought that the driver of the car behind was like him, painstakingly slow and safety minded, he had gradually become irritated as time wore on, the same image in his rear view mirror becoming rather tiresome. Thus he muttered quietly, not wanting to wake Naimh, "I'm glad that bastard's overtaken us; he was getting on my nerves."

His relief was wiped out almost instantaneously, the car in front suddenly braking hard as soon as the man had got in front. "Shit!" exclaimed Brendan, shocked, "What the fuck is he doing?"

Naimh stirred but did not wake from her sleep.

Abdullah pressed hard on the brake pedal, keeping his hands firmly on the wheel, fighting the tyre resistance as the wheels pulled first to one side than the other, fighting to ensure that his braking pressure did not drive his car off the road. He glanced in his rear view mirror, anticipating the impact of Brendan's car.

With his foot almost sunk to the floor, pushing with all his might on his brake pedal, his car initially slowing in a squeal of tyres, Brendan was thinking he was going to avoid hitting the maniac in front; then nothing, the brakes not working, the vehicle seeming to increase in speed. In his blind panic he had also put his right foot back on the accelerator, increasing his speed in the same instant that the brakes finally failed.

He screamed, "Christ, Naimh! Wake up, the brakes aren't working!" The blood pounding in his temples, he swerved, desperate to avoid the idiot in front. Glancing off the right hand bumper of the car in front, Brendan's car swerved into the middle of the road and it looked as if he was going to be okay, for by some miracle he had drawn level with the idiot's car and had every chance of overtaking and getting by. Abdullah glanced over, smiled, but then calmly increased his speed not allowing Brendan the opportunity of getting past, Brendan still on the wrong side of the road.

"The stupid bastard!" yelled Brendan, "He bloody smiled at me! What the hell is he doing?"

"What; what's up? What's the matter?" murmured Naimh awaking from her sleep, her gummed up eyes not focusing properly.

"The brakes have packed in," yelled Brendan, "I can't slow down and that idiot in front won't let me back in." Brendan pressed furiously on his brake pedal, hoping against hope that they would finally work, that by some miracle they would suddenly free themselves from the reason for their failure. Not only was Brendan not a particularly good driver he also knew nothing about the mechanics of a car.

With sweat pouring from his brow he accelerated, trying to pass the moron driving alongside. He almost got past but the other vehicle increased its speed, its front bumper catching the rear nearside of his car causing his vehicle to swerve, skidding along the highway. Brendan fought like fury to correct his swerve, Naimh screaming like a wailing banshee alongside him. Her screams certainly didn't help his ability to remain cool and calm.

With Brendan's car at a right angle in front of him Abdullah accelerated, driving his vehicle, hard, into the side of Brendan's car, Naimh's terrified face peered out through the glass; her eyes now fully working, wide in fearful terror.

Abdullah's car hit with such force which, combined with Brendan striving to turn his wheels to the right, caused Brendan's car to tumble. The impact had mostly been against the rear passenger door but never the less stove in the panel on Naimh's door, breaking her hip and an assortment of bones on the left side of her body, her femur, three ribs, comminute fracture of the radius, ulnas, and humerus bone of her arm, as well as her scapula and clavicle bones. Cut and bleeding, her bones shattered - although she did not know the extent of her injuries - Naimh screamed, initially in shock, then in excruciating pain, her discomfort not being helped by the car rolling over and over.

The impact and the first roll caused Brendan's head to smash against the frame of his door, his air bag cushioning any further possibility of impact from the steering wheel but did not save him from the shard of broken glass as his window shattered, the first roll having taken him over onto a small raised bollard, a water marker, the bollard impacting into his window.

The glass shard cut into him, severing his jugular, his blood gushing forth in a river of scarlet fluid. Brendan didn't have time to say another word, no time to ask Naimh if she was okay, no time to say goodbye. He died instantly.

Naimh was knocked unconscious, her mind yielding to the shock and fear, its defence measures drowning out the pain racking through every nerve in her body.

Abdullah smiled, an immense feeling of well-being and satisfaction spreading over him; stopping his battered vehicle he walked over to inspect Brendan's broken and mangled car. The pool of blood, the stillness of the occupants, the only movement being one of the rear wheels still spinning slowly, its momentum not yet completed, caused him to smile grimly, then he departed. His next stop would be Brendan's and Naimh's home in England, the only other place where his Dhow must surely be.

Chapter 37

Armani suit, blue shirt, yellow silk tie, Ray Maloney slicked down his already immaculate hair. He checked his reflection in the glass of the hallway door and partially satisfied with his appearance, pressed the intercom button outside Kerry's office. Whilst waiting, he coughed nervously, clearing his throat, and straightened his tie as he heard the door lock being released; he pushed open the door and stepped inside.

It was Siobhan who he had spoken to on the intercom and she smiled up at him as he entered the room but Kerry ignored his entrance, choosing to occupy herself on whatever task it was that kept her focused on the screen of her computer; eventually she glanced up, almost with disdain. Ray's cheerful and ebullient mood evaporated, his practiced speech having withering on his lips. No longer confident, he hesitantly muttered, "Hi...um...Kerry, you look, um, great; much better now that you have had a few days' rest."

Kerry merely snapped in response, querulously retorting, "Oh, cut the crap!" Her face contorted with contempt. She rose from her seat, brushed past Ray and exited the office, leaving Ray totally crestfallen. Bemused, stared forlornly at Siobhan, Ray stammered, "What did I do? What did I say?"

Siobhan smiled up at him, her face full of sympathy, but her eyes were sad, vacant.

"You don't look very happy yourself," queried Ray, his embarrassment at the perfunctory dismissal from Kerry quickly being overshadowed, surpassed by his concern for Siobhan. "Are you worried about being in danger too?"

"No," Siobhan smiled warmly, "And I wouldn't mention it again. Kerry thinks that you're being incredibly stupid and that there's no reason for anybody to be after her. She was also a bit cross that you discussed it with me - she feels that you're trying to put me off having her stay at my place until she can find a new flat for herself."

Ray sat down, his brow furrowed, his legs feeling weary. "I honestly do feel that there has to be some connection." He looked into Siobhan's eyes, quickly adding, "Not that I feel you should be overly worried, I don't feel that there is a threat against you, and at least you've got your Danny to look after you."

Siobhan's face fell, a tear forming in her eye. She turned her head away.

Ray leapt up from his seat, concern etched across his features, "Oh God, Danny is alright, isn't he? Nothing's happened to him, has it?"

Siobhan turned back to Ray, the sorrow written into her face, her eyes moist with tears. She smiled wanly. "No, nothing's happened to Danny, thank God, but it's just the same if it had."

"Why, what's going on?" Ray queried solicitously, genuine concern evident from his tone.

"Danny and I have split up," she almost cried, "The bastard's taken a job in Spain." She paused, determined to regain her composure before slipping into a deluge of emotion, "And, apparently, the shit's being seeing someone else; he and that 'cow' have moved in together, in Barcelona." This time, she couldn't stop herself and burst into tears, the teardrops tricking down her cheeks.

Ray rushed forward to console her, holding the sobbing Siobhan in his arms. But at that moment Brian rushed out from his office, furious, berating the hapless Ray for upsetting Siobhan. Ray was taken aback, bewildered and perplexed, Siobhan unable to intervene on his behalf, her crying making her intercession utterly useless. It took a few minutes to straighten the situation out, Brian on the point of ejecting Ray from his office; good friend and good customer he may be but he couldn't have him upsetting a member of his staff.

The ensuing argument between Ray and Brian quickly brought Siobhan to her senses, an amused smile taking over from her earlier sorrow. Through her drying tears she explained to Brian the reason for her crying, her explanation leaving Brian mortified and Ray crimson with embarrassment. In the awkward silence that ensued Brian thought of what to say, what to do to alleviate and appease the awkwardness that he had put Ray through. "Can you join us for a drink tonight Ray?" his tone apologetic, "It's my birthday next Saturday, the big four-zero; we're going to the Rock Island Diner at Leicester Square. I could do with some male support against this female rabble."

Mollified, Ray eagerly retorted, "Um, that'll be great, I'd love to join you, thanks." But then his face clouded, "But I think that I may have unintentionally upset Kerry for some unknown reason; as soon as I arrived she stormed past me and left the office."

"Oh take no notice; it's nothing to do with you," soothed

Siobhan, "Kerry's been like a bear with a sore head. You know that her close friends Naimh and Brendan were in a car accident in Ireland?"

Ray's stupefied expression told her that he obviously didn't know.

"You didn't?" Siobhan quickly related details of the accident, Brendan's demise, and the fact that Naimh was still in hospital in Dublin, out of intensive care but with assorted bones broken. It would take weeks before she was well enough to return.

Ray whistled, shocked, dumbfounded, wondering out loud, "You don't think it's anything to do with Sean and other recent related deaths, do you?"

"What are you gabbling on about?" queried Brian which left Ray with no option but to hastily explained his theory to Brian, summarising all the events that seemed to connect Kerry to Sean's killer or killers.

Brian shivered unintentionally, uttering, "Wow, I had no idea!" He turned to Siobhan, "Did you know *all* this, about Ray's suspicions?" He asked with a mixture of curiosity and self-concern, not wanting to be in any firing line himself.

Siobhan sighed, "Yes, Ray has continually expounded his suspicions and fears to both Kerry and me," she smiled with reassurance on seeing the quickly forming lines of anxiety spreading across Brian's brow. "But, none of us, including the Police, can see any link." She grinned at Ray, "And as for Brendan's crash in Ireland, it was just an unfortunate accident. Apparently some crazy loony was overtaking Brendan's car, causing Brendan to skid and turn his car over."

"Oh, I see," replied Ray softly, not convinced, determined more than ever to protect Kerry and, now, Siobhan too.

Chapter 38

Abdullah stepped out of the shadows and nodded casually to the figure lurking under a shop awning on the other side of the road. Without any overt gesture, he utilised slight nuances of his head and eyes to indicate the group of people that he and Saeed were to follow. Abdullah was glad that he elected to take only Saeed on this task, the younger brother Fawzi being far too impetuous for his liking. If it wasn't for the fact that Fawzi was destined not to return from this mission, being expendable, Abdullah would have sent him back to his homeland, feeling that the young man would turn out to be a liability. Although fervent enough, the impetuous youth needed more training; much more training.

Also, this morning, he had caught Fawzi watching a DVD, a disgusting film with three blonde white women performing unseemly sexual acts on a window cleaner. Although Abdullah's loins had stirred at some of the pictures he has witnessed, the seemingly bored female office workers living out their fantasies with the muscular workman, Abdullah had quickly switched off the television, removing the offending DVD from the machine.

Fawzi's protest had died on his lips when he saw the anger and venom evident in Abdullah's features. He had been convinced that Abdullah was about to kill him.

On learning where Fawzi had acquired the offending material, Abdullah had gone through the younger man's meagre possessions, tumbling the few items and crumpled clothing on the floor. Discovering two pornographic magazines carefully hidden within the fold of a pair of trousers, Abdullah had let rip, verbally abusing Fawzi but stopping short of pounding the man to a pulp. He still needed Fawzi, so Abdullah reined in his anger, merely slapping Fawzi, hard, across each cheek, sufficient to split the young man's lips, a trickle of blood dribbling down his chin.

Although Abdullah had not given Brendan's life, or death, a second thought, now he felt glad. Glad that he had rid the world of such a man who kept such vile material, for both the magazines and the DVD had been found by Fawzi when they ransacked Brendan's home, tearing through the property like three whirling dervishes, quickly destroying or discarding any obstacle that came in their way.

Without removing his venomous eyes from Fawzi, he ripped up

the magazines, tearing the pages into tiny shreds. Fawzi's last glimpse of the wanton beauties within, being of some busty redheaded woman, her nipples being split in two by the tear across the page. Despite his fear of Abdullah his face fell. "God," he thought, "Hurry up with my virgins."

Abdullah brought his thoughts back to the present. The Dhow had not been there, not at that man's house. And now time had run out. He, together with Saeed, would follow the woman - the slut - who had resided with that man Sean and one way or another they would drag the information from her. Tonight they would find out where the Dhow was located. Tonight he would have his Dhow back, finally!

So now here they were, waiting outside Kerry's office building. Saeed, on seeing his leader's signal, had fallen in behind the group of three men and five women who had just exited from the office building. Having been trained on covert operations he knew how to trail the Westerners without being observed himself.

Equally adept at stalking, Abdullah kept pace on the opposite side of the road.

Feeling uneasy, a feeling of dread, a shiver shooting up his spine like a dead man walking over his grave, Ray glanced over his shoulder but could see nothing untoward because Saeed had melted into the shadows, into the throng of the heaving population leaving their offices for their long and arduous journey home, or on to their next watering hole. Ray's nerves tingled, his hair standing on end, a feeling of foreboding and impending disaster washing over him.

Chapter 39

Despite Kerry's contempt for his opinion Ray was growing increasingly afraid for her well-being; he had totally convinced himself that she was in danger. He didn't know if it was because of the macabre thoughts that he was experiencing or if it was because he was feeling increasingly tired but he kept looking over his shoulder, glancing around the room, the hairs on his nape tingling like a prickly cactus. Eventually his melancholic mood was assuaged as he enjoyed watching the waitresses as they danced on the bar counters. The distraction of the dancing girls, with the help of quite a few beers, was helping to alleviate his feelings of foreboding, of unease. Happily ensconced with Kerry, Siobhan, and the rest of Brian's crowd of birthday revellers, he had been in the Rock Island Restaurant for nearly three hours, the drinks flowing and the meal, of three courses, now long since consumed.

The dance record reaching its climax, the attractive waitress staff clambered down from the bar counters and hastened to their various duties, their own unbelievably gorgeous waitress making a bee-line for their table. Seemingly out of nowhere she was joined by a second, younger girl, the newer girl's pony tail bouncing across her back as she followed the leading waitress. The second waitress had glossy, dark hair, her features exotic, almost of Asian origin. Ray squinted, alert, his obscured vision barely discerning that the second woman was carrying something in her hands, his nerves becoming taught, his mind warning him that something was about to happen.

But it was okay; as the young waitress pulled level with her senior colleague, Ray could discern that she was merely holding a large brandy goblet, the contents of the glass brimming to the top, threatening to overflow as the girl approached them. He hadn't realised that he'd been holding his breath until he heard the strange sound of air being expelled from his lungs, the noise emitted akin to a wheezing smoker or of someone making a 'dirty phone call'.

Siobhan shot him a sideways glance, looking at him askance.

Their waitress, who had previously introduced herself as Martina, now introduced her younger colleague, "This is Jenny; she's come to give me a hand." The younger waitress was holding the glass which contained a special cocktail, the house 'special', and her face lit up like a Belisha beacon, a smile that seemed to spread from ear to ear. The resident Disc Jockey played 'Happy Birthday' and the two waitresses joined in the song, the younger one feeling slightly awkward at having to sing along, her cheeks turning a shade of crimson. Brian was both pleased and yet embarrassed, muttering, "You buggers! I hate this kind of thing; I'll get you back for this." But his smug tone belied his supposed dislike of the attention lavished on him.

When the song had finished the restaurant went almost quiet, the sound of silence quickly being replaced by the hubbub of voices from their fellow diners. Martina then took the glass from Jenny, grinned at Brian, and placed the goblet in front of him, beaming, "Here you go birthday boy." She glanced in the direction of the Disc Jockey, then added, "You have to 'down' this cocktail – we call it our 'Knockout Surprise' – before the D.J. finishes a count from seven downwards."

Martina nodded in the direction of the 'D.J.' and his dry, throaty voice was heard almost immediately over the sound system, "It's a 'Happy Birthday to...," he paused, looking down at a scrap of paper in his hand, "Brian; forty today, eh?" With a throaty chuckled he added, "And we know what you won't be doing tonight if you drink that! Tee-hee."

Taking a box of matches from her pocket, Martina lit the surface of Brian's drink. "Now!" She exclaimed, the 'D.J.' commencing his count at the same instant. Ray watched, wide-eyed as Brian scooped up his cocktail and without pause put the glass to his mouth, swallowing the contents. The restaurant diners joined the 'D.J.' in his countdown, Brian emptying his glass just as the number 'one' was shouted out. Coughing and spluttering, he wiped his mouth with the back of his free hand and grinned inanely, the now empty glass being thumped back, triumphantly, onto the table. Both waitresses, having seen it all before, politely clapped, removed the glass and went about their other business, Brian quickly forgotten.

Rheumy eyed from the effort of his endeavour, Brian smiled sickly, muttering breathlessly, "That was no problem."

"Yea, sure!" retorted Kerry, with wry amusement; having imbibed a few drinks she looked wistfully in Brian's direction, wanting to forget her woes, she wished that she had one of those drinks. "Actually, that looked like fun. Can I have a go?"

Concerned for her friend, Siobhan interjected, "Kerry, I don't think you should; you've had enough already. It doesn't show on

Brian yet but that was a strong cocktail which would go straight to your head and probably knock you out cold; that's why they call it a 'Knockout Surprise'. *And* you'd have an almighty hangover tomorrow."

Kerry's snapped petulantly, "Oh, who cares about tomorrow? I want to live for today. There's so much I need to forget, to put out of my mind." She stared pleadingly at Brian, adopting her most sexy and alluring demeanour, pleading coquettishly, "Please Brian. I know it's your tab, but I don't mind paying for one myself. You surely wouldn't object to me trying one of those 'Knockout Surprises'. I'd really love to try one."

Despite Siobhan's protest, supported by the extremely concerned Ray, who was quickly told by Kerry in no uncertain terms to mind 'his own fucking business', Brian relented and ordered Kerry one of the in-house 'Knockout Surprises', which duly arrived at their table, this time delivered by the younger waitress only.

Jenny sighed, not sure if she should be delivering this drink to this particularly lady who already appeared to be drunk, but following her senior's instructions, she placed the glass in front of Kerry and immediately glanced up, looking at the D.J., who nodded in response. "He won't be a second," she said with almost disdain, "You know what to do, don't you?"

Kerry nodded nervously, no longer feeling bold. Ray shook his head anxiously; he felt that Kerry was in enough danger without getting totally pissed out of her head as well.

"Hello again, party people," called out the supercilious D.J., "There's another brave soul who reckons that they can finish a 'Knockout Surprise' before the count of seven. Who is it then?" He asked peering out into the dining area.

Brian yelled out, gesticulating like a child, pointing at Kerry, "It's her!"

"Great," retorted the D.J., "But who *is* she - what's her name?" Without waiting For Brian's answer, he persisted, "What's your name darling?" Ray groaned inwardly, not wanting more attention focused on Kerry, more people who might be putting her life in danger.

Kerry's response was squeaky and awkward, "Um, Kerry," Her high-pitched response making even herself squirm.

"Go for it then, Kerry! I hope you've got someone to look after you?" Cried out the D.J., who added as a mischievous afterthought, "If not, come and see me later!"

Ray scowled but Siobhan mumbled, "You're not good enough mate!" This brought a smile to Ray's lips, who nodded wholeheartedly at Siobhan's words.

The waitress lit Kerry's 'Knock-out Surprise' and the countdown commenced, the D.J. having allowed Kerry an extra second to prepare. Kerry, hands trembling, picked up her glass and started to gulp. Her eyes watered, she spluttered, dribbles of liquid escaping from the rim and trickling down her chin. But undaunted, she persevered, the D.J. and the Diners counting down relentlessly ...three, two, *ONE!* At the same instant as a drawn out 'one' was sounded Kerry drained her glass, replacing it with triumph on the table. Wiping her chin, she smirked with self-satisfaction.

"Wow, well down baby," Called out the impressed D.J., the admiration evident in his tone, "That *was* a really close call!" He paused, adding, "Don't forget, if you need me later!" He chuckled, a new record already playing on the decks.

Kerry broke into a coughing fit, her upper body swaying. Ray grimaced, aghast, and muttered to Siobhan, "Bloody hell! She is well on her way to being totally rat-arsed!" Annoyed, he remonstrated with Brian, "I think you've been irresponsible Brian. With all that Kerry's been through, it's not drowning in alcohol that she needs, it's tender, loving care!"

"I'm okay," retorted Kerry, snapping at Ray, and hiccupping. "As I said before, hic, you're not my mum. I'm big enough to look after myself."

Siobhan sharply interjected, "No Kerry, you're obviously not!"

Brian surprised at Ray and Siobhan's rancour, meekly responded, "Hey don't spoil the mood, it is my birthday."

Unmoved, Ray looked daggers at Brian, who tetchily returned his stare, a peeved expression on his face. Realising that his anger was being misdirected at Brian who had only been trying to help Kerry in his own way, Ray muttered, "Oh, just forget it! But I hope that you're not sorry later." Kerry scowled petulantly, her lips no longer able to form coherent words of protest.

Siobhan scrutinised her friend, "Are you sure that you're okay? Do you want a black coffee?"

Kerry's vision was becoming increasingly unfocused, her words slurring, "No; uh no. I feel - a bit high - but I'm okay." Delighted that she had found words, she fooled herself into believing that she was okay, gleefully declaring, "I feel...I feel like dancing; who wants to dance?"

Emboldened by the alcohol, Kerry pushed back her chair, rose, swayed, and almost lost her balance, saving herself by placing both hands flat onto the table.

Ray leapt up, ready to assist.

"Oh for Goodness sake Kerry, are you sure you're okay?" Siobhan sighed, exasperated.

Kerry nodded but then shook her head negatively. "Um, I...er, I, need the loo, I think," she slurred.

Ray rushed to her side, "I'll give you a hand," his voice heavy with concern, his arms supporting her swaying body.

Siobhan smiled, her eyes twinkling, "And how do you propose to do that? You take one step inside the ladies loo and I'm sure that two or three of those bouncers," Siobhan glanced in the direction of the entrance, "Will leap about you like a ton of bricks."

Ray smiled ruefully, "I guess I hadn't thought of that."

Siobhan smiled kindly at Ray as she went to Kerry's side, "It's okay, I'll take her," and she took her drunken friend's weight, relieving Ray of the need for his support. "C'mon, I'll give you a hand," she spoke softly, reassuringly, to Kerry, "Sure, we've all been in this state before."

Kerry raised her head, staring fixedly into the distance. "I'll be fine," she slurred, "I'm not pissed. I just got up too quickly." She tossed her head, pulled free from Siobhan's support and pushed herself off from the table. Big mistake; the alcohol fused confidence belying the ability of her legs to carry her weight and she staggered, almost fell, but then through some miracle, continued her journey to the toilet, swaying across the restaurant, her body sashaying in and out between the tables in an unruly manner, everyone giving her a wide berth, the Staff looking on with concern.

Both Ray and Siobhan followed her from a safe distance; not too close as to cause an argument but ready to leap to her assistance should she finally succumb to the power of the alcohol. As Kerry entered the ladies room, banging unceremoniously into first one side of the door frame then the other, Ray peeled away leaving Siobhan to follow her drunken friend into the inner sanctum. Feeling slightly sheepish under the staring eyes of the accusing restaurant staff, Ray retired to Brian's table.

*   *   *

"Kerry?" pleaded Siobhan, listening against one of the closed cubicle doors, "It's me, Siobhan; are you okay? Open the door. Please."

Kerry merely groaned.

Siobhan persisted, her voice soft, concerned, "Kerry, just open the door. I'll help you."

"I can't...Christ, my head," Kerry slurred, her voice wretched; then she was violently sick, spewing forth copious amounts of mixed solids and liquids, her body retching, making her feel as if she was about to burst. The violent retching spasms did nothing to soothe the throbbing that was growing in her head, a crescendo of blinding pain that seemed to drive like shooting nails into the back of her eyeballs.

"Oh, balls!" cried Siobhan, frustrated and helpless. Scanning the room, inspiration hit her and she entered the empty cubicle to the right of Kerry. Putting down the toilet lid, she stepped up onto the closed seat and then pulled herself up on to the dividing partition; with her stomach on the dividing wall, she reached in, unbolting the fastening on Kerry's door. In trying to regain the floor of her present cubicle Siobhan gave herself a massive whack on the ankle, the porcelain of the bowl making contact with great force causing Siobhan to swear out loud, a stream of profanities drifting out from her mouth, any pretence of trying to act like a lady long since gone.

Siobhan gently eased open the unlocked door of Kerry's cubicle. The sight that greeted her was not very pleasant.

There was vomit on the floor, in Kerry's hair, and all around the ceramics of the toilet bowl, inside and outside. Kerry's head was deep within the bowl, her groans echoing out in a hollow, yet muted sound.

Siobhan recoiled in disgust. "Christ, what a mess; she's bad," she muttered, then continued out loud, her voice authoritative, "Kerry for God's sake, get your head out of the bowl!"

"Can't" Kerry mumbled, "Feel dreadful." And with that the retching spasms took over her body, spewing forth yet more bile of the seemingly endless supply from her stomach.

Siobhan was beginning to feel slightly queasy herself. "God, what a sight and what an unbelievable mess!" She thought and put her hand to her nose in defence against the smell. "The vomit's everywhere Kerry," Siobhan complained, "It's in your hair, on your top. Everywhere! You *have* to get your head out of the toilet bowl!"

Kerry ignored her, groaning, "Ahhh, I just want to die. Let me die."

Siobhan persisted, her voice soft, cajoling, "Come on Kerry, get your head out of the bowl. Lie down on the floor for a second. I'll clean you up."

"Can't...ugh...I keep...being sick."

"Please," Siobhan pleaded, taking a step forward, "If you feel that you're going to be sick again then we can lift you to the bowl."

Kerry slightly, almost imperceptibly raised her head, gasped for air, but instantly lowered it again, retching into the bowl, only a tiny trickle of bile escaping, contradicting the abundant retching of her body.

Siobhan was becoming exasperated, snapping impatiently, "Come on Kerry, we'll get you sorted, you daft thing, but you must take your head out from the bowl; you're getting covered."

*   *   *

It was some time before Siobhan returned to Brian's table and though she had thoroughly washed her hands and arms, the odour of Kerry's vomit still seemed to pervade her being. Brian decided that it was time to call it a night, concerned for Kerry's well-being; he was convinced by Ray and Siobhan that they would both make sure that Kerry got home safely. Settling the tab, Brian and the rest of his party departed, leaving Ray to wait whilst Siobhan checked on Kerry's progress, Kerry apparently cleaning herself up in the ladies toilets.

Ray thought it would be opportune to order three strong coffees, hoping against hope that they could slightly sober Kerry before taking her to the outside air. Siobhan eventually returned to the table supporting a very wan looking Kerry, her hair wet and matted, the odour of something unpleasant still on her being.

Kerry was apologetic, "Sorry Ray, I should have listened to you."

"Are you feeling slightly better?" he queried.

Kerry smiled thinly, her hollow eyes and ashen skin making the question unnecessary, so Siobhan responded on her behalf, "I think her stomach's settled, but Kerry says she's got a head like a steamroller pounding inside."

"Sorry," Ray sympathised, "I've ordered some coffee and I've got a couple of aspirins."

"Where the hell did you get them from?" mused Siobhan, surprised.

Ray grinned ruefully, "I occasionally keep a strip in my top pocket for nights such as these; I've been caught out a couple of times myself."

Kerry stared at him through her hollow, heavy lidded eyes, her earlier repugnance replaced by a new awareness, "You're not quite the quiet old fart that you make yourself out to be, are you?"

Ray didn't know whether to be annoyed or pleased, replying gently, "Never pretended to be, it's just what you perceived me to be like. Because I don't make a lot of noise, announcing my presence from the rooftops, doesn't make me a boring person."

"No, I can vouch for that." Siobhan smiled affectionately, "I, for one, have never labelled you boring; sweet, yes, but not boring."

"Anyway," interrupted Kerry, displeased at the exchange of smiles between Ray and Siobhan, "I am sorry for not listening to your advice and for screwing up the evening. You were right Ray, and I should have known better."

"It's okay, but it wasn't just me who was recommending you to take it easy," he glanced at Siobhan, "I'm just sorry we failed."

"Yes, that goes for me as well," interjected Siobhan, feeling that Kerry was attempting to marginalize her. Kerry ignored Siobhan's interruption, her eyes focused on Ray, drawing him into her web. Kerry didn't like competition and although Ray was not her type she didn't like the thought of Siobhan coming between her and one of her admirers.

"Thanks anyway," she cooed at Ray, ignoring Siobhan.

Feeling awkward and disconcerted under her hard gaze, Ray turned his head away. "It doesn't matter, so long as you're okay now."

After a moment's pause - all three lost in their thoughts - Ray looked up, "Kerry, I'm still concerned. Um, you know how fond of you I am and I do think that you need to take seriously the thought that your life could be in danger."

"And not just in danger from excess of alcohol," grinned Siobhan.

Ray shot her a withering glance of contempt, perturbed that she too was not taking the situation seriously enough. "It was only a joke," protested Siobhan, annoyed at Ray's glance of disapproval.

Picking up his drink, Ray consumed a large swig of coffee and continued hastily, "Look, I know it is none of my business but please will you be careful. Be alert at all times, at least until the Police catch Sean's killer or killers."

A tear formed in Kerry's eye. "Oh, I'm sorry," soothed Ray, "I didn't mean to upset you by mentioning Sean."

"It's not that," responded Kerry, her voice tearful, "It's because of Spratt...*me*...and Spratt."

"What!" exclaimed Ray, totally taken aback, not expecting Kerry to mention her indiscretion.

"Kerry!" Shrieked Siobhan, "Be careful what you're saying!"

Ray glanced from one to the other, a look of shocked disbelief on his face, hoping against hope that, despite the gathering evidence, Kerry hadn't actually formed a relationship with Spratt. "What, what do you mean, you and Spratt?" He almost spat out the word 'Spratt'.

"Don't say any more," cautioned Siobhan, her eyes pleading, warning.

But Kerry ignored her, blurting out the facts of her relationship, or 'liaison' with Pete Spratt. Ray sat there stunned into disbelief, his face crumbled; devastated, he absentmindedly picked up his drink, downing the contents in one, long continuous gulp.

Siobhan groaned both as a result of the repetition of Kerry's story, her stupidity in succumbing to Spratt, and secondly, because of her friend's indiscretion in revealing all the details to Ray.

Feeling relieved at having got the events off her chest Kerry looked up at Ray, looking into his eyes, expecting the sympathy and support that the poor sap had always given to her. But not this time; no, the look on his face was a mixture of anger and dismay. The smile that was beginning to form on her lips, a smile framed to match the expected mutual smile of sympathy from Ray, was quickly frozen.Her face hardened, Kerry blurting, "I know I've been a bit silly, sleeping with Spratt whilst still living with Sean, but it only happened on two occasions! Yes, I made a stupid mistake."

Ray's jaw had sunk so low it was almost on the table. Involuntarily, he groaned, "I thought it was just a one off, a mistake, but obviously not. I thought that you had better judgement, but then I'm biased," he bitterly blurted.

"What!" thundered Kerry, not prepared to accept such admonishment from this boring twat.

"I just can't understand it," retorted Ray bitterly, "I knew that you and Sean were engaged to get married but I felt that you could do better. I even hoped that...that I could win your heart." He paused, looking helplessly into her angry face, "But a relationship with Spratt, I can't believe it; you know he's only after one thing."

Kerry, initially dumbfounded by Ray's response, brusquely wiped the tears from her eye, "How dare you!" She snapped, "I didn't have to tell you! I thought that you would give me some moral support. How dare you judge me as well, you twat!"

Siobhan sat still, wishing a hole would open up and swallow her.

Ray was shocked at the vehemence of Kerry's words, eventually managing to mutter in response, "I'm sorry; it's just that it was a shock, you know, Pete Spratt. I just can't believe it."

Kerry pushed her chair back, leaping to her feet. "Come on Siobhan," she ordered, "We're going now." Glaring contemptuously at Ray, she snarled, "We'll leave this insignificant twat to his own devices." Turning to Siobhan, she glared at her friend, her eyebrow raised questioningly to reinforce her point, "Are you coming or not?"

"Um," Siobhan felt extremely awkward and got slowly to her feet, smiling ruefully at Ray. She mumbled an apology which only served to infuriate Kerry even more.

Glancing back at Ray, Kerry declared through clenched teeth, "And if you ever think that I could get involved with someone like you...hah! I wouldn't even consider it for a second! You're so *fucking* boring!"

Shocked at the vehemence of Kerry's words, Ray sat white-faced, bemused and hurt. But in spite of her words and despite the inner turmoil raging inside him, he quietly uttered, "No, I'll see you both safely home. You can't go on your own, especially not in the state that you're in."

Kerry snapped, "What do you mean, 'the state I'm in'? You cheeky bastard!"

"Kerry please," protested Siobhan.

Ray sighed, "I didn't mean it like that. What I meant was that with the amount of alcohol that we've all consumed, makes us - especially you - more venerable."

"Oh, cut the crap!" snarled Kerry, "We don't need a useless twat like you looking after us. What on earth use could *you* be?"

Siobhan put her hand on Kerry's arm, softly interjecting, "Kerry, I want Ray to see us home. If not for your sake than for mine; I don't feel safe with everything that's gone on."

They stood motionless, Kerry glaring at Ray; she turned on her heel, marching towards the exit. "If you must Siobhan, let the useless prick watch over us."

Siobhan smiled apologetically, muttering kindly, "She's been through a lot Ray. She doesn't mean all the nasty things that she's saying."

"I know," Ray responded softly, his kind tone belying his inner emotions. Crestfallen, dejected, yet scared for Kerry and Siobhan's safety, he followed them as they exited the restaurant.

Hardly a word was spoken between the three of them in the taxi cab on the way to Siobhan's home. Travelling with a lump in his throat, Ray kept a watchful eye, twice convinced that they were being followed but each time the assumed pursuing vehicle turning off.

Initially leaving the restaurant he had tensed up, ready to defend the girls as a dark figure loomed out from the shadows but the man in question was obviously just another night time reveller, staggering towards the kerb, then regaining his composure before proceeding on his drunken path.

When they reached Siobhan's place Ray insisted that the Cabbie waited whilst he escorted his female companions to their door, then glancing round once more, he bade Siobhan a good night, warning her to lock the door behind them. Kerry had already stalked away, stomping into Siobhan's Flat, no word of farewell being imparted from her lips.

Thanking Ray, Siobhan pecked him on the cheek and assured him that she would make sure that they were secure. Ray hated to leave them alone but knew that there was no way that Kerry would countenance him staying overnight, regardless of his genuine intentions.

Heartbroken and bitterly disappointed, yet fearful for the safety of both females, he climbed back into the cab with a heavy heart. "Damn, damn, damn!" He muttered, thumping the door with his fist.

The Cabbie turned round, glaring, his voice almost a low growl, "Oi mate, carry on like that and I'll kick you out."

Ray looked up, a vacant expression in his eyes, "What? Oh, sorry; Waterloo Station please." He gnawed at his knuckles, the fear and sadness eating within him.

The Cabbie glanced into his rear view mirror, shivered, and firmly shut the glass partition, muttering, "Frigging nutter!"

Chapter 40

The midnight blue Volkswagen Passat taxi pulled away from the kerbside, the driver following Ray's cab. The Passat's two occupants were barely visible, even the occasional light when passing a street light failing to pick out their shapes or features. Keeping a respectable distance they followed Ray, the Passat driver determined that this night would see the true beginning of the fulfilment of his mission.

*   *   *

It had been a long wait outside the 'Rock Island' and after two hours Abdullah had left Saeed on sole watch whilst he went off to secure a vehicle. Saeed was given instructions that if the group left the 'Rock Island' then at all costs he must follow Kerry, phoning back only when he was sure of her location for the night.

Deciding not to use a mobile phone because of the possibility of being traced, Abdullah located a public phone box, making a quick phone call to the businessman 'Banker'. His demand was firm, baulking no resistance; what he wanted was a taxi, which would be necessary for the next stage of his plan. He had then sat in a nearby café, impatient, drinking odious cups of weak western coffee, and had twice had to harass his businessman contact to ensure that the vehicle was being arranged.

It was almost an hour before the vehicle arrived, the delivery driver, after demonstrating the necessary controls to Abdullah, soon dispatched with a flea in his ear.

Still not au fait with UK driving Abdullah hesitantly drove the Passat to the point where he had left Saeed on watch. Pulling in to the pavement, his indicator flashing, the 'Taxi for Hire' sign still not switched off, caused Saeed to jump out of his skin. The sudden appearance of the taxi screeching to a stop right beside him made him ready to flee, panic written all over his face. Saeed suspected a trap, the security forces ready to detain him. Then he caught a glimpse of the driver, Abdullah smiling out at him. That smile sent shivers down Saeed's spine; he had never seen Abdullah smile before but the smile did nothing to improve the man's aura of evil.

Saeed's relief was short lived. As soon as he opened the door to climb into the taxi a young policeman approached the vehicle, a look of determination on his face Abdullah discerned the sudden look of fear on Saeed's visage and looking up in the direction of

Saeed's vision, he froze. A mixture of wariness and anger flowed through his veins. He was not going to be stopped this early into his mission and he reached down into the door pocket, feeling for the comforting reassurance of his trusty, sharpened dagger.

The Constable reached the vehicle, knocked authoritatively on the window, indicating that the driver was to wind down the window.

Tensing, ready to grip the dagger and thrust it upwards into the policeman's chest, Abdullah did as instructed, the policeman's face now inches from his own.

"Are you aware of the regulations regarding hire taxi's and black cabs?" demanded the Constable, "You are not permitted to pick up passengers on spec.; bookings must be arranged from your control."

Abdullah almost breathed with relief. This stupid young policeman was stopping him for something insignificant, something so utterly pointless. It would not be difficult achieving his mission in such a backward country where they put more emphasis on the little things rather than the major issues.

"No Sir, I know" responded Abdullah obsequiously, having no idea what the policeman was talking about but quickly picking up on the key words. "But, Mr *Saeed* here was booked by the office."

Saeed scowled, startled at the mention of his name. What was Abdullah doing giving his name away for, he thought.

"Is that correct?" demanded the Constable to Saeed. "Can you tell me your name?"

"Saeed...Saeed Younis," hastily responded Saeed, realising now why Abdullah had given up his known name. The second name, Younis, was made up, a name that Saeed had seen over the newsagent's shop near their dwelling.

"That's okay then," smiled the policeman.

As the policeman was pulling himself back up to his full height, Abdullah said, "But Sir, I now have a problem. The car is in trouble - it keeps stopping. I am afraid to drive it anymore."

"You can't leave it here," instructed the Constable. "Or I'll have it towed away."

"No Sir, I understand. But can I phone my office to send a mechanic?"

The policeman considered the request then reluctantly agreed. "Okay, so long as you're not causing an obstruction for too long."

Walking away, he called over his shoulder, "But turn off your 'For Hire' light!"

It took Abdullah a few minutes to locate the correct switch, eventually turning off the taxi 'For Hire' light. Twice Saeed had to shoo away prospective punters whose initial joy at finding an available taxi was turned to angry words at finding they couldn't make use of the vehicle.

To further assist in their ruse Abdullah raised the bonnet. They both then sat quietly, eyes firmly fixed on the entrance to the 'Rock Island', Saeed now extremely grateful for the warmth and the comforting rest for his weary legs.

The tediousness of the situation was getting to both men, not helped by the reappearance of the young policeman wondering why they were still there and why no one had turned up to fix the car. Abdullah had assured him that someone was on the way and the Constable had agreed to wait a few more minutes before he was going to call up a tow truck, charging them for recovery of their vehicle at the police pound.

When the Constable appeared for the third time, a grimace of determination on his face, Abdullah had to make a quick decision. Did he abort tonight's mission, letting his target disappear once more from his grasp or would he have to rein in the young policeman? The dilemma was running round in his head as the policeman approached. Making a snap decision, he leapt from his vehicle, the same fixed smile on his face that had made Saeed so uneasy earlier. "Sir, they have fixed the car and we are just going."

Not sure whether to take any action or not the Officer was pleased that they would now be removing the problem from his beat area. What he didn't understand was why the passenger, having waited so long, now decided to leave the vehicle, adopting a waiting posture as he leant against a nearby lamppost. "Why aren't you taking your passenger?" he demanded.

"I couldn't take the risk Sir," replied Abdullah, self- effacingly, "I'm just going to take the taxi back to the depot."

"Bad luck," mouthed the policeman disinterestedly to Saeed and then continued on his repetitive beat, looking forward to his meal break.

A few minutes later, turning the corner into a silent side road, the policeman was dismayed and annoyed to see the taxi parked up once again, this time its boot was now open. Striding purposely forward, determined that he was no longer going to brook this clear flouting of justice in his patrol area, he failed to notice the shadow that stepped out from a recessed shop doorway. His first indication of being in trouble was the hand being firmly clamped over his mouth, a sharp blade being driven up into his back, piercing through his clothes and flesh in a matter of seconds. Having no time to respond, to defend himself, he was bundled forward into the open boot, his eyes registering shock and fear as Abdullah sliced through his neck, the blood spilling from his carotid artery in a mini fountain of spurting fluid.

Abdullah slammed down the boot lid on the dead Constable. He was pleased on two counts; first, the man could no longer identify them, and secondly he was becoming a bloody nuisance with regard to tonight's mission. Aware of his blood stained clothes, the liquid also congealing in his hair and on his face, Abdullah looked around for some method of cleansing himself and the car. Almost at once the heavens opened, a sudden thunderous fall of water from the skies, and Abdullah stood, his arms upraised, grateful for the sudden rain downpour that helped to cleanse him and to wash away the blood from the rear of the car. He was convinced that Allah was looking after him, helping him to fulfil his mission in this God-forsaken land. With a renewed zeal and resisting the urge to get down and pray, Abdullah climbed back into the taxi.

Arriving back outside the 'Rock Island', Abdullah was dismayed to see Saeed furiously flagging him down, the man's frantic actions sure to bring attention to them both in this busy thoroughfare. "What an idiot the man is, he will wish he never came on my mission when I have finished with him," thought Abdullah, but his thoughts of admonishment were quickly swept away when Saeed explained that Kerry and two others had just departed from the restaurant, Saeed unable to find Abdullah or to flag down another cab in order to follow them.

With Saeed barely in the passenger door Abdullah sped off in hot pursuit, Saeed having pointed out that Kerry's taxi was stuck at the traffic lights ahead. Although his initial idea of being the first taxi on the spot when Kerry left the restaurant was now out the window he knew that he would have to formulate a new plan, following the woman as best he could. Wherever she lay tonight, then that place would fulfil the beginning.

It had been extremely difficult for Abdullah to keep pace and follow Kerry's Black Cab, twice having to jump red traffic lights. Somehow, with Saeed's eagle eyes, they had managed to follow the cab to Siobhan's address, where Abdullah steered his vehicle into the kerb, ignoring the 'Resident's parking only' sign, squeezing in between a Mini and a Cabriolet. Watching as Ray, Kerry and Siobhan exited the cab, he was about to switch off his own engine when he noticed that Ray was returning to the taxi, the man climbing inside.

Thus it was that Abdullah made an instant decision. They would follow this man who he had observed a few times in the company of Kerry and if the Dhow was not at the woman's current address, then Abdullah would have another option. He sighed, wearied by the continuous, convoluted options of getting back his Dhow.

Instructing Saeed to write down the street name and house number, he told his acolyte of the revised scheme. When they found out where the man lived they could then return to this street, search the woman's home and interrogate the 'slut'. Although he was convinced that his Dhow was in the house that they were now departing from, Abdullah knew it could wait for a little longer, his forward planning making sure that there was always another option. If not at the woman Kerry's current home, then the next casualty would be the man they were following.

Abdullah felt almost excited, so sure that the dénouement was coming, his glory to be written in annals and read over and over again by those who kept to the faith, his heroism and martyrdom recounted by many in the years to come.

Failure would not to be considered.

Chapter 41

Pete Spratt, inebriated, staggering, almost falling, just managing to grab hold of the railings, lolled against them, his right hand firmly gripping one of the iron bars for support. He could hear a voice mumbling, "Pete, I reckon you've had it. We'd better get you a cab. I think your evening is over! You're as pissed as a fart, you silly old sod."

Spratt slurred, "Nah, I'm not." And to prove it, he pushed himself, determinedly, off the railings, stumbled, legs all over the place, almost toppling to the ground. Quickly re-grabbing hold of the railings he swung himself, gracefully drunk, back to the railings for support, but facing away from the voices that were talking to him. He could hear women giggling, one muttering affectionately, "Silly fart, you're drunk; you aren't going to much use to us tonight."

Holding tightly on to the railings, he protested "Nah, not drunk," his legs giving way. "May...maybe a little pissed...can I cadge a bed for the night?"

The two women exchanged glances, the one with dyed blonde hair then glancing around at other available males exiting from the club. "I don't know, Pete. I need a man tonight and by the look of you, you're not the kind of man that's going to be of any use to me."

"Ah come on girls, you know that Pete Spratt has never let down a lady before."

"There's always a first time," riposted the dyed blonde, eyeing two likely males who were grinning inanely in their direction. "Pete," the dyed blonde smiled, "Sorry mate but we have to go." And the two women departed leaving Spratt holding onto the railings for dear life.

"Slags," he yelled after them, "Bloody slags!"

Oblivious, the two women linked arms with the two grinning males and disappeared off into the night.

Spratt sunk to the ground, the effort of holding onto the railings proving too much for his tired arm muscles. "Need a woman," he mumbled, "Need a woman, and a bed." Slumped on the ground, ignored by passing revellers, the cool night breeze massaging his temples, he felt a cold shiver travel through him then his stomach rumbled and his chest heaved. He had to find somewhere for the night.

It was a hell of trek back to his place and he knew from past experiences that very few cabbies would be happy to take someone in his condition, so he needed somewhere closer. Who? Struggling, he managed to pull the mobile phone from his pocket, his glazed eyes barely able to focus as he ran down the names. "Kerry," he mumbled, "She won't refuse me."

*   *   *

"Who's that phoning you at this time of night?" grumbled Siobhan as she poured two cups of strong black coffee, Kerry having left the kitchen with her mobile phone glued to her ear.

"Um, it was Spratt," she uttered quietly, unsure of herself. "He's nearby, a bit tipsy, and begs a place to sleep tonight." Kerry looked pleadingly at her friend.

"No, absolutely not," grumbled Siobhan. "No way!"

"Why not?" demanded Kerry, her voice heavy with petulance, like a daughter grounded by her mother.

"You *know* why Kerry," re-joined Siobhan, "And besides, I've already had to cope with one very drunk person tonight!"

"Actually, I've already said yes," snapped Kerry staggering out of the kitchen; she called over her shoulder, "I've given him the address and he's already in a taxi on his way."

"You have no right!" shrieked Siobhan storming after her friend, "This is *my* place, not yours!" Furiously grabbing Kerry by the shoulders, Siobhan shrieked into her friend's face, "He's *not* staying!"

"Ow, you're hurting me," protested Kerry, "Let go!"

The two friends glared at one another, both equally angry and very close to ending their friendship. Realising how strongly her friend felt, Kerry relented, her anger being replaced by cunning. Forcing a tear to her eye she petulantly wailed, "Okay, I'm sorry. I didn't think. I've been through so much recently." She sniffed, wiping the tear from her cheek and seeing the anger dissipate from Siobhan's eyes, she murmured, "But please, you tell Pete when he gets here. I couldn't face him now."

Siobhan searched long and hard into her friend's eyes, and then relented. "Oh, bloody hell, all right then Kerry. Although I don't like the idea of you and Spratt being in the same place at this time of night, he can stay...but on the couch!"

Kerry almost snapped an angry response back at her friend but quickly bit her lip, forcing a "thank you," instead of the stream of petulant invective that she really wanted to utter.

When Spratt arrived he was in a worse state than Kerry had imagined, she and Siobhan having to use all their strength in helping him into the Flat. With the women either side of him Spratt was half pulled, half supported towards the living room.

Staggering along the hallway, supporting Spratt as best they could, the two women managed to drag him to the sofa where all three fell in a tangled heap. He managed to plant a kiss on Siobhan's cheek whispering in her ear, "You're my favourite, Siobhan; why won't you give me a chance?"

"Sod off!" she hissed in reply

"What's...what's going on?" demanded Kerry, her eyes narrowing suspiciously.

"Oh, nothing," Siobhan hissed through clenched teeth, "Spratt's just pissed, he's being a prat."

Kerry glared angrily at Siobhan, blaming her friend, knowing that something had been said between them. Siobhan, exasperated, shook her head despairingly. Kerry managed to prop Spratt up but he gradually slide sideways, his torso spread over Kerry and his legs pinning Siobhan on the sofa. He fell asleep.

"Ah, bless him," soothed Kerry, lovingly, "He's fallen asleep."

"Bless him, my arse." Siobhan moved sideways, squirming, and managed to release herself. Pleased that Siobhan had removed herself from the sofa, Kerry wriggled until she was more comfortable, with Spratt's head resting in her lap.

Siobhan hovered over them, concerned both for her friend and her furniture, "What do you intend to do with him?" She quickly checked herself, realising what she'd just said, "No, I don't mean that; I *know* what you'd like to do with him. I'm more concerned with my stuff - I don't want to risk him dribbling, or spewing on the sofa or on my carpet."

"Show a bit of concern," retorted Kerry caustically, "He's not very well."

Siobhan favoured Kerry with a withering stare, which was totally ignored, her friend not in the least concerned regarding her lack of support.

Kerry gently caressed Spratt's hair and temple. "He looks so gentle and peaceful when he's asleep, like a lost little boy," she purred.

Kerry's words served only to annoy Siobhan, who snapped, "At least we know we're safe from his wandering hands when he's like that; at least we have to be grateful that he's not trying to get into our knickers!"

"He doesn't have wandering hands, but he does have charm and sex appeal." Kerry's eyes remained lovingly fixed on Spratt.

"Yea, right!"

Siobhan's tone caused Kerry to glance up and she snapped with feeling, "*You* wouldn't know what he's really like! I know him *intimately.*"

"Kerry, I don't want to be part of this conversation anymore. I'm going to leave you to sort the pig out. Just make sure that he isn't going to be sick; you'll find a bucket under my sink. Use it!" And Siobhan, angry, turned away, determined to leave Kerry with the responsibility of the problem that she had created.

"Jealous cow!" muttered Kerry under her breath but loud enough for Siobhan to hear. But Siobhan swept from the room, ignoring Kerry's childish remark. Shaking her head, she returned to her bedroom, sitting on the bed in silent, controlled anger.

Only a few minutes passed before Kerry knocked on her bedroom door and entered as Siobhan sat motionless, still furious, tensing, her lips pursed.

"Siobhan darling," Kerry voice was mellow, placatory, "Please don't be pissed off. I couldn't leave Spratty to his own devices in the state he's in and I promise that nothing will happen. I'll put him in my bed." Siobhan was glaring up in horror before Kerry hastily continued, "Of course, I won't be in the bed. Er, if it's okay with you, I'll sleep in your room?" Her eyes pleading, she implored, "Please Siobhan. You know it's the best thing. There's safety in numbers and Spratt will be out of harm's way; he can be safely tucked up on his own in a proper bed." She smiled cheekily, "Isn't that what you want? We can both be safe from the sex mad demon! Please agree, Siobhan. Please!"

Siobhan relaxed her stiff posture, a weary smile beginning to form. "You could always charm the birds from the trees. Alright then, but don't forget the bucket - leave it by the bed."

Delighted, Kerry almost skipped from the room.

Chapter 42

The Black Cab deposited a fatigued Ray in his home street, the fresh air making him feel slightly woozy. Paying the cabbie, he ignored the fine drizzle that spattered gently against his hair and shoulders, and paused, resting against a lamppost.

He remained stationary, not only to re-gather his thoughts but also because the combination of alcohol and reflected street lights - one of which seemed very bright, it's mazy, myriad shards of light reflecting off the droplets of rain as they zigzagged their way to the ground - finally caught up with him, causing his head to spin. Whilst he waited for his head to clear the sharp shards of light were gradually replaced by opaqueness as his eyes focused into the gloom. Instinctively, he picked out an unusual movement, a sudden freezing of a moving image. Rubbing his eyes Ray desperately tried to clear the fuzziness that now clouded his vision and straining, he focused into the distant murky, rain sodden night. Although nothing seemed to be moving he was sure that he had seen something, a frenzied movement, instantly stilled as the reason for the movement became aware that Ray had noticed its presence.

The hair on the back of his neck stood up, the skin on his nape beginning to prickle. A prehistoric feeling of danger and foreboding swept through him like a raging torrent, his mind quickly becoming alert, body sobering, Ray instantly becoming alive to danger, ready to fight or flee.

There was something there, an imperceptible movement, a slight nuance that yelled out a warning. Nothing that he could clearly see or discern but nevertheless, there *was* something.

Ray quickly glanced around him, determining his next course of action. He was utterly convinced that he was being watched, every nerve in body screaming out in unison. Some were urging him to run, turn and run for his life. Others were urging caution, to be careful, to make a plan for a secure and safe withdrawal. The nearest option was his flat but even if he did make it, open his door, escaping within, bolting the door behind him, then his pursuer would know his address and hunt Ray down at his leisure.

No, local knowledge was going to have to be Ray's saviour. He would lead his stalker away from his flat, his home, leading who he assumed might be a murderous bastard away through the alleys and byways that Ray knew intimately. He was determined that he was not going to be yet another victim of Sean's killer, for he was now utterly convinced that whoever was out there in the gloom must be the same individual who had done for Sean. But why? Why Sean? And now, why him? What was the connection? It couldn't simply be because they both knew Kerry; it had to be something else, something that no-one seemed able to figure out.

Ray knew all the various short cuts, the hidden obstacles that he would have to overcome to make his escape. Having taken many diverse routes to his home in the past, particularly on those occasions when he had imbibed too much and had had to find his way, almost blindfolded, to his front door, made him familiar with the local terrain like the back of his hand.

Girding his loins, he breathed in a lungful of air and stepping forward, immediately broke into a sprint, lurching forward across the silent, sodden road, entering a pedestrian alleyway on the other side. With his heart beating from the sudden exertion he could hear the blood pounding through his temples, the roaring in his ears matching the hurried thumping on the ground as his steps forced him onward, his shoes splashing, scattering the recently formed puddles of rain water, displacing the now dirty liquid into rivulets of brown, muddy water that flowed in an assortment of directions, the spray flying off before dispersing and dying into tiny trickles of fluid.

Ray ran and ran, ducking and diving into side streets, alleyways, leaping over back garden walls, tumbling over dustbins and across a disused builder's yard. With his lungs crying out for air, his legs no longer able to withstand the heavy and frenetic pounding of his escape, he finally came to a breathless stop outside a silent, closed launderette, his body almost doubling over as he wheezed air in and out through his vibrating lungs. Sucking in a desperate lungful of replenishing oxygen he calmed his beating, racing heart, listening, listening for sounds of his pursuers or pursuers.

He was aware that more than one person had been chasing him, initially hearing the sound of at least two pairs of feet. They had almost caught him but then something had happened, an almighty row sounding in his wake, a noise of metal containers being disturbed and accompanied by strange profanities that were beyond Ray's comprehension. As he continued his escape he had been cognisant that his potential enemies had fallen further behind, the sound of their footfalls receding into the distance. But not wanting to take any chances Ray had kept going, his legs pumping for all they were worth, running like he hadn't done for years, his feet having covered almost two miles through the side streets and alleyways of his familiar territory.

At last Ray felt safer; convinced that he had outrun his pursuers. Slowly recovering his composure, he straightened up, glancing in the direction of the normally busy premises of the launderette that now stood eerily silent, its earlier buzz and activity now a distant memory. The place was usually crammed with students, busy working mums, or bemused middle aged men, all trying to accomplish a successful turn round of their dirty clothes; the noise from the dryers competing with the rumbling drums of the washing machines. But now it was silent. Eerily silent, a silence that initially appeased Ray's racing heart but soon the stillness began to disturb him, the unreality of the situation beginning to gnaw at his being.

Ray sat down on a low wall outside the launderette and considered his options. Everything was becoming surreal.

Before, it had been others involved in this strange world, this dark, murky, sinister world of murder and intrigue. But now it was his turn; somehow he had been dragged into this situation, the scenario feeling him with an overwhelming feeling of gloom. How had he become involved in this situation? And what to do; Oh God, what to do?

*　　*　　*　　*

Abdullah had been convinced that he and Saeed would catch Ray. The pursuit, at first, had been a close run thing. Initially he was caught on the hop, surprised that the inebriated Ray had got wind of their discreet approach, his sudden turning away and legging it into the distance coming as a bit of shock to Abdullah. But almost as quickly he and Saeed had set off hot on Ray's heels; three pairs of feet pounding over the ground, six legs stomping down on the rain filled puddles at almost the same pace.

Indeed, Saeed was almost upon Ray, reaching out to grab the infidel's shoulder but then he stumbled, his foot catching on an unseen, discarded plastic bottle. Saeed went tumbling to the ground and Abdullah, immediately behind but at a slightly slower pace, had collided with Saeed's prostrate body, tripping over the man and was sent flying, clattering into a line of three, tall, metal bins that housed the waste from a Chinese restaurant. Momentarily dazed, he had allowed Saeed to help him to his feet then angrily shook off Saeed's supporting arm, swearing at the man, both for initially falling and subsequently for not keeping up the chase.

They had, fruitlessly, kept up some form of pursuit but Ray had long since disappeared into the night and after running round in no particular direction they had eventually given up the chase. Leaning against a brick wall of an end of terrace house Abdullah was breathing heavily, great streams of hot, moist air shooting out from his over-laboured lungs. He stood, breathing deeply, glaring at the younger but inept Saeed who was standing, watching him, the man's hands nonchalantly on his hips, the insolent dog seemingly already fully recovered from his exertions.

Abdullah scowled and pushed himself off the wall. "Right," he said, his voice almost rasping, "We'll get the woman first then we'll return for this man; he must live somewhere in that street where the taxi dropped him off." With a malevolent gleam growing in his eyes he continued, "By Allah, if my Dhow is not with the woman then we'll make her tell us where it is...and what number that man resides at!" He added, his voice ending in a vicious growl.

Saeed glanced around, his expression one of rising bewilderment. "Um," he pondered, doubtfully, "Do you know the way back to our car?"

Abdullah glared at Saeed, the dreadfulness of their predicament hitting him like a ton of bricks. "Of course," he thought, "What a fool. We're lost." But he wasn't going to admit that to Saeed, instead riposting, "You idiot!" he almost shouted, "Haven't you kept track of where we've been going; imbecile!"

Saeed stared with dismay at Abdullah, his bottom lip dropping in surprise. "Why is it my fault?" he thought, but wasn't about to argue with his psychopathic leader.

Thus rather than leaping straight into their car and speeding away to Kerry's current abode Abdullah spent what seemed like an eternity as he and Saeed trawled through the streets until, finally, they managed to locate their vehicle.

Fortunate that the unlocked car, keys still in the ignition, had not been stolen Abdullah climbed into the driver's seat. Picking up the London A-Z he threw it at Saeed, commanding, "Now guide me, idiot, and this time remember where we are and where we are going!"

In the darkness Abdullah was unaware of the look of pure hatred that Saeed pitched in the direction of his leader.

With Abdullah snarling at him as he turned on the small vanity lamp above the sun visor - how the hell did Abdullah expect him to read the A-Z in the darkness? - Saeed managed to locate the street where they had left Kerry's place earlier that night. This second journey had been an utter waste of time as far as Saeed was concerned but he was not about to voice his opinion or displeasure to his leader.

The return journey to Siobhan's flat was undertaken in total silence, other than the occasional profanity from Abdullah as Saeed had misdirected them a couple of times, and they finally made it back to the street where they had last seen Kerry.

"Now," mused Abdullah, "Now that Western harlot will pay. Oh, by Allah, she will pay!"

*　　*　　*　　*

Ray's initial feeling of euphoria, his triumph and joy at having escaped his pursuers was soon washed away. A sudden thunderbolt hit him. Obviously he was being targeted, pursued - the memory of the pursuers' pounding feet still echoing in his ears – but if they had been following him...then...they must have seen him drop Kerry and Siobhan off. "Oh my God," he cried out with sudden alarm, "Kerry must be in a danger. I have to ring her, warn her, and Siobhan!"

He reached into his pocket for his mobile but it was not there. He must have dropped it! Panic began to sweep through Ray as all sorts of weird and horrible images filled his mind. "What would those bastards do to his beloved Kerry...and Siobhan?" He barely noticed but subconsciously his thoughts showed equal apprehension for Siobhan, her welfare becoming almost of identical concern to that of Kerry's.

Running even faster than before he speed through the streets, stumbling and falling as he caught his foot on a kerb, grazing his cheek and spraining a finger as he tumbled. Regardless and without a second thought he picked himself up, calling out the girls' names in a futile warning gesture as he ran.

Finally, breathless, his sides aching, his lungs almost bursting, he reached his front door and tried to barge the door open barely before having inserted the key. Turning the handle, he flew head over heels into the hallway, almost cracking his head against the inner wall. With a bruise on his forehead to match the graze on his cheek he ran to the telephone and depressing the digits with a force that almost broke the buttons, hastily dialled Kerry's mobile.

With his breath slowly returning, he waited, phone pressed hard against his ear, desperately wishing Kerry to answer.

But there was no reply, the phone eventually transferring to Kerry's message service. With a sinking heart, he ranted, "Answer your phone Kerry; answer the bloody phone!"

Searching his mind, he tried to think of Siobhan's surname; he didn't know her home number or her mobile number, so the only chance was via directory enquiries. "But shit!" he muttered, "I can't ask for 'Siobhan' at her street, with no house number or surname!"

In desperation Ray dialled 999, but after being transferred to the Police, the Operator was most unhelpful, particularly as Ray's tale seemed fanciful and he didn't know the girls surname or house number, and he wasn't entirely sober either. The more the Operator tried to fob him off the more irate Ray became, the Operator threatening to send round a Squad Car, that is, if one had been available anyway! Finally losing interest, the woman at the police desk pulled the plug, determined that as she knew the caller's name and address, she would make sure that he did receive an unpleasant visit as soon as a car and crew were available!

Ray ended up shouting abuse down a dead line. Eventually realising that the operator had disconnected he threw down the receiver in anger and picking up his house keys flew out of his house, slamming the front door as he exited.

There was only one thing for it; he would have to go round to the girls and warn them. Dear God, he hoped he was not too late.

Chapter 43

Kerry stirred; she could hear Siobhan gently snoring, her breath gently sucking in and out whilst she slept on the other side of the double bed. But it wasn't Siobhan's snoring that had disturbed her sleep, it was something else. Tired and hung over, she barely opened one eye, confused as to why a dim light was penetrating the bedroom and almost instantly she discerned a figure suddenly blocking out this new beam of light. Abruptly both her eyes sprang open as she saw that the entering figure was Spratt, totally naked, approaching the bed whilst shivering, Kerry wasn't sure if he was shivering from being cold or in anticipation of the pleasure to come.

Spratt muttered, "Lovely; two warm women."

Kerry stared, disbelievingly but excited as Spratt walked to the base of the bed, lifted the duvet and gingerly slide his way under the covers, positioning his legs between the two sleeping women. Kerry couldn't resist a smile as Spratt muttered under his breath, "Ah, that's so much better, warm at last." He snuggled down, stretching his legs up the bed. Siobhan murmured, gently stirring in her sleep.

Kerry worked her toes down Spratt leg, stretching as far as she could, working her way up his inner thigh. Spratt reciprocated, both he and Kerry moving closer towards each other. Unfortunately Spratt's other leg made contact with Siobhan, his foot sliding up her thigh, under her nightdress. Siobhan murmured, slightly stirring, "What's going on?" But then sighed pleasurably..."Mmmm."

Feeling warm and comfortable, amorous and beginning to be aroused and with the growing belief that he was being encouraged, Spratt slide up the bed, his hands now caressing both Kerry's and Siobhan's thighs.

Siobhan woke, startled, "What the hell are you doing?"

Not realising that Spratt has been feeling them both, Kerry merely replied quietly, "Nothing; just stretching, sorry. Go back to sleep."

"Well do you mind not touching me up when you're stretching, you kinky bitch," Siobhan responded sleepily.

Spratt's hand rose higher on her thigh and Siobhan almost screeched, her head finally rising from her pillow, "What the hell are you doing, you pervert!"

"Oh, don't get your knickers in a twist; I'm a healthy female, with urges," snapped Kerry, determined that she was going to enjoy

Spratt and not realising what Spratt had been up to.

Siobhan virtually leapt from the bed, scared stiff that Kerry had lesbian tendencies. Rather than being angry she almost laughed with relief at discovering another shape in her bed. Siobhan's eyes darted from the shape under the duvet to Kerry's guilty eyes and reaching forward she smacked her palm down on where she considered the uninvited guest's genitals might be under the duvet.

Luckily she missed, Spratt's head emerging, a wide, boyish grin spreading over his face.

"You cheeky bastard!" Siobhan whined, mostly out of tiredness, "What the hell do you think you're doing?"

Spratt smiled, "I'm sorry; don't throw me out. I was bloody cold when I woke up in the other room and not knowing where I was I just wanted to get warm. Besides," he paused cheekily, "One of you girls needs to shave her legs!"

"You cheeky little shit!" Siobhan attempted to slap Spratt but he dodged away, edging closer to Kerry, Siobhan's hand swishing harmlessly through the air.

Kerry grinned.

Aware that Siobhan was now annoyed, Spratt pleaded, "Come on Siobhan; I really am freezing. I'll stay down the bottom of the bed. You're safe up at that end. Pleeeease." His pleading was that of a little lost boy, causing Siobhan to almost relent.

"Sod off Spratt," she decided firmly, "I'm not falling for that; come on, get out." And pulling back the duvet she recoiled in shock when she realised that he was naked, "Oh gross, you're stark bollock naked!" she shrieked, before forcing Spratt from the bed and from the room. "Bloody hell, I'm just too knackered for this crap. If you wake me up again Spratt, I'll stick my foot right up your naked arse!"

Ignoring Kerry's look of bitter hatred, Siobhan defiantly stumbled back to her side of the bed, climbed back onto the luxuriant warmth of her sheet and pulled her duvet over her shoulders, sinking her head blissfully onto her pillow.

Kerry, now wide awake, waited in the darkness, her breathing soft, quiet, waiting for Siobhan to go back to sleep. She was determined to get some action tonight and her stuffy, boring friend was not going to be allowed to stop her, Siobhan's flat or not! After what seemed like an eternity but in fact was only a few minutes

214

Kerry was satisfied that Siobhan had dropped back into her deep sleep. Gently, she rolled to the side of the bed and edged herself off; then softly tip-toeing, she left the bedroom, closing the door firmly but silently behind her.

Entering her own room, where Spratt was tossing restlessly, she stepped to the bed. Dropping out of her nightdress she gently tapped Spratt on the forehead, waiting excitedly for his eyes to open, her finger to her lips indicating him to be quiet. Her heart almost leapt, her loins almost melted, as her expectations soared at the eager and animated expression that spread across Spratt's face as soon as his eyes had focused on her naked body.

Without a word being spoken, she almost leapt into the bed, falling onto Spratt, their mutual lust devouring them with unbounded desire. Spratt's face, alight with anticipation, matched the desire written on Kerry's features; their bodies ready to engulf one another.

*   *   *   *

Ray ran down the street desperately seeking a taxi to get him to Siobhan's flat. It was at times like these that he wished he had bought himself a car but he hadn't had much use for a car in town up to now, going everywhere by bus, tube, or cab, and besides, parking the vehicle would have been a problem anyway. At this hour of the night the roads were virtually deserted and with no hope of seeing a passing taxi Ray stepped into the road, attempting to flag down a couple of passing motorists who swerved to avoid him, yelling profanities as they drove away from the maniacal figure of a man, wildly waving his arms up and down.

Almost pulling out his hair in desperation Ray ran back to his home, nearly ripping the front door off its hinges in his desperation to enter. Rushing to his dining room he yanked open one of the drawers of the welsh dresser and pulled out his copy of the yellow pages phone book. Hastily locating the page for taxis, he scrolled down the list until locating a twenty-four hour taxi firm that he knew was fairly local.

Not wanting to alarm the Controller he moderated his breathing, making sure that his voice was calm before anyone answered the call. Thinking quickly, he decided to say that he needed to get to his pregnant wife as a matter of some urgency, the wife staying at a friend's but now going into labour. Could they send round a car straight away?

The Controller, tired and beginning to feel slightly drowsy in the early hours before dawn quickly became alert at the urgency of the call. Yes, she did have one driver available and yes, the driver could be dispatched straight away. Haven been given the address by Ray the Controller stretched, lifted herself slowly and rose stiffly from her chair and went into an adjoining room where she gently kicked a dozing male reclining across a dirty threadbare sofa.

Grumbling, the man, bleary eyed, struggled to his feet then quickly regaining his composure, reached for a set of car keys hanging on a hook by the hatch in the Controller's room, and exited. His only thought being that when he dropped off his fare at the intended destination he would immediately drive away, for there was no way that he was going to take a heavily pregnant woman to maternity. Once before he had had a pregnant female passenger who had decided to give birth in the cab and he hadn't been happy at the clearing up he had to do, nor with the woman's constant pleas for God!

Chapter 44

Although it was still dark a dim glow from one of the street lights permeated Siobhan's room, fighting hard to overcome the blackness. Gently stirring from her deep, deep sleep, Siobhan thought that she could hear birds singing outside her bedroom.

But it wasn't really birds that had woken her; of course not, not at this time of night. It was something else. There it was again, a knocking sound. She turned over, turned away from the light that was creeping through her curtains, determined that whatever it was she was going to ignore it. She was going to enjoy her weekend lie-in come what may.

But the sound wasn't going to give in, the knocking growing louder, more persistent, more aggressive. Shit, she'd have to do something or else the neighbours would start to complain. With her mouth feeling like sandpaper, she muttered, "Drunk too much again - will I ever learn? I'm getting too old for boozy evenings." She licked her lips running her tongue over their length, and stretching, let out a gentle sigh. Siobhan resigned herself to getting up, seeing who was at the front door at this unearthly hour, get a glass of water, then get back to bed as quickly as possible.

Suddenly remembering Kerry, she thought, "Shit, Kerry disturbed my sleep last night, I'll make her get the door." Opening her eyes Siobhan was surprised to see that Kerry was no longer in the bed - nor in the room!

The heavy persistent knocking was replaced by the sound of broken glass and her bedroom wall vibrated at the same instant, an increasing rhythm, a tempo that beat against her wall. The new noise was accompanied by a loud moan of pleasure that increased in volume, a high pitched voice soon equalled by a deeper voice echoing equal happiness.

Realisation hitting her like a smack in the face Siobhan sat bolt upright, anger building within. It wasn't that she minded what Kerry was doing but who she was doing it with. She knew that Kerry would be hurt and that she was going down a road of futility and heartache. But suddenly Siobhan became confused; the sound of broken glass had been momentarily forgotten in the wake of the noise of Kerry's bed banging against her wall, her screams of ecstasy drowning out other thoughts. No, there was something else and Siobhan's blood froze as she heard the sound of footsteps pounding up her stairs.

Sweeping back the duvet she flicked on the bedside lamp, swung her feet onto the floor and stood up, hastily pushing her arms into her dressing gown barely seconds after her feet touched the carpet.

*   *   *   *

Abdullah leapt up the stairs and though tired through being up all night he felt a surge of energy, suddenly alive and recharged, zeal lighting up his eyes, his determination, his forthcoming triumph, etched on his face.

Reaching the landing, he went to open the first closed door. Expecting no resistance he was shocked when the door did not yield. It was locked! Snorting in anger and not wasting another second he charged to the next closed door along the landing and this time the door swung open, Abdullah almost falling headlong into the room in his haste. His eyes immediately focused upon a female, desperately securing her dressing gown as he entered.

Pulling the sides together to protect her modesty, the woman screamed, a blood curdling scream of abject terror and surprise.

Momentarily dazed by the woman's scream, Abdullah paused for a brief second, then he went for her, his blood lust up. She wasn't the woman he was after but he had to shut her up before his real target was overly alerted.

Through his subconscious he was aware of a noise, a banging on the bedroom wall, the sound and ferocity increasing in tempo with the moans and yells of a woman from the next room. Confused because he thought someone else was meting out justice to his intended target, he only paused fractionally before leaping on the frozen, static form of the terrified Siobhan.

As he grabbed her, the woman's legs buckled, the fear instantly turning her muscles into jelly. Taken off guard Abdullah fell forward, his grip on the falling woman loosened and he hit his head with a thump against her dressing table.

Abruptly shaken from her stupor of fear - the man's obvious profanities in a language she did not comprehend - somehow awakened Siobhan's instincts for survival; screaming desperately for Kerry, she scrambled to her feet, evading the desperately lunging hands of the man she assumed to be a potential rapist.

Leaping past her assailant, Siobhan almost bounced out of the bedroom, desperate to reach the protection of Kerry's room and yes, for the first time in her life, she would sink into Spratt's arms for protection. But Kerry's door was locked; thumping on the door and screaming in abject terror to be let in she could almost hear the sound of her pursuer's breath as he came after her.

Turning on her heels Siobhan ran across the landing, heading for her kitchen in the hope of grabbing a heavy pot, or a sharp knife...yes, a sharp knife, and sod the consequences from the police! She continued to shout for Kerry whilst running to the kitchen, where she pulled out a carving knife from a drawer. A bright shiny bladed knife that made her pursuer pause only inches from grabbing her as she had turned to face him.

The deadly glint in Abdullah's eyes was replaced, the eyes becoming wary but underneath he was calculating, working out in his mind if the woman had the courage to plunge the weapon into him and if she did, would she be able to strike a debilitating or mortal blow. His eyes reflecting equal measures of cunning and evil Abdullah was convinced that Allah would guide him.

Biting her lip, Siobhan held her breath, knowing that the next move could be her last or could be the one that saved her, getting her out of this mess. Either scenario was terrible, she equally did not want to be raped, violated, and similarly did not want to be a killer. "Bollocks! Double bollocks!" She thought, "Where the fuck is Kerry? Why isn't she or that prick Spratt helping me?" Running her fingers through her hair, her eyes roamed the room, Abdullah taking a step closer as he noticed her eyes wavering from him. She waved her knife at him, the intent to defend herself evident in her motions.

Slowly, through the ecstasy of their overindulgent love making Kerry became aware of Siobhan calling her name; her first thought being that Siobhan was furious with her for sneaking off to be with Spratt. Voice heavy with resignation she called out, "What's the matter, what's happening? What's all the cacophony about?"

"Help me! Open the bloody door!" screeched Siobhan, "I've got a rapist here!"

"Oh piss off," retorted Spratt gruffly, "Grow up you jealous bitch; just because you're not with a man."

"For Christ's sake, I need help. There is a man! An evil looking fucking pervert - please help me!" Siobhan pleaded.

Ready to take his chance, ready to lunge forward, convinced that he could swerve away from the intended knife thrust, Abdullah paused, his eyes flicking sideways, realising the someone could come up behind him.

Seizing her moment, the man's vicious eyes no longer fixed on her, Siobhan stepped to her right, ducked under his lunging arm and virtually flew from the kitchen, her feet barely touching the floor. She ran to the stairs, aware of the sinister figure only inches behind her. But then she stopped in her tracks. Her heart almost stopping, her adrenalin fuelled vision of escape blowing out like an extinguished candle, all hope sunk without a trace. For coming up the stairway was another figure, a dark, equally sinister shape, a companion to the evil behind.

Siobhan screamed involuntarily, a scream of dread and hopelessness, at the same time she could feel her attacker's hot breath on the back of her neck. About to spin round, to dig the knife, hard, into the evil rapist - at least she would get one of them she fleetingly thought - the man gripped her from behind, his hard, calloused hands firmly gripping the wrist of her knife wielding hand.

Abdullah, angry, fuming, determined, his energy channelled, focused, his goal nearly in sight, and forced her forearm firmly downwards. With an iron grip, fingernails gouging into her flesh, he twisted Siobhan's forearm, the pain excruciating, her grip loosening, the knife tumbling from her hand and almost skewering into her foot.

She emitted one final scream of frustration and fear before a sweaty, foul smelling hand was clamped firmly over her mouth. "Why hadn't Spratt and Kerry helped?" was her final thought before she passed out, the fear and dread having overtaken her other functions, her body deciding to shut down, to faint.

Abdullah almost lost his hold on the fainting Siobhan but quickly regained his composure, and with the assistance of the reluctant and dubious help of the belatedly arriving Saeed, who had seemed to take an eternity to mount the steps, he dragged the limp woman back towards the locked bedroom door. He could hear the frantic rustle of movement from within the bedroom, the muted whispering, voices tremulous, fearful, questioning but obviously unsure of what to do. They were also obviously cowards, not prepared to come to their friend's aid, their own safety being of paramount importance. He knew now that the rest of the task would be easy, he had the measure of his last two protagonists. Ah, the sweet rewards to come.

"Open the door!" he commanded, "Or I will kill the woman."

After what seemed like an intolerable pause, a terrified, quaky voice eventually responded, Kerry squeaking out, "Who...who are you?"

"Who I am is of no consequence," growled Abdullah, "But you have stolen something of mine and I want it back."

"I don't know what you're talking about; I haven't stolen anything," Kerry tremulously responded.

"My Dhow, stupid woman!" growled Abdullah, "My Dhow! *You* have my Dhow."

"Your Dhow?" queried Kerry, afraid and confused, racking her brains, trying to figure out what the man was talking about. "I don't know what the fuck you're talking about; what's a fucking Dhow?" Having grabbed the bed sheet to cover herself she stepped closer to the locked door but recoiled as Abdullah pounded his clenched first against the brown wood.

On her knees with her left shoulder propped against the wall Siobhan slowly regained consciousness, Abdullah's harsh voice reverberating through her ear drums, resounding through her gradually awakening brain. Her eyes flicked open, then quickly closed again, her brain telling her that it hadn't all been a nasty dream. This was reality, this was life, but not as she had ever envisaged. Nothing in her past had prepared her for this moment and although she wanted to scream again she resisted the urge. Scrambling to her feet and making a run for it would be no use; she knew that she would be no match for her protagonists. So she remained still, playing possum, her nerves tingling, her body aching to flee but her mind fighting, resisting the urge of the keyed up muscles, anxious in preparation of their attempt to make her body escape.

She couldn't understand why none of the neighbours had intervened, then she remembered that the neighbours on her left were on holiday and the woman on the other side always slept with her Walkman 'glued' to her ears, the woman's habit encouraged by too many years of light sleeping.

"My boat, my boat!" yelled Abdullah, tired of this game. "I am weary of this nonsense. If you don't give me my boat now, I will kill this woman then I will break down this door and make you both suffer!"

Realization suddenly hit Kerry as she croaked through the closed door, "Oh, you mean the silver boat that Sean gave to me?"

"Of course I mean *my* Dhow," boomed Abdullah, "You have no right to it."

"But Sean told me he had paid for it."

"It was not for sale; he did not buy it from me!"

"Oh, you can have it. I don't give a shit about it, in fact, I gave it to Pete...he's with me now," she turned to face Spratt just in time to see him sliding out of the bedroom window.

Kerry hadn't been aware of him slipping on his underpants, sneaking to the window, sliding it gently open and climbing over the sill.

"Pete...?" she queried, dumbstruck, her mouth agape, not knowing what to say. The little shit was abandoning her, jumping out of the window, leaving her to her fate.

"Come on babe, follow me," Spratt muttered belatedly and he had the gall to smile at her as his face disappeared below the window ledge.

"Pete, Pete!" she yelled as she ran towards the open window, "Don't leave me, you bastard." At the same instant the heavy thump of Abdullah's shoulder hit the closed door, his guttural cry resonating through the hallway as the doorframe rattled, the door shattering, shards of broken wood twisting inwards,

Kerry screamed in utter terror as she saw a sinister, hulking, fiendish looking brute leap through the broken door into the bedroom, his maniacal eyes boring into her and spittle of rage dripping from his mouth.

Chapter 45

Ray was relieved to see to see that Siobhan's street was still quiet as the taxi pulled into the curb. He hadn't been sure of the number but knew roughly which house and he knew he would recognize Siobhan's front door; it had a green Leprechaun door knocker - the only one in the street according to Siobhan.

As the taxi driver pulled up, he quickly garbled off the price shown on his meter, explaining to Ray that he had to rush off to another pick up. Ray was barely out of the cab, money paid, before the Cabbie drove away in a squeal of wheels, Ray staring aghast at the man's hasty withdrawal.

Then all hell seemed to break loose, a person dropping down from an upstairs window, quickly followed by the piercing scream of a female. Momentarily frozen, Ray stared in horror. "Oh God, that's coming from Siobhan's place...or at least I think it is!" he muttered, aghast.

Running forward as the body impacted on the ground with a resounding crunch, he could hear the crack as the person falling landed very heavily, obviously breaking a bone. The upstairs scream was matched by the howl of pain emanating from the fallen figure, a shirtless man, wearing only underpants and who quickly attempted to scramble to his feet but instantly sunk back to the ground, his broken leg unable to support his weight, a fresh howl of pain shrieking from his lips.

Ray's first thought, recognizing Spratt as the street light illuminated his love rival, was to wonder what the hell the man was doing here. Then quickly realizing what must have been going on - Kerry and Spratt spending the night together - he turned away, bitterly disappointed, angry at Kerry, but also peeved with Siobhan who had obviously allowed the liaison to take place in her home despite all her protests of disapproval of the relationship. Having turned away, Ray didn't see the shadowed face peering out from the bedroom window or notice that the man held a woman firmly in his grasp, his hand clamped forcefully over her mouth.

Spratt tried to crawl away, a splinter of broken bone pierced through the skin below his knee, the fibula having shattered under the impact of the fall onto the concrete paving slabs. He crawled, blood beginning to ooze from his wound, the pain bringing tears to his eyes and causing him to whimper like a beaten dog. "This is so unfair," he wailed to himself, "All I wanted was a guaranteed shag!"

*　　*　　*　　*

Dragging the terrified Kerry across the room, Abdullah yelled to Saeed to take hold of the woman whilst he pursued the injured man who had jumped from the bedroom window. "The man who was escaping, running away, is *the key*...he has the Dhow! I must get him," yelled Abdullah.

Unfortunately in the mayhem Saeed misunderstood and charged away down the stairs, intent on catching the escaping man, Abdullah's furious voice ranting in his wake.

Squinting through tiny slits in her eyelids Siobhan seized her moment and scrambling to her feet she pounced on Abdullah, leaping on his back, her hands gouging at his face. But she was no match for her powerful adversary. Shaking her free, he rushed forward with Kerry still in his grip and drove the whimpering Kerry's head forward, hard, into the banister.

Kerry was knocked out cold.

Abdullah turned to face the winded and dazed Siobhan, whose head had grazed the door frame when she had been sent flying. With an ominous, manic grin spreading on his face, his enraged eyes contradicting the apparently friendly lower half of his face, he clenched and unclenched his fist, then his eyes flicked to the discarded kitchen knife.

*　　*　　*　　*

Partially crawling, half rising on one leg, supporting himself against parked cars, Spratt managed to drag his body a considerable way along the street before he noticed Saeed flying out of the house, a vicious looking knife glinting in the man's hand.

Quickly realising that everything was not as it seemed, but still not sure what was going on, Ray had ducked down behind one of the parked cars, intent on determining the lie of the land before deciding on a course of action, for he knew that he couldn't abandon the girls; hoping above hope that Kerry and Siobhan were still alive. Also, if they were harmed then it would serve no purpose by him changing into the house; but he determined that if the bastards had hurt or killed the girls, then...

Spratt cried, pleading, as the sinister figure approached him. Unable to support himself any longer he slumped to the ground, the wincing pain of his broken leg once again hitting the ground causing him to cry out in unbelievable agony.

"Please don't kill me," he cried, tears rolling down his cheeks, "All I wanted was sex."

When the charging Saeed drew level, Ray leapt from his hiding place, launching himself at the surprised, unprepared enemy, his fist raised and connecting on the unsuspecting foe's temple. Saeed crumpled to the ground like a pack of cards, the blow knocking him unconscious. Ray's momentum caused him to land on top of the collapsing Saeed and rolling clear in one swift movement, he scrambled to his feet, prepared to continue his assault on the bearded stranger. His fists clenched, he took a wary pace towards the prone man, the wariness quickly succumbing to relief and joy when he realized that his enemy was not about to rise up. Unbelievably, it didn't register for a second but then it sunk in; he had struck lucky, inadvertently knocking the man out cold!

Ray turned away from the prone Saeed, towards the cowering figure of Spratt.

Spratt looked up, his expression bewildered, surprised, the tears still rolling down his cheeks, his sunken eyes expecting the worst. Slowly, comprehension began to dawn and he pleaded through his sobs and pain, "Quick, the fuckers were about to kill me. Help me get away. There's still another one of the bastards in Siobhan's flat!" And he reached out his arm in anticipation, expecting Ray to help him and support him out of this mess.

Ray stood looking down at the pathetic figure of Spratt. "What about the girls? What's happened to Kerry and Siobhan?" he demanded.

"Dunno mate," muttered Spratt unconcernedly, "These guys are complete fucking nutters! Just help me get away." He looked up imploringly, his arm still outstretched whilst he partially attempted to pull himself up by using the door handle of a car.

Ray remained motionless, lips pursed, feeling nothing but contempt for Spratt.

"Look, you prick!" grumbled Spratt, "Your life is in danger too. If you don't help me then we're both fucking dead!"

"I'm not leaving without Kerry and Siobhan," snapped Ray.

"You're too late you prat," snapped Spratt, his words subdued, the pain making his attempt at shouting back at Ray ebbing into almost a wail. "They're dead and you will be too! Help me."

"You bastard!" snapped Ray, his eyes blazing, "You bloody little shit; you've just left them. I've got to go and check." He turned contemptuously away from Spratt just as Abdullah was exiting the building, Siobhan held tightly in his grasp, his hand cupped over her mouth. Whispering in her ear, Abdullah removed his hand from her mouth and pulled the kitchen knife free from his belt.

Ray's heart almost leapt when he saw that she was alive; she looked pale, ashen, her hair matted with sweat and blood; he noticed the graze on her temple. Her terrified eyes pleading for help. But she was still alive! He couldn't believe the feeling of euphoria and was about to rush forward when he realized that Abdullah held a knife in his hand.

Abdullah quickly took in the fact that Saeed had been incapacitated, Saeed's knife lying by the side of his body. The fool had allowed himself to be killed he thought. A momentary doubt flashed through his mind but was quickly replaced by renewed resolve. He still had this woman and would use her. He advanced towards the stationary man, the man who initially had seemed about to charge towards him but had suddenly stopped in his tracks. Perhaps the Westerner coward was afraid.

Glancing downwards Ray also spotted the discarded knife and in one swift movement bent down to retrieve it. He then looked up in the direction of the menacing eyes of the approaching Abdullah, still dragging Siobhan, her feet scuffing along the pavement.

Abdullah paused. This was not going to be as easy as he had thought. The man was going to fight, not flee.

They were both distracted as Saeed's leg suddenly twitched, the man releasing an unearthly groan.

"The fool is still alive," joyfully mumbled Abdullah in Arabic, "I can still make use of him."

Seeing his foe's eyes light up Ray hastily stepped over the prostrate figure of Saeed and raising the man's concussed head, he held the blade of the knife against Saeed's throat. "Release the woman or I will kill him!" demanded Ray, his voice much more stern, more commanding than he actually felt.

Abdullah merely grinned, the evil, maniacal grin that had earlier caused Siobhan to shiver uncontrollably.

It was a stand-off, both men determined, their eyes locked in an equal measure of resolve and purpose.

Ray began to have doubts, his bravado wavering. He could see Siobhan getting weaker, the colour almost drained from her features, her face expressing utter despair, defeat. Thinking furiously, he came up with a proposal. "Look, we both have captives. If you release the woman, I will let you take your friend away."

Abdullah did not respond, merely staring relentlessly into Ray's eyes, weighing up the options, the possible alternatives in his own twisted mind.

A frown began to spread across Ray's forehead, the lines growing into deeper grooves. He wondered why no one had intervened from the nearby homes but it was still early dawn and the weekend to boot. No doubt most people were sleeping off hangovers. He hoped above hope that one of the neighbours may at least have telephoned for the police. "How long before they get here?" Ray hopefully speculated.

"I have a proposal my friend," said Abdullah, his words slow, deliberate, "Your friend over there," he nodded his head in the direction of the slithering Spratt's body, Spratt trying his utmost to crawl under a parked 4X4 Range Rover, the closer Crossfire Sports car not providing him enough protection.

Pulling Saeed's head further back, almost breaking the man's neck, Ray allowed himself a quick glance in Spratt's direction.

"If you give me what you friend has stolen I will release the woman," continued Abdullah.

Ray called over his shoulder, "If you've stolen something from this guy, Spratt, I suggest you give it back - now!"

"I ain't got nothing of his," replied Spratt weekly, his voice muted as he crawled under the car.

"He has my Dhow!" thundered Abdullah, "Give me my Dhow and I will let her go."

"Your Dhow?" queried Ray.

"Yes, my Dhow," snapped Abdullah, "It's an Arabic boat."

"I know what a Dhow is," responded Ray, "But I don't understand?"

"It's a silver Dhow, mounted on a wooden base!" retorted the exasperated Abdullah.

"Ah, now I follow." Ray called over his shoulder. "Have you got his Dhow, Spratt?"

"Kerry gave me a fucking silver boat if that is what this is all about," Spratt responded weekly, his wish to be elsewhere growing with every second.

"Well, give him the Dhow, you numbskull."

"It's in my flat," Spratt didn't want to talk any more, his words fading to a whisper.

Abdullah's eyes lit up at the confirmation of the location of his Dhow. But now, how to get hold of it, at the same time disposing of these infidels?

"We'll give you the man's address and his keys," advised Ray, "And you can let the woman go."

"He's not having my address...or my keys," retorted Spratt, fearful of what may occur in the future, a maniacal dark skinned man entering his house and plunging a six inch blade into his chest.

"Shut the fuck up Spratt," growled Ray, "You don't have a fucking choice!"

"It's not that simple my friend," smiled Abdullah, the smile making Ray wince. "If I release the woman, get the keys, then go to the man's flat, who do you think would be waiting for me - the police." He scowled. "Don't take me for a fool!"

"Well, how do you propose..."

Abdullah impatiently interrupted, "I will take the woman and your cowardly friend back into that house," he pointed by nodding his head in the direction of Siobhan's flat, "And you can take my friend with you to secure the Dhow, bringing it back here. Then we will do an exchange. You can use my vehicle." He indicated the car that had brought him and Saeed to the location. "But if you betray me or call the Police, I will slit their throats," he added with growling menace.

"Bugger off," muttered Spratt, "I'm not going back in that place with the fucking loony!"

Ray pondered the proposal and despite Siobhan's pleading eyes pleading with him not to leave her, he reluctantly nodded his agreement.

Abdullah reached into his pocket, pulled out the car keys and threw them at Ray.

"How do I know that your friend won't attack me when I'm driving; he's not fully conscience now, but when he recovers, I..."

"You can tie him up," interrupted Abdullah, "There's a roll of cord on my back seat; I was going to use it to secure the woman Kerry when I abducted her."

"You bastard," growled Ray, his hackles up again.

Abdullah's eyes flashed in anger, "Don't be stupid," and with the knife indenting but not piercing Siobhan's neck, growled, "Let's get this over with."

Reluctantly, Ray hastily secured Saeed's hands and feet and then dragged the man, placing him in the passenger seat of Abdullah's vehicle. To be doubly sure, Ray also tied Saeed to the seat itself; he was not about to take any chances with these murdering bastards. Fortunately, Saeed's concussed brain was still not functioning correctly and he allowed Ray to manhandle him without too much protest, but his eyes registered confusion and doubt, his brain not understanding why his leader was letting him be treated like this. Ray slammed the passenger door shut.

Dragging Spratt from under the car was not too much of a problem despite Spratt's breaking finger nails embedding in the tarmac being testament to his initial resistance as he desperately tried to claw beneath the surface of the road. Surprisingly, and despite his injuries, he fought like a tomcat, the fear of being left with Abdullah making him hysterical with fear; Ray had to thump him, a swift blow to the chin knocking the already fading body into a welcome respite from the excruciating pain. Even though it was not the best of circumstances Ray felt an immense amount of satisfaction, doing something to Spratt that he had wanted to do for many months!

Looking up, Ray considered the option of attacking Abdullah but the man's cold, venomous eyes seemed to read his mind, the evil eyes flicking from Ray to Siobhan, and then to the kitchen knife which was gently caressing Siobhan's exposed neck. The message conveyed by the eyes was explicit; any attempt on Abdullah would result in the woman's life being instantly terminated. Ray knew that the man would have no qualms.

Abdullah stepped aside as Ray dragged Spratt back into the house, dropping him just inside the front door. Racing up the stairs his heart stopped a beat when he saw Kerry lying lifeless on the carpet, a trickle of blood oozing from her head. Quickly touching her neck he felt for a pulse and was ecstatically relieved when he realised that she was still breathing. Noticing that the sheet was revealing more than it should, he pulled it up to Kerry's shoulders, protecting her modesty as best he could. Finding Spratt's jacket and trousers in the front room and fumbling through the pockets he located the key to Spratt's flat and then flew back down the stairs and out, almost in the waiting arms of the increasingly impatient Abdullah.

Having found Spratt's driving license Ray new the address he was heading for but he drew from Siobhan the best and quickest way to get there, departing on the assurance that not only would he certainly be back but that the exchange would take place only if both women were still alive, unharmed and, reluctantly added, also if Spratt was kept alive.

Chapter 46

The journey to Spratt's address was fitful; Ray's brain working furiously, thinking of ways how to notify the police yet keep Kerry and Siobhan safe.

Twice he had inadvertently jumped a red light, his eagerness to secure the Dhow and return to the girls of paramount importance. Luckily for Ray his dangerous, reckless journey had been carried out in the latter part of night, just before the early embers of dawn, thus he avoided harming other members of the public, the traffic being almost non-existent at this time of the night/early dawn. Navigating through the main roads and on to the even quieter side roads his cornering at breakneck speeds resulted in the heavy squeal of tyres, the burnt rubber smouldering on the cold tarmac as he turned each successive corner.

Luckily for Ray the traffic police were also non-existent, their reduced manpower resulting in a lack of visibility, men being replaced by eerily silent speed cameras and the occasional CCTV unit, all currently useless to either stop Ray in his tracks or to subsequently mount a successful traffic prosecution; the vehicle in which he was traveling did not exist in the computer at the DVLC in Swansea.

More through luck than judgment Ray made it, gripping the vehicle's steering wheel, his knuckles white, his fingers firmly locked around the leather cover of the steering wheel, his brow knotted in intense concentration. Sweeping into Spratt's road he counted down the numbers, quickly locating Spratt's home, then turned to face the now more attentive Saeed, the slightly concussed man's malevolent eyes gleaming through the darkness at him, his arms pulling restlessly at his bonds. Now looking closely at his captive's face something about him seemed familiar; he knew the face but how, where, when? However for the moment he had more important issues to deal with.

Ray was facing a dilemma. "What to do?" he mused, "If I leave the man here in the car he's more than likely to be noticed before I can get back with the Dhow or he could yell out, attracting attention, and I don't know where in Spratt's flat the Dhow may be so I don't know how long it'll take me."

Saeed seemed to sense his captor's thoughts; his eyes began to gleam brighter and a twitch of a wicked smirk began to form on his face but was quickly replaced by an almost vacant, sullen expression.

Ray was not fooled; he had discerned the awakening of thought in the man's eyes. He had seen a glimmer of hope, a preparation of a plan. "Even if he escapes I'll still have the Dhow and that seems to be the key in getting the girls released," Ray pondered. "But if he does escape will the other man believe that his friend has escaped and that I haven't turned him over to the police? Would he still release his captives or would he harm the girls?"

Ray was motionless with indecision.

Then his mind was made up for him, the indecision being swept away in a sea of action, the indecisiveness, the dithering no longer an issue. Saeed had loosened his bonds, Ray's ability to tie secure knots being found out at the worst possible time. Pulling himself free from his restraints and in one continuous action he lunged forward, his freed arms reaching out for Ray's vulnerable neck, the man's hot, sour breath on his cheek, permeating Ray's sensory facilities. Ray's head, despite the fierce grip of the man's hands clamped on his neck, recoiled, backing away from the man's pungent breath.

The impetus from Saeed and the natural reaction of his recoiling, forced his head against the driver's window, the crown hitting the glass with a heavy thump. He tried desperately to break free from his attacker's vice-like grip but the man's hold was too strong, the man's fingers getting tighter round Ray's neck, forcing the air from his windpipe. His breathing at first heavy and energetic was now becoming increasingly shallow and laboured and he knew he was losing and had to do something quickly.

Ray struggled desperately, frantically, knowing that he was running out of time, the man's initial surprise attack having given his opponent the advantage; he kicked out against the floor of the car, his ankles scraping on the brake and accelerator pedals, his right foot trapped between the two pedals. Ray desperately pushed down, the sides of the pedals gouging out abrasions and cutting into his ankle, but getting his foot pressed against the floor, he pushed up with all his strength, managing to raise his head higher against the backrest of the driver's seat, Saeed's grip slightly reducing, the man's position making his frightening hold impossible to maintain. To compensate, Saeed shuffled his body forward and upwards but in doing so he slightly released the intense pressure on

Ray's neck.

Sucking in a huge mouthful of air Ray made one last concerted effort and with his only available weapon, his head, he slammed it forward, crashing the forehead into his protagonist's temple. The crack of the man's bone, Ray's head hitting in the same weakened point of flesh where his earlier punch had rendered the man unconscious caused his attacker's eyes to glaze, the man losing focus, his grip on Ray's neck almost released.

Although his head was swimming in a hazy swirl of growing incomprehension Saeed was not about to give up and with a final vestige of fanatical determination, copying his opponent's tactics, he smashed his head forward intending to inflict a knockout blow just as the infidel had done to him. Ray dodged, tilting his head sideways, breaking free from Saeed's grip, the man's thrusting head missing its connection, his cheek merely brushing against Ray. Saeed knew he was losing consciousness from the effect of the renewed blow to his head but before his brain finally succumbed, reducing his body to its earlier comatose state, his mouth made contact with Ray's ear and he snapped his teeth together, biting down hard on Ray's earlobe.

Ray inadvertently howled in pain, the man's teeth sinking deeply into his flesh. Pulling free, the pain was excruciating, the blood beginning to trickle then stream onto the shoulder of his shirt. Furious and in pain he pushed Saeed away, the man's jaw still locked on a tiny part of Ray's earlobe now no longer part of Ray's body, the man's teeth haven bitten deep, ripping a tiny section of Ray's ear clean away.

Ray couldn't believe how much it hurt and with pent up fury he punched the unconscious Saeed in the face, breaking his attacker's nose in a crunching sound of tissue and cartilage.

Rummaging in his trouser pocket he pulled out a handkerchief and pressed it firmly against his ear, stemming the flow of blood. He then sat motionless, recovering his thoughts, his breathing returning to normal, his mind becoming aware of the first twittering of the early morning birds and in the distance the very early glow of dawn's light. He knew that he had to move quickly and had to come up with a plan that would guarantee the girl's safety.

Discarding the handkerchief he climbed from the vehicle and went to the front passenger door. Without any ceremony and no longer interested in niceties he dragged Saeed's body from the car, the man's head hitting the hard tarmac with a thump. With total disregard and anger he dragged the limp body to the rear of the car with the dual purpose of keeping his antagonist hidden from any unsuspecting member of the public and, most importantly, to prevent further any further altercation taking place.

Raising the boot lid he froze, his arms lifeless, Saeed being unceremoniously dropped to the ground adding a few more bruises to the man's already battered body. Ray's mouth was agape but instantly he recoiled in shock and horror as three flies flew off from a body in the boot just missing contact with his left ear. The shock was quickly replaced by revulsion and a nauseous growl from his stomach, the foul horrific smell explaining fully the pungent odour that he had been aware of during his journey but which was now released in its full gut wrenching stench.

Opening and closing his mouth, both as a combination of keeping the rising bile in his throat and from the horror and revulsion of seeing a dead policeman, the man's face frozen in shock and obvious pain, the body having released fluids and solids in its dying seconds. Repugnance flowed through him like a river bursting its banks and now he really did feel sick, sick to the core, the policeman's eyes staring up at him in macabre death mask.

Not knowing what to do, his mind churning, the knowledge that the people chasing Kerry really were this ruthless; stomach heaving and temples pounding, he walked round in circles, confused, afraid, shocked, almost delirious. But the thought of Siobhan and Kerry reasserted themselves in his mind and he began to calm his brain bringing it back to rationality; without any consideration he hauled Saeed's body into the boot and slamming the lid shut and turned away, striding purposely to Spratt's home. His mind was working furiously, mulling over every possibility of ensuring the safety of the hostages.

An idea hit him; the man who might just be the key, Detective Sergeant Morris, a non-politically correct policeman. A policeman who had learnt his job the hard way and had come up through the streets; a proper policeman who would put thoughts of saving members of the public over and above a macho, ignorant attitude of shooting first and asking questions later. "Where did I put his number?" he mumbled.

Fumbling with the keys as he unlocked Spratt's front door Ray stumbled, feeling his way inside the flat. Desperately groping for a light switch and praying that Spratt lived alone he felt both walls of the hallway, his fingers eventually connecting with the raised metal base of the light switch. Turning on the light he paused with bated breath, ready to meet head on any new challenge that might present itself; but all was quiet. Hurriedly pulling out his wallet, he rummaging through the contents in desperate hope that he had left D.S. Morris' card inside; he almost cried with relief when the card was located.

Rapidly exploring Spratt's deserted flat Ray located a telephone in the sitting room and dialled the number; whilst waiting for a response his eyes scanned the room, seeking out the sought after boat. It wasn't in the sitting room.

Detective Sergeant's Morris' mobile phone rang and rang but there was no reply; finally Ray was switched to voicemail and he swiftly explained who he was, giving a brief summary of the situation, "Hi Sergeant Morris, its Ray Maloney. We met after Sean O'Malley's murder. Sean's girlfriend and two other people are being held hostage by a murderous thug. He's more than likely the person who must have killed Sean. They've also killed a policeman; I've got his body in the boot!" Ray gave Siobhan's address and added, "He sent me to collect a boat, a Dhow, which apparently belonged to him. But it's imperative that I get back, for Siobhan and Kerry's safety! I've also got the thug's accomplice locked in my boot; will explain more later. If you get there before me be careful for the girl's sake because I'm sure the guy will kill the hostages without a moment's thought. I'll meet you at..." then the phone cut out.

Ray felt that that was all he could do for the present and locating the bathroom he found a small first aid kit, stopping his bleeding ear with a small plaster. Speedily searching the rooms, he found the Dhow sitting on a dresser in Spratt's bedroom. Staring disdainfully at the unmade bed a lump formed in Ray's throat, his mind working overtime with thoughts of the antics that Kerry and Spratt must have got up to in this room. Shaking his head free from such unpleasant thoughts he scooped up the Dhow, rushed out from the flat, slamming the door behind him as he exited.

*   *   *   *

The return journey to Siobhan's home was even more fraught than his outward journey. The dim glow of the dawn was fighting hard to overcome the blackness, the roads beginning to fill up with the early morning traffic. Ray had jumped two red traffic lights and had been extremely fortunate that a white van had missed him by inches, the irate driver gesticulating out of his window, his face grimaced, a tirade of obscenities pouring from the man's wide mouth, the words lost on the preoccupied Ray.

Reaching Siobhan's street Ray brought the car alongside the kerb in a screech of brakes, the available kerbside parking spaces now easier, a couple of the street's residents having already departed on their way to weekend retreats.

Leaping from the car Ray was dimly aware of the early morning sounds of nature, the nascent dawn stirring the hungry birds into life. He could hear the chirruping birds, singing, a pair of nesting starlings exchanging pleasantries with a nearby flock of starlings perching in a London Plane tree located outside Siobhan's back bedroom; the soft tune incongruously pleasant against the background of dread that was building within Ray's chest. The starlings were rudely and suddenly disturbed by a marauding magpie, it's warbling call disturbing the calm, its appearance foreboding, a warning of portent danger.

Ray paused, realising that he was being reckless and far from saving Siobhan, Kerry, and that arsehole Spratt, he would probably only get them all killed. There was no sign of Sergeant Morris or any other police presence so it was all down to him to extricate his friends. He realised that he was scared, terrified, not for himself but because if he made the wrong move it would result in the death of the woman he loved. "Oh Kerry, I hope I make the right decision," he mumbled to himself but confusingly the picture in his mind was not of Kerry but that of Siobhan.

Ray shook his head trying to clear his thoughts and the growing feeling of dread. He looked up at Siobhan's windows; the place was in darkness, the curtains drawn back but none of the lights switched on. Although the early efforts of the dawn light were attempting to light up a new day, Siobhan's flat remained in an eerie darkness.

Ray returned to the car, locked the doors, and made sure that the boot was still secure. He listened quietly, his ear pressed against the metal of the boot but it seemed that his prisoner was still unconscious, or dead! Ray shuddered at the thought; although his life had been in danger it was not in his nature to take someone else's life.

Glancing back at the Dhow resting on the passenger seat he stepped away from the car, taking in his surroundings, looking for a suitable place to hide the key. He had to have a bargaining tool and there was no way that he was going to march into Siobhan's flat with the car keys in his pocket. It would then have been a reasonably simple matter for the evil protagonist to overpower him, take the keys, and kill them all. It was evident to Ray that his adversary would show little or no mercy, the man's cold, evil eyes confirming the nature of his previous killings.

Ray noticed a dustbin positioned just inside the railings of a house three doors down from Siobhan. Crouching down and reaching inside he pressed his hand against the side of the dustbin, resulting in the dustbin tilting slightly, leaving a small gap underneath. Stretching with his other arm he placed the car keys underneath the dustbin and then let the dustbin gently drop back to its resting place. Standing upright, he glanced around but the street was still deserted, no one seemed to have noticed his actions.

Girding his loins, his heart thumping inside his chest, Ray made his way to Siobhan's flat and tentatively knocked on the broken door. Getting no response he tentatively knocked again, slightly harder, but the door remained closed, only a deafening silence emanating from within. The delay seemed interminable and now he desperately needed to use a toilet. Shuffling from one foot to the other he banged firmly on the front door, his fist pounding against the hard wood. Ominously there was still no reaction, no reply. Throwing caution to the wind, his dread of the girls' fate now overtaking his fear, he grabbed the handle, pulling it down, the door slightly opening; surprised that the door was not locked and full of trepidation, he pushed the door fully ajar. Silently, gently, Ray slowly entered, his muscles tensed, his fists balled, ready to fight.

It was eerily quiet and still, other than an overpowering smell that invaded his nostrils; Ray had a flashback to the policeman's face in the boot of the car and an intense feeling of dread enveloped him. An overwhelming sense of sadness swept over him, his pulse racing, the hair tingling at the back of his neck, his worst fears being realised almost instantly, a large pool of crimson fluid on the hallway carpet.

Letting out a wail of anguish, heedless of his own safety, he ran up the stairs, charging blindly forward. Reaching the landing, Ray stopped in his tracks, the gruesome sight of Spratt's pained, tearful face staring up at him. The face, although etched in fear and pain, was clean and clear, in stark contrast to the jagged, ugly tear that stretched almost entirely round Spratt's throat. The body tissues mixed with skin and congealing blood, a pool of the darkened liquid on the carpet by Spratt's head, the surplus blood having trickled through the banisters and down onto the hall carpet. Spratt had obviously vacated his bowels, the foul smell surrounding his dead body pervading the air, incongruously reminding Ray of a trip he had made to an abattoir with his school many years ago. His school teacher had been a vegetarian and it was her idea to put all her pupils off eating meat; it hadn't worked with Ray then, but it might now!

He gagged, wanting to vomit but instead let out a wail of anguish before charging into one of the bedrooms, desperately afraid, terrified of what he might find; the room was empty. Searching the other bedroom and the rest of the flat he soon concluded that it was empty, deserted, with the exception of Spratt's lifeless body.

No longer able to contain himself Ray rushed to the toilet, managing to relieve himself before his feeling of nausea took over. Barely finishing peeing, he lent forward into the bowl, his gagging and retching enough to disturb the sleep of the dead, barely pausing before wiping his mouth with toilet paper, he flushed the loo, then turned back staring morosely at Spratt's body locked in rigor mortis.

He had to discover Siobhan and Kerry's fate? Surely the homicidal bastard wanted his Dhow, he wouldn't have left without it; surely not? A sudden thought struck Ray and he rushed to the front bedroom window. "Of course, what an idiot!" he thought, "The man was obviously waiting, hiding somewhere nearby, and now he's probably got the car, having watched me hide the keys. What an idiot I've been. Bollocks!"

Ray fully opened the window, expecting the car either to be gone or at the very least its window smashed and the Dhow gone. But now, through the growing brightness, he could clearly see the car, untouched, undamaged, and parked exactly where he had left it. "It doesn't make sense," he mused, "Why would the man leave with the girls but without the Dhow?"

Fatigued, weary, an immense feeling of dread and sorrow enveloping him, Ray turned away from the window scratching his head, not knowing what to do. He'd have to dial 999 that was for sure but would it be too late for Siobhan and Kerry?

Stepping towards the telephone residing on a table in the landing, he abruptly noticed that there was a sheet of notepaper placed under the phone. Snatching it up, he quickly scanned the contents. It was from the homicidal maniac, the paper dirty with blood stained fingerprints, the man either careless or contemptuous of being caught. "Or perhaps he doesn't care?" thought Ray.

The message triumphed over the vindictive killing of Spratt and warned that an equally similar fate would meet the women if Ray didn't follow instructions; no police were to be called and any sign that they were involved would result in the immediate death of the western harlots. There would be no mercy.

One of the women's mobile phones had been left and Ray was to leave the premises and await a call from Abdullah. The man was also not afraid to leave his name, seemingly having no fear of the authorities or of being caught. The murdering bastard certainly had absolutely no fear of his enemies or of death, stating that his mission - yes, he confusingly wrote the word 'mission' - was blessed by Allah. "What the hell is that all about?" mused Ray. "How can you fight against such people?" He agonized.

Glancing around the room his eyes fixed on the mobile phone discarded carelessly on the sofa. Scooping it up, he hurried from the room; he had to get out of Siobhan's flat before Sergeant Morris or any of his colleagues reached the place. Now it was entirely up to Ray to save Siobhan and Kerry, for he knew that his adversary would have no mercy, no compassion, and if any suspicion was aroused that the authorities were after him he would end the girls' lives in a twinkling of an eye.

The man was pure evil, but more than that he was obviously a zealot, believing that his evil deeds were actually sanctioned by a God. Perhaps he was a terrorist? There was no reasoning with people such as him.

Ray knew he would have no choice but to kill his adversary. There was no other way. Stepping over the stinking remains of Spratt's body, Ray could not help thinking of the price that Spratt had paid; all the man had wanted was a bit of fun.

Chapter 47

Abdullah had made Siobhan drag the unconscious Spratt up the stairs, the strain of partially supporting, partially dragging Spratt's deadweight body putting an intense strain on her every muscle and sinew. She thought that her heart was about to burst but the fear, and the adrenaline, gave her the energy necessary.

Aware that she was no match for the thug who kept his malevolent eyes on her, the sharp knife gripped menacingly in the man's hand, she determined that their only hope was to do as the man said and hope and pray that Ray could find the means to rescue them. After all, he was bound to get help. Besides, she was absolutely exhausted from her efforts and even if the opportunity had arisen for her to either pounce on the thug or to make a break for it she knew that she would have been no match against him; but regardless, she wouldn't have deserted Kerry anyway.

Having made the reluctantly obedient Siobhan tie up both Spratt and Kerry with dressing gown cords obtained from the women's bedrooms, Abdullah positioned the two captives sitting on the landing, their backs against the stair banisters.

Abdullah had searched Siobhan's flat, the woman held securely in front of him, his knife against her neck as he shuffled her from room to room, tipping her flat upside down. His search was for two purposes, firstly to ensure that his precious Dhow was not on the premises but also to find a suitable means of tying up his third captive. Having failed to find anything equal to the two dressing gown cords he pulled out three pairs of tights from one of Siobhan's drawers. They would have to do.

Forcing Siobhan back into the landing, he ordered her to lie face down on the floor before securing her hands behind her back, the material of one pair of tights proving particularly successful, the tightness of the bound pinching Siobhan's skin and making her wince with the pain. Using the remaining two pairs of tights he tied her legs together and also those of the now awakened Kerry who began whimpering and crying, trying to understand what was going on. Abdullah was not too bothered about securing Spratt's legs as he knew that the man could hardly walk let alone run.

The wait had been interminable, the man who had gone with Saeed seemingly to take for ever. Abdullah began pacing up and down with increasing nervousness, his mood reflecting on his three captives, Kerry beginning to sob with uncontrollable anguish. Spratt stirred, the aching hurt in his leg and his bleeding finger tips making him moan in anguish and pain. Gingerly opening his eyes, hoping against hope that he had been dreaming, he almost let out a scream of terror when he saw the Arabic man's face peering into his, inches from his nose, the man's hot, strong smelling breath making him blanche and recoil, his head thumping against the wood of the banisters in a futile effort to pull away.

Cringing and whining, Spratt pleaded for his release, promising the Arab every penny he owned and not only the man's boat but everything in his flat. If he let him go he wouldn't tell anyone, not even the police. After all, this was nothing to do with him, and having glanced with hatred and contempt in Kerry's direction, he had said that it was all *her* fault; *she* had given him the stupid boat even though she knew it had been given to her with love and affection by her fiancé. Abdullah could keep the women, who were nothing but trouble anyway.

Kerry's sobs became louder, her wailing building to a howling crescendo.

Abdullah stepped to her, his knife hand poised inches from her head, the anger blazing in his eyes.

"Please Kerry," pleaded Siobhan, "Try to control yourself. Keep calm and we all may get out of this."

But Kerry, terrified, didn't stop howling and Siobhan winced as Abdullah drew his hand down, sharply, the blow smacking with a resounding crash on her cheek, causing Kerry's head to loll to one side. Siobhan had screamed involuntarily, her nerves no longer able to withstand the torment; her good friend Kerry was hurt and she had done nothing to help her. Closing her eyes not wanting to witness any more thuggish brutality from this bloody and foul interloper, she bit her tongue, fearful, petrified, awaiting the next sadistic action that would probably put paid to her good friend.

But Kerry's howl stopped, the wind knocked out of her, the blow from Abdullah in mid exhalation causing her to exhale on an already empty lung, her body desperately short of air for the next breath; she almost stopped breathing, her mouth flapping like a landed fish. Sucking in mouthfuls of air Kerry began to wheeze and then breathed normally, her body shocked but her howling abated.

Hearing Kerry suck in her breath Siobhan opened one eye, then the other, glancing with fear and trepidation at her friend, expecting the worst. Kerry wasn't dead; she wasn't even cut or bleeding! There was a nasty weal on her cheek, a bright bluish hue spreading like wildfire from Kerry's temple down to her chin, but she wasn't dead! Siobhan relieved at Kerry still being alive was never-the-less secretly pleased that the wailing woman had been shut up. She tore her eyes from Kerry, aware that the man was now glaring in her direction, his bruised, white, tensed knuckles locked in a fist, his eyes wary but malevolent.

He was staring at her with threatening malice, waiting for her to scream again and if she did so then she would get the same treatment as the other western harlot. He didn't need to say any words, the look was enough. Siobhan apologized for calling out, muttering that she thought he had knifed her friend; she promised to remain calm.

Satisfied, Abdullah turned away from his captives, momentarily calmed, and went to the kitchen to get a drink of water.

Despite Siobhan shaking her head negatively, her eyes warning of the potential danger, Spratt seized the opportunity to roll over, stumbling partially to his feet, and limping with support against the banister, had made his way to the top of the stairwell before Abdullah returned, the man's cold frown of hatred causing Spratt to stop in his tracks. A wail of fear began to form on his Spratt's lips.

Abdullah didn't utter one word, the man's cold, assertive silence sending a shiver down Siobhan's back. She was terrified, for the man's face and eyes had spoken volumes to her. Something in his visage told her that the game had now changed, the intruder having made up his mind on his next, brutal course of action.

Without uttering a word, he forced Spratt back down towards his earlier position against the banister. Then, surprisingly, he undid the bounds securing Siobhan and Kerry's legs. "I do not want another sound from any of you," Abdullah ordered sternly and, subsequently calmly, without emotion, began to tie the tights across the women's mouths. Initially when the tights were pulled hard, almost cutting the corners of her lips, Kerry gagged, almost retching uncontrollably until Siobhan had told her friend to calm down and to breathe normally, gently. Then he had gagged the silent, terrified, but controlled Siobhan.

Opening one of Siobhan's wardrobes, he pulled out a long sleeved dress, untied Kerry's hands and ordered her to put it on, his eyes never leaving her body as she reluctantly dropped the bed sheet and scrambled into the dress, the stare not of desire but of revulsion. Re-securing her hands, he also untied Siobhan, passing her another dress, but refusing the offered dress, she reached for a pair of joggers previously thrown over the back of her chair and, under Abdullah's fixed gaze, pulled a top from a drawer. Both women were trembling, unsure of what was to happen next as the man tied Siobhan's hands once again.

Satisfied, Abdullah turned his attention back to the whimpering, cowering Spratt and with a maniacal look in his eyes, grabbed him by the head, pulling a handful of the man's hair as he stretched him upwards, Spratt's jugular exposed. Without a second thought, Abdullah brought his knife sharply down, slicing into Spratt's throat, Spratt's initial scream of fear, anguish and pain ending in a gurgling and incoherent babble, the man's blood pouring forth like a pipe that had just had an air bubble removed.

Oblivious to the mess spewing onto his face, hands and clothes, Abdullah sawed through Spratt's throat, the knife not as sharp as he would have usually used; the semi blunt weapon causing a jagged tear of skin, muscle, vein, and bone.

Kerry gagged and fainted.

Siobhan almost choked on her own vomit, quickly managing to swallow the bile before it totally filled her mouth, the excess fluid streaming from her nostrils.

Having completed his task, Abdullah went to the bathroom and quickly swilled his face and hands, calmly drying himself on Siobhan's red and black coco-cola towel, then used the towel to wipe the wet blood from his clothes.

Insensitive to the frantic, terrified, and quivering women, he went to the telephone and made a call. Then noticing Kerry's discarded mobile phone, he forced the woken, terrified, sobbing Kerry to give him her number. Hastily scribbling a note for Ray's return, Abdullah removed the blood-stained dressing gown cord from Spratt and used it to doubly secure Siobhan's bounds. He knew that this woman would pose the most danger but until he had the Dhow, he couldn't afford to kill her.

Following an interminable, nervous wait, there was a sound of a car pulling up outside, its driver keeping the vehicle in the middle of the road, not making any attempt to park.

Threatening the women with the same fate as Spratt if they

didn't do what they were told, he forced them from the flat. Siobhan supporting Kerry as best she could, Kerry's terrified, jelly-like legs barely able to carry her body.

Abdullah made the women lie in the floor-wells behind the rear seats, and climbing onto the back seats, one of his legs resting on each woman, he forced them to remain secured uncomfortably on the floor.

Without a word to the obedient, subservient, and fearful car driver, he nodded, his brain now fixed on the next course of action.

The car sped away in a squeal of burnt rubber.

Chapter 48

Ray stumbled, almost falling head over heels as he raced down the stairs, desperate to put as much space between himself and Siobhan's flat. He didn't want to be stopped by the police. He had to get clear, far away, to be unencumbered; he was surely Siobhan and Kerry's only hope.

Racing from the flat he paused momentarily and then pulled the door gently too behind him. It seemed silly trying to creep out of the place after all the noise that must have occurred earlier but he was determined not to get noticed, to be as discreet as possible as he exited. Scurrying towards the dustbin where he had earlier hidden his keys, he dropped to his knees and reached inward through the railings as he had done so only a few minutes earlier. Alas, some sixth sense told him he was not alone; he was being watched. The hairs on the back of his neck stood up, his skin tingled, his muscles tautened.

With one hand tilting the dustbin and his other reaching for the keys, his eyes swivelled, glancing sideways, straight into the staring, gawping eyes of a young, half naked, blonde woman. For an instant, their eyes locked, neither moving, the woman's fearful expression and feeling of exposure matched by his inward groan.

Ray grinned, self-consciously, but the young blonde let out a rip roaring scream of untold intensity, the noise reverberating through the window glass, hitting Ray like a tsunami of sound. The shock of the woman's reaction startled Ray, causing him to drop the dustbin, the base of the bin falling heavily on his trapped arm, the key falling out of his hand.

The woman's face was quickly replaced by that of a large muscle-bound man, a look of anger and menace on his face. As quickly as the man's face appeared at the window it disappeared; Ray could hear the sounds of the front door being unbolted as he scrambled hurriedly to retrieve the key, the dustbin toppling over in his haste.

The metal dustbin lid fell free, rolling across the tiny patio area before clanging noisily against the metal railings. The contents of the dustbin, now released, poured forth in an ugly stream of colours; egg shells mixing with milk cartons, plastic packaging, left-over food, including some obviously decomposed potatoes and tomatoes, and an old shoe with chewing gum stuck on the sole.

Key grasped tightly in his hand, Ray clambered to his feet, the door of the flat flying open and the large well-built man strutting out, a look of determined anger on his face, shirt unbuttoned, the shirttails flying behind. The man was intent on retribution, intent on punishing this pervert who had been spying on his woman.

"Let me explain..." smiled Ray, but got no further as the burly man grasped his neck with one hand, the other poised to punch Ray in the face.

"Fucking peeping tom; scumbag!" yelled his assailant, "I'll teach you to perve on my wife; filthy fucking pervert!" And glancing at the spilt dustbin, he added, "And not to steal from my bin, you thieving little tosser. Get a bleeding job!" And with that the man's fist flew at Ray's face.

Ray twisted his head sideways just at the right moment, the intended blow scraping his already sore ear. He pushed against the burly man, getting inside the man's reach before the huge oaf could attempt to administer another punch.

Breathless, Ray wheezed into his assailant's ear, "I'm not a pervert; I was just trying to retrieve my car key."

"Fucking likely!" shouted his assailant as he resisted Ray's push, the burly man also pushing forward, intent on obtaining sufficient distance between the two of them to really punch the lights out of this fucking creep.

Seizing his moment, Ray dropped to one knee and grasping the man's shirt, he tugged, his assailant flying forward; as they toppled Ray fell onto his back and still grasping his assailant's shirt, he used his feet to propel his opponent over his head, the man flying forward, smacking his head with a resounding thump against the rear door panel of a parked Audi.

Ray quickly scrambled to his feet, just in time to meet the charging blonde, now clothed, as she ran forward, intent on gouging at his face. Charming people, mused Ray as he sidestepped, the blonde tumbling forward, collapsing in a heap against her dazed partner.

"Look, I was trying to explain." Ray started to say but got no further because Mr 'Burly Oaf' was getting to his feet, his face scarlet, his eyes bulging with venom, the man's woman tossed carelessly on the ground. If he had been mad before, now he was apoplectic.

Realizing that an explanation would meet without any favourable or reasonable response from monolithic man and his blonde, Ray scoped up the car keys which he'd dropped during the tussle and ran away as fast as he could, the oaf shouting after him, the blonde screeching obscenities. Aware that he would not have time to jump into his car and manoeuvre out of the parking space, Ray decided that discretion was the better part of valour and he hot footed it down the road, rounding a corner, only stopping when he found a large tree trunk to hide behind.

Pausing to suck in a lung-full of air, and not hearing the heavy footsteps of pursuit, he peered round the tree trunk. Other than a few peculiar stares from a newspaper delivery boy and some passing cars, all seemed to be quiet from his recent pursuers. "That's all I need," he thought, "As if I haven't got enough to deal with!"

Girding his loins, he made his way back to the end of the street and cautiously looked round the corner. Monolithic man and his blonde were nowhere in sight. Tentatively, Ray made his way to his parked car, unlocked the door, and slid inside.

He didn't dare check the boot to make sure that both bodies were still inside - that would cap Ray's day if he opened the boot to find a wide-awake Saeed launching an attack whilst monolithic man crept up on him from behind. No, he would have to take the risk, drive away, subsequently checking on his prisoner at a later time.

He very nearly determined to drive to the nearest police station but Siobhan and Kerry's lives were still in danger and, reluctantly, he knew that he couldn't gamble with the girls' lives. Their fate was inexorably in his hands.

Chapter 49

Returning to his original lair in the Mosque, Abdullah covered both women with 'Jilbabs' that the driver had brought with him, and making Siobhan and Kerry wear the Khimar/veil, he forced his two captives through a back entrance of the Mosque.

With morning prayer already in progress, Abdullah was not too concerned regarding any noise that the captives might make as they made their way via a side passage and onward down into the cellar rooms below the Mosque. Forced into a room that was obviously below ground level, Siobhan and Kerry, terrified beyond comprehension, were made to sit on a wooden bench whilst Abdullah made a series of phone calls in Arabic.

The car driver, having accompanied them into the cavernous, sparsely furnished room, removed their veils and the outer clothing that had covered the women during their forced entrance. He then waited in the background, silent and obedient, never once taking his eyes off Siobhan and Kerry, his obvious duty being that of their gaoler.

Kerry was weeping, her earlier wails being curtailed after a sharp slap across the face from Abdullah. She had peed herself and was biting her lip to prevent herself crying out again, her misery and pity not for the now demised and forgotten Spratt but more because of her own fear.

Although desperate for the toilet, Siobhan stared sullenly at her captors, her ears straining to pick up any words, clues of where they were and what the murderous brute's intentions might be. Well, she *knew* what his intentions would be but she was looking for a light in the tunnel, not at the end of the tunnel. If she was forewarned as to their possible fate she could at least try to formulate some kind of plan, a possibility of evading what appeared to be certain death. If this was the same man who had carried out the previous killings, in addition to Spratt's murder, then he was bound not to show her or Kerry any mercy.

But she couldn't discern anything, the man speaking in a strange language. She though she heard the names of one or two familiar landmarks but couldn't be sure, the man's pronunciation giving her cause to doubt.

Finally attracting Abdullah's attention, Siobhan indicated that she needed the toilet. The murderer called Abdullah - the driver had used the man's name - scowled venomously but then turned to his colleague, barking out commands in that strange tongue of his, the words rapid, the instructions harsh.

She rose to her feet, expecting to be taken to a toilet where she could release the immense pressure building in her bladder; but the former driver shouted at her, yelling in a furious torrent of unidentifiable, angry words, and rushing forward, he shoved her back onto the hard bench, his aggression making her sit with a bump, her bladder almost giving out at the same instant.

"I am human," protested Siobhan, "I need to pee!"

But Abdullah ignored her indignant, embarrassed protest and continued with his phone calls, firing out instructions in those strange words. Tears formed in her eyes but she was determined not to end up in the same state as Kerry, a pool of yellow liquid on the floor under their bench, the urea trail stained on Kerry's leg.

The car driver left the room, firmly shutting the door as he exited.

Gritting her teeth, Siobhan tried to hold on, knowing that it was only a matter of time before she would lose control. She was sure that her pee would dwarf Kerry's puddle, but at least the thought of trying not to let herself go, not to give in, helped take away some of the fear of her impending death.

Siobhan at first indignant, almost cried out in relief as the driver reappeared, an old bucket and four sheets of tissue paper in his hand. Without a word, the man passed the bucket to Siobhan and stood waiting, his eyes fixed on her. Abdullah barked out a command and the man trembled and faced away.

Barely had Abdullah turned his own back, before Siobhan, her hands still bound, had tugged down her pants and squatted over the bucket, her liquid being released in a furious torrent, Siobhan almost purring with relieved pleasure.

Allowing a small pause after the temporary stream, Abdullah waited for the sound of silence then turned to face his captives, a look of contempt and deep disgust on his face.

Her ears pricked up when Abdullah started speaking in English but seeing her eyes watching, he moved to the other side of the room, the only words Siobhan catching were 'Oxford Circus', Abdullah repeating the words in an angry and frustrated tone. Having completed his call, Abdullah barked another command to the driver, the man rushing forward in instant obedience.

The driver grabbed the handle of the bucket and picked it up, the deep yellow liquid sloshing inside. He offered it to Kerry, who stared back with a bewildered expression on her face, her eyes glazed and fixed in the distance.

"Toilet!" demanded the driver, but met with no response.

Siobhan gently tapped Kerry on the shoulder, asking, "Do you need another pee?" Kerry merely shook her hand.

Disgusted with his task, the driver left the room, the bucket sloshing as he exited.

It wasn't long before the room filed with a motley crowd of people, all pausing momentarily to stare at the two women. Some of the new-comers protested at their presence but Abdullah quickly shut them up, his anger dissipating into explanation, the justification meeting with a few sharp intakes of breath followed by understanding nods of approval.

Siobhan stared wild eyed at the sudden influx of people, her hopes raised that with so many witnesses the murderous Abdullah could no longer afford to kill them. Unfortunately, her upbringing had never taught her about religious fundamentalism, everything being swept under a carpet of political correctness during her years of education at both school and university! She had both studied and worked with some lovely people, Muslims from England and abroad but, other than in news reports, had never come across such zealots as she was now involved with.

In every walk of life, in every religion, there was good and bad but unfortunately, the authorities, the decision makers, had no idea how to differentiate between the two. Everything was blanketed in a cloak of supposed righteousness, with little true understanding, flexibility of purpose and will, or accurate knowledge being utilized. Siobhan, listening intently, picked up words such as 'Jihad', 'Allah', and the names of some tube stations as well as some famous London landmarks.

She was intelligent enough to discern that something major was being planned, and that these dreadful people were scheming, arranging some atrocity. Unfortunately she and Kerry were caught up in the midst of it and not only could she not warn anyone, she knew that they were both in utmost peril, unlikely to survive.

Glancing at the silently sobbing Kerry, she couldn't help shuddering.

Chapter 50

It hadn't been long before Ray received the phone call from Abdullah, instructing him to meet up on the westbound platform of the Central Line Tube at Oxford Circus station, at 10.30 am.

No later, or the women would die!

There had been no mention of Abdullah's accomplice; Abdullah's apparent disinterest in the fate of his colleague producing a welcome surprise. Not asking regarding Saeed's whereabouts or his well-being caused Ray some relief, for he had no idea if the man had recovered or not - maybe he was dead? He had still not dared to open the boot; there were no sounds of movement from within, and he didn't want the risk of explaining to the homicidal maniac that his accomplice was either injured or dead.

It was the second phone call that made Ray almost jump out of his skin. Oblivious to the 'strictly no stopping' red zone markings, he quickly pulled the vehicle into the kerbside before answering the phone. This time his heart started pounding, the sweat rising on his brow. Obviously Abdullah had remembered Saeed and now the stakes were about to increase.

What was he to tell Abdullah? What the hell would the madman do if he thought that that his colleague was dead?

With a voice that croaked more than spoke, he tentatively uttered, "Hello?"

The relief washed through Ray when he realized that it was Sergeant Morris on the other end of the line. Although Morris was bawling at him, berating him for the actions that Ray had taken, putting people's lives at risk, etc, etc, Ray was never-the-less relieved that it was Morris and not Abdullah on the line.

Morris demanded to know where the hell Ray was, and not to do anything else until the police could step in.

"But I can't involve you directly at the moment," pleaded Ray, "Siobhan and Kerry's lives are in danger."

"I know that, you idiot," growled Morris, "But we're the professionals, we know what to do. Just tell me where you are and wait until we reach you!"

"There's no time," Ray whined, "I have to be at the Oxford Circus Tube by 10.30 am."

"Don't go on your own; wait until we get to you," insisted Morris.

"Please Sergeant, I need to press on. The people I'm up against are ruthless."

"I *know!*" snarled Morris, "We suspect that you're up against part of a fundamentalist network. Just do as I tell you. You have no idea what you're getting into!"

"Ah, that's where you're wrong Sergeant, I do know." A sudden thought hit Ray. "But how did you know where to ring me; where did you get this number?"

"You see," explained Morris, "That's what I mean by leaving this to the professionals. You left the terrorist's note at the address you gave me. Now just do as I say and wait!"

"Can't Sergeant, just can't," riposted Ray, "No time; meet me at Oxford Circus, Central Line...at ten thirty!" And with that Ray cut off the vehemently protesting Morris.

Ray looked up to see a Traffic Warden noting his registration details in a book. Without waiting for the ticket to be pinned to his screen he sped off, cutting into the hooting traffic, an aggrieved and aggressive Mercedes driver flashing his lights and hooting at him. The mobile began to ring again but Ray ignored it, knowing that it would be Morris still trying to remonstrate with him.

His nerves were raw, his muscles taut, his eyes straining, his head ached, none of his feelings being helped by the incessant ringing of the mobile or the hooting, headlight flashing maniac behind him.

Incongruously, he wondered who would foot the various bills for illegal stopping, not to mention the congestion charges incurred. Glancing up in the rear view mirror he spotted the irate traffic warden waving the penalty ticket in his left hand, his right hand reaching for a mobile phone. The Mercedes driver zoomed past him, middle digit raised, and almost hit Ray's vehicle as he pulled back in in front of him.

It was certainly already one of those days, and it had hardly started! With his heart in his mouth, he turned off towards Oxford Circus.

Chapter 51

Abdullah stared down at his hand. Despite the years of preparation and the many previous times that he had experienced danger, or the anticipation of a kill, he had never experienced this; never expected it.

A frown crossed his brow and he glanced sideways at the driver, wondering if the man had noticed. Abdullah quickly tucked his hand into his pocket, feeling the comfort of the sheathed, sharp-bladed knife, his favourite weapon of termination. The frown remained on his brow; he could still feel his hand shaking. Why had nerves suddenly got hold of him? Why was he allowing the culmination of his life's dream to affect him so? His mind mused whether it was a cowardly fear of death or the tingly thrill of anticipation of the 'Jihad' that he was about to fulfil.

Whatever the reason, he could not let the visibly trembling and very terrified driver know of his own weakness, his own emotions. Unbelievably the driver was visibly quivering, the perspiration dribbling down his thick, hairy neck. "Such a coward!" thought Abdullah.

He turned in his seat, his eyes meeting with those of Fawzi. He hadn't told Fawzi that his brother had been captured, was as good as dead, for he still needed Fawzi's unquestioned loyalty and support. All Fawzi had been told was that his brother had already taken up his allocated position, and was playing a full and integral part in the operation, the final phase of their 'Jihad' now set in motion. He wouldn't tell Fawzi where and why, using the pretence of confidentiality in case any of them were captured.

Eight teams were now either in position or would shortly be at their appointed rendezvous points, Abdullah having earlier triggered the necessary call out messages via his acolytes who had assembled in the Mosque basement. Very few of the eight teams, nor the members of Abdullah's current party, knew the names of the other team members or their locations, and none knew of their specific targets. Thus if any of them were caught or apprehended, then none of the other teams or targets could be betrayed to the authorities.

Everything was now in place and the instruction for the final acts would come from him. Many months of planning, of preparation, could be brought to fruition, to completion, the decadent westerners finally paying for their continued insults to Islam.

Abdullah could feel his heart beating faster, the passion and pride rising within his bosom. He was the only member of the U.K. operation who knew of the existence of the eight teams but even he didn't know the target locations, just the general areas.

Yes, he knew it was in the heart of the infidel's capital, and he knew that thousands would die, including all his people (what martyrs they will be, what accolades they will earn!); but he didn't know of the actual finite points, the 'trigger' locations.

For that information, he needed his Dhow.

Putting thoughts of his martyrdom out of his mind, he concentrated on the immediate task of getting to the venue on time; he just hoped that the fool, Ray, would bring the Dhow with him. The two infidel women clothed from head to foot in full 'Abayas' and 'Khimers', their faces heavily veiled, their hands secured with thick bracelets in the form of heavy bangles, with sturdy chains of 3 inch length allowing only minimal hand movement, sat trembling on the rear seat.

Around their ankles, Siobhan and Kerry also had heavy duty bangles connecting their feet together also by a very decorative, but strong, chain that, although not unbreakable, did reduce their chances of a quick escape. Abdullah had told them that any such attempts at escape would only last a second or two because, by that time, they would have his knife impaled in their backs. He took great pleasure in taking out the dagger from its scabbard, secreted inside his trousers, his pocket having already been removed to allow easy access to his favourite weapon of death. At the sight of the obviously sharp, now shiny, cleaned, glistening blade, Siobhan had recoiled in horror.

Kerry gasped and then reverted to her wailing; Abdullah's sharp slap across her face this time having no effect. The car driver stopped the vehicle, turned round, and using a spare, reserve, 'Khimar', raised Kerry's veil and stuffed the material into her mouth, making her momentarily pass out, the enforced sound proofing being forced from her mouth as she slumped forward.

Abdullah discarded the dagger's scabbard and wrapped his weapon inside a cloth, the metallic tip barely visible until a shaft of light caught it, making it glint like the eye of a malevolent spirit.

Knowing he could not trust the women not to panic or call out for help, he secured gags under their veils, the slumped Kerry's head being forced back and up, whilst he quite physically and firmly ensured her silence.

*   *   *   *

Discarding his borrowed car, Ray grabbed the Dhow and snatching a carrier bag from a street vender's stall, he used his oyster card, rushing through the station check in, and tore down the passageway, hurtling down the escalator, sometimes two steps at a time, virtually knocking people out of his path. He was lucky that he caught most of the travellers on a good morning; for generally most of the early morning late 'rush hour' commuters or early morning shoppers were not always of a good frame of mind, easy to upset, and ready to snarl an unpleasant comment at any bad mannered fellow traveller. He shoved the Dhow into the bag.

Reaching the designated crowded platform he could not see Siobhan or Kerry anywhere. Checking his watch, he tore halfway along the platform, leaning out over the tracks so that he could get a better view. But there was no sign of the girls. "Shit; stupid bastard," he muttered, "Must have got it wrong!" He rushed to the eastbound side, running as best he could on the crowded platform, up and down its length. But still there was no sign.

He decided to return to the westbound platform, panic beginning to eat at him, a cold sweat enveloping his body. "I'm so sorry, Siobhan," he almost cried, a few startled passengers backing away, wary of him, "I've let you down."

Two trains pulled in virtually one after the other, the crowd on the westbound platform momentarily thinning out to a sparse mixture of eclectically dressed individuals. But still Ray couldn't see Siobhan or Kerry, or indeed that bastard Arab thug.

There were two Islamic looking females at the far end of the platform, dressed from head to toe in Burkas, and for some reason Ray decided to approach the women. He was so upset, so unreasonable, that he was going to remonstrate with these innocent Moslem women, blaming them for the strife that now prevailed upon him. But as Ray neared, two men stepped out from behind the women, one smiling contemptuously in Ray's direction. It was Abdullah! Ray recognised his antagonist instantly and clenching his fists, he was ready to pounce, ready to beat the shit out of the bastard.

"Careful," Abdullah warned, fully aware of Ray's intent, "It won't be that easy to vanquish both of us." He smiled sardonically, glancing at his companion, then at his companion's hand in the man's coat pocket, an unnatural bulge denoting a hidden weapon.

Ray assumed the man had a gun, and he stopped, poised, clenching and unclenching his fists.

"Oh Ray," wailed Kerry, her voice distorted, muffled, the gag not secure in her mouth, "Help us! *Please*!"

"Shut up woman," growled Abdullah, "I did warn you that if you tried to get help, then...!" He left the words unspoken.

Ray startled, gasped, his fists unclenched. His vision concentrated on the two women dressed in 'Abayas', instantly his eyes locking with those of Siobhan. With most of her face hidden behind the material of her veil, Ray was nevertheless aware of Siobhan's beautiful green eyes, gorgeous yet pleading, enticing yet warning. If a woman had had such beautiful eyes as those he now recognised as Siobhan's, then all the camouflage in the world would not make a difference; eyes like that would entice any man.

"Siobhan?" he asked unnecessarily, "Is that you?"

She nodded affirmatively, yet regretful, meek.

"Of course it's us, you prat!" snapped Kerry, the muffled voice not disguising her anger.

"Shut up woman," hissed Abdullah from the side of his mouth, the closest of the re-filling crowd on the platform beginning to stare in their direction.

"Do you have my Dhow?" demanded Abdullah, his eyes swivelling to the carrier bag firmly grasped in Ray's hand.

Ray nodded.

"Then pass it to my friend," ordered Abdullah.

Ray tore his eyes from Siobhan, glancing in the direction of Abdullah's sidekick. There was something vaguely familiar about the man, but Ray could not make out why?

"First let the women go. Then I'll hand over the bag."

"The bag," reiterated Abdullah, Fawzi's hand extended, ready to receive it.

"No, I'm sorry," Ray retorted firmly, "Let the women go, up the stairs, before I hand over the bag."

Abdullah smiled. Not a warm smile, but a smile of malice and contempt.

"Do you think that I'm that stupid? Because I'm an Arab, you think I'm stupid?"

"No," protested Ray, "It has nothing to do with stupidity or ignorance; it's merely insurance. I need to be sure that before I hand over my bargaining tool, the women are safe."

Abdullah swore; the Arabic word used of no meaning to Ray.

At that moment another train pulled into the station and Ray, seizing his moment, threw the carrier bag holding the Dhow into the face of Abdullah's assistant. At the same moment he reached for both Siobhan and Kerry, pulling them towards him.

Kerry decided to scream, the fear overtaking the more sensible side of her emotions. Before Ray knew it, far from being the saviour, the defender of the women, there were many hands laid upon him, one individual in particular grabbing him around the waist and swinging him onto the hard concrete floor of the platform.

"*No*, you fools!" he cried out, trying to break free, "I'm rescuing them. I was..." But his words became muffled as the throng enveloped him.

He watched helpless from the bottom of the melee as the crowd assisted Abdullah and his sidekick in dragging the obviously offended and afraid two Muslim women away, for this was London and no white racist bigot was going to be allowed to attack these women just because they were different.

He watched as the girls were dragged away, frustration and tears of anger building inside; Siobhan silent, but the howling Kerry dragged to sanctuary by the good folk of London, the misunderstanding throng also inadvertently restricting Siobhan, driving her back into the arms of Fawzi, her restless, violent struggling being totally misconstrued..

*   *   *   *

Abdullah, knife camouflaged within a roll of cloth, the tip pressed sharply in Siobhan's back, had tried to stab her, but the rush of the crowd and Siobhan's quick step sideways had saved her from a mortal blow. When the crowd had jumped forward to supposedly save her, Siobhan had desperately wanted to cry out, to tell them who she was, but the gag that Abdullah had secured in her mouth, hidden under the all encasing face mask, and now wet with saliva, allowed her only to mumble indecipherable words. She knew that Kerry had somehow loosened her own gag, but instead of yelling out, explaining their situation, all she did was scream and holler.

If Siobhan could have hit her, she would willingly have slapped her friend, firmly, across the face!

Luckily, the sudden forward rush of the throng caused Abdullah to drop his knife but no longer concerned with the fate of his captives, all he now wanted was to take possession of his Dhow. He snatched the carrier bag from Fawzi's hand and with the crowd driving them on, they were driven along the platform and up towards the exit. Momentarily separated from Fawzi he could see that the fool still had hold of one the women, dragging her along with him.

The fool! The women were no longer necessary. He had the Dhow and even if the authorities had any idea of his intention, the women would have been clueless as to the location of their hide-out. Somehow Kerry had been left behind in the mad rush for the exit and she remained, cowering on all fours, partially hidden by one of the ticket machines.

Reaching the surface Abdullah ran towards their waiting vehicle, a Telecoms van, the driver dressed as a BT engineer, supposedly fixing the wires in a telephone junction box. The fool Fawzi was still running after him, one of the women still firmly in his grip.

The Telecoms van driver, aware of their presence, slammed shut the junction box, Abdullah immediately jumping through the rear doors of his van, closely followed by Fawzi and one of the women who he had brought earlier to the station. Calmly, the driver closed the rear doors and climbed into his vehicle just as Sergeant Morris and the police anti-terrorist units arrived separately, the squeal of brakes almost as loud as the blaring of the sirens.

Chapter 52

Sergeant Morris, having alerted his superiors at Scotland Yard, arrived at Oxford Circus literally seconds after the initial arrival of the Police SO13 and SO19 units.

Two police SO19 ARV units skidded to a stop, each of the three-man specialist armed response vehicle units pulling across the road, effectively blocking off Regent Street. Almost simultaneously, five further vehicles arrived, SO13 and SO19 units coordinated from Scotland Yard. They blocked off Oxford Street, armed SO19 officers disgorging from the vehicles with practised haste.

The area was sealed off, other AVR units being sent to the next stations up and down the tube line. There was to be no escape. Having secured the area, the armed police teams, carrying Glock 17 pistols and MP5 sub machine guns, charged inside the station; their colleagues - some with HK G36F Carbines more suitable to penetrate vehicles – were left on guard outside.

The specialist teams worked through the station, efficiently, quickly, but with a practised well-drilled expertise. After the disorganisation and apparent lack of coherent leadership or communication, where mistakes had been made at Stockwell, and wherein an officer had been put in a difficult position, this time there was to be a clear and precise plan of action, targets clearly identified before lives were to be put at risk.

*　　*　　*　　*

Fighting in frustration to break free, Ray was punched, hard, on the jaw, the blow jarring him, making his eyes momentarily glaze over.

"You! I know you, you racist!" remonstrated one of the men holding him down, "You're that guy that Pete Spratt can't stand; Pete said you were a nasty piece of work!"

Ray's glazed vision focused, taking in the aggressive face of one of Spratt's crowd. He knew the face, but not the name. "You bastard," Ray spat in response, "I might have known that a friend of Spratt's would be involved with a Muslim fanatic!"

"A Muslim fanatic; don't make me laugh" mocked the man holding him, "It's just an excuse for you to pick on Muslims and attack our women because they wear the Burka."

"You stupid fool," Ray shouted, "They weren't Muslim women; they were Siobhan and Kerry - kidnapped by a zealous madman!"

The man was taken aback, "What? No; bollocks. That's

nonsense."

The throng around Ray suddenly became doubtful, wondering what they had got involved with; some disappeared quickly along the platform, others slinked away.

Armed police, yelling their heads off, telling people to get down, came charging down the platform, scattering anybody who stood in their path. It was chaotic, frenetic, terrifying for the bystanders, but considered necessary; their superior officers considered the men to be disciplined, well-organised units in control of the chaos, and the frenetic approach was allegedly designed to destabilise their enemy or enemies. But weapons were not to be fired unless there was a clear danger or lives at risk.

*   *   *

Spratt's friend, Ibrahim, crouching on the ground by Ray, armed weapons pointing at his head, had been manhandled brusquely, forced face down to the ground, his hands secured behind him with plastic cuffs. The same fate quickly befell Ray, both men and a scattering of the other apprehensive looking individuals who had been on the platform, were all under suspicion, all being restrained.

The officers stood over them, some armed with cut-down MP5, low capacity fifteen 9mm single fire machine guns, most with torches attached to their gun's fore grip. A few of the potential suspects began wailing, in fear of their lives; they were just in the wrong place, at the wrong time. Satisfied that the area was secure, but with the knowledge that some of the suspects maybe having escaped, the police took their prisoners in for questioning.

Chapter 53

Saeed kicked hard against the boot lid, trying his utmost to force the lock. Not only was it impossible, it was also very difficult to get any momentum, any force, in such an enclosed area. He called out in his broken English, pleading for help, begging for freedom.

Eventually two bystanders, hearing his muffled cries, went to investigate. Saeed kicking up at the boot lid at the same instant startled them, making them back away. But the cries persisted; emboldened, they went closer, tried the catch, the lid springing open.

Saeed leapt up, a blood soaked ogre rising from the darkness inside, terrifying and scattering his rescuers, and rolling out from the boot, he dropped to the ground. Unsteady after being cooped up for so long, ignoring the looks of astonishment, mixed with wariness and fear from his rescuers, he forced his way through the small crowd that had gathered around him. Ignoring their questions and cries of "Wait!" he pushed past and ran. Just ran. With no idea where he was going and what he was going to do.

He ignored the pandemonium, the hubbub that was brewing in his wake, the horror of his blood stained body running from the scene, a second body, a macabre corpse, quickly discovered in the boot.

After wandering aimlessly for nearly half an hour, Saeed saw a sign for the 'Bank' tube station, and recalling his previous forays with Fawzi, he knew how to make it back. Luckily, he had some money in his pocket. He was safe.

Then he thought of Abdullah and trembled; one way or another he was in trouble. He had failed. He just hoped that everything was alright and that Abdullah had got his Dhow; otherwise it would be too horrible to consider. And if Abdullah was captured or Allah forbid, his brother Fawzi, then Saeed would be all alone, with nowhere to go, for his refuge in the Mosque and other addresses would be of no use.

With trepidation, uncertainty, he boarded the train.

*   *   *   *

Abdullah stared with venom at the captive woman. If he hadn't dropped his knife in the mad scramble then he would now take great pleasure in slitting the harlot's throat. But he had no knife on him; ridiculously, none of them had any weapons.

He just stared with malice at the woman.

She would die; soon, but not now.

Aware of the venomous eyes boring into hers, Siobhan quaked in fear. She was glad that Kerry had somehow managed to escape but now she felt alone. So very alone, and terrified...more afraid than she had ever been in her entire life She knew it was only a matter of time. In a way she was grateful for the gag still in her mouth, for if it wasn't there, she knew that she would scream. And, of course, that would only serve to exacerbate the situation.

Fawzi had been berated, angrily in Arabic, for not having disposed of the woman whilst they were underground. The least he could have done was to strangle one and push the other onto the track. But to try and bring both women back, that was madness. They were not needed, they were expendable. And to cap it all, he had then lost one on route! He was useless; like his brother, he was a danger to this mission.

Fawzi on the receiving end of Abdullah's tirade began to question where his brother was, what had happened to him. Abdullah's evasiveness, his shifty eyes, his defensive response, made Fawzi realise that all was not going well. He began to question Abdullah, demanding to know more, demanding to know exactly what had happened to his brother.

The two men squared up to one another and it was only the braking of the van, causing Abdullah to lose his footing, which stopped an open fight from taking place. Lying on his back where he had toppled, Abdullah refocused his mind on important issues, his eyes glaring sternly at the young Fawzi.

"Strangle the woman!" he ordered, "She is of no use to us; she will only endanger us and our holy 'Jihad'. Strangle her!"

Taken aback, Fawzi gawked at his leader, the rebellion killed in his soul. He glanced at the whimpering woman, who although not understanding Arabic, was obviously terrified of the two men looking in her direction.

"This is it," though Siobhan, "But I don't want to die yet." A tear tricked down her cheek, unseen under her veil.

Fawzi turned away from Abdullah, his hands clenching and unclenching. He had never killed anyone before, and certainly not with his bare hands.

His mind still seething at the early open rebellion from Fawzi, Abdullah clambered to his feet and picked up the bag with the

Dhow. It felt lighter than it should have done; he didn't remember the Dhow being this light. He peered inside the bag before immediately emitting a scream of anguish, a howl of protest, his voice raised in a despairing wail, "*No!*"

He reeled round, desperately yelling at Fawzi, Fawzi's hands round Siobhan's neck, squeezing the life from the frantically struggling woman.

"My plinth is missing!" he yelled, "The Dhow's wooden stand!" Charging towards Fawzi, he screamed, "Let the woman go - we still need her!"

Fighting furiously, but ineffectual against a superior antagonist, memories flooding her thoughts; her life – and imminent death - swimming through her mind, dying, gasping for breath, struggling desperately, Siobhan stopped breathing. It was over; she could feel the spirit escaping from her shell, her being evaporating into the ether. She passed from cognisance, succumbing, powerless, her body giving up.

As she succumbed, she felt sadness for the life that she was not going to experience, sorrow overtaking her fear and pain; but then she felt a peace washing through her, calmness, an acceptance of what was to come.

Chapter 54

Ray received a very rough ride, the police threatening to charge him for withholding information. It was only the intervention of Sergeant Morris, plus the rescue and survival of Kerry that got him off the hook. He was almost re-arrested, screaming abuse at the anti-terrorist officers when he could not get them to mount a rescue operation for Siobhan.

No-one knew where to begin.

Convinced that Siobhan would be killed - if she wasn't already dead - didn't help his mood. Gutted, desolate, not wanting to go anywhere, he and Ibrahim left the police station, independently, at little after two p.m. in the afternoon.

*   * *

Ibrahim had been shocked to the core when he learnt about Spratt's murder and the tie-in to Kerry's partner's death; it seemed that although the antagonists were fundamentalists, they were nevertheless part of Ibrahim's own faith. He was mortified. It was not the true way of Islam.

Having made his peace with Ray, he offered whatever help he could, both men knowing that although the offer was genuine, it was futile. There was nothing that they could do between them.

*   *   *

Kerry, with nowhere to go, the stress of her confinement causing her palpitations, had been admitted to Guys Hospital. She was in a secure wing, a private room, where she could use her well established ability, her spoilt persona, and her well drilled expertise in extracting maximum comfort for minimum input.

Delighted, she revelled in her current status, her selfish qualities coming to the fore.

*   *   *   *

It took some time for the various messages to filter through.

The team operating as 'EDF' electricians, their 'EDF' branded lorry with its access platform raised outside Embankment Tube station, disengaged the winch. The men, who supposedly were working on repairing a street light, quietly lowered their access platform, and drove way.

The 'Transco' Gas van, parked in Trafalgar Square, manhole cover raised, two men apparently working below ground, replaced the manhole cover and folded away their work barriers. They smoothly packed away their tools and drove off.

The 'BT' Engineers, fixing a wall mounted telephone connection box on a building next to Liverpool Street station, clambered down from their ladder, repacked, and departed.

Another 'BT' team, repairing a PCP telephone multi-connection unit outside Waterloo Station, also quietly put away their equipment, and slinked off.

Similar scenes were played at other venues, various teams at Euston Station, Victoria, St. Pancreas, all discreetly packing up and slipping surreptitiously away, their missions aborted.

Each team knew of their target area, the kind of equipment they would need, but not the finite location. They had all received rudimentary instructions, with a basic level of necessary skill, in the areas of their proposed operation. Even their I.D. cards were correct, their alibis covered in the event of premature questioning from the police.

They had been told that the mission was not lost, not aborted, merely in abeyance, merely delayed. The vehicles were driven back to a warehouse in north London, a secure building in a cul-de-sac not overlooked by any private houses.

Now, slightly in confusion, some not knowing whether they were to return to their homes or not, most made their way back to the Mosque, to its cellar, to sanctuary. Others slipped away to the refuge of known friends and sympathisers. All were now nervous of discovery, no-one knowing the reason for abandonment of their mission.

Abdullah knew that their presence at Oxford Circus had been compromised but it was a small price to pay, the operation still feasible, the catastrophe still possible. Each target, the Semtex explosive teams, and the follow up final denouement operatives were still operational, still undetected. Obviously, Oxford Circus itself would now pose a problem but there might still be some possibility of achieving that target. It all depended on the exact location of the hidden container; but first, he had to find the necessary information.

Chapter 55

It was very late in the afternoon, almost early evening, before Ray got back to his flat. He should have been alerted by the very unwelcoming stares of his neighbours and the coolness, aloofness of their welcome, but it wasn't until he entered his flat that he realised the reason for the approbation of his neighbours.

His home had been turned over, wrecked, the flat a tip; mess everywhere.

His flat had been searched, fine tooth-combed by a team of police investigators, finesse not part of their operational techniques. He felt lucky that at least they had had his door key, avoiding the need for a forced entry, the front door still intact, still able to shut in one piece, and still lockable.

The neighbours were now wary of him, a police suspect, maybe part of the major incident that had taken place at Oxford Circus tube, the media awash with all kinds of lurid rumours. Too tired to care, weary beyond measure, almost falling asleep, Ray had collapsed into bed, ignoring the mess around him.

*　　*　　*　　*

Confidentiality was the key, a major debriefing taking place. Although not part of any of the Police Force's specialist or anti-terror squads - SO13 or SO19 units, nor indeed SO12, Special Branch - Detective Sergeant Morris had been called to Scotland Yard and was ensconced in a major incident room, a Deputy Commissioner in the chair. Because Morris had been on the trail of the suspects for some time he was now an integral part of the investigation.

Things had stepped up a level from the previous incident, and leaps and bounds from the initial flagged murders. The authorities were now concerned that something major was afoot, Morris and his investigation part of a brewing major incident; but what? That was the key, that's what they had to find out, and urgently!

Evidently, the intelligence services had received various warnings from their overseas sources, warnings of impending doom, a major disaster to be unleashed in England. London was the supposed choice. Activists were being sent or were already in place. In fact, alarm bells had already begun to ring when a couple of known potential terrorists living in the north of England had disappeared from surveillance; disappeared, totally 'off the radar'.

It was red-alert time, warning messages screaming out from the Middle East.

Although he had not been introduced to the two individuals sitting in the darker recess of the room, it had been whispered that they were military, a Brigadier no less, the actual DSF of the UK's Special Forces. The Director Special Forces was accompanied by a man, taking notes, rank unknown.

To involve the SAS caused a shiver to run down Morris's spine.

The DSF Brigadier was not normally involved in such routine, his job normally that of decision maker at the top of the chain. He was usually distant, weighing up the options, the facts, planning and balancing, and commanding from a distance. But today he had been at the Yard, meeting with the Commissioner, and being at the right place at the right time felt that he should sit in; first hand. This was an almost unique situation for him.

And this *was* serious!

The CCTV cameras had picked out the two Arab suspects leaving Oxford Circus Station within a gaggle of people, and also a woman, totally clad in an 'Abaya', being dragged along by one of the men. The men had been quickly identified as Arabs by piecing together all the data; witness and bystander statements, one person in the crowd identifying both men as Gulf Arabs by their accents. That quickly subdued the possibilities of Iranian or Syrian connections.

The police also knew that the woman was not involved, a hostage only, but the likelihood of her now being alive almost nil.

However, none of the MI5, MI6, or police files had anything flagged. The suspects were termed as 'clean skins', nothing to point them out as potential threats. They knew, through gentle interrogation of the hysterical and histrionic Kerry, that there was a large cadre involved, and a major operation planned.

Time was now of the essence; although they had a pretty good idea, a theory, they still had to find out the what, the where, and the how - and quickly!

Kerry had been shown numerous pictures, I.D. data, and sketches of known Islamic fundamentalists, potential threats, but she could not identify anyone. If her information, her judgement, could be relied on then everyone involved in this potential terrorist strike appeared to be 'clean', unknown.

It was desperate.

It was also known that the suspects escaped in a BT van, but that was found abandoned in a side street not very far away. Despite appeals in the media, there were no witnesses, no information of where they went after that. The trail had gone cold. Ray's earlier abandoned car had been taken to the 'Yard', fingerprinted, gone through with a fine tooth comb, but nothing concrete thrown up.

Morris cursed the individuals who had let Saeed escape from the boot. But at least they did have his fingerprints and his DNA from the blood in the boot. The Security Services were sure that they would get their men, for there was to be no escape from the UK, but would they be in time...

Chapter 56

Sneaking in to the basement below the Mosque, Saeed was relieved to find not only his brother and Abdullah, but a host of fellow activists. There was some truth of the saying of comfort in numbers.

Fawzi was angry, immediately demanding vengeance against Ray; his brother looked a sight. Two black eyes, livid bruises on his forehead and cheek, a lurid cut on his temple - the blood having dried in an unsightly smear - and a series of minor cuts and bruises all over Saeed's body. Fawzi was livid, wanting revenge, now, regardless of the current mission failure. It took some while for Saeed and Abdullah to calm him down, the three of them retiring to a semi-detached house adjacent to the mosque.

Away from the throng, the conversation continued in a more subdued manner.

"I don't understand why we need the Dhow?" demanded Fawzi.

"Not the Dhow but its base, its stand!" Abdullah retorted.

"Yes, I know...the Dhow's stand; but I still don't understand why?"

"Because it has the necessary locations hidden inside, fool."

Fawzi was not satisfied with Abdullah's reply. "But we knew the various target addresses anyway."

Abdullah sighed, frustrated, finding Fawzi extremely aggravating. "Only *I* knew of all the target addresses!" He snapped exasperated, "But no one, other than the individual men who hid the containers, knows of the precise hiding place in the target areas. Now those men have gone, they have left the Country, and many have died in Syria and Iraq. They were not been permitted to communicate with one another. There was only one master copy of all the hiding places, and *that* was in the Dhow!"

But as you had the Dhow's base before you went back to Saudi, why didn't you open it then and find out the hidden locations?" Fawzi was not giving up, he had to vent his anger on something, someone.

"Confidentiality, in case I was caught, stopped by Immigration or the other authorities," growled Abdullah impatiently, tired of trying to explain himself to this imbecile. "If I didn't know, then I couldn't betray our 'Jihad'".

"I'm sorry Abdullah, I still don't understand. If you had the Dhow and the addresses, why didn't you use them before?"

"Because - not that is of concern to you - the nerve gas was not to be the beginning. First our martyrs would cause explosions at the targets, and when panic erupted - with the infidel security and fire services rushing to the scene – that is when the other martyrs were to break open the gas containers! It has been the delayed arrival of the 'Semtex' that deferred our 'Jihad'." What Abdullah had not explained to his acolytes was that many of those who had planted the containers knew they would not only have no chance to survive when the containers were opened, but also that their death would be gruesome beyond belief; there was faith, but there was a greater knowledge of excruciating pain. Only Saeed and Fawzi knew but Abdullah envisaged that the brothers thought they could release the containers from a safe distance, escaping themselves, from the potential horrors.

"So we are lost, the mission is over?"

"No, fool," Abdullah snapped, "We have to find that man...Ray. He must still be the key. He must have our Dhow Stand with the hidden data."

Abdullah attempted to phone Ray on Kerry's mobile but this time there was no response, the line dead. Kerry's phone, battery now lifeless, was being held in Scotland Yard.

"We know his name and his street," Abdullah uttered determinedly, "The businessman, Salman Khan, can help us find the house number; he has helped before pretending to carry out credit checks. Let us go - *now*!" And leading, closely followed by a very exhausted and battered Saeed, plus a vengeful Fawzi, he set off once again in pursuit of the hapless Ray.

*   *   *   *

Ray tossed and turned, his body crying out for sleep, but his mind was overactive, desperate to know the fate of Siobhan. He felt dreadful, so guilty, for not having saved her. If only he had been bolder earlier; it was all his fault!

The crumpled sheets were damp with sweat, his legs kicking out, jerking in reaction to subliminal messages from the brain. He was running, but not getting anywhere. Suddenly he felt strong hands around his neck, the cruel, malevolent face of Abdullah inches from his face. With a mocking expression, a look of malicious intent, eyes bulging in hatred, the homicidal maniac squeezed tighter, pressuring the passages, blocking any air reaching Ray's lungs.

His assailant's eyes bored into Ray, the eyes full of rage, spittle dripping from the corners of the mouth. Desperate, struggling, trying to break free, Ray was aware of a second face, a man sneering, the man's face visible beyond Abdullah's shoulder. It was the man from Oxford Circus who had dragged Siobhan away!

With one final desperate kick, Ray lashed out, breaking free, his momentum tumbling his body off the bed, falling on the carpet with a thump. Dazed, surprised, shocked, but ready to fight, the jolt on the floor made him wake up; still clutching the pillow that had been his wrestling partner, he lay still, gathering his thoughts.

It had only been a dream...a nightmare! Although the adrenalin was still pumping through his body, he breathed a sigh of relief.

Then, he recalled! The face behind Abdullah; he knew that face! He'd seen that face before the struggle at Oxford Circus, but where? Racking his brains, it finally hit him. The flight back from Bahrain, the man had been the sick passenger...in the next seat!

"The bastard; if only I had known then, I would have made him choke on his own vomit!" he thundered. With the memory of the flight traversing his brain, Ray suddenly recalled the face of the second man, and he whistled in astonishment. Also, he remembered that he still had their 'Koran'; there had been a note inside, in Arabic.

Maybe, just maybe, there might be a clue.

The Book was in his office. He'd left it in on the cabinet with the intention of sending it back to the Airline, but just hadn't got round to it.

But now he knew just the man who could decipher the writing!

Dialling Ibrahim, Ray arranged to meet at Rosie's bar, hoping to get there before closing time.

Chapter 57

The man named Ellis stood up. Except for a very few 'in the know', most had no idea exactly who he was, other than the fact that he worked for one of the UK's Intelligence Services.

Ellis explained the authorities concerns regarding a possible terrorist attack in the UK – in fact, it was more than possible; the reality of the situation, the growing evidence, the high level of intelligence data collected, making it more than probable that something of major proportions was planned. Indeed, the Intelligence Services believed that a Gas attack was imminent, with London as the most likely target. A vast quantity of 'VX' gas had 'disappeared', gone off the radar, last tracked being transported on a ship from Yemen to Rotterdam. The shipping documents had proved to be false, the Liberian flagged Vessel going down on its subsequent voyage, sinking off the coast of Nigeria.

There were no survivors to question.

After Rotterdam, the scent had gone cold; the consignment vanishing into the ether. "No pun intended," added Ellis, but not eliciting a laugh from anyone. On a more sombre note, he explained that he'd 'lost' one of his colleagues in Aden, Yemen. "Our Agent, hot on the trail of those we believe were controlling the operation, disappeared, his head appearing on one of the prolific websites now used by terrorists. He had been described in the media as an operative with the Yemen Hunt Oil Company, but of course the web site identified him as an Agent of the West."

A boffin then took the 'chair', a Professor from the Government's 'Defence Science & Technology' department. He explained further about the suspected 'VX' gas and its effects. "Ironically," the boffin started, "'VX' nerve gas was first produced in the UK; accidentally discovered whilst research was being carried out at 'ICI' in the North of England; it was developed at the Government's Porton Down facility."

"VX gas..." he paused..."Actually - it's normally kept in liquid form - is a lethal nerve agent that operates by cutting off the nervous system. It works by binding to the enzyme that transmits signals to the nerves, causing the nerves to become isolated and uncontrollable."

"Being odourless and tasteless, it is difficult to detect," the Boffin adding an unnecessary sober note.

"Well, how the fuck are we supposed to find it?" muttered a voice behind Detective Sergeant Morris.

"Poisoning by 'VX' nerve gas leads to contraction of pupils, dribbling, convulsions, involuntarily urination and defecation, with death finally arriving by asphyxiation - the respiratory muscles unresponsive to the body's need for oxygen."

The room went silent.

"The bad news is that as little as 10mg can be lethal, and we are pretty sure that 'VX' is the nerve gas used by Saddam Hussein to wipe out thousands of Kurds in the north of Iraq. Unfortunately, if the terrorists have sufficient quantity of 'VX', and given the right conditions, 'VX' will be difficult to stop in this environment. Tens of thousands of people could - no, *will* - die." The Professor's brow furrowed, it was almost as if he was going to burst in tears; his mind puzzled as to how some of his erstwhile colleagues could have produced such a deadly gas.

Even given the fact that the UK had long since ceased its experimentation did little to sooth his internal anger.

The Professor's summation elicited gasps of amazement, everyone in the room fully aware of the potential threat. Of course, the current threat may not be involved with 'VX' gas, but if not today, then...

Ellis took the floor again. "After the British decided not to continue with development or use of nerve agents, the technology was traded with other countries, particularly America; swapped for additional nuclear technology. We know that production was subsequently carried out in America, France, and Russia. Somehow, Iraq's Sadam Hussain got hold of the gas, and as the Prof said, it's believed that he used the gas against the Kurds in the north of Iraq as well as against his fellow Iranians." Ellis took a sip of water.

"However, we believe the missing batch is of French origin, originally 'borrowed' by a Frenchman of Algerian origin. He was a scientist at the French research facilities but disappeared shortly after a shortfall was discovered in the French stockpile of 'VX' Gas. We believe it was initially intended for Saddam Hussein's use, but was stolen shortly before the Allied invasion of Iraq. As I said earlier, we know it went from Iraq to Yemen, then possibly to Rotterdam. But that's it. Although we have everybody possible involved, searching, we cannot trace what happened after that."

Ellis looked directly at Sergeant Morris, "I don't know why, but we believe that the man you are after for kidnap and murder is a part of the cell that is holding the gas. Although he is 'clean' in our system, with the data you collected, we checked him out. He has been in and out of the country for a few years, yet none of our Agents can find a trace of his family, and his supposed contact addresses do not check out. We have, however, found connections with Yemen, which sent alarm bells ringing. So, now he's well and truly on the radar, a real potential lead!"

Sergeant Morris didn't know what to say, how to respond with all these bigwigs staring at him. "So, Sergeant Morris," Ellis continued, "I think our first course of action is to bring in that man Ray Maloney, and the woman Kerry, for further interrogation. There is more to them than meets the eye."

Chapter 58

Desperate to assist, Ibrahim had already been waiting a little while in Rosie's Bar before Ray arrived. A drink was already ordered for Ray, a table secured in the corner. Thus, when Ray entered the bar, Ibrahim waved him over, desperate to help, mortified that he had probably paid an unwitting part in Siobhan's death.

Without niceties, both men being aware of the desperation of the situation, Ray showed Ibrahim the copy of Fawzi's note. "Can you read it?" he demanded, "Can you make out what it says? Is it anything to do with those murderous Islamic bastards?"

Ibrahim, not offended by Ray's manner, muttered, "Of course I can read it, its Arabic!" He smiled, his glance quietly rebuking Ray, "It is unfortunate that some in my faith do not know how to behave, but we are all not bastards."

"I'm sorry, that was out of order," Ray repented, "It's just that I am so shit scared of what may have happened to Siobhan." He looked plaintively at Ibrahim, "Do you think they've killed her?"

Ibrahim, a good man, didn't know what to say. He looked sorrowfully at Ray, his eyes speaking volumes.

"She's dead, isn't she?" lamented Ray meekly, grief stricken.

"Regretfully, I would think so," responded Ibrahim reluctantly, "I'm afraid fanatics such as the man you described don't have respect for any of the human niceties. They are unashamed and are repulsive to us."

"Well, can this note help me to find the Islam...sorry, the fanatical bastards?"

"Yes, if the address written on this note is correct, and if they are still there," Ibrahim replied, adding, "I know the area well; it is very close to a large Mosque in north London, in Islington."

Mouth dry, Ray took a quick sip of his beer and then shot to his feet. "Let's check it out. See if we can find Siobhan."

"Shouldn't we tell somebody first?" questioned Ibrahim, "Shouldn't we tell the police?"

"Come on, there's no time to waste. Siobhan may still be alive!" Virtually tugging Ibrahim from the bar, he added, "I'll phone that Detective Sergeant Morris as we drive. He's the only policeman I can get any sense out of."

*   *   *   *

Reaching the address garnered from Fawzi's scribbled note, Ray was grateful for Ibrahim's Lexus, the leather seats providing warmth and comfort. He was glad that his new friend owned a luxury car, and pleased that he had taken the spare mobile phone from his London office. Ibrahim had only been imbibing sparkling water in the bar, so the journey, although hasty, had been relatively calm.

The person who owned the target house was obviously fairly well off; the five bedroom house situated down an exclusive road, in an expensive area. On the circular drive a 4 wheel drive Chevrolet truck and a Daimler Sovereign car were parked.

If Ray and Ibrahim had been aware that the owner worked for the Social Services, then they may have wondered where the money came from. However, they didn't know who owned the house or what to expect as they drove in.

Ray remained in the Lexus, the darkness hiding his skin colouring. But taking no risks, he sunk low in his seat, no longer being visible from the outside. Disregarding the hour, Ibrahim knocked on the door, apologising, in Arabic, for disturbing the occupants at this late hour. A man of Asian extraction opened the door, his sleepy face and expression revealing his unhappiness at being disturbed at such an hour.

Ibrahim explained that he had just arrived from Bahrain and had expected someone to meet him at Heathrow. In the event of something going wrong, if there were any problems, he had been given this address.

The man remained silent, just staring at Ibrahim, a wary look on his face.

"I'm sorry," Ibrahim continued in Arabic, "I've obviously come to the wrong place." Looking undecided, uncertain, he half turned, as if weighing up his options, obviously lost, alone.

As he turned to go, the man spoke, "No wait." Reverting to Arabic, he uttered, "I don't know who you are or where you're from, or why you've been given my address. No one told me about you." He was angry. "But I suggest you contact Imam Qureshi, who helps people such as you."

Without giving too much away and without admitting that he was part, albeit a 'hired' part, of the terrorist organisation, he managed to direct Ibrahim to Imam Qureshi's Mosque. As far as the man was concerned, he was doing his job. After all, Social Services paid his salary, and if he kept strangers such as this one from the door of Social Services, then he was saving the country money. His conscience salved, he turned on his hells, shutting the door behind him.

With the information they now had, Ray left another message on Sergeant Morris's voicemail.

*   *   *   *

Arriving outside the Mosque, the Lexus pulled into the curb.

Ray and Ibrahim sat still, watching the Mosque, determining their next possible course of action. Fortunately it was a bright, moonlit night; almost a full moon, with very little cloud cover. Their luck was definitely in, for almost immediately they spotted two individuals peering out from a side door of the Mosque.

Satisfied that the coast was clear, the two figures exited the building, making their way in the shadows, heading for a smart looking semi-detached house, adjacent to the Mosque.

Ray watched as the two individuals knocked on the door of the semi, the door being opened almost instantly. They entered, closing the door behind them.

"What should we do?" queried Ibrahim, "Should we knock and see what we can find out?"

"No, let's wait a couple of minutes; see what's happening," Ray replied, not knowing why his reply was whispered.

It was approximately only three minutes before the two men exited the building, making their way back to the Mosque.

"They're not the same men who went in," Ibrahim observed.

Ray studied the men as they stepped out from the shadows. "My God, you're right; one is smaller, the second quite overweight!"

"I wonder what's going on, what are they doing?" Ibrahim questioned.

"Oh well, I guess it's time to check it out, to take the risk." Ray smiled nervously at Ibrahim, "You can lead as you speak Arabic. Pretend you're looking for a man called Saeed."

"Oh cheers," riposted Ibrahim.

"You don't have to do this," Ray responded, "It could be dangerous. It's not your battle."

"Of course I'll do it. You're not getting all the glory," Ibrahim joked. "Besides, these people are damaging my religion, my faith."

Ray switched his phone to vibrate mode and following Ibrahim, picked up a loose brick from the small garden wall as they entered the tiny front garden of the property. Ibrahim knocked gently on the door, the response almost immediate, the door opening a crack, an eye peering out.

"I need to speak to Saeed," Ibrahim stated, his voice abrupt, trying to signify authority.

"Not here," the man responded doubtfully, not sure who Ibrahim was and ready to close the door.

"No fool," Ibrahim growled, "I need to come in and check something for Saeed."

The man remained staring, doubtful. A muted voice called out from inside the house asking what was happening, and the man who'd answered the door turned to respond. Seizing his moment, Ibrahim shoved on the door, sending the man flying backwards in the hallway, and charged into the house, Ray hot on his heels. As they went passed the fallen man in the hallway, he reached up, trying to grab Ray's legs.

Ray smashed his brick against the man's crown, a crack sounding seconds before the blood spurted from his victim's head, the splinter of bone jutting through the skin. His assailant fell, caught by a lucky blow from Ray, the edge of the brick slicing into the man's head as he hit the hard buffer of the wall. Eager to press on, Ray didn't realise that the man had died instantly.

Charging ahead, Ibrahim encountered a second man entering the hallway, but using his momentum, he dropped his head, butting the surprised man in the chest, both of them toppling to the floor. They fought, viciously, like rabid dogs, no holds barred, rolling into the lounge.

Ray tried to intervene, but firstly the doorway got in his way preventing him getting behind Ibrahim's foe, then when the fighters had rolled into the lounge, each time he attempted to swing his brick down, the terrorist rolled, leaving Ibrahim vulnerable to the brick.

When Ibrahim eventually managed to hold his foe's arms, Ray saw his moment, a window of opportunity, and he smashed the brick on the enemy's head, splitting his brick into pieces, but the assumed terrorist slumped forward, knocked out cold.

Ibrahim got to his knees, gasping for breath, Ray helping him to his feet.

"I hope these guys are something to do with the fanatic Abdullah, otherwise I'm in trouble," Ray muttered surveying the scene of his carnage against the two men.

"I hope so to," panted Ibrahim, "Or else I'm likely to get deported!"

Breathing heavily, recovering from their exertions, Ray heard a noise, a soft whimper, a strange strangled sound, human, yet eerie.

"What's that? Did you hear that?"

"Hear what? No..."

"Shush!" ordered Ray, "I can hear it again."

Both remained silent, the whimper sound reactivated. Already psyched up, the unnatural noise alarmed them, making them shiver, the hairs on Ray's arms tingling

"Yes, I heard it that time," Ibrahim whispered, "What is it?"

They turned, looking around, straining to follow where the sound emanated from. Leaving the room, they trailed the whimper to the hallway, to a closet, a cloakroom under the stairs. Tentatively opening the door, afraid of what he would encounter, Ray could dimly discern a shape, a figure, gagged and bound, tied to a chair. Glancing round to make sure that they were not going to get jumped on by a third party, Ray opened the door wider, the light beginning to illuminate the shadowed figure.

His heart leapt with unbounded joy as he experienced such a surge of emotion, from utter desolation and despair, to unbridled relief and euphoria; the captive figure was Siobhan! Still alive, but looking very bedraggled, but smelly!

Their eyes met, she continuing to murmur, the whimper turning from despair to a tone of joyful liberation. With eyes filling with tears of relief, glistening in unexpected salvation, she would have cried out in exhilaration if the gag was still not fixed firmly across her mouth; the elation and ecstasy of her rescue by her newly found knight in shining armour made her emotions run amok, giving her such a high feeling of elation. In her rapturous state she now had a new love in her life, the happiness washing all her woes away, all her earlier feelings of despair vanishing in a new found infusion of joy. Unfortunately, from such a 'high', she was unaware of what fate had in store for her, the grim reaper ever expectant, ever demanding; life's recurring cruelty ready to reappear at her door.

Ray hugged her desperately, joyfully, gleefully, not letting go, Ibrahim gently prodding him. "We have to get out of here, now! We've found Siobhan and we don't want all of us to end up as prisoners as well." Ibrahim prompted. "We don't know how much time we have before they relieve the guards, for that's obviously what those guys were here for. It'll probably not be very long before they're replaced. Come on!"

Reluctantly releasing his grip on the tremulous Siobhan and with Ibrahim running back to them with a knife he'd found in the kitchen, Ray hastily cut her ties, the blood flowing freely through her restricted veins, pins and needles prickling her skin. Siobhan was close to bawling, happy but still terrified, and with tear filled eyes, she grabbed hold of Ray not wanting to let go, not wanting to be alone.

"I thought I was going to die," she softly sobbed, "It was horrible, terrifying. Oh God, I was so scared. First, they took me back to the same place where Kerry and I were held before but, unlike before, this time it was full of people. They were horrible, resenting me, despising me. Some spoke in English; I heard the word 'Semtex' at least once. There was a wall which everyone was wary of, behind which they obviously stacked weapons or explosives. It was really horrible, scary." She tucked her head into Ray's chest.

"Don't worry," he soothed, "It'll be alright now; I'm just so sorry that we couldn't help sooner."

"Then when some of the people started objecting to my presence in the Mosque - I was being held in the basement – the man called Abdullah moved me to this house."

"We have to go," Ibrahim urgently reminded them.

Ignoring Ibrahim, Siobhan continued, "The only reason they didn't kill me is because you kept part of Abdullah's boat. They still needed a bargaining tool."

"What?" Ray was stunned, "I didn't!"

Siobhan looked up at him, her eyes registering shock, stunned; the horror of her lucky escape sending a tremulous shiver down her spine. "You didn't?"

"No, I gave the Dhow to Abdullah's sidekick," Ray replied softly, Siobhan's fortuitous survival beginning to dawn on him, "I handed it over in a carrier bag."

"But...but," she blurted, "They said you'd kept the base, the wooden plinth!"

"It must have dropped out from the bag; thank God!" Ray raised his eyes to the heavens, "It saved your life!"

Siobhan sank into Ray's arms, weeping like a child; her body riven with a mix of relief and horror of what might have been.

"Come on guys," Ibrahim pleaded, "We're not out of the woods yet!"

Consoling Siobhan, hugging her tightly for all he was worth, Ray glanced at Ibrahim. "The missing Dhow base must have been dropped at Oxford Circus in the kerfuffle."

He gently released Siobhan, "It's obviously important, somehow critical to what these fanatics are planning. We have to find it."

Ibrahim sighed, resigned to helping, "I guess I'm roped into this search as well." He smiled benignly.

"Thanks," responded Ray, "But first we have to get Siobhan to safety. We can drop her off on the way."

She gripped him tightly, holding on like a limpet. "Ray Maloney, I'm not letting you out of my site. I'm going everywhere where you go; from now on you're my guardian angel." Smiling wanly, she stared doe-eyed at Ibrahim, "And you too."

Chapter 59

Detective Sergeant Morris had been instructed not to take his mobile into the briefing room, confidentiality was of paramount importance. No one was to leak data to the media or their families. Thus, he had left the phone at the duty officer's desk, switched off. The briefing over, Morris was dispatched from the 'Yard' in a squad car, in full emergency mode, 'blues and two's, lights and sirens, priority over anything or anyone else.

The security services were playing for serious stakes; something was going down, but where and when? Situation critical.

At Ray's home, seeing the front door jemmied open, Morris and the police constable accompanying him rushed inside, expecting the worst, anticipating that their man had been dispatched, terminated.

The place was a tip, far worse than when the police had carried out their own search earlier. Nothing had been left in cupboards, drawers, wardrobes, or shelves. Every conceivable area had been searched, ransacked, piles of discarded clothes, crockery, utensils, pots, shampoo, all personal effects, books, etc, on the floor.

Each room had met with the same fate.

Luckily, there was no sign of a body or of anyone having been killed on the premises. The initial relief on believing that Ray may not have been killed was soon tempered by the knowledge that Morris was no nearer finding the man critical to intervening in the terrorists' plans. Checking from room to room, stepping over the debris, crunching broken glass under foot, Morris and the Constable double-checked, looking for clues, ideas, anything.

There was just nothing that could point a way, no idea of what happened to Ray, nor why the terrorists were pursuing Ray, or indeed where the terrorists where. Morris pulled out his mobile, ready to report back to the 'Yard'. He cursed himself; he'd forgotten to switch his phone back on subsequent to leaving the briefing room.

Preparing to dial the priority number given to him, 'message waiting' flashed up on his phone. With his heart in his mouth, he immediately identified that the voice on the first message was Ray's. Listening to the message, angry that Ray hadn't waited for him - the idiot acting on his own - he was doubly furious when he listened to the second message. Ray was taking matters into his own hands, with all kind of potential unfortunate repercussions.

Pressing return call subsequent to listening to the second message, it was Sergeant Morris' turn to access a voicemail message only. "Damn, damn, shit!" He swore, frustrated, angry, yet concerned for Ray's safety. Ray had no idea of the danger that he was in, or the calibre of people that he was up against; they were fanatics.

"Bollocks!" Morris hated fanatics almost as much as he hated politically correct police officers, or members of the public who felt they could operate as a private police force! He quickly connected with his new contacts at Scotland Yard.

Chapter 60

Returning to the semi, Abdullah initially couldn't comprehend the carnage that greeted him. Already perturbed that the front door was not locked, the guards not answering his knock, he was apoplectic, enraged, when entering the dwelling.

If either of the men had been standing he would probably have plunged his knife in there and then; retribution, punishment, anger, all three emotions swimming in equal volume in his head. But both guards were down, seemingly dead. He was livid, furious; why had he been given complete incompetents to support him in the 'Jihad'?

Saeed and Fawzi, running into the dwelling directly behind Abdullah, were gob-smacked, the scene totally unexpected; profanities exchanged, their language very un-Islamic. What the hell had gone on?

They quickly checked the closet, their worst fears being realised, the woman captive was gone! Her cords obviously cut, pieces of rope lying on the floor in the under stairs cupboard.

Frustrated, angry, Abdullah kicked the door, the brothers backing away, avoiding his fury. "Why!" he screamed, "Why? I left them with a pistol. Why couldn't they manage a simple task?"

The man lying on the lounge floor moaned, Abdullah stepping in his direction, ready to kick his frustration away. The man raised his head, "They tricked us," he croaked, "The person who attacked me was an Arab like you Abdullah – a brother – he tricked us."

"Fool," snarled Abdullah, "You still had a weapon, why didn't you use it?"

"Not me, Abdullah," croaked the wounded individual, "It was Naeem who carried the weapon; they overpowered him before he could use it."

"You dog, you have destroyed this mission!" Abdullah's eyes narrowed, "And now you must pay." He took his knife from its sheath.

"No Abdullah, please, have mercy. Don't kill me like this; I wish to die a martyr."

"You're not worthy!" Abdullah virtually spat in response. "The mission is lost. It is over!"

The wounded man tried to rise to his feet, desperation in his battered face, "It may not be over; I heard them speaking of the thing you were seeking. One of the men said it was still at Oxford

Circus."

"What! What did you say?" Abdullah cried out, renewed hope beating within his bosom.

The wounded man, fearful of his premature demise, sunk back to the floor, repeating his information.

Re-animated, feeling reborn, Abdullah turned away. "Quick!" he ordered to the brothers, "There are two pistols hidden in the kitchen cupboard, under the sink. It is no longer time for secrecy or discretion; this time we will take the weapons we need."

Rushing to the cupboard, almost leaping over the kitchen table, he pulled out two Glock 17 pistols, the same as used by the security services, but cut down versions, and two 17-round magazines.

Fawzi reaching out his hand for one of the guns was ignored, Abdullah keeping one weapon and handing the second to Saeed. If Abdullah didn't mean business before, he did now; the missionary zeal lit up his eyes, the 'Jihad' once more on track, his God renewing his hope, the promise of salvation and glory. Oh, what a martyr he would prove to be!

Meanwhile, Fawzi seethed in frustration; they would have to trust him soon. He was a warrior to Islam, an integral part of the 'Jihad', a martyr-to-be. Dejected, he trudged behind his brother and Abdullah.

Chapter 61

Scheduled to replace the guards in the semi, Hassan chose Ahmed to accompany him, but not having been forewarned by the departing Abdullah in his haste to get to Oxford Circus, they inadvertently put themselves in direct danger. Entering the house, as Abdullah had done, they were astounded, shocked, to discover the fate of their colleagues.

Hassan was informed by the injured man that Abdullah had gone to Oxford Circus. There was hope that the 'Jihad' could be salvaged; the thing that Abdullah needed for them to fulfil their holy task was potentially located at Oxford Circus Tube.

Feeling joyous, buoyant, they helped their surviving comrade to his feet, preparing to take him back to the Mosque.

* *

Before the terrorists had had the opportunity to leave, returning to give the joyous news to their colleagues in the Mosque, the first Police Anti-Terrorist unit arrived. The vehicle, on silent approach, pulled up some distance from the front entrance of the Mosque.

Two of the SO19 personnel from the arrived ARV quickly decamped from their car. Armed with HK G3K Assault Rifles, they took up secure positions behind the vehicle whilst their colleague radioed in; his job being that of communications as well as back up. All the men were equipped with fire-resistant overalls, Kevlar body armour, assault vests, and ceramic helmets. In addition to the assault vests they carried stun grenades, tear gas, and additional magazines for their Rifles.

But they didn't move in, waiting for support, having been advised not to enter the building due to the possibility of chemical exposure. Also, somebody had to make a final decision if the Mosque was to be assaulted, the political ramifications of the impending action making the commanders at the top of the chain very nervous.

Additional police teams, equipped with chemical protective suits and masks were on their way, the first three officers having adopted their assigned positions, the approach areas appearing secure.

* *

Although the police approach had been almost silent, something had alerted Hassan. Peering out of the partially opened front door he could make out a dim glow, the soft interior light of the police

BMW, two men exiting causing the internal light to light up momentarily. Those few seconds were enough to warn Hassan and, initially panicking, he stumbled back into the hallway, falling over his dead colleague Naeem.

The collision knocked Naeem, turning him over, revealing the piston still tucked behind him in his belt. Grabbing the gun, Hassan almost dropped it in his panicked haste. It had been years since he had received a rudimentary training in the camp in Pakistan and he just hoped that his nerves would allow him to aim properly.

Quickly ushering Ahmed into the hall, he pointed out the silhouette of the police car in the distance. Ahmed was to make his way back to the Mosque, warn the others, and by mobile phone, alert everybody hiding in the other safe houses. They had obviously been betrayed. Now it was a question of survival and regrouping.

A second police vehicle arrived at the far side of the Mosque, the tell-tale glow of the internal light as the officers exited, informing Hassan. This was a larger vehicle, with many officers disgorging. The newly arrived police Jankel armoured Land Rover had taken up its designated position at the far side.

Hassan realised that they were in danger of being cut off if any more police came to their side of the Mosque. Ahmed was instructed that he was to warn their brother martyrs, Hassan adopting the role of leader. Ahmed was told that if he stayed close to the wall, he should be able to creep back unseen, keeping low, this area of the street being relatively dark, the moon having slipped behind a large cloud. It was to be now or never.

Hassan would give covering fire if necessary.

Ahmed set off as directed, his progress slow, but then he panicked when a further two police Land Rovers arrived. Rising to his haunches, he ran in a crouch, his shape becoming visible to an officer in yet another approaching car, this one a BMW ARV.

Leaping from the car, the SO19 Officer called out, "Stop, halt; armed police officers. Stop or I'll fire!"

Aware that the Mosque was now surrounded on all approaches, the alert police officer knew that advertising their presence was no longer a secret, and he now had an 'object', a target that was attempting to skulk away.

Ahmed, panicky and terrified, glanced over his shoulder, and just ran, the officer yelling at him being totally ignored.

A bullet hit him in the back and he slumped to the floor, but continued, half crouching, partially dragging himself. A second bullet was followed by a hail of firearm fire, all aimed in his direction. He was hit twice more, once in the shoulder and another in his leg. He howled in pain, desperately dragging himself forward to the sanctuary of the Mosque.

Hassan chose that moment to step out of the house, the two officers from the BMW directly ahead of him, their focus totally on stopping their target. Close to the 'kill' they disregarded one of the tenets of their training, to be aware, be alert, of everything around them. Depressing the trigger, Hassan shot and killed one officer, the bullet entering his temple. He wounded the second, the policeman dropping to the ground the moment he realised he was a danger. Although too late to save himself being incapacitated, his leg and knee receiving direct hits, his quick reactions were just in time to save his life, another bullet thudding into the side of his vehicle at a height where his head was milliseconds previously.

A spotlight from the roof of one the Land Rovers instantly picked Hassan out, and he died in a murderous hail of bullets, vengeful officers filling his body with lead, but the diversion was the split second that Ahmed needed as he crawled the final few inches to the side door of the Mosque, a pair of friendly hands pulling him inside.

The mortally wounded Ahmed relayed Hassan's message regarding Oxford Circus. Although it initially heartened them, it didn't do much to aid their mission. Other than one man knowing that his brother's widow was involved, and phoning her with the data, no one else knew of how to contact the other fighters involved in this 'Jihad.' For most of these people in the basement, this was the first time they had ever met; the teams that did know each other consisted of a maximum of two or three in each cell.

Thus, the necessary secrecy would also cost them, for they did not know who to forewarn. Only Abdullah knew. Of course there were others outside the country who knew, but that served no benefit in their present situation.

Chapter 62

Abida terminated the phone call and swung out of bed, silently moving in her room. Staying at her friend's family home in London, she had no wish to disturb her hosts.

Today would be her last. The moment she had been waiting for, for many years; she had been patient but now it was time. Her husband and her father had died as martyrs in Afghanistan and now she could join them. That's all that she had been living for, the only reason for her existence. Her mother had died many years ago and now she was not interested in anything or anyone else. She had resisted the urging of her brother-in-law's family to move in with them. No, she had only one purpose remaining in life.

Strapping the canvas bag containing the Semtex round her waist, she quietly finished dressing, and then took two detonating caps. She only needed one detonator but took the second as a spare. She didn't mind using the Semtex, knowing her own death would be quick, and unlike other explosive material she had handled in the past, the Semtex was odourless. Odours and colours had subsequently been introduced by the makers of Semtex but Abida had been given hers from an older batch illegally supplied to Libya some fifteen years previously.

Prepared, she didn't see the need to eat or drink anything and, as silently as possible, left the house.

*   *   *

The fanatics trapped in the basement room of the Mosque were in a quandary. With the room stacked with enough explosive to blow the Mosque to kingdom come, their options were limited. They could wait for the police to break in and then blow everybody up, including themselves, or individually they could strap the explosives on their bodies and then charge at the police. Those who chose the suicide, the martyr option, would give others the chance to escape in the mayhem.

Deciding that they would go out as martyrs, fighting the infidel, those who were originally scheduled to carry the Semtex took up their carefully wrapped bundles, which in turn were secured in the thick canvas pockets of canvas vests strongly sewn with leather belts; each muttering prayers to Allah, they fastened the vests tightly to their bodies. The Semtex martyrs would charge out first, the remainder slipping out after the explosions occurred. Then, at least some could escape in the resulting chaos, allowing them to carry out the main mission. The five men put on oversize overcoats, buttoning the front to camouflage their canvas vests.

There were seventeen of them left in the Mosque, excluding the dying Ahmed, five with the Semtex canvas vests, who led the way to the exit. Two men, armed with their two remaining Glock 17 pistols, would position themselves either side of the door as soon as the five Semtex volunteers exited; once the explosions occurred they would fire at any remaining police officers, thus allowing for at least ten of them to escape. At the very worst, if their attack failed, the ten unarmed men could claim that had been held hostage; there was a chance to salvage something from this disastrous mess.

The officers in the police cordon ring waited, weapons poised, cautiously watching the first trickle of emerging men, hands raised in surrender. The order was that no shots were to be fired unless targets were clearly identified; they had to be sure if the men were friends or foe. A Police Commander with a loud hailer was bawling a message, advising the approaching men that they had to drop to the floor, **now**, hands placed on the back of their heads, but to the terrorists it was an indecipherable message.

The first men emerging seemed to be extremely rotund and although their hands were raised above their heads, they fanned out in a semi-circle, wide gaps spreading between them, and then they began to trot forward, still arcing as they increased their speed.

Quickly realising that the men were charging at them, their intent obvious, the police Commander gave the order to fire, teargas and firearms, the police secure behind their armoured vehicles.

Mr & Mrs Javaid, having raised their three boys as devout Muslims could not comprehend how their sons had become radicalised. Their youngest boy, Bilal, barely seventeen, having been prevented from leaving the family home in Leicester - his two older brothers having previously escaped the net - had managed to slip out from his home two days previously. Reports of his brothers having successfully joined the 'fighters' in Iraq had made him even more determined to help the 'cause'. Because he was the brother of proven potential martyrs, and because his older brothers, Idrees and Tariq, had received firearms training, it was easy for Bilal to convince the others that he was more than capable of handling one of the Glock 17 pistols. As one of the two men positioned just inside the door, he gripped his pistol fiercely, finger on the trigger, ready to fire as the five 'heroes' exited before the others. But, with absolutely no firearms training, as soon as he depressed the trigger, the recoil force jerked him backwards, his finger still locked on the firing position, the bullets smashing widely in those around him. Zain, the second man with the Glock had no choice but to change his aim, a shot piercing Bilal's forehead, the boy dying in a bloody mess of flesh and splintered bone, the gun slipping from his hand. Mr and Mrs Javaid were to hear later that week that all three sons were no longer with them, Idrees and Tariq part of a group targeted by an American Drone.

With virtually nothing to obstruct their aim, the police marksmen' bullets hit their targets, the fanatic fundamentalists dropping in a hail of fire. The first Semtex explosion sent the dismembered remains of the leading fanatic into the man just behind him and slightly to his left. A chain reaction was set in motion, a series of cataclysmic explosions erupted as each man's Semtex was ignited, all hell breaking loose, the night lighting up in an amazing myriad of colours and brightness, windows in the adjoining streets shattering, doors buckling as if they had lives of their own, and shards of deadly debris flying through the air. To those residents in the nearby streets, it looked like a major public firework display was occurring, but far louder and far more terrifying.

The SO19 Officers scattered, diving for cover, the air filled with debris of brick, glass, wood, bones, skin and blood, a gory bloody mess. With the force of the blast a river of flame swooped through the air, engulfing two of their vehicles, which were lifted off the ground, the tyres melting, the cacophony of cracking metal and shattering glass adding to the mayhem; the vehicles crashed down on their sides a good two metres from their earlier positions. The blast force blew in the front wall of the Mosque, the wall disintegrating with a mighty roar; those who had survived Bilal's trigger happy action, struck by crumbling debris, initially trapped, then dying in a hurricane force of air, followed by flames that scorched the flesh from their bodies.

Fortunately, the police lost only four officers wounded, one severely, his hand blown off, one with a piece of shrapnel imbedded in his thigh, and the other two with third degree burns; the Commander's quick appraisal of the situation and his instructions to his well-trained men allowing them to hit most targets before the terrorists had got too close and the following subsequent immediate instruction to adopt recovery positions. All in all, they had got off lightly,

But of their assailants, none survived; those outside either riddled with bullets or blown to smithereens and the others inside crushed or in fragments, making subsequent identification well-nigh impossible for the authorities, except for Bilal, whose provisional driving license, tucked in his trouser pocket, allowing the authorities to give Mrs Javaid the awful news in the future to add to her other forthcoming grief.

Chapter 63

Ray was impressed with Ibrahim's driving skills, reaching their destination in record time. Leaving the Lexus in a 'taxi only' parking spot in Hanover Square Gardens, they ran into Regent Street and onward to the nearest access to Oxford Circus tube. The area was still relatively quiet, with only a couple of work/maintenance vehicles on the road, plus a limited few delivery trucks. The occasional bus and taxi sped by, Ray almost being hit by a speeding Cab as he ran across Regent Street.

Nearing six am, the tube had already opened and Ray tore into the station, closely followed by Ibrahim with Siobhan bringing up the rear.

Time was of the essence; they had to search quickly and thoroughly. Ray, being the only one of the three who knew exactly what he was looking for, didn't hold out much hope of finding the Dhow base; more than likely it would have been swept up during the routine cleaning of the tube station.

A Tube employee prevented Ray leaping over the turnstile, insisting he purchase a ticket. Fortunately Ibrahim had some change in his pockets and rushing to the ticket machine, procured three 'travel zone-one' tickets.

With Ray leading, they rushed through the few early morning travellers, searching, scanning the terrain, as they went. Reaching the Central Line platform where Ray had originally handed over the bag containing the Dhow, he leant over, checking to see if the wooden base had fallen onto the track.

About to leap down onto the track, Siobhan pulled him back. "Don't be so stupid Ray," she cried, "You'll get yourself killed."

"But I need to check...to make sure; I've looked everywhere else," he protested.

"I guess it's gone; either destroyed or taken by the cleaners," Siobhan soothed, "We tried our best. At least that bastard Abdullah hasn't got it."

"Let's go," supported Ibrahim, "We need to contact the Police; tell them everything that's happened."

The three made their way back towards the surface, this time the disgruntled Ray dragging behind, shoulders hunched, a feeling a failure. "If only I knew why the Dhow base had been so important; important enough for so many to die?" he mused.

*   *   *

Sergeant Morris's head almost hit the rear seat window, the police squad car effecting a three point turn, the police driver's advance driver training effecting a prompt one hundred and eighty degrees turn in the narrow road.

The information over the radio had resulted in Morris, almost screaming, yelling at the driver to turn round. Their car had been on its way to the Mosque in north London when reports had come through that Ray and Siobhan were spotted on CCTV entering Oxford Circus tube station. It looked as if they were being held hostage by a man of Arabic appearance, the man appearing to have some sort of package in his right hand and what looked as if it might be bloodstains on his shirt. Other anti-terrorist teams were on their way, diverted from the operation at the Mosque in Islington, North London.

What wasn't registered was that the man of 'Arabic appearance' was the same individual previously detained with Ray and that, following extensive enquiries, he had already been ruled out as a potential suspect. Also, the 'package' in his right hand was not a package but was actually a 'man-bag'; Ibrahim favouring tight, contoured, high fashion jeans, was loath to spoil the effect by putting anything in his pockets.

At Scotland Yard all hell was breaking loose, the Assistant Commissioner and the Intelligence Teams in near blind panic. It looked as if it was all going down and that the Islamic fundamentalists were targeting the tube again, and Oxford Circus to boot. Maybe the 'VX' Gas was to be loaded on trains and sent over the entire underground network!

A judgement had to be made whether to shut down the entire Tube system, causing chaos, virtually closing down London, urgent calls being made, a decision demanded. Homeland Security was in near meltdown, the dithering inexperience of its leadership – public elected amateurs and unqualified civil servants - potentially resulting in mass disaster.

*　　*　　*

Ray stopped in his tracks.

There, a few yards in front of him, was Abdullah! The terrorist was approaching the Oxford Street entrance; both of them instantly stopped, rooted static in surprise, their eyes meeting and the loathing and hate mutual. Ray couldn't help glancing sideways, to make sure that Siobhan was safe, her back departing towards the Regent Street exit.

Unfortunately, Abdullah also picked up on Ray's eye movement, his eyes lighting up. He had both his enemies, cornered, a malicious smile breaking out on his face.

Ray twisted his head, yelling, "Siobhan; run!"

She half turned, about to return.

"No!" he cried out, "Don't stop! The fucking terrorist is here! Run!"

Panic shot across Siobhan's face, spreading like a wind through her body as she looked in horror just beyond Ray's shoulder; there was her gaoler, the bastard who would easily have slit her throat without any qualms. Her legs almost gave way, the fear and terror drowning her like a torrent, a knot howling in her stomach.

She ran past the momentarily static Ibrahim, Ray a few paces behind.

Someone screamed.

Ray, glancing over his shoulder, tripped over the leg of a woman who was standing still, frozen in fear, mouth agape. He fell just as Abdullah fired his Glock 17 pistol, the bullet shooting over Ray and hitting the Ticket Inspector, innocently going about his tasks.

"He's got a gun," someone cried unnecessarily.

"Get down, there's a mad gunman; we're all going to die," a female bystander cried out as she burst into tears.

Ray rolled across the floor, fortunately evading the next two bullets fired by Abdullah.

Ibrahim and Siobhan jumped round the corner, diving to the ground, the ricochet of bullets reverberating round the tube station. People were running past them, heading for the Regent Street exit.

"The next one will kill you," pronounced Abdullah, only two paces from Ray's prostrate body.

"Frigging nutter!" yelled a commuter.

Another early morning worker attempted to sneak up behind Abdullah, briefcase poised to smash against the gunman's head, but Abdullah coolly ducked, swivelled, and shot the public spirited man in the face at point blank range, blood and flesh splattering across Abdullah's already maniacal face. Oblivious, and in a millisecond, he had his weapon re-directed at Ray's head.

The screaming grew to a crescendo, the horror terrifying. Two females were wailing in terror. Without taking his eyes off Ray,

Abdullah growled, "If anybody else tries to be clever, I will open fire on everyone, male and female!"

The screaming continued, but everyone froze, even those attempting to crawl out of the station. No one dared move a muscle.

"Now," uttered Abdullah, voice heavy with menace, "Where is the base for my Dhow?"

"I don't bloody know!" Ray shouted, Abdullah's finger almost depressing the trigger.

"One last time," the terrorist growled, "What have you done with the wooden base of *my* Dhow?"

Terrified, trembling, legs like Jelly, Siobhan whispered in Ibrahim's ear, "What do we do?" Although petrified, she had to find a way of helping Ray.

Equally terrified, Ibrahim shrugged, not from disinterest and certainly not from cowardice; he just didn't know. "You go...escape," Ibrahim murmured, "I will stay to see if I can do anything."

Siobhan shook her head. "I'm not leaving him." She smiled courageously at Ibrahim, the smile not reflected by the beating of her terrified heart, "He came to save me; I must do the same for him."

Ibrahim sighed, "You're crazy; the madman will kill you as well."

Looking round for a potential weapon, Siobhan spotted an oblong peace of highly polished wood, partially jammed, tucked behind a 'Metro' newspaper stand. She rolled across the floor, pulling the oblong piece of wood free. Her feeling of elation quickly dissipated, disappointment hitting her. The piece of wood was too short, it couldn't be used as a weapon, but then her eyes lit up. "Do you think this it?" She asked Ibrahim, "Although it just looks just like an ordinary piece of wood to me."

Ibrahim shrugged as Siobhan rose to her feet. "I'm going to ask," she almost croaked, her throat dry with fear, and before Ibrahim could prevent her, she went to the corner, calling out, "Hey you bastard, I think I've got what you're looking for."

Abdullah's eyes flicked from the prostrate Ray to the direction of Siobhan's voice. "Bring it to me," he demanded.

"Yea, sure," she riposted, "And then you'll just kill us both."

"I can kill him regardless," growled Abdullah, "Now bring my

Dhow base!"

Siobhan was doubtful, not knowing what to do.

Ray shook his head. "No, don't do it. He'll just kill you too Siobhan."

"I'm running out of patience," snarled Abdullah.

Siobhan was in a dilemma, unsure, wanting to save Ray but having experienced Abdullah's evil machinations, she was also afraid for her own life.

"Please Siobhan," whispered Ibrahim, "Let me take the Dhow base. I am of the same race and religion as the man threatening Ray; he will not shoot me."

Siobhan looked doubtful but not able to think of any alternative that might get them out of this situation she reluctantly passed the lump of wood to Ibrahim.

Abdullah cried out, his voice full of anger and venom, "Now your friend dies. I wait no more!"

"Patience friend!" responded Ibrahim in Arabic, "I'm bringing what you need now. Don't shoot."

"Show yourself," demanded Abdullah, "Who are you...and remember I have a gun pointed at this man. I will kill him without hesitation if you attempt anything."

"Yes brother, be calm," Ibrahim responded, not feeling in the least bit calm himself, his heart pounding ten to the dozen as he stepped out from the corner, the Dhow base held clearly in front of him.

"Who are you?" growled Abdullah.

"I am a friend to the man who you pointing the gun at, but I am also a brother of Islam," responded Ibrahim, reverting to English.

"You cannot be our brother," spat Abdullah, also in English, "Otherwise you would not have friends such as him."

"Because I break bread and speak with such as him," responded Ibrahim, looking distastefully at Ray, "Does not mean that I do not support you, my brothers, in your beliefs."

Ray fidgeted, fear racking his body, perspiration leaking from every pore, his shirt damp; he glanced from the pistol pointed in his face to Ibrahim. "What is he playing at?" thought Ray. "Is he betraying Siobhan and me?" Ray tensed, prepared to do something, to fight for his life.

The pistol moved millimetres closer to his face, Abdullah menacing, "Attempt to move or escape and I will shoot!" Ray froze, the slightest nuance of movement alerting his adversary.

"Give me the base," demanded Abdullah, his eyes flicking from Ray to Ibrahim. Then he remembered. "Are you the man who went to the house in Islington earlier this morning?" Haven taken a step closer, Ibrahim stopped in his tracks, the question unexpected, catching him unawares.

The look on his face was sufficient evidence from Abdullah. "You *were*! You killed my people, my friends!" he shrieked, and lifted his Glock 17 in Ibrahim's direction.

Ray took the split second to punch, hard, into Abdullah's groin, making the connection in the same instant as the terrorist fired at Ibrahim, the shot shooting deep into the ceiling. Although crippled in pain, Abdullah brought his pistol down to finish off Ray, but Ibrahim pounced, virtually flying through the air. With the Dhow base in his hands, he connected with Abdullah, knocking the gunman's arm sideways, the bullet missing Ray's temple by less than a centimetre. The impact caused Abdullah to drop his weapon, the Glock 17 flying out of his hand, clattering across the station floor. Ibrahim's forward momentum propelled his body into Abdullah and both men grappled, falling to the ground.

With Ibrahim and the terrorist wrestling, fighting and gouging, rolling across the floor, Ray clambered unsteadily to his feet, his legs shaking. He picked up the discarded slab of wood and crashed it down on Abdullah's head, the terrorist toppling off Ibrahim and falling to the floor.

Relieved, pulse still racing, afraid, yet adrenalin still pumping, Ray dropped back to his knees, his body trembling. Ibrahim lay on his back, panting, exhausted, bruised and dazed.

Peeping round the corner, Siobhan rushed towards them, whooping in delighted relief, both her friends alive! She helped Ibrahim to his feet and then rushed to Ray, dropping to her knees. With eyes momentarily meeting - no words being necessary - she wrapped her arms around Ray, both of them holding tightly to one other.

After a while, Ray pulled back slightly, gazing into her eyes. He smiled; she responded with a warm, loving grin and then kissed Ray passionately, their lips locking like limpets. They were unconscious to the sound of the approaching police, sirens blaring, a maelstrom of noise beginning to grow louder, reverberating in the confines of the station entrance.

Ibrahim dragged the dazed Abdullah to his feet, Abdullah's right arm held behind his back, the fingers almost touching the terrorist's neck. "Right, you piece of shit," he murmured into Abdullah's ear, "You are a disgrace to my faith, our people, and you do not represent the true Islam."

Ibrahim was angry, berating the fanatic, "If we were back in Saudi I would look forward to seeing you executed but, unfortunately, these Western people, who your kind tries to destroy, are more civilized than scum like you will ever be." Furious, Ibrahim manhandled Abdullah through the exit, towards the growing noise of the sirens, the police arrival imminent.

*   *   *

Ray glanced up at the departing Abdullah. "At least we're safe; it's finished. Thank God it's all over." He embraced Siobhan ever tighter. "And mostly, thank God, that *you* are safe; I was so afraid."

It all happened in a blur; simultaneously a scream, a shot, and Siobhan gasping in shock, then instant pain. She screamed, the agony intense, the blood seeping through her clothes and then she collapsed, her breathing still, her eyes closed.

Fractionally frozen in shock, Ray cried out in anguish, "No, Siobhan! No; oh my God!" With tears forming in his eye, he looked up, staring into the aimed pistol held in Saeed's hand.

Chapter 64

Morris arrived at Oxford Circus just as the initial police cordon was being set up. He had a real case of déjà vu, rubbing his eyes just to make sure he wasn't dreaming. The armed Officers were screaming at two men of Arabic appearance who were just outside the Oxford Street entrance, screaming for them to raise their hands and drop to the ground.

The second of the two Arab men, holding the first in a vice-like grip, was hollering in protest, trying to explain something.

The Police, oblivious to his cries of protest, his dismay, not needing an excuse or an explanation at this critical juncture of the operation, aimed their weapons, threatening to shoot. Most of the remaining bystanders ducked and scurried way and the fast arriving police reinforcements corralled the very few remaining voyeurs to places of safety.

Chaos, pandemonium and panic ensued, Oxford Street, Regent Street, and surrounding areas coming to a standstill. The frightened, but watching public, consisted of the usual participants, the gory, thrill seeking onlookers, the curious, and the majority, who were terrified, desperately fighting their way through the increasing throng of gawping spectators. None of this made the police operation any easier, Inspectors and Sergeants yelling instructions, officers being delegated to clear the area.

Police officers, using loud hailers, began instructing the public to keep off the streets, stay indoors, the situation dangerous.

A warning shot, inches from Ibrahim's head, forced him to release Abdullah, the pair raising their arms and sinking to the ground.

"But I'm trying to help!" cried Ibrahim in frustration, raising his head off the floor, "I don't need this treatment."

"Shut the fuck up," countered the nearest police officer, his MP5 sub machine gun poised, "And keep your fucking head down!"

All trains in and out of Oxford Circus were halted, the operation resulting in absolute mayhem and chaos all through the Underground tube network. But at least the potential was there to save lives, to keep as many people as possible clear and, most importantly, to allow the security service unbridled access to the vermin in the target area.

*   *   *

Saeed had run up the escalator, Fawzi hot on his heels. Searching the platforms, they had got themselves lost, twice ending up at the wrong exit. The sound of the gunfire had driven them on, knowing that something was happening on the surface.

There was no sign of Abdullah, but hearing the approaching police sirens, Saeed knew that they were in trouble. Reaching the ticket barriers, Saeed saw his arch-nemesis, the man Ray, on his knees with a woman just getting to her feet next to him. He stopped in his tracks, instantly angry, Fawzi banging into his rear. Now was the time for vengeance; he would kill the man who had mistreated him yesterday.

Pulling the Glock 17 from his sports bag, he fired at Ray, a look a pure malice in his eyes as he depressed the firing mechanism. Revenge felt so sweet. Execrably, the shot missed, hitting the woman. Not pausing to think, he re-fired, but this time Fawzi, attempting to look over his shoulder caused him to lose aim, the shot going wide.

Ray gently released his hold on the still Siobhan, her hair draped across her unmarked face, and raced towards Saeed, not caring if he got shot or not. All he wanted to do was to kill the man who had killed Siobhan and if he also died in the process, then what did it matter.

"What's happening?" demanded Fawzi.

"It's the man who has caused us so many problems. The one who attacked me yesterday," replied Saeed, coolly aiming.

Fawzi pushed level, recognising Ray, but once again making Saeed miss, the bullet smashing into the discarded wooden base of the Dhow.

Furious with his brother, Saeed hit Fawzi across the cheek with his pistol, the brother recoiling in surprise. "Keep back," yelled Saeed, "You keep stopping my kill - making me miss!"

The third reprieve gave Ray time to launch himself at Saeed, jumping on top of the ticket barrier as Saeed fired again. This time, too close to miss, the shot hit Ray, knocking him back momentarily, the bullet penetrating his abdomen. Undaunted, subconsciously aware of a sharp pain just above his hip, initially akin to being hit by hammer, then like a screwdriver driven inside, Ray kept going, grabbing Saeed's face, his body now within the outstretched arm of Saeed's gun hand.

Saeed fired again, his arm forced wide by Ray's impact, and this time his shot hit the advancing Fawzi rushing to his brother's aid. The shock and surprise stopped Fawzi in his tracks; he put both hands to the hole in his chest, a look of horror on his face. Then he toppled forward.

Saeed screamed in rage, bringing the weapon to bear on Ray's head. But Ray grasped Saeed's arm, forcing it away, upwards, the bullets being fired into the ceiling causing no harm to the remaining prone, but terrified travellers.

They fought like cat and dog; Ray initially more successful because Saeed's other hand was occupied in trying to use the gun to fire or to beat Ray across the head; neither tactic succeeded. Then rolling towards the escalator, Ray managed to force Saeed to loosen his grip on the Glock, the back of the man's hand pressed against the moving stairway, his skin being caught in the downward momentum.

Yelling in pain, Saeed released the weapon, but then he brought his free hand into play, punching and slapping Ray's head with brutal force. Ray realized he was taking damage and his wound didn't help. Although now hurting like hell - it had hadn't been critical, the bullet passing straight through flesh – but never-the-less he was weakening through loss of blood. Desperate, knowing he was losing and with Saeed now on top, pinning him to the floor, the man's punches wearing Ray down, he gripped Saeed's coat; raising his legs he pushed upwards as hard as he could, hoping to kick his opponent down on the descending escalator.

Initially it seemed to pay off, Saeed tumbling backwards, but just as he was about to drop down the escalator, he pulled at Ray's leg, dragging Ray with him. They tumbled down the escalator, gouging, scratching, biting and punching as they clattered and banged their way to the bottom; both combatants banging their heads against the metal sides as they descended. Fate was kinder to Ray; he landed on top of Saeed, winding his already breathless adversary. Barely able to stand, Ray hauled himself to his feet and, without compassion, kicked Saeed in the head. Although groaning and groggy, Saeed scrambled to his feet.

"No, you murdering shit!" screamed Ray, "I've had enough of you and your kind!" With that he kicked the rising man in the balls, making Saeed double up, his head level with Ray's knee. Then Ray kneed him in the head, just above the nose, hearing the already broken nose crack again. Saeed howled in pain as he dropped to the floor.

Not wishing to take any further chances for his enemy to rise 'from the dead' and subconsciously intent on his own vengeance, Ray kicked with fury at his opponent's body, sending Saeed into a bloody mess of defeat.

"You bastard fanatic," he cried out, "Now you'll pay for Siobhan's death!"

It was his turn on the night duty rota, and when not working in the vicinity of the tracks, Micky always had his ear phones lodged firmly in his ears, AC/DC tracks pounding in his head, the sound deadening the loneliness and stillness of the night, not to mention comforting him against the eerie flickering of shadows in the murky light. Having completed a routine maintenance job, rewiring an electrical fuse box, and having completed his work report, he exited the staff workroom oblivious initially to the lack of people – the fire alarm siren not having penetrated through the volume of the rock music. Slowly, it dawned on him that the morning rush start was belied by the lack of people and then he suddenly looked up, mouth agape, as he saw three men fighting at the top of the escalator. As soon as he saw the gun flash, and a man falling, he knew something was wrong. Diving to the ground, he peered over the side of the escalator as two of the men continued their fight even though they were tumbling to the bottom.

Fortunately for Ray, quickly apprising himself of the situation, Micky pulled himself up by the hand rail and reaching out, soothingly, he calmly pulled Ray away from his victim, all sanity, reason, and compassion having departed from Ray's mind. The now off-duty electrician gently berated Ray for his brutality whilst also cajoling him that his adversary no longer offered any threat.

Still trembling with anger, Ray looked at the bloody mess he had left of Saeed and coming to his senses, he then felt dreadful, the bloodlust dissipating. His enemy's evil had rubbed off on him and he immediately felt ashamed; all he wanted now was to get back to Siobhan's body and get away from this place and from these dreadful people.

Chapter 65

Trapped within the initial police cordon set up around Oxford Circus tube, Abida pressed her back against the glass of the shop display window.

The police were yelling at people at the edges of the cordon to run clear of the marksmen taking aim. Those too far away to escape, or in danger of being shot in the crossfire if the two Arab terrorists resisted arrest, or if the target suspects attempted other tactics, were told to get down, hit the floor. Despite being yelled at, there were a few like Abida who appeared not to understand the instruction, apparently panicking, their bodies pressed against the walls of the buildings.

But in Abida's case, she was not panicking. She wanted to be there; needed to be there. She had been told that the man known as Abdullah might need her assistance at Oxford Circus, but she didn't know what he looked like. She had spoken to him a few times but they had never met. Ignoring the almost histrionic yelling of the police officers, she scanned the entrance to the Tube and in particular the two men on the ground, their hands on their heads.

Armed police officers were approaching the two suspects, further marksmen ready to give covering fire.

Dressed in western clothes, an overcoat, thick woollen blouse and corduroy trousers, a normal ladies headscarf covering her head, she was attempting to blend in better than if she had been wearing her traditional clothing. She felt sure that Allah would not mind in this instance. As a precaution, she had put on three extra pairs of pants – the larger sized garments better described as pants than knickers – but despite the four pairs, she was afraid that her bowels might betray her objectives.

This was it, her moment. She was needed; this was what she had agreed to do; to die for the cause.

A small group of police officers edged towards Abida and six other whimpering bystanders with the intention of escorting them to safety.

Abida took the detonator cap, undid her overcoat, and calmly called out, her eyes already dead, "I am armed with explosives. Let them go," she pointed her head in the direction of the two prone suspects, police gunmen virtually standing over the two Arabs. "Let them go, or I will blow us all up." The six people by Abida screamed, five women and one man, all petrified, frozen to the spot, two immediately bursting into tears, wailing in abject misery and fear.

The approaching police officers stopped in their tracks, uncertain, glancing at each other for guidance or instruction.

Abida repeated her threat.

The police had been forewarned of what they might be up against, Semtex and nerve gas, but only a few present were equipped with the appropriate protective clothing against the gas. A female Inspector, leading the 'rescue' mission, ordered her twitchy colleagues to remain still. Without taking her eyes off Abida, she radioed in.

Ibrahim and Abdullah, still face down, hands behind their backs, were in the process of being handcuffed, other armed police still with weapons pointing at their heads.

Abida screamed, "Release them now...or I will detonate!" She added, "Tell the police to back away from them!"

The female Inspector spoke hurriedly in her radio, instructions from on high still not given. Her eyes narrowed not quite knowing what to do as Abida seemed intent on blowing them all to kingdom come. The Inspector knew that if the terrorist did have Semtex than they were all goners anyway. It was the gas threat that she was more concerned about.

The officers, in the process of securing and arresting the suspects, received a communication via their radios, immediately glancing over in the direction of the female Inspector. Reluctantly, they released Abdullah and Ibrahim and with their colleagues' weapons still aimed at the suspected terrorists, they backed away.

The female Inspector, using her initiative, negotiated with Abida, securing the terrorist woman's agreement that her team could take away the six other people, three of whom were now on the ground, wailing hysterically, convinced that their lives were measured in seconds.

The police loud hailers instructed everyone to get down, the SO19 cordon moving slightly away, their guns still trained on Abdullah and Ibrahim, but now also on Abida. There was to be more police support soon, very soon, coming from the direction of the underground; officers already running on the tracks, approaching from the bowels of the earth. But caution was the key, the fear of the potential release of nerve gas prevalent in the senior officers' thoughts.

*   *   *

Confused and angry at his treatment, Ibrahim rose cautiously, but he almost sunk back to the ground when he realized that although his hands had been released, he was still a suspect, a target. So many weapons seemed to be trained on him, the eyes of the police officers indistinguishable behind their goggles.

Abdullah looked up, looked across in Abida's direction, and smiled. For the first time in many hours things appeared to be going his way.

"Please," called out Ibrahim, "I'm not with him!" He gestured furiously at Abdullah. "I was working with Ray Maloney to rescue a woman, and to stop these maniacs."

No response. The guns remained pointed.

Abdullah grinned, maliciously, delighted at Ibrahim's misfortune.

"Please," Ibrahim repeated, taking a step forward.

A voice commanded, "Stay where you are. Ask the woman to remove her explosives and we can talk."

"Please, for Allah's sake please," pleaded Ibrahim, "I have nothing to do with these terrorists!"

Sergeant Morris, kept well back by the anti-terrorist officers, squinted through the throng of police and police response vehicles. He recognised Ibrahim. "I know that man," he called out, "He's an acquaintance of the terrorists' kidnap victims; we need to talk to him."

The police personnel surrounding Morris looked blankly at him, not comprehending.

Morris got to his feet, tugging his arm free from a restraining hold put on him by an armed SO19 officer. "Stop! Don't shoot that man in the tight trousers," Morris called out, running forward, "He is not part of the terrorist group."

The SO19 officers looked over their shoulders whilst their colleagues restrained the obviously mad man who was running in the direction of the terrorist suspects.

Abdullah smiled grimly; he knew Morris, had watched the policeman on a few occasions. The pathetic man was no match for him. He almost laughed as he saw SO19 officers holding Morris back.

Suddenly, he pulled the knife from a sheath in his unstitched trouser pocket, and grabbing hold of Ibrahim, he pulled him backwards, towards him, the knife pricking into the back of his intended victim's neck.

Chapter 66

The senior Commander arrived on the scene, a Deputy Assistant Commissioner, fresh from his operation at the Islington Mosque. He was mad; furious as hell. What the hell had his officers, his Commander on the ground, been doing?

His subordinates had released two of the prime suspects and also left the woman who might, or might not, be primed with Semtex. Disregarding the potential of local devastation and loss of life, the Deputy Assistant Commissioner knew that the subsequent repercussions if the Semtex was merely a prelude to the release of VX nerve gas; the ultimate body count would be immense, unacceptable. They should not have released the suspects; he was furious and scared for the people of his City.

The Deputy Assistant Commissioner harangued his juniors, their future promotions, if any of them survived, looking extremely dubious.

The order was given to take out all three suspects. A ten second warning for all police personnel to get their heads down.

Ten seconds. That's all he was giving his men and the public. Maybe he would die too.

But it had to be done; a decision made.

*   *   *

Abdullah vengefully duplicated Ibrahim's earlier actions, forcing the right arm up on the person who he considered as a traitorous Arab, Ibrahim's right arm forced up high behind his back. Grinning, delighted, almost ecstatic in his chance of retribution and in his twisted belief of the glory of his 'Jihad', he deftly repositioned the knife in his right hand. Murmuring softly in Ibrahim's ear, he bragged, "I am a Yemen, just as Osama truly was, not a Saudi."

Before Ibrahim had the chance to turn, to move, to struggle, Abdullah drew his sharp blade across Ibrahim's exposed throat, the sharpened knife slicing through the skin and flesh as easily as a heated knife through butter.

Ibrahim's cry was cut off, the gurgle in his throat spewing out blood and torn tissue, his carotid artery severed, the life draining from him in seconds.

The SO19 officers, given the long awaited, long desired order, opened fire.

Their initial shots hit the fast deceasing Ibrahim, then Abida. She blew apart, milliseconds after being hit, a vicious explosion ripping through the street, a whirlwind of fire and heat, tearing through buildings and people. Nearby cars, buses, taxis all ending up as burning wrecks; splintered glass, shards as long as two feet in length spewed into the air, skewering the preliminary surviving bystanders and security personnel.

Whatever was left of Abida would not have been enough to provide her with a respectful Moslem burial, her tiny fragments of body scattered over a wide area. Even in death she had betrayed the tenets of her Islamic faith. The female Police Inspector and her colleagues were considered as collateral damage, sad, but the decision absolutely necessary to protect the greater good.

The blast saved Abdullah's body from being drilled by bullets, the force knocking him backwards, still holding on to Ibrahim. As the force of the explosion drove him backwards, back into the entrance of the Tube Station, the limited number of shots that the police marksmen had manage to loose off thudded into Ibrahim's body, the dead man protecting him.

The few SO19 personnel that were still in a position to fire - well back, and not affected by the blast - were too late. Abdullah was winded, but safe within the confines of Oxford Circus Tube. Caution was now the word as the police re-grouped, carefully sifting through the living and dead remains of both their colleagues and members of the public. Wails and cries of pain served to accentuate their anguish and remorse.

Scrambling to his feet, Abdullah's eyes lit upon the wooden base, its end shot off, something metallic visible within. He ran to the lump of wood and working the fragments loose at the end of the wood base, pulled out a used cigar cylinder. Sighing with satisfaction, Abdullah glared at a recumbent bystander who was about to get to his feet. The man hastily lay down again, terrified.

Sticking the cigar cylinder in his shirt pocket, Abdullah ran towards the ticket barrier, intending to escape through the underground network.

He stopped in his tracks. Deep from within the bowls of the Underground he could hear police bellowing, "Stay down; armed police! Stay very still; don't move until we identify you!"

Abdullah looked around, unsure; there was no escape. The police were outside and also deep within the bowels of the station. Maybe he could open the container and read out the details to the businessman? The man could subsequently take over the final act of their 'Jihad'?

But then he remembered that the businessman did not know all the names of the operatives; all *that* data was coded in the mobile that Abdullah had in his coat pocket and, of course the Imam in Yemen knew.

He could hear the re-commencement of activity outside the station; the temporary lull subsequent to Abida's explosion now being replaced by a cacophony of sounds. He could hear the jumbled sirens of Ambulances, Fire Engines, and more police arriving. Order was being reassembled through the outside chaos; his time was running out. There would be time for one call only, after which he would then destroy his mobile and the data. Nothing could be permitted to fall into the hands of the Westerners.

He quickly dialled the number and left the message with a 'sleeper', a man who was being kept back for future targets. The mission had failed. He would destroy all the evidence. They would have to rebuild the 'Jihad' with a new team, supplemented with those that survived this mission. He was devastated on hearing about the police attack on the Mosque in Islington. Now he knew that he had really failed!

Disconsolate, Abdullah understood that he had to destroy the information revealing the various hiding places of the eight nerve gas containers. The Imam in Yemen knew the locations; he could rebuild their 'Jihad'. Calmly, through the increasing crescendo of mayhem outside the station he unscrewed the cigar cylinder, removed two sheets of tightly woven paper and unravelling them, he turned them over in his hands, a frown creasing his forehead as he realised that it was not the information that he expected. His jaw dropped, enlightenment suddenly hitting him; what he had in his hands was not merely the code to decipher the exact data where each gas canister had been secreted, but was in actual fact data showing the *actual* locations of the nerve gas canisters. Now he really did understand that only he had the information to unravel the various locations, each of his fellow martyrs merely being provided with a sheet of data which was meaningless. The Imam had not been totally honest with him and now his brothers would not even have had the vaguest idea of which tube station they were to be at. All their previous preparation and training had been meaningless, their targets totally different to the ones they had imagined.

It was vital that Abdullah passed on the data that he had discovered and he quickly re-dialled the 'sleeper's' number, sweat now pouring out of his pores. He fidgeted, waiting, and then bawled at the man to keep quiet as he read out the information, ensuring the 'sleeper' had correctly noted the actual tube stations and then a summary of various passages, verses from the Quran that, un-encoded, ,would reveal the precise hidden locations. Faced with the inevitability of his fate at least Abdullah could stop the infidels laying their hands on the information. Removing the Sim card from his phone, he crushed both the card and phone, repeatedly stamping hard down with his heel until just tiny fragments remained. Then he took a few deep breaths and, resigned to his fate, he separated the sheets, crunching the first one into a ball and put it in his mouth. He determined that swallowing the paper would be the answer.

There would be no evidence left.

Now he was really calm again, glad that he was not to be the architect of their absolute failure. Others could fulfil the intended 'Jihad'.

Chapter 67

Hurting, wounded, exhausted and bleeding, Ray staggered to the escalator. He could hear the police approaching from somewhere beneath him, ordering people to stay put, remain calm – as if – but he had to get back to the surface, to Siobhan's body. There was no way he wanted to leave her for people to trample over. He would carry her out with the courtesy and respect she warranted.

He felt very emotional, very sad, but was too exhausted to think of anything other than emitting a howl of despair. Siobhan had not deserved her fate and he, useless as he was, had been unable to save her.

Hearing the ear-splitting thump of the explosion, immediately followed by other strange, deafening, but unidentifiable sounds, a tremendous commingling, a bedlam of noise from above, he was filled with trepidation, uneasy at what he would find on reaching the surface. Warily and with as much resolution as his weary state would allow, he mounted the upward escalator but almost got blown backwards, a whoosh of air running through the station, the reverberations of Abida's explosion rocking in from the outside.

Managing to grab the hand rail, Ray pulled himself forward, first on his knees, then almost lying face down. Tired, he just lay on the first few steps of the now static escalator but quickly rousing himself, he crawled upwards towards the surface. The sound of screams and wails, cries and issue of commands, assailed his ears. He really had no idea what to expect, what had happened, but he could surmise, a look of utter despair sweeping through him.

Somehow he felt partially responsible. Approaching the top, he got to his feet, making his way to the exit.

There, right in front of him, his back facing Ray, a man peering out from the exit of the station was Abdullah. The utter exhaustion dropped from Ray like a cloak, rage instantly replacing his tiredness, adrenalin flushing through his system like an oil change.

The fanatical terrorist, concentrating on something in front of him, had no inkling of Ray's approach. He was fiddling with something in his hands, which he then put to his mouth. Ray crept up behind Abdullah, grabbing him round the neck with a stranglehold grip; at the same moment, he brought his knee up, sharply, into his enemy's back.

Abdullah, caught totally by surprise, the blow in his back driving the air from his lungs, his windpipe also restricted, nearly choked on the ball of paper; involuntarily, he spat it from his mouth, the paper shooting out as he half turned his head at the last moment.

Ray forced Abdullah back, almost breaking the terrorist's spine but Abdullah, with ferocious strength, managed to twist and then turn, relieving the pressure on both his windpipe and his back. His fingers dug into Ray's arms, digging deep, trying to twist Ray's grip free. Abdullah appeared to be losing, his right hand no longer involved in the fight. Ray almost had his adversary subdued, his enemy dropping forward onto his knees, the man gasping for breath.

The pain when it came was unbelievable, the shock and surprise almost causing Ray's heart to stop.

Abdullah had used his free hand to pull out his knife, and before Ray realised what was happening, the fanatic had sliced deeply into Ray's left forearm, almost cutting to the bone. Ray cried out in pain, instantly releasing his hold before desperately attempting to grab Abdullah's knife hand before the man could administer a killing blow.

Abdullah's eyes flicked down to the second sheet of paper that he had dropped in the struggle and this gave Ray the milliseconds to act; he feinted as if he was going to punch Abdullah's face then suddenly side-stepped as Abdullah lunged with the knife. The knife sliced through Ray's trouser belt but didn't reach the skin as Ray stuck his foot out and pulled Abdullah's outstretched arm as it swooped inches from him. Managing to trip the fanatical terrorist with his foot, the man went tumbling forward, sprawling face down on the floor.

With time running out Abdullah had two options; get the papers and destroy them, or fight this man to the death. He had to destroy the paper. Furious, livid, he scooped up the loose sheet and almost in the same movement, aimed the knife at Ray, throwing it, his arm swinging forward, before diving towards the discarded paper ball.

Ray's eyes flicked towards the earlier discarded Glock pistol, fallen next to the murdered man. He dropped to the floor just after Abdullah released the knife from his hand. The blade shot through the air at exactly the same spot where Ray's face had been a fraction earlier. Ray rolled across the ground towards the pistol.

The race was on, Ray striving to reach the gun, Abdullah grasping for the paper ball but missing it as it rolled agonizingly clear from his grasping fingers and under the ticket barrier. Enraged, Abdullah got to his feet. Now he knew he had to deal with Ray first; he turned back to face his nemesis, to finally put an end to this ridiculous and worthless human, this unholy non-believer.

The Pistol was pointed at him but the man called Ray didn't seem sure, didn't seem confident how to use it. Abdullah launched himself at Ray confident that the infidel did not have the knowledge or balls to fire the pistol. Three bullets hit him in total as he charged forward, each one smacking him in the chest, his momentum keeping him going.

The gun was now empty! Ray thought that he would never stop the fanatical maniac, but then Abdullah, reaching forward, an evil malignant, determined expression on his face, collapsed at Ray's feet, and died.

Almost falling on top of Abdullah, Ray girded his loins, drawing up a reserve of strength from somewhere within his inner being; he knew that whatever Abdullah had been trying to destroy must be of importance. Dropping the pistol, his legs finally given out, he dropped to the floor, picked up and pocketed the loose sheet, then crawled towards the ticket barrier. Sliding under the barrier, he retrieved the ball of paper, grasping it in a tightly closed fist.

Now that it was all over, his body had no reserves left; it switched off, all his energy spent, and his mind closed down, the body finally resigning to utter exhaustion. He passed out, the ball of paper tightly clenched in his hand.

*   *   *

When Ray came round, his ears were buzzing with strange sounds, frenetic activity all around him. His eyes tried to focus, his head lying on the floor, dust and a discarded chocolate bar wrapper inches from his nose. He had to think where the hell he was, his fuddled mind confused, his eyes blinking ten to the dozen. The surrounding panoramic chaos of sight and sound soon brought him back to the present, his heart sinking when a picture of the dead Siobhan flashed across his brain.

Dimly he became aware of a shadow over him, a person leaning down.

"He's still alive! I saw his eyes move."

Ray recognised the voice; it was a friendly voice, not an enemy's voice.

"Are you okay?"

Ray stirred.

"Don't move; the medics are on the way."

He knew the voice; it was Sergeant Morris. Ray tried to rise but Morris held him down. "I said to lay still." Quickly discerning that Ray's arm was leaking too much blood, Morris took off his jacket, pulled off his shirt and used it to fix a tourniquet round Ray's deep wound.

"Thanks," Ray muttered. "Afraid I've been shot as well; in the stomach area, but I guess not too badly."

Morris, concern furrowing his brow, put his jacket over Ray to keep the man warm. "Anyway, I don't really care," Ray was morose, close to tears, "I failed; they killed Siobhan."

Morris placed a consoling hand on Ray. "She's not dead yet, pal. But she is critical. The Ambulance has just taken her away."

"But I saw her shot dead," said Ray trying to get to his feet, the hope, belief, exultation expanding within. "I've got to go to her."

Morris gently restrained Ray. "There's nothing you can do; she's already in the best hands possible," Morris stated consolingly, "Besides, you're not in such a good condition yourself."

An ambulance crew set their stretcher down ordering Morris to give them space.

Before backing away, he asked, "There are four terrorists dead, including the woman outside. Were there more?"

Ray shook his head, "Don't know." The pain was really biting deeply into his psyche, his body craving repair and recovery, "I was aware of three only. Sorry."

Before Morris backed away, letting the Ambulance crew in, Ray grabbed his arm. "The bastard was trying to destroy this." He handled the soggy, crumpled ball of paper to Morris and then pulled the other sheet from his pocket. "It may be of interest."

Ray blacked out, the beginning of a smile on his lips; maybe Siobhan was okay.

Chapter 68

'Blondie's' song 'Maria' was playing gently in the background; Kerry, listening to the song's lyrics, drifted, feeling sexy and desired. This was *her* song.

Ray smiled, the tension draining from him.

It had been two months since the incident at Oxford Circus and the first time in ages that he had had to participate in one of these dreary marine exhibitions. Ray had been forgiven by the police for taking the law into his own hands and had eventually been rewarded for his bravery and gallantry, the information given to Sergeant Morris of huge importance, saving many lives. They never did tell Ray exactly what it was all about; besides, he didn't really want to know, sometimes too much knowledge can be disconcerting. All he knew was that the sheets listed eight tube stations and under each tube station name was a verse from the Quran, which Ray knew as the Koran; apparently the verse numbers gave the locations of whatever it was that the terrorists had hidden, for example 19 Maryam 30 gave paces forward and to the left, and the experts soon deciphered the Arabic code for the starting point for each one, some locations starting within the tube and others at premises adjacent. Anyway, everyone had been ecstatic at what they recovered.

Now he and Kerry were sharing a coffee in the exhibition restaurant. Kerry looked at him, her eyes questioning, "You don't look all that friendly towards me? Have I done something to upset you?"

"I'm fine." Ray responded, his voice apathetic.

Kerry became beguiling, adopting an innocent expression, "Are you sure? Have I done something to offend you?"

"Not really, not anymore."

"What do you mean?" she snapped.

"Oh for goodness sake, leave it."

"Tell me what the matter is!"

Ray, reluctantly, responded, "You weren't straight with me from the word go; always lying about your life, and of your feelings for Spratt. Anyway, it doesn't matter anymore. Anyway, I have to go." And getting to his feet, with a spring in his step, he left the exhibition, the thought of meeting Siobhan, and their intended dinner assignation making him feel like a teenager on a first date.

Now, life could really begin, but he still couldn't resist glancing round, never quite sure if someone was going to leap out of the shadows. It was going to take a long time before he could truly relax again.

Printed in Germany
by Amazon Distribution
GmbH, Leipzig